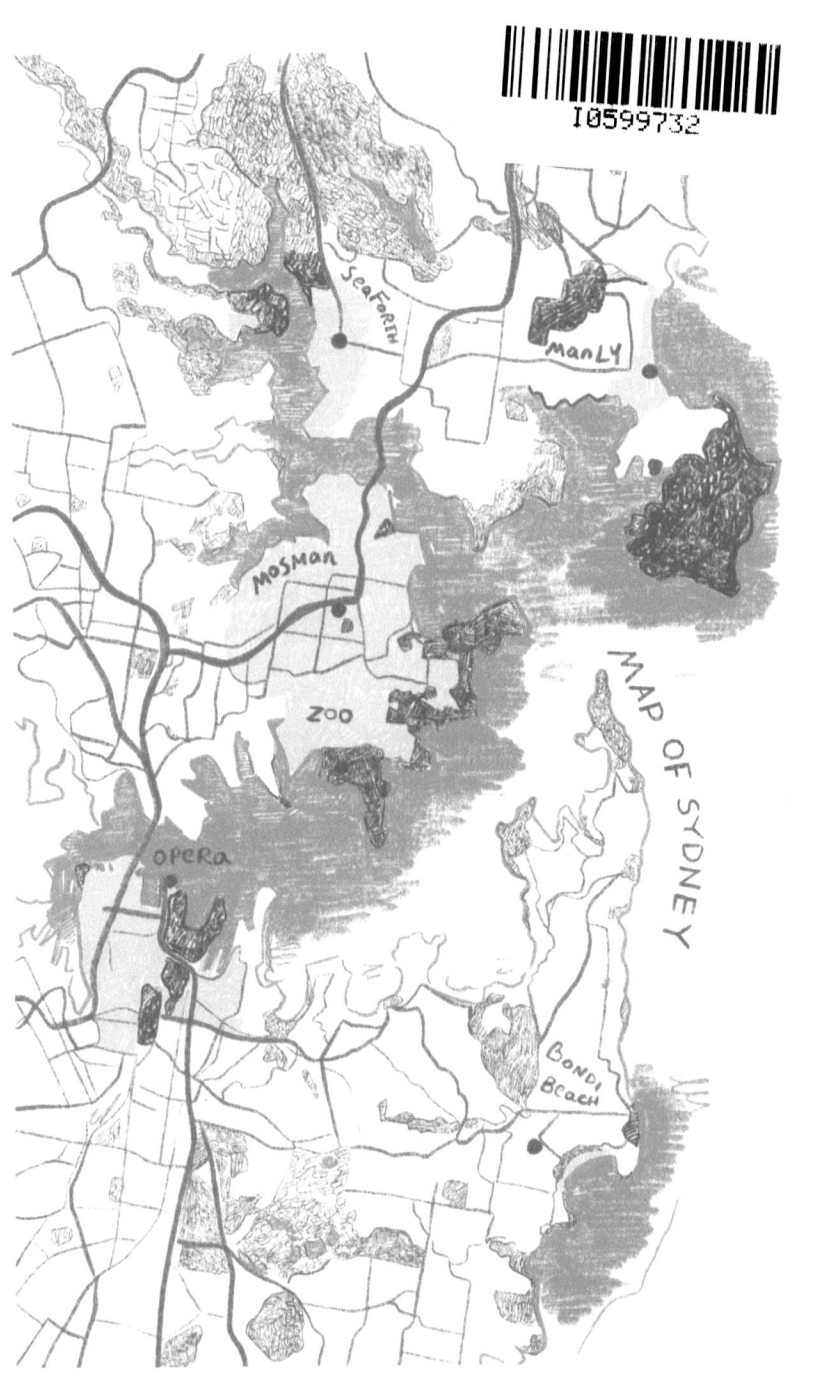

I0599732

SeaForth

ManLY

Mosman

ZOO

Opera

MAP OF SYDNEY

BonDi
Beach

TWIN SUMMIT
PUBLISHING
est 2024

M. E. Flatow

OCEAN CHILD

a novel

Ocean Child is a work of fiction.
The story, all names, characters, and incidents are the product of the author's imagination or are used fictitiously. Any resemblance with actual persons (living or deceased), places, locales, buildings, corporations and products is entirely coincidental.

Copyright © 2025 by M. E. Flatow
All rights reserved.

Published in the United States and worldwide by Twin Summit Publishing, LLC.
www.meflatow.com

No part of this publication may be reproduced, distributed, disseminated, or transmitted in any form or by any means, including photocopying, recording, or other electronic or mechanical methods, without the publisher's prior, express written permission, except as permitted by US copyright law. For permission requests, contact Twin Summit Publishing, LLC: flatow.publishing@gmail.com.

NO AI TRAINING: Without in any way limiting the author's and publisher's exclusive rights under copyright, any use of this publication to "train" generative artificial intelligence (AI) technologies to generate text is expressly prohibited. The author reserves all rights to license uses of this work for generative AI training and development of machine learning language models.

Library of Congress Registration No.: TXu002504394
ISBN: 979-8-9928593-6-2 (special edition)
ISBN: 979-8-9928593-0-0 (hardcover)
ISBN: 979-8-9928593-1-7 (paperback)
ISBN: 979-8-9928593-2-4 (ebook)
ISBN: 979-8-9928593-7-9 (audiobook)

Book cover and illustrations by Zuza Miśko
Edited by Jamie Flatow, Lauren Finger, Alyssa Matesic, and Enchanted Ink Publishing
Readers: Sydney Flatow, Maria Boisvert, and Jessica Scotto

First Edition

For Jamie, with Love

"The tyrant is always in danger of losing his hold upon the victim when the latter begins to think."

— HORATIO ALGER, JR. *RAGGED DICK*

"No sympathy for the devil; keep that in mind. Buy the ticket, take the ride ..."

— HUNTER S. THOMPSON. *FEAR AND LOATHING IN LAS VEGAS*

OCEAN CHILD

Ray had three daughters, continents apart: one he raised, one he loved, and one he denied altogether. To his eternal disappointment, these are their stories, not his.

CHAPTER 1

Sunday, October 3, 2010 | Sydney

Julia hated Sundays with every fiber of her being.

She was stuck in a holding pattern, her life stagnating somewhere between adolescence and adulthood, a reality her father, Ray, made sure to point out at every opportunity. Julia's days were spent surfing, working side jobs, and avoiding her formidable father. On good days, he was merely irritating. On bad days, she detested him. Their clashes were inevitable, her free spirit constantly colliding with his rigid world order. Their relationship had been beyond repair for as long as she could remember, but of all her father's flaws, it was his haughty certainty—the way he carried himself as if he had never made a mistake—that Julia despised most.

During the week, she steered clear of him; their schedules rarely aligned. But on Sundays, she was trapped by the Corning family's weekly brunch. Julia's attendance was expected, or as Ray put it, *compulsory*. Most weeks, a rotating guest list of neighbors, coworkers, and friends arrived at precisely midday to eat, drink, and boast. Julia suspected her father's greatest disappointment was that she didn't provide him with a steady stream of triumphs to showcase.

Julia opened her ancient laptop and sat on the floor of her cramped bedroom, passing the time. At twenty, she still lived at home—a compromise brokered by her mother, Alice. Julia's mood instantly soured as a whiff of roasting meat drifted from the kitchen, confirming it was Sunday.

Today's version of brunch was the worst—no guests, no distractions, just the three of them picking at an overly prepared meal. With no audience to entertain, Ray's attention would land squarely on her. These private family gatherings exposed her to his relentless criticism thinly veiled as fatherly advice—or, as her mother preferred to call it, love.

As Julia waited for brunch, she absentmindedly scrolled through her inbox, deleting spam with a few quick clicks. Her bedroom was a blend of childhood nostalgia and her love for surfing. The pastel dresser, schoolgirl desk, and narrow bed clashed with the vibrant surfing posters covering the walls. Her most treasured possession, a surfboard named Floating Sky, rested in the corner.

At eleven, Julia had bought the used board, determined to hone her skills and take on bigger, more challenging waves. Floating Sky was an elegant, custom-shaped shortboard with a smooth white deck and a vibrant turquoise underside. She had spent hours restoring it to near-pristine condition, finishing with a personal touch: an airbrushed waratah—light red, almost pink—the iconic Australian flower and emblem of New South Wales, her home state.

An email caught her eye:

Catrina and Julia,
I apologize in advance if this email is jarring. My name is Miriam Worthington, and I am your sister. Growing up in London, I did not know our father. As I got older, my curiosity led me to hire a private investigator. An exhaustive search of birth records over three continents identified Raymond Corning of Sydney, Australia. The report also listed you two, Catrina, 22, from Southern California, and Julia, 20, from Sydney, as my biological sisters. I have attached the report.
I'm truly excited to discover that I have sisters. I've included my

*contact information below if you want to connect. If this intrusion
is unwelcome, please disregard.
With love, Miriam*

Julia entered Miriam's name into a search browser, and her mouth fell open in shock as the results revealed her sister's celebrity. On the screen was a tall, light-skinned blonde actress she instantly recognized as the star of *Night Nurses*, a campy British TV show her father insisted on watching every Sunday night. She'd never understood Ray's strange fixation with the show—until now.

She stared at the screen, taking in the promotional photos from *Night Nurses*, the red-carpet appearances, and images of Miriam posing with other famous people. Julia was in awe of her . . . sister? This was too much to process. She was stunned.

This was new—different—a break in the monotony. The idea of having a famous sister was an unexpected thrill. Julia's pulse quickened, a restless energy taking over as she reread the email. A grin crept onto her face, her cheeks flushed, and a strange, giddy laugh bubbled up in her throat. She bounced to her feet, pacing the room, too charged to stay in one place.

Julia excitedly ran into the kitchen of their home in the Mosman neighborhood of Sydney to find her mom preparing Sunday brunch. The aroma of the roasted lamb shoulder filled the 1980s-era kitchen, mingling with the buttery richness of mashed potatoes and the tangy freshness of cucumber salad. Julia leaned against the counter, watching her mom braid a challah loaf, her fingers moving methodically over the glossy dough. Alice worked tirelessly in the home, a role her husband insisted upon, though she accepted it with contentment rather than resentment. Her purpose was prescribed: to keep the home, ensure Ray's satisfaction, and raise their only daughter, Julia.

"Smells good," Julia said.

Alice looked up briefly. "Thank you, darling. It's nothing fancy, just the usual. Your father likes everything prepared by hand."

"*Your* hands . . . Still no guests today?" Julia asked as she adjusted her short sandy-blonde hair that was kept off her face by a small pink clip.

"Just the three of us."

"Are you and Dad watching *Night Nurses* tonight?"

"Of course, every Sunday," Alice said, carefully brushing egg wash over the challah. "Your father wouldn't miss it."

"Why does he even like that show? Rubbish dramedy about British nurses doesn't exactly scream *Dad*. He only watches the news and cricket. What's special about this program?"

"I suppose he finds it amusing. Like those old BBC shows *Fawlty Towers* and *Blackadder*."

"Righto," Julia said, unconvinced, as she jumped to sit on the counter, "because he's such a fan of situational comedy."

Alice's hands stilled for a moment before she returned to the dough. "Not everything needs to make sense, Julia. We just like it . . . And get off the counter," Alice said, exasperated.

As she dropped to her feet, Julia studied her mother. She couldn't figure out if Alice was simply busy or avoiding the topic. "You and Dad doing okay, getting along?" she asked.

"What kind of question is that?"

"He isn't the easiest guy to live with. You two ever have issues?"

"Where is all this coming from? Your dad and I are fine," Alice said as she maneuvered her rounded frame around the kitchen.

"He never gets on your nerves? All his preaching about the *right way* . . ."

"He's a great husband. Always has been. Your father is under a lot of pressure. He runs a prestigious school and is a local leader. I'm proud to be married to him."

"What about when he was younger? Did he stay out late with his mates?"

"He always prioritized us," Alice said while pursing her lips and turning away from Julia. Through gritted teeth, she continued, "He was home if he wasn't working or at the cricket oval or his social club."

Julia let the silence linger for a moment before asking, "Why only one kid?"

Alice sighed, her hands smoothing the edges of the challah. "Oh, Julia, you know why. We had trouble conceiving."

"Remind me," Julia said.

"Years of trying . . . we'd nearly given up when we took that holiday—P&O Cruises from Sydney to Nouméa. You were our little miracle. Our Child of the Sea."

"You never wanted another?"

"After you, we decided not to try again. It was too painful, all the waiting, all the heartbreak. And you were perfect, Julia. Our family was complete."

"Perfect? Dad doesn't think that. He was always yelling about my marks in school. And now he's having a go about getting *real* job. I'm tired of it. I need to move out . . ."

Alice sighed and returned to her work. "I'm sorry if he doesn't love you the way you want to be loved . . . You and your father . . . Stubborn. Passionate. That's why you clash."

"Maybe," Julia said, unconvinced.

"Don't forget, he rescued you at the beach years ago. Dropped everything to help you. He was terrified you'd drowned. That's love," Alice said, placing the bread on a baking sheet and wiping her hands on her apron.

"Eight years ago . . . Not what happened . . ." Julia said as she walked away. A memory surfaced—her father's voice, deep and commanding, cutting through the crashing waves. It was the day he allegedly rescued her, a story he never tired of retelling. But Julia's version, the real version, was far less heroic.

As Julia remembered it, she was twelve and surfing alone at Manly Beach. A wave caught her and she popped up, carving along its face. A blur of movement caught her eye too late—a tourist on a rental board, clumsy and oblivious, dropping in on her wave from the side. The collision was swift and brutal, the tourist's board smacking into her knee with a sickening thud. She gritted her teeth and dragged herself back to the beach. Walking to the bus stop was out of the question, so she hobbled to the nearest payphone and dialed home. Alice answered, listening with concern as Julia had haltingly explained the accident.

Ray arrived in record time, his car screeching to a stop at the edge of the promenade. Without a word, he marched toward Julia, his hand-waxed shoes crunching on the sandy sidewalk. "What were you thinking?" he asked, grabbing the board and shoving it into the backseat. "This is exactly why I told you surfing is dangerous." Julia sat quietly as Ray continued lecturing her as he got in the car. "Netball, athletics, swimming—those are sports with structure, discipline, and proper coaching," he said. "Surfing is an excuse to waste time: no goals, no accountability, no measurable achievements. You're a natural in the water. You've got the talent to win swimming medals, but you never apply yourself."

Julia shook off the bitter memory and glanced at her bedroom mirror. Her seashell-blue eyes reflected as she smoothed lotion over her sun-kissed skin freckled from countless hours on the water. Her thoughts returned to Miriam's email: a sister—*sisters*—out in the world. Suddenly, Julia's life was less ordinary. The tedium fell away as questions swirled. Who were they? What did they know about her? What lives had they lived, untouched by Ray's impossible standards?

Julia reopened the web browser. The first headline read, *Rosalind Leighton Worthington, Mother of Actress Miriam Worthington, Dies Suddenly of an Apparent Heart Attack at Age 47*. Rosalind, described as from a prominent family in London's high-class social circles, had passed away overnight in her home. The article, dated a year ago, noted that Miriam, her only child, had declined to comment.

Julia's heart sank for her newly discovered older sister. The news story intensified her long-standing contempt for Ray. Julia couldn't reconcile how this boring and predictable man had such a sinister secret, how this self-righteous community pillar could abandon two children.

Julia's initial intrigue and excitement about Miriam had given way to anger, and her father was the target. Her mind raced over half-formed thoughts and questions without immediate answers. *What kind of man does this? Pretending to be the perfect husband and father ...*

She opened the attachment Miriam had sent, containing the investigative report, and read the summary.

> *Married with three daughters, one by marriage and two estranged with different mothers. Son of a British father and an Australian mother. Father struggled with alcoholism and was abusive. Channeled his energies into academics and sports—cricket, specifically—and excelled in both. At the top of his class, he earned a doctorate in education. Head of school at a Sydney grammar school by the age of thirty-three.*

She shifted in her chair, nails pressing into her palms, her body warm. *And my sisters ... did they grow up wondering where he was? Did he ever bother to write to them or call them? I bet he ghosted them.*

The hypocrisy stung the most. All his moralizing, his lectures about the *right* way to do things, the *right* way to act—and yet he'd had affairs. *And poor Mum ... she has no idea.*

"Julia! Brunch is ready!" Alice yelled from the hallway.

As Julia processed her stirring emotions, she printed the email and folded it into the back right pocket of her jeans, itching for a confrontation. She wanted to knock her father off his moral pedestal. She had no specific plan but would hit back if provoked.

Ray sat at the head of the eight-station table, his posture as rigid as the lines of the pressed tablecloth. At forty-eight, with his thick mustache, dark brown streaked with dignified gray, he was a cliché from a history book. He was dressed in a blazer, starched shirt, and pressed trousers, his precise presentation another tool in his arsenal of authority. Alice sat to his left in a floral dress with a modest pearl necklace. Julia, a sartorial contrast in jeans and a faded T-shirt—a visible rebellion—slid into her seat, which faced Alice, creating a triangle of tension that made the expansive table feel smaller. Julia could count the seconds until Ray's opening remark about her informal appearance.

"Mum prepared another magnificent meal for our enjoyment. It's a shame you didn't have time to get ready."

Julia flashed her mom a devilish smile as she stabbed a piece of meat.

"Julia, any proper job prospects this week?" Ray asked.

"Nope," Julia replied, her eyes fixed on her plate.

"This happens when you don't apply yourself in your studies. How often did I tell you that you wouldn't have good options if you didn't work harder?"

"Twenty? Thirty? Don't recall the exact figure," she said, cutting her food with deliberate slowness.

"Watch your tone."

"Sorry, Dad."

"If you're going to live under my roof, you will respect your mum's Sunday meal. Do I make myself clear?"

"Understood. To be clear, I respect the meal. It's excellent. Thanks, Mum," Julia said, turning to Alice.

"By not showering or dressing properly, you disrespect your mum. By talking back, you show disrespect to me."

As Ray's face darkened, Alice interjected, looking at Julia. "Honey, try the potatoes. They're your favorite."

"Thanks, Mum." Julia took a bite. The salt and butter balanced the creamy richness of the potatoes. "They're top-rate," she added.

Ray, undeterred, continued, "I work with young adults at the school who are not putting in the necessary effort. At least they can fall back on the trades. Honest work. You surf all day. I don't know where it all went wrong."

"Sounds like it's time for me to move out. I was telling Mum the same thing earlier. I'll find a flat this week."

"Who would rent you a flat? You don't have a job. You don't have money."

"Incorrect. I have twenty-four dollars," she said in a naked attempt to set him off. Then she sat back and watched his face redden further.

"You don't understand how hard it is to earn a living. You think this is all some big joke. I had high hopes for you, and now you're an adult with no plans and no purpose."

Julia's fork clinked against her plate as she met his gaze. "I do have a purpose. I surf."

"Surfing . . . another example of failing to reach your potential. You could have been a national champion."

"You mean to reach your expectation . . ."

"If I could go back in time, there are many things I would've done differently. I should've sent you away to school. Far from the coast."

"Regrets? Interesting. Are there any others you'd like to share?" Julia said, her arms crossed defiantly.

As Ray pushed back his chair and began to stand, ready to unleash his next missive, Julia pulled the folded email from her jeans and slid it across the table to Alice.

Ray froze, his hands moving to his hips as he stared at the paper suspiciously. His voice rose, loud and commanding, the full force of his headmaster tone unleashed. "What is that?"

Julia, ignoring Ray's theatrics, gestured toward Alice. "Read it, Mum."

Alice looked toward Ray as she did during times of stress. Julia's eyes didn't move off her mother as Ray lorded over them from the head of the table. Alice picked up the email, her face falling upon reading it, then turned back to Ray, her shoulders slumping as though burdened by an invisible strain. Her hands fidgeted with the edge of her cloth napkin. She avoided meeting Julia's eyes, her focus flitting to the floor before returning to Ray, her posture shrinking with every second of silence. In disbelief at her mother's muted reaction, Julia turned to Ray. His face was an explosive shade of red.

"What is it? What's going on here?" Ray asked, pointing at the email.

"Mum . . . Mum . . ." Julia said, leaning forward on her elbows.

"WHAT DOES IT SAY?" Ray demanded as he grabbed the email out of Alice's hands.

"Mum . . . did you know?"

Alice's gaze remained fixed on Ray as he started to read the email.

"You *knew*? I can't believe . . ." Julia said, pressing her interlaced fingers on top of her head.

"Ray, she knows about the other girls," Alice said, tears forming.

"Wow. How is this okay? Mum?"

Ray lowered the email and stared at Julia. "You come to *my table*, in *my house*, and spring this on your mother? How dare you? You have become a rotten child. *Truly rotten.* All I've done for you. All we've done for you. Letting you live under this roof. You have been nothing but a burden—an embarrassment!"

Julia sat frozen, her mother still refusing to look her way, while Ray continued, his words growing crueler with every breath. "And look at *her*," he said, holding up the email and referencing Miriam. "She's a smashing success. A legend. She's an award winner in her field of study. Respected. You're a *surfie bum*. I can't fathom how a daughter of mine—"

"ENOUGH!" Julia interrupted while standing. "I'll be out in ten minutes . . . for good," she said, grabbing the email from his hands and leaving.

Ray didn't respond. His face contorted with rage as he stormed out of the dining room. The heavy slam of the study door echoed through the house, rattling picture frames on the walls. Alice remained seated. Her sobs were audible. She'd witnessed many blowups, but this one was different—final.

CHAPTER 2

Sunday, October 3, 2010 | London

Miriam couldn't sleep. She had a terrible headache and an overpowering sense of dread. It was four in the morning, and she kept refreshing her email. A few hours ago, she had emailed her two sisters for the first time, desperate for a response. She was feeling particularly lonely, with today being the first anniversary of her mom's sudden passing. Fortunately, her agent Linda was flying into London on Monday to spend the day with her.

While packing for her upcoming move to Los Angeles, Miriam picked up a framed picture of her mother. She desperately wanted to discuss this career-redefining relocation with her. Rosalind would have had tremendous insight; Miriam was the only topic she had enjoyed discussing. As a child, Miriam had asked her mother about their family, her father, and Rosalind's upbringing. Her questions had been met with a dismissive smile and a vague "That isn't interesting, dear. Let's focus on you." It wasn't just secrecy—it was avoidance, a refusal to be vulnerable. Miriam had longed for even a glimpse beneath her mother's hardened surface. Rosalind had never opened up, and Miriam had stopped asking, but the questions remained. She had collected scraps of information where she could, piecing together fragments of her mother's story.

As Miriam understood it, Rosalind Worthington had been born into the British aristocracy. She had lived a charmed and privileged life until a brief reckless moment while overseas on vacation, a one-night stand with a charismatic young Australian, had left her pregnant. Her parents, mortified by the breach of decorum, had cloaked the pregnancy in secrecy, removing Rosalind from public view. Miriam's birth had passed without grand announcements or celebrations, and Rosalind had raised her daughter as a single mother, an outcast in a world where she had once been revered.

Miriam couldn't reconcile the mother she knew with someone who would have a one-off encounter. It had never made sense to her.

Mother and daughter had built a fine life together in London. Their generational wealth had ensured comfort, but free from the obligations of high society, they had lived as they pleased. Rosalind had poured everything into her daughter, nurturing Miriam's intelligence, refining her talent, and believing in her with an overwhelming and absolute devotion. Miriam had never doubted that she was the center of her mother's universe. She had never imagined a world where that wouldn't be true. And then, without warning, her mother had been ripped away. Rosalind's consistent presence, which had grounded Miriam her whole life, was gone, leaving a hollow, unfilled void.

The framed picture Miriam was holding blurred. She was supposed to be packing and moving forward, but she couldn't move at all. She was adrift.

She wanted to sleep, but the medicine she needed to do that would leave her spacy, and she wanted to be at her best on Monday for her final day on set.

As Miriam went to refresh her email, her computer screen suddenly lit up with a video call from Australia. She hurriedly clicked *Accept,* and Julia's perky face appeared on the screen. Julia was sitting in what appeared to be a dimly lit internet café with rows of computers placed in open-air cubicles. A surfboard was leaning against the wall, drawing Miriam's eye. Julia didn't speak, her mouth agape.

"You're staring," Miriam joked, breaking the ice. "I'm so happy you reached out. When did you read my email?"

"I got it a few hours ago. I was surprised. I'm excited, though."

"That's excellent news. I was nervous to send it. I didn't want to disrupt your lives." Miriam was trying to downplay her eagerness to connect with Julia, with family, but the wide grin on her face betrayed her.

"I'm glad you did. Has Catrina responded?" Julia asked.

"Not yet. But she's in California, so who knows what time it is over there?" Miriam said, laughing.

Julia nodded. Miriam was still adjusting to seeing her new sister, suddenly real, on the screen. "I called you on a whim. Didn't expect you to pick up . . ."

Miriam waved a hand dismissively. "I've been up for hours. Moving day is approaching, and there is too much to do." She gestured to the boxes behind her. "I'm heading to LA—a new city, a new start."

"LA?" Julia asked. "Why there?"

"After eight years on the same show, it's time for a new challenge. My agent will have auditions lined up. Also, I selected a house in Laurel Canyon. West Hollywood is beautiful. You need to visit."

"That's . . . big. Sounds like you've got a lot going on. Is that a stuffed koala behind you?"

"Ah, yes. I can't forget to pack Taronga the koala. Our dad sent it to me when I was a baby. Not sure why I keep it."

"Did you name it Taronga because of the zoo?" Julia asked.

"Yeah. The koala used to have a shirt that said 'Taronga Zoo.'"

"I'm sorry about Dad. He's a scumbag."

"Forget him," Miriam said, waving her hand. "What's happening in your world, Jules? May I call you Jules?"

Julia smiled, and Miriam felt a spark of connection. "Jules is fine. Nobody calls me that . . . but it sounds distinguished with your accent."

The nickname created a tiny bridge, closing the distance between them.

Julia continued, "It's been . . . a lot. Dad freaked out after I showed him your email, and things escalated. So I left home—for good. I'm figuring it out."

"You left the house? Now I feel terrible. I did not want to create drama."

"I'm twenty. It's time to get on with it. I considered it for ages, but Mum kept convincing me to stay. I needed a reason to go, and when he yelled at me over the email, it got me off my arse."

"I'm so sorry. Are you okay?" Miriam asked.

"More than okay. I feel free. I've known you for half a day, and you've already changed my life."

"Ugh. I can't believe one email . . . Well, leaving home is a big step. Do you have a plan?"

"You haven't lived till you slept on the beach," Julia said, laughing as she fell back in her chair.

"Seriously?" Miriam asked. The idea of sleeping anywhere but her home or a high-end hotel was foreign to her.

"I've done it before. No big deal. No scarier than moving from London to LA."

"Sure, but I already have a place . . . Do you need anything? Anything at all?"

"Nah. I'm pretty resourceful."

"Please be careful," Miriam said with a concerned look on her face.

"Always."

"Thank you for calling me so quickly." Miriam paused. "It means a lot—more than you can know. I've been floating since she died. And . . . it's a chance to have a family again. No pressure, though . . . I must sound like a crazy person."

"Not at all. This is great. Can we do it again tomorrow?" Julia asked.

"Of course."

They said their goodbyes, and the call disconnected.

Miriam burst into tears. She had hoped for a response to her email, but receiving a video call from her baby sister was more than she could have ever hoped for. Suddenly, she felt better and looked forward to seeing Linda.

CHAPTER 3

The call with Miriam was delightful. The actress Julia had seen on telly so many times was suddenly real and relatable. Miriam looked different than expected, her flowing golden waves replaced by a severe blonde pixie cut. Julia marveled at her movie-star blue eyes and instantly admired her older sister. After a tough morning at her parents' house, the call lifted Julia's spirits, energizing her to face her new challenges.

Julia stood on the Manly Promenade, ready to start her new life. The Northern Beaches community was alive with a distinct laid-back Sunday vibe. The lively promenade connected Manly Beach to the surrounding coastal trails. It stretched along the iconic beachfront, lined with Norfolk pines, and provided uninterrupted ocean views. The waves rolled in as surfers dotted the water like distant shadows. The promenade was crowded with joggers, cyclists, and families. Julia paused to take it all in. This was her scene. These were her people. And unlike the unfriendly confines of her father's house, there was freedom here.

She found a community bulletin board near a popular café and approached it, her duffel slipping off her shoulder. She scanned the pinned advertisements. Job ads, apartment listings, and flyers for surf lessons crowded the board. She considered offering surfing lessons to children, but the volume of ads on the board was discouraging. Perusing the rental market, she gagged—the prices were far beyond anything she could afford.

She hadn't thought this through.

Right when she was about to turn away, a flyer near the bottom of the board gave her hope.

> *Waitress Wanted: Greek Taverna.*
> *Experience preferred but not required.*
> *Apply in person.*

Julia liked the taverna and its owner, Gus. After early-morning surf sessions, Julia occasionally ate lunch at the taverna and found it casual and friendly. Gus had a big personality and was a local institution. Everyone in town knew him, and he knew their business. Another benefit was that the taverna was two blocks from the beach and only one block off the promenade, a short walk from where she stood.

As good a lead as any, Julia thought. If she could land the waitress job, she'd eventually be able to get a small flat. In the meantime, she'd find one of the girls she surfed with—someone would have a couch she could crash on for a few weeks until she'd saved enough for a deposit.

Things were falling into place.

She didn't regret leaving home, not one bit. The only thing that bugged her was leaving her giant trophy behind.

Saturday, November 20, 2004

Julia wasn't sure what had compelled her to enter the Sydney Junior Surf Classic at fourteen. It had been a whim, an impulsive decision, something she had never done before and wouldn't do again. The entry fee had been steep, but she had paid it with her money. Her hands rested lightly on Floating Sky, its smooth surface comforting as the bus inched closer to Bondi Beach. The board had been her companion for years, a constant through injury and frustration. She used the bus ride to focus on the task: delivering a measurable achievement to her dad.

The air at the competition was electric, alive with the sound of crashing waves and the chatter of spectators and competitors. Bondi Beach stretched before her, a sunlit expanse bordered by the turquoise sea. Tents and banners bearing the logos of major surf brands such as Rip Curl, Billabong, and Quiksilver lined the sand. Surfboards of every shape and size dotted the canvas. Julia couldn't help but smile at the sight.

She found a spot near the competitors' tent, laid out her things, and took in her surroundings. The other surfers, older and more experienced, moved with an air of confidence. Some chatted in groups, while most stood alone, scanning the waves as they mentally mapped out their runs. Julia was in awe of the scene but wasn't intimidated.

The event organizers set her heat for midmorning, giving her time to watch the other competitors. She learned the competition rules and observed the experienced surfers, studying their techniques, noting how they navigated the waves and chose their lines. The announcer's voice amplified over the loudspeakers, calling out scores and rankings. Julia ignored the spectacle on the beach and focused on the water and how the swells broke.

When her turn came, Julia zipped up her wetsuit and grabbed Floating Sky. She went to the water's edge, the sand cool beneath her feet. A long, steadying breath calmed her as she paddled out, and the familiar pull of the ocean centered her. The waves were perfect— clean, consistent, and powerful. Julia relaxed her body, her movements fluid and instinctive.

When the first set rolled in, she caught the wave, carving a clean line as she sped down the face. The crowd's cheers were distant, muted against the ocean's roar, but Julia didn't need encouragement.

She was at home, weaving through barrels and slicing expertly through the water. Julia won her heat decisively, securing a spot in the finals.

As Julia waited for the finals, Bondi Beach unfolded like a living postcard, its yellow sand framed by jagged cliffs on either end. The light-blue water sparkled under the midday sun, and the crash of waves filled the air, blending seamlessly with the crowd's murmur. To a surfer, Bondi was more than a beach—it was a proving ground, a stage where the ocean demanded respect and skill. It was one of the world's most iconic beaches, drawing a blend of elite surfers, international travelers, and Sydney locals who converged on its shores for the electric energy it radiated. Its fame came from the perfect intersection of natural beauty, cultural significance, and world-class surfing conditions.

The beach's unique geography—the way the shoreline curved into a perfect crescent and the reefs off the southern end—created ideal breaks. The waves were crisp, shaped by the offshore winds that blew in from the cliffs, giving them a distinctive quality. On this day, the afternoon water conditions were ideal: clean, consistent, and breaking to the right. Julia could see the sets rolling in from her vantage point, forming tapered peaks that promised long rides.

The finals began in the early afternoon, and the waves were fast and unpredictable, their steep walls demanding razor-sharp reflexes and commanding respect. Julia waited patiently, floating on the water, her eyes scanning for the perfect swell to close out the competition. When it came and she started her final run, the wave loomed larger than she'd expected. Its face shifted unpredictably as the offshore wind picked up. Doubt crept into her mind—had she misjudged its power? Hesitation had no place here. She paddled hard, and the water surged beneath her as she lifted.

Julia popped to her feet, her balance instinctive, but the wave pitched into a hollow, threatening to close out entirely. The lip curled abruptly, casting a shadow above her as the tube formed. Julia had no choice but to act. She dropped low with a powerful shift, crouching deep into the barrel. For a pulsating moment, it appeared she would be swallowed whole. The roar of the water surrounded her. The world was reduced to the barrel's thundering tunnel and the sunlight at its far edge.

Julia didn't panic. She held her line and adjusted her weight. Floating Sky responded as an extension of her body, and spray lashed her face as she emerged cleanly from the barrel. The crowd on the shore erupted in cheers, but Julia wasn't done. The wave's surge flattened, losing momentum, but Julia didn't let the run end. With a quick pump of her board, she regained speed and carved hard into a tight bottom turn, spraying an arc of water behind her.

As she raced toward the end of the wave, its face crumbled, threatening to knock her off balance. Julia leaned back, slicing her board across the collapsing lip in a sweeping cutback, reclaiming control with natural fluidity. The crowd's cheers grew louder as she transitioned into a final maneuver—a soaring, artistically executed aerial that sent her flying above the ocean. Floating Sky was momentarily airborne before they landed together with a triumphant splash.

Julia knew she won.

The awards ceremony began as the sun descended, casting a bronze glow over the beach. When the announcer declared Julia the winner, a surge of satisfaction washed over her. The victory was sweet. As Julia walked up to be honored, she plunged Floating Sky into the sand next to the stage and then accepted the comically oversized trophy from the competition director. The crowd cheered, cameras flashed, and Julia let herself bask in the accomplishment. Yes, it was about winning—delivering a measurable surfing achievement—but it was mostly about her love for the ocean and her connection to something larger than herself. Standing there on the stage, trophy in hand, Julia was thrilled. The applause and cheers were surreal. She curled her fingers around the trophy's base and posed for the cameras.

The long trip home, consisting of two buses and a ferry, was euphoric. Julia stared out the window, watching the city blur as she replayed the events of the day, but as the final bus wound closer to

Mosman, a different thought crept in—her parents hadn't seen the competition. Ray had had an important event at the Men's Club, and Alice, as usual, had been consumed by preparing for the next day's brunch. Julia tried to brush it off, telling herself their absence didn't matter, but the sting was undeniable.

When Julia arrived home, Ray was at the door, bouncing on his heels like a kid waiting for a birthday present. His eyes locked on the trophy, and he lit up with an excitement she hadn't seen before.

"There she is!" he exclaimed, stepping forward and grabbing the trophy out of her hands before she could say a word. "Let me see this beauty!"

Julia barely had time to adjust Floating Sky, which was awkwardly balanced under her arm, before he turned the massive trophy in his hands and inspected every detail. She dropped her duffel bag by the door and headed toward the kitchen. She had forgotten to eat all day and was famished.

"I can't believe you won. Quite the achievement!" Ray said, giddy.

"Yeah," Julia said, propping Floating Sky against the wall.

Ray's grin widened. "I've been hearing about it all day. The phone hasn't stopped ringing—friends, colleagues, everyone's talking about you. It's all over the radio!" His delight was evident. He strutted into the dining room, trophy in hand, and said, "Alice! Come and look at this!"

Julia had barely reached the kitchen when she had to change direction to the dining room as Ray called out.

He set the trophy on the dining table as if it was the crown jewel of the Corning household.

"Our daughter is back! You need to see this trophy!" Ray yelled to his wife.

Alice wiped her hands on a dish towel as her eyes widened when she saw the trophy, but her enthusiasm was subdued. "Oh my goodness, Julia," she said. "That's . . . incredible."

Julia noted how her mother's gaze darted back toward the kitchen, distracted by whatever she was cooking or prepping for the next day's brunch.

Ray didn't notice Alice's lackluster reaction. He was still smiling as he turned to Julia with a gleam in his eye. "I heard sponsors approached you—Rip Curl, Billabong, Quiksilver. They want to sponsor you! Do you have their business cards?"

Julia hesitated, reached into her pocket, and handed them over. "Yeah, they gave me cards," she said, devoid of the excitement from earlier at the beach.

Ray grabbed the cards with both hands, flipping through them like they were winning lottery tickets. "This is huge, Julia. Do you know what this means? Sponsorships, endorsements, opportunities!" His words came in a rush, as if he was piecing together a master plan.

Julia rolled her eyes as Ray paced, rattling off ideas about sponsorship meetings and turning her win into a "launch pad." The trophy she had earned with every ounce of her strength and skill was now sitting on the dining table, no longer hers. It was a centerpiece in Ray's imaginary future, a blueprint for his ambitions rather than a monument to her achievement. She considered interrupting him, asking him to stop, reminding him this was her win, her life. But she didn't. She stood there, silent, as his excitement filled the room.

"I'm glad you're excited, Dad. And today was a rush. But I'm not interested in any of the sponsorship stuff," Julia said.

Ray looked at her, his face faltering. "Not interested? Julia, do you realize what this could mean?"

"Today wasn't about all that. It was just . . . surfing."

"I don't understand. You have a gift, Julia. A talent most people would kill for. You're the best junior surfer in Sydney. You're eligible for nationals now. You could be the best in Australia with proper coaching and training. Sponsors will pay for the best instruction and cover the expenses for the major events."

"I was curious about how I would do at a competition, so I signed up. Turns out I'm pretty good. It was a cool day. But I have nothing else to prove."

"You have a lot left to prove. There are rumors that surfing will become an Olympic event. You could be an Olympian if you dedicate yourself. You have a special talent. Let's call these people and see how far you can go. I'm so proud of you."

"Here's the thing, Dad: I'm glad I did it, but it was a one-off."

"You're going to throw away your gift?"

"I'm not throwing anything away. I don't need sponsors and competitions to love surfing."

"Julia, my love, you're just exhausted. Today was a long and emotional day. We can discuss everything later. Tonight, we celebrate." Ray turned his head toward the kitchen. "Alice, cancel supper. Let's go out and celebrate," he said, lifting the trophy once again.

The trophy stayed in the dining room for weeks, a testament to her win and his parenting. Alice was forced to work around it when setting the table for Sunday brunch, and Ray recounted the competition to visitors as if he had witnessed it. Ray toured the trophy around the Men's Club, boasting about his daughter's talent to anyone who would listen.

Whether to preserve the purity of surfing or as a reaction to her father's response, Julia never competed again.

Sunday, October 3, 2010

Julia shook off the memory and headed toward the restaurant to see if the waitress job was still available.

The Manly Corso, a vibrant pedestrian walkway lined with shops and restaurants, stretched from the beach to the wharf on the harbor, a sensory bridge between the relaxed surf culture of Manly Beach and the commerce of the bustling city of Sydney. The storefronts teemed with focused locals and meandering tourists. Baby strollers weaved through the crowd, skillfully avoiding sightseers clutching ice cream cones.

Julia spotted the pastel-blue walls of the restaurant she sought, which stood out against the muted tones of the other shops on the quiet side street. The wooden sign above the door swayed in the breeze with faded paint: *Greek Taverna*. The restaurant looked old, but it was full of charm. From the sidewalk, Julia could smell the sizzling souvlaki and lemon-drenched potatoes combining with the salty air through the open windows.

The place was alive. A small cluster of regulars lingered near the door, chatting and laughing over their takeout bags. Inside, Julia could see families seated at the booths, their discussions rising over the occasional clink of plates and forks. The checkered floors added to the taverna's old-school charm. The walls were a gallery of Gus's life—black-and-white photographs and yellowed newspaper clippings captured moments from his childhood in Greece, his arrival in Australia, and the taverna's opening. Among them was a faded photo of a younger Gus standing beside his brother Nico, both grinning widely in front of the city's famed opera house. It was Nico's memorial, a quiet tribute to the brother who had died in a construction accident in 1977—the one topic Gus didn't discuss.

Opening the heavy glass door, Julia was greeted by the unmistakable baritone of Gus Alexopoulos himself. "Tzoúlia! *Havayiou*?" he bellowed from behind the counter, his thick mustache twitching as he grinned widely.

Gus made everyone feel like family, and Julia was no exception. It had been weeks since she had last stepped inside, but Gus treated her like a regular, giving her a unique nickname. He bustled around the counter, wearing his usual grease-stained apron and rolled-up sleeves. His stocky frame filled the space with his distinguished, slicked-back white hair. His hands, rough and weathered from years of hard work, moved efficiently as he delivered plates of food to a table of tourists.

"Gus," Julia greeted as she perched Floating Sky against the wall, ensuring it wouldn't topple over. She placed her duffel bag beside it and approached the counter, weaving past the crowded tables.

Gus's bushy eyebrows rose in curiosity as she approached. "So, Tzoúlia, what brings you in? Hungry, eh? Sit down. I'll get you something. Lemon potatoes, fresh pita, maybe a little souvlaki?"

Julia shook her head. "I already ate, Gus. But thanks. Actually, I saw you're looking for a waitress. Is the position still open?"

Gus laughed, his mustache twitching as his shoulders shook. "The job? For you? You know, the pay is no good!"

Julia couldn't help but smile. Gus's humor was infectious. The few patrons in proximity chuckled along with him. "I figured as much," she said, "but I need the work."

Gus studied a copy of the flyer on the counter as if he hadn't written it himself. "No experience required, it says. Ha! You ever waited tables before, Tzoúlia?"

"Not exactly," she said. "But I'm a fast learner. And I know how to handle people."

Gus nodded thoughtfully, scratching his chin. "That you do. You've got Greek taverna spirit—tough and no-nonsense." His eyes twinkled with mischief as he gestured toward an empty seat at the counter. "Alright, sit down. Let's make this official. A formal interview, Tzoúlia—very formal!"

Julia slid onto the counter stool that Gus had gestured to as the taverna buzzed with late-afternoon energy. Gus moved to the stool next to her, pausing only briefly to holler, "*Shurup*, William!" to a regular, teasing him before turning his attention back to Julia. "Alright, Tzoúlia. Let's talk. You want the job, huh?"

"Yes," Julia replied. "I'm a hard worker. I can handle long shifts, and I've been in enough restaurants to know the rhythm. I'll keep up."

"Hmm," he murmured, scratching his chin as he leaned against the counter. "Hard work is good, but this isn't about slapping plates on tables. This taverna is my home. My soul. People come here for the food, sure, but also for the family atmosphere. You think you can be that for them? Part of the family?"

Julia was unsure how to respond. "I . . . I think so. I've surfed in Manly since I was a kid. I know the locals, the regulars here. This beach is my family, too, in a way."

Gus's mustache twitched into a grin. "*Alo dali mou*, that's what I like to hear. Family. The people, not just the job." He signaled to an employee to make a coffee. "You want a coffee?"

"No, thanks," Julia said, "I'm all good."

"Aye, Tzoúlia," Gus said with a laugh. "You're too polite. It won't last long here. So tell me—what's your story?"

"My story?" Julia echoed. She hadn't expected this to get personal. "Uh, well, I left home . . . like, today."

Gus's forehead creased, but he didn't interrupt.

"I brought my board, a bag of clothes, and twenty-four dollars in my pocket. Actually, I spent four at the internet café, so now only twenty," she said, forcing a wry smile. "I'm winging it."

"Hmm," Gus said, stroking his mustache. "And the home you left? No good?"

Julia hesitated. "It was . . . complicated. But I'm here now, and I'm not going back. I'm ready to work hard and build something for myself."

Gus nodded. "Good. Sometimes, a fresh start is what you need. So you surf every day?"

"Just about," Julia said. "Manly is my spot. I love it here."

Gus's eyes twinkled. "Ah, that's good, Tzoúlia. The locals will like that. They'll see you belong." He slapped his hand on the counter, making her jump. "Alright, you've got the job."

"*Really?*"

"*Naí*," Gus said, grinning.

"That means *yes*, right?" Julia asked.

Gus nodded as the employee placed a coffee in front of Julia. "But where are you staying? Can't have my new waitress sleeping on the street."

Julia bit her lip. "That's . . . my next project."

"Well, lucky for you," Gus said, "my wife, Maria, and I lost our tenant in a one-room flat we own a few weeks back. It's five blocks from the beach. Not much—actually, it's quite terrible—but it's available."

"Wow," Julia said. "That'd be amazing, but . . ." She reached into her pocket.

Gus held up a hand, shaking his head. "Nah, nah, none of that. Remember when I said the pay is no good?"

Julia nodded cautiously.

"Well, if you take the flat, the pay becomes more-not good." Gus laughed. "Though when we get American tourists, they leave good tips." Gus paused and raised his voice, "Unlike these locals, who never leave my waitress a decent tip."

The restaurant cackled in unison.

"That's great," Julia said. "I don't need much. Do I get a meal with my shift?"

"*Fysiká*. All my workers must be experts in Greek food."

"Perfect, then *more-not-good pay* and occasional American tips are enough. Surfing is free."

"Ha!" Gus barked, slapping the counter again. "You've got it all figured out, eh? Alright, Tzoúlia, it's a deal."

Julia stood and extended her hand. "Thank you, Gus. I won't let you down."

"I know you won't," Gus said, shaking her hand. "Now, finish your coffee, and let's get started. I'll show you around the place. This is the start of something good. I can feel it."

Julia blinked, taken aback by the sudden declaration. "Wait—right now?"

"What better time to start? The dinner crowd's rolling in soon. You'll get a feel for the place and meet the regulars. Then, after we close tonight, I'll hand you the keys and take you to the flat."

"You're throwing me into the deep end, huh?"

"Tzoúlia, you're a surfer. Deep water doesn't scare you. You'll do fine."

"Sure . . ."

"The schedule is six days a week—three until closing, usually around eleven. Sundays are your day off. Don't be late. Work for you?"

"*Naí*," Julia said.

"That's the Greek spirit! Alright, let's get you set up," Gus said, motioning her to follow him behind the counter. He handed her a clean apron, and she smiled. "You'll start by shadowing me," Gus said, retying his apron to demonstrate for Julia. "Watch how I take orders and interact with customers. By tomorrow, you'll know everyone's names and Bruce's dreadfully dull life story," Gus said, pointing to a gray-haired customer who feigned outrage. "This place runs on community. Now, let's go. Dinner rush waits for no one."

Julia tied the apron strings around her waist as shown, centered herself, and followed Gus. The past few hours had been a whirlwind —leaving her parents' house, starting fresh in Manly, having a great talk with Miriam, and now walking straight into a new job that came with housing. Everything was coming together.

CHAPTER 4

Catrina had lived twenty-two years without a father, and now, out of nowhere, a purported half sister wanted to chat. She cleared her inbox before heading to work and read the note from Miriam. Catrina was at a loss. She wasn't missing a family. She had her mother, Morven—ever-present, constantly in her business. She had Sam and the rest of her friends. Her instinct was to ignore the email and let it rot in her read folder.

She left for work without telling her mother about the email intrusion. Morven would have all the feelings and opinions, and Catrina didn't want to hear them. Her mom had been twenty-two when she'd gotten pregnant, a topic they had discussed openly. A distant relative had died, leaving Morven a small inheritance—not enough to change her life but plenty for one grand adventure to Australia. *The first of many faulty financial decisions*, Catrina mused. Sydney had been warm and the drinks strong, and a local named Ray had charmed Morven's pants off, literally. Morven had gone home to California pregnant and, *like always, without a plan,* Catrina thought.

Morven had reached out to Ray not for love or partnership but for help. Subsistence-level child support would have made everything more manageable, but he had made it clear he wanted nothing to do with them. Morven had consulted a family law attorney, only to be told there were no options since he was a foreign national. She had let the matter go and never contacted Ray again.

To Catrina, Raymond Corning was nothing more than a name on her birth certificate.

As a teenager, she had found pictures of him online, and to her annoyance, she looked like him. She had inherited her mother's short stature, but Catrina's darker complexion and light brown hair came from Ray. Morven, with her fair skin, long auburn curls, and effortless smile, was every bit the daughter of Scottish immigrants.

Catrina had never thought about her absentee father. Her mother wasn't perfect—not even close—but she was present. Available. Morven's life may have been chaotic, her vocational choices incoherent, and her financial planning nonexistent, but she provided unwavering maternal support. Catrina had a home, people who cared about her, and a budding career. She didn't need sisters scattered across the globe; her life felt complete. Catrina was ready to ignore the email, but before she did, she wanted Sam's opinion—in case she was missing something.

Nestled in the middle of Carlsbad Village, the Break was a female-owned coffee shop that conveyed local charm. Its sprawling outdoor patio was a hub that other independently owned businesses gravitated toward. Known for its ethically sourced coffee, including a signature blend from its small-batch roastery, the Break exuded an artsy vibe that drew locals and well-researched tourists. The decor was blog-worthy without chasing trends, focusing on a creative, welcoming environment paired with consistently excellent drinks.

Samantha Bouchard, known to her friends as Sam, put people at ease. Her shoulder-length brunette hair, often loosely tucked behind her ears, framed deep-brown eyes that noticed the little details. She was a thoughtful barista whose knack for recommending the perfect book and crafting a comforting cup of coffee had earned her a devoted following in Carlsbad. Openly and confidently living as a lesbian, Sam channeled her creativity into making the Break an inclusive and inviting space.

Sam looked up and greeted Catrina. "Hey, Cat! Are you excited for your second anniversary at work? Will they throw you a big party?"

"Yeah, and Tim will pat me on the back."

"Eww. A pat or a rub?"

"Cute—I meant metaphorically," Catrina said, smiling

Sam reached for a cup. "Usual today?"

Catrina nodded and pulled a folded piece of paper from her back pocket. "Want to hear something bizarre?"

"Always."

"I got this email Saturday, but just saw it this morning before leaving the house," Catrina said while handing the paper to Sam. "It's from an actress in London claiming to be my sister. I googled her —she's on a hospital show over there."

"Your sister? Oh—another daughter from your MIA. dad?" Sam asked, with a smirk, but her tone suggested empathy.

"Yeah, and it gets weirder," Catrina said, awkwardly picking at her jacket sleeve. "She emailed me and another girl, Julia, from Australia. She's claiming all three of us are sisters—same dad."

Sam's smirk turned into a grin, seemingly trying to lighten the mood. "Are you sure this isn't one of those scams where you have to send money to a prince to save his kingdom?"

"Ha. No. She attached a report from a private investigator. It was comprehensive. Everything appears to be true. The investigator somehow obtained our birth certificates. Couldn't have been cheap. It was a lot of work."

"Well, actresses are rich, and in this day and age, investigators can track down anything." Samantha finished the email and put it down. Her voice softened. "I wonder why she reached out now," she said.

"From what I can tell, her mom died last year. She was very enthusiastic about having sisters. I guess she's looking for a family connection."

"Pretty cool. New pen pals, and if you ever travel overseas, you'd have a place to stay . . ."

"I hadn't thought of it that way," Catrina said as she looked down, now fiddling with the edge of the table. "They didn't do anything wrong."

"Exactly," Sam said, tucking a loose strand of hair behind her ear.

"The report aligns with what Mom told me. My dad is the villain here, not them. I'm surprised he only has two other kids," Catrina said, finally smiling.

"How crazy is it that you have half sisters in Australia and London? Are you going to respond? Tell Morven?"

"Yeah, I'll tell her. She loves drama," Catrina said. "And my instinct was to ignore it, but after talking to you, maybe I'm open to talking to them . . . but not if it means dealing with the deadbeat. I want nothing to do with him."

"Fair enough," Sam said, reaching over and squeezing Catrina's hand. "Your boundaries are nonnegotiable. How can I help?"

"You already have," Catrina said with a sense of relief, Sam's reaction putting her at ease. "I'll think about it some more. I've got to get to work. Still good to run this evening?"

"Of course. Wanna grab a sandwich after? I hate going to the deli like a sweaty mess, and I have nothing in the fridge at home," Sam said.

"Sure. But how will I make you less sweaty? Want me to towel you off?" Catrina said without thinking. When she realized what she had said, her cheeks flushed.

"If you like . . . Ha . . . No, I meant when two of us look a mess, the embarrassment is spread thinner."

Catrina nodded. As she walked out of the coffee shop, she was mortified at the towel comment but thankful for Sam's help in putting her sister's email into perspective. She'd talk to her mom about it and decide whether to respond. It might be fun to have sisters.

In the meantime, she was eager to get to the office. There would be an anniversary party to commemorate her milestone. What had started as a college internship had turned into a career, and she loved it.

———

Catrina, a junior in college at the time, stepped out of her car, clutching her bag, and marveled at DeltaTech's headquarters. The tall, modern building had a buffed glass exterior that gleamed under the blue sky. The landscaping was pristine, with trimmed hedges, vibrant California poppies, hibiscus, and bush sunflowers lining the walkway to the automatic sliding doors. A bold, minimalistic company logo etched into a steel panel beside the entrance gave the building a professional look.

Inside, the lobby floors were seamless gray slate, while the walls featured a mix of neutral tones accented by bold splashes of color—greens and blues that evoked trust and innovation. The receptionist's desk was an elegant minimalist piece in steel and glass, and the large LED screen behind it displayed DeltaTech's up-to-date product line and recent achievements. Everything about the space exuded efficiency, progress, and ambition.

Catrina straightened her chin-length wavy hair and approached the elevator bank, where an HR representative was waiting. Rachel, a no-nonsense-looking woman in her early forties with dark eyes and a professional air, greeted her with a brisk smile. "Catrina McDavid, right? Welcome aboard," she said, extending a hand.

"Thank you," Catrina replied, shaking Rachel's hand. Her nerves were frayed, but she pushed them aside, determined to make a good impression.

Rachel led her through bright, open hallways illuminated by overhead lighting. The carpet was a subtle pattern of blue and gray, softening the footsteps in the bustling office. Glass-walled meeting rooms with large screens and ergonomic furniture lined the corridors. Employees moved through the space with purpose. Some gathered in collaborative hubs featuring modular seating and digital whiteboards. It was a hive of activity that perfectly reflected the fast-paced world of medical device sales.

They arrived at a small desk tucked into the corner of an open workspace. It was modest but modern, with a dual-monitor setup, a standing desk option, and a streamlined docking station. "This will be your spot for the internship," Rachel said, gesturing toward the desk. "You'll find everything you need to get started in the top drawer. If you need anything else, let me know." Rachel hesitated as if considering her next words before saying, "Tim Brockwell will be your direct supervisor. He should be coming by to give you an orientation shortly." She paused again. "If you have any issues *at all*, you can always come to me."

Catrina tilted her head. "Thanks, Rachel. I'll keep that in mind."

Rachel nodded briskly and gave her a small, encouraging smile. "Good luck, Catrina. I'm sure you'll do great." With that, she turned and walked away, leaving Catrina alone.

Five minutes later, Tim Brockwell strode over, cutting through the office like a spotlight through the fog. His confident gait, crisp polo shirt that hugged his athletic frame, and pressed slacks immediately caught her attention. Catrina straightened instinctively as he approached.

"Catrina McDavid," Tim said, his demeanor playful yet commanding. He extended a hand, and when she took it, his grip was firm but not crushing. "Welcome to the team. I've heard good things about you."

"You have? And call me Cat." The heat rose to her cheeks as she realized she had just flirted with him. Embarrassed, she glanced around the open-plan office, trying to mask her discomfort and wondering who could have already mentioned her to him.

Tim leaned in, lowering his voice as though sharing a secret. "I make it my business to know who's joining my team. I've been told you're sharp, hardworking, and capable. I see a lot of smarts behind those blue eyes. That's exactly what I want in my interns."

His words lit a spark of satisfaction in her, and Catrina smiled.

Tim pulled a chair from a nearby desk and sat across from her, his movements smooth and deliberate, his body language open but powerful.

"I'm glad you're here," he continued, his hazel eyes locking on to hers. "DeltaTech isn't any medical device company. We're shaping the future of healthcare. And I see people like you as part of the future." He leaned back, spreading his arms in a casual yet commanding gesture. "Tell me, what made you want to work with us?"

Catrina hesitated. "Well, I'm still in school at UC San Diego," she began, "but I've always been interested in the medical field. I thought this internship would be a great way to—"

"Smart move," Tim said. "Starting young and building a foundation early—that's how you succeed. I did the same thing, you know. I worked my way up from nothing." He gestured around the office as if to emphasize the empire he was building. "This place? It's not a job. It's a springboard. You can go as far as you want if you're willing to put in the work."

Catrina was captivated by his energy. Tim had a way of making everything sound more significant. It was no longer just an internship but a stepping-stone to greatness.

Tim shifted gears. "What about you? Tell me about your goals. What do you want to achieve?"

"I'm not sure yet. I want to learn as much as possible and figure out where I fit."

Tim grinned. "That's a great answer. Honest, humble. But let me give you a tip: Never tell people you don't know where you fit. Tell them you belong. Confidence, Cat. It's the key to everything. But here's the thing," he said. "Success isn't only about hard work. It's about relationships. That's the real game, Cat." He smiled again. His casual use of her nickname sounded intimate. "Your job here is simple: Make me look good. Help me shine in front of the clients and the bosses. You do that, and I promise you'll go far."

Catrina blinked, unsure how to respond. Tim didn't leave room for awkward silences. He rested his forearms on the desk between them, and his tone changed. It was vaguely conspiratorial when he said, "You've got promise, Cat. But let me tell you something most people won't: The corporate world isn't about who's the brightest in the room. It's about who can command attention and make people believe in their vision. You help me do that, and we'll be unstoppable."

She nodded.

Tim was magnetic, a tsunami of confidence, a nonstop ball of charisma. He wasn't talking about himself—he was talking about her potential, her future. Catrina appreciated his self-assurance, which helped her overcome her first-day insecurities. She was in the presence of someone who had figured it all out, somebody she could shadow and who would have her back.

Tim glanced at his watch and stood from the chair. "I've got a meeting in a few minutes, but before I go, let me give you a piece of advice: This job is what you make of it. You've got a clean slate here, a chance to prove yourself. Don't waste it." He touched her back with his hand and let it linger a second or two longer than appropriate, though Catrina didn't mind.

"And if you ever need anything—advice, help with a project, whatever—come to me. My door's always open for people willing to do the work," Tim said.

"Thank you," Catrina said with genuine gratitude. "I appreciate it."

Tim nodded, flashing one last, dazzling smile. "Welcome to DeltaTech, Cat. You're going to do great things."

Catrina was appreciative of the attention and mentorship he promised. Still, she took a moment to reflect on her tendency to people-please, which was the only reason she still lived in California.

During her senior year of high school, she had received a scholarship offer that was a dream come true: a full ride to Davidson College, a small school in North Carolina that promised a future far removed from the uncertainty of her life in Carlsbad. It was her chance to reinvent herself and escape the constant pressure of being the responsible one, the fixer, the rock. But when she had told her mom about the opportunity, her mom's excitement had been more complicated than the expected maternal pride. Catrina's mom had smiled brightly, but her eyes had betrayed a different emotion. It wasn't sadness—it was panic, poorly disguised.

Despite loving Morven, Catrina was frustrated by her mother's impulsivity and lack of foresight. It wasn't only financial problems, but the emotional toll of being the responsible member of the relationship. Catrina had often come home from school to find her mother crying over a bad breakup, lamenting a failed business venture, or scrambling to find their next physical address.

Catrina's decision to attend UC San Diego hadn't been made lightly. The Davidson scholarship had been her ticket to freedom, to a life where she wouldn't have to hold everything together, but Morven had given up so much for her. She had put her dreams on hold—whatever they may have been—to raise a daughter alone, juggling multiple jobs and constant stress. How could Catrina justify leaving her behind now? Ultimately, she had rationalized her decision: UC San Diego was a good school, and the proximity to home meant she could continue to help her mother. It wasn't the escape she had dreamed of, but it was the right thing to do—or so she told herself.

CHAPTER 5

Night Nurses was filmed at a sprawling utilitarian studio tucked into an industrial pocket of London. Miriam arrived expecting a grand send-off fitting her contribution to making the show an international success.

Though it wasn't announced publicly that this was her last season, it was well known on set. To Miriam's surprise, before filming started, there was no acknowledgment—no speech from the director, no red English roses, no parting gifts, no mention of her final day. It didn't bother her, as she figured they were saving it for afterward. She got into wardrobe, ran through her lines, and stepped onto set.

The hospital corridor set was bright, sterile, and lined with gurneys and monitors positioned to mask the flimsy plywood walls. The cameras rolled, and she delivered one last booming performance as Greta Simmons, the quick-witted, loose-tongued nurse supervisor.

Then—cut.

The set dissolved into routine. The crew moved on to the next setup. The director studied his notes and storyboards. Her co-stars whispered to each other, unhooked their mics, and wandered to their dressing rooms.

Miriam scanned the studio, waiting for a nod, a handshake, a "We'll miss you." Nothing. The same people who had worked beside her for years packed up and moved on as if she had never been there.

Three years ago, when the cast's collective contract had expired, Miriam had refused to participate in group negotiations. In retrospect, that had been the final splintering with her castmates.

During negotiations, Rosalind had been adamant that Miriam receive her full value. And she had. She had secured a substantial raise over the other actors and had agreed to a three-year extension. The British tabloids had devoured the drama, siding with her and anointing her as the show's indispensable star, further widening the divide.

A year into the new contract, Miriam had soured on the show and the cast. The tension on set had been intolerable. Miriam vividly recalled her conversation with Linda at the time.

"I want out of *Night Nurses*. It's not the same anymore," Miriam said. "The cast can't stop whining about my success. Whenever I win an award or receive a positive review, they act as if I've stolen something from them. The role is creatively stifling, Linda. I have been playing Greta Simmons for six years now. Six years! There is nothing else for me to explore with Greta. I'm not progressing as an actress."

"I get it, Mir. I do. You're ambitious, and that's part of what makes you so good. But let's be practical. You've got two more seasons on your contract, and the show remains wildly popular. Walking away would burn bridges—and they're hard to rebuild."

After a pause, Miriam asked, "And what about me, Linda, my career? Am I supposed to keep playing the same character until I'm typecast?"

"No, of course not," Linda answered. "But this show is the reason you're a household name. It's given you a platform to negotiate the roles you'll want once it's over. Look, I hear you. The cast is jealous—that's their issue, not yours."

"I'm stuck."

"I get that. But you'll leave on top if you finish these last two seasons. No bad blood, no unfinished business. Then you move to Hollywood, focusing entirely on film and prestige television. Trust me, Mir, you'll have producers lining up to work with you."

There was a pause, and then Miriam sighed. "You always make the bitter pill go down easier."

"It's my job," Linda replied. "So can I take this as you agreeing to stick it out?"

"Fine. But promise to find me something big and challenging after this."

"I promise," Linda said.

───

Now, standing on set for the last time, Miriam told herself it didn't matter; she didn't need their appreciation. But as she lingered, doubt crept in. This hurt. Being iced by her coworkers of eight years stung more than she wanted to admit. Maybe she had been too blunt, too demanding, too selfish, too unwilling to meet them halfway. She tried to shake off the feelings and walked off set with her head high.

Miriam went to greet Linda in the lobby, but Nigel, the showrunner, was already talking to her agent. Miriam hung back and watched the interaction.

Nigel's face was a mask of angst and frustration. "How did you let Miriam cut her hair before the season finale?" he barked at Linda. "We spent unbudgeted money on a wig, and it doesn't look right. She's been an absolute nightmare this year, and this haircut is her final . . ." Nigel turned the back of his hand toward Linda with two fingers raised, an unmistakable gesture in Britain that would have been lost on the American agent.

"Nigel, her mom died last year. Give her a break. She's carried this show for years. A little gratitude and understanding are appropriate," Linda said, hands on her hips.

"We've been patient with her and adjusted last year's shooting schedule to accommodate. Enough is enough. The audience has expectations, and she shows up to the final week of shooting with a completely different look. It's very unprofessional."

"My sources confirmed she'll be nominated for another BAFTA this year. Based on the competition, she'll win it too. How dare you complain about her look. What the fuck do you know about women's hairstyles? I bet half of London cuts their hair to match her after the tabloids run pictures."

"Look, Linda, I bet she didn't even tell you. She's out of control."

Linda didn't back down. "Nobody else in this building has won a BAFTA. She has three. Soon to be four. You should be kissing her ass, not complaining."

Nigel groaned and stomped off in a huff. Miriam was irritated by his tone but proud to have an agent who vigorously had her back, always.

Miriam instinctively reached into her purse, opened a discreet bag of pills, took a handful, tilted her head back, and dramatically threw them into her mouth before fully entering the lobby, still in costume, and wrapping Linda in a hug.

"Do you love my hair?" Miriam asked, faking a smile while removing her wig. "This will help my Hollywood rebrand."

"It's great, but the producers aren't happy about it," Linda said.

"They have no vision," Miriam said dismissively. "It would've been a great way to write me out of the show, but the writers are lazy and a little stupid. Hey, I know a great place to eat. Give me twenty minutes, and I'll be out."

Miriam went to her dressing room to change. With her mother gone, she realized, Linda was the most important person in her life. She trusted Linda completely. She decided at that moment to let Linda guide her career in Los Angeles.

She wouldn't repeat the mistakes she had made in London. She wouldn't talk to the press, especially about her co-stars.

As Miriam stood, the pills took effect. Her body went numb, she began to sway, and she leaned against the wall.

It was decided.

Linda would be her mouthpiece.

Linda would tell her story.

Miriam sat in her dressing room chair as her mind went blissfully blank.

Linda

Linda Edelstein sat upright in the lobby of the television studio, the soft leather chair creaking as she glanced at the clock. Ten minutes until her lunch with Miriam. Meetings with Miriam required a certain level of preparation—not professionally but emotionally. Miriam was brilliant and magnetic but often exhausting.

Linda was a homebody and missed the comforts of Los Angeles. She closed her eyes and pictured her office in Beverly Hills, the framed posters lining the walls—films and television shows she had helped bring to life by supplying the talent. Each piece of memorabilia was a reminder of the countless battles fought and won in a notoriously cutthroat industry. Now in her late fifties, she had spent nearly three decades in a business that prized youth and ambition.

She had witnessed many bright stars burn out, their potential snuffed by the pressures of celebrity. But Miriam was different. She had the talent and the resilience to weather the storms of fame. Miriam struggled with the loss of her mother and wore her grief. She had always been driven, clever, and ambitious, but after Rosalind's death, her affect had become flat. Her once keen focus had dulled, and her behavior had become unpredictable; her moods were erratic, and her performances on set were uneven. Linda feared that medication abuse was contributing to Miriam's personality changes. In addition, the contempt Miriam had long hidden for the show that had made her a household name was now obvious. The timing was right for a split. Miriam was tired of playing Greta Simmons, and her castmates were tired of her. After years of being the standout in an ensemble cast, Miriam was ready to move on to bigger things, to become a star in Los Angeles.

As Miriam sat beside her in the car, silent with arms crossed and sunglasses masking her expression, Linda couldn't help but reflect on the eight years she had represented the actress. She recalled the night she had first seen Miriam on stage in London. It had been a chilly evening, and she had nearly skipped the small community theater production in favor of an industry networking event, but something had told her to go. She lived for these moments—the thrill of discovery, the anticipation of finding someone incredible. And Miriam was outstanding. At seventeen, she had commanded the stage with a confidence and grace that belied her age. Her portrayal of Barbara Fordham in *August: Osage County* was electrifying. Linda had found a prodigy in an unlikely venue.

The memory still gave her satisfaction. Signing Miriam was one of the best decisions of her career. The girl was all perfect angles and luminous beauty, with a mind that moved as quickly as her tongue. Linda witnessed plenty of young talent, but Miriam was different, extraordinary. Her greatest asset and Achilles' heel was confidence that bordered on arrogance, depending on the recipient's perspective.

Linda thought about what she wanted to say at lunch and how to guide Miriam through her latest challenges without stepping on her pride. Miriam didn't take criticism lightly, even when it was constructive. But Linda knew her client—when to push and when to pull back, letting Miriam figure things out. Whatever the meeting would bring, Linda was ready. She had built her career on navigating the unpredictable, and Miriam was worth the effort. She would guide Miriam because Miriam, like all her clients, wasn't a name on a roster but was part of her family.

By the time they reached Sartoria on Savile Row—a recommendation from Stanley Tucci, as Miriam was fond of pointing out—the actress was disoriented. Her usual poise had slipped, leaving her disheveled, distracted, and verbally scattered. Miriam seemed oblivious to the restaurant's high ceilings, marble surfaces, soft leather banquettes, and brass accents.

The restaurant was impressive. Impeccably dressed waiters delivered handmade Italian dishes to tables on crisp white tablecloths, accompanied by sommelier-paired wines. Everywhere she turned, high-dollar business deals were negotiated over al den*te* pasta.

Linda and Miriam started by discussing Miriam's call with Julia. After a year of prompting, Linda was glad Miriam had finally made the connection. Miriam seemed genuinely excited about the conversation, and Linda encouraged her to keep that line of communication open—it was healthy—before shifting to work. "I know the answer, but I'm not doing my job if I don't ask it. *Night Nurses* will be doing another season—"

"No chance."

"Okay, I agree. But it's my job to remind you we don't have any firm offers in hand."

Miriam, her eyes unfocused and wandering around the restaurant, audibly sighed. "Linda, you're the best agent in the world. I told you two years ago when I agreed to stay in London that you had to get me something big. You promised. What have you found? What are my options?"

Linda pulled out her notebook and began outlining some of the projects and promising opportunities available. As she discussed the pros and cons of movies versus television, Miriam interrupted. "Should I start with a big-budget movie? I'll only consider studio movies or prestige TV shows on HBO, Showtime, or AMC."

Linda ignored the petulant interjection. "Movies are hit-and-miss. A good prestige television show means years of income. Movies are high risk, high reward. They offer big paydays when they hit, but they don't always pan out. A few great movie roles don't necessarily guarantee long-term stability. You're not yet in a position to secure leading roles above the marquee, so you're at the mercy of the headliners. The industry is fickle, and one flop can set you back. With TV, a solid, long-running show—especially the kind of series we're discussing—provides consistent work. It keeps you in the public eye. It's income you can count on for years, not a one-off check." Linda paused for a moment, making sure Miriam was with her, then continued.

"And beyond the financial benefits, consider the opportunities that come with a successful series. A prestige show can open doors for film roles, endorsements, modeling gigs, and other projects. It can elevate your profile in ways a single movie might not. It's about building a sustainable foundation. This is about the bigger picture, Mir. You're not looking for a quick win. You're looking for long-term success." She studied Miriam's face closely, waiting for a reaction, hoping she was getting through.

"Sounds like you want me to do TV," Miriam said, with a dismissive eye roll.

Linda, frustrated by Miriam's tone, twirled a forkful of silky pappardelle, the fresh pasta coated in a rich, velvety ragu. "Yes. I would prefer you become a regular on an American show rather than be the fifth lead in a movie. The money is better."

"Linda, Mum is dead, and I inherited everything. I'm proper posh. I have more money than I could ever spend. It's not my priority." Miriam then began rambling incoherently about the West Hollywood home she'd just bought with Rosalind's money. She pulled out her phone to show Linda the kitchen, pool, state-of-the-art theater, and lush landscaping.

Miriam's words were out of character. She was usually polite, sophisticated, and careful with language. She would never discuss money or her financial situation in such a crass manner. This version of Miriam—detached, crude, and dismissive—was unrecognizable. Linda attributed the behavior to whatever medication Miriam was on, but it was still unsettling, and her patience was wearing thin. It was time to discuss the unpleasant topic.

"Mir, I've received complaints about your behavior. What's going on?"

"Nothing. That's absurd. Who complained?"

"That doesn't matter. I'm concerned. How can I support you?"

"Nothing is wrong. I'm just tired of being in London. I'm all alone. I need a fresh start. Have for a while now."

"That's understandable. And you're getting one. I want to make sure you're okay before we add the stress of a new project. What medications are the doctors giving you these days? Perhaps we should get a second opinion in LA."

"I do want an LA doctor. These Brits—"

"Mir, please answer me. What medications are you on?"

"I don't know—a few different ones. Klonopin is the main one. It helps me sleep, which started being a problem after Mum died. And anxiety—especially from those arsehole producers who ambushed you at the studio. Can you imagine dealing with those pricks every day?" Miriam grabbed her glass of wine and took an exaggerated gulp before excusing herself to use the bathroom.

While she was gone, Linda googled on her phone and found: *It is important not to mix Klonopin and alcohol, as they can quickly enhance each other's effects, which can lead to a higher risk of overdose, hospitalization, and death.*

Miriam returned and took her seat. She appeared disoriented.

"Did you take Klonopin before we left the studio? You're not supposed to drink—"

"I'm careful. You know me, Linda."

The constant interruptions and Miriam's overall attitude shut Linda down, and the lunch devolved into Miriam's disjointed, unproductive rambling, uninterrupted by Linda. Miriam bounced from one topic to another, from her new house in Laurel Canyon to an offhand comment about a random film project, her frustration with past roles, and a fleeting mention of a restaurant she had visited in Paris. None of it was connected; it had no substance. When Linda tried to engage, Miriam didn't listen. Instead, she was in a cycle of self-indulgence, lost in her thoughts, unaware of the time passing.

Flying to London to discuss Miriam's future had been a waste of time, Linda decided. Her irritation was hard to shake. Here she was, trying to help Miriam take the next step in her career, but Miriam didn't have herself in order. Linda recognized the behavior—a client unwilling to confront personal issues, thinking past success and charm would be enough. They weren't.

As Miriam wound down, Linda decided to give her some tough love. "Mir, I love you, and I've got your back, but you need to be clear-headed when you arrive in LA. You'll have to audition for these roles. If you're not at the top of your game, at least two dozen actresses will take the jobs from you."

Miriam waved off the concern with a casual flick of her hand. "Linda, trust me. I'm ready. I'll crush it. Get me auditions, and I'll get the parts."

With that, the lunch was over. Linda helped Miriam into a cab and texted her assistant to book the next available flight to Los Angeles. The original plan to spend a few days in London was now intolerable. She headed straight to the airport, determined not to linger another minute.

Linda made it through security and customs in record time and arrived at the British Airways International Wing Lounge at Heathrow, her body weighed down with exhaustion. This day had been one of her least favorite in recent memory. She was ready to leave it behind, starting with a glass of wine and a new book. She approached the bar, glanced at the flight board, and saw an upcoming flight to New York's JFK airport. For the briefest moment, she considered taking the flight and visiting her brother Avi in Brooklyn, but she dismissed the idea just as quickly.

Wine in hand, she found a quiet corner and grabbed her book, eager to sit down, detach, and let the day go, but before she could settle in, her phone vibrated. The screen flashed with Nigel's name, and, with a sigh, she braced herself.

"Hello, Nigel. Miss me already?"

"Linda, I'm making this call out of respect for you and your agency. I wanted you to hear it directly from me—*Night Nurses* will not offer Ms. Worthington a new contract. Her behavior—"

"Let me stop you there. I was about to hit Send on an email telling you Miriam wasn't coming back. I think you expected that, hence your call." Linda was obfuscating, but she couldn't resist the *you can't fire us, we quit.*

Nigel continued, "We get it. The personalities weren't right on set. It's best for all parties to go in separate directions."

"I agree. Thanks for calling—"

"Wait, wait."

"Yes, Nigel?"

"Miriam, when her head is screwed on straight, is a telly star—"

"I'm done. I'm not going to listen to you shit talk. Bye, Nigel."

"I'm sorry. Give me a minute. What I'm trying to say is LA is a mistake. She's not a movie star or cut out for Hollywood."

"Absurd. Talented, attractive blondes with top representation don't struggle for work in LA. Hell, she can make a fortune modeling between movie roles if she wants."

"Maybe, but she could be on British television for the next thirty years. She's perfect for what we do. She's funny without trying, has perfect timing, and can handle dramatic moments—a rare combination. What about a spin-off show? We can keep her character going but remove all the problematic castmates. We hire supporting actors who know their place. With proper expectations set, no one will grumble. They'll be thrilled to have work and will credit Miriam. A Greta-centered show will be a success. I ran it up the flagpole at the BBC. They'll do a full-season pickup, no questions asked. No pilot needed. Netflix will acquire the US rights, and Foxtel will pay for the Australian rights. This is a big payday all around. What do you say?"

"Nigel, that's a nice offer. But Miriam's mind is made up. She bought a house in LA. She's moving—"

"She can work in LA during the off-season."

"Your shows have such long shooting schedules, and it'll be the same problem. The opportunity is good—*really* good. But Miriam's done with Greta, no way around it. Thanks for trying, but it's a pass."

Linda was past tired. She sipped her wine and reached to turn off her phone, ready to close the workday, when a new email notification popped up across the screen: *Linda, I love you. Thank you for everything. I can't wait to see you in LA.* —*Miriam.*

As she read the email, a sense of amity spread through her body. The note was a small gesture, but it meant a lot. Even at her absolute worst, Miriam was a good person. She was family.

CHAPTER 6

A s the workday came to a close, Catrina straightened her desk. She was looking forward to her run with Sam and the chance to finally talk through whether she should contact her newfound half sisters. She had been going back and forth all day. Her initial reaction to the email had been negative, but now she was leaning toward responding, if only out of curiosity.

She was halfway through aligning the edges of a stack of documents when she heard Tim's footsteps approaching. Sure enough, he came bounding over, his high-energy stride tempered by a hushed tone. Two years of working for him at DeltaTech taught her to be cautious when he acted in this manner.

"Hey, Catnip, what's going on?" he said, lurking over her desk with a grin.

Catrina tensed at the seemingly playful nickname. She hated it and considered correcting him but let it slide, once again, since Tim took corrections poorly.

"Just wrapping up," she replied.

"I've got the opportunity of a lifetime," Tim said as he lorded over her.

Catrina paused, unsure where this was going. "Okay . . ." she said, glancing at him to gauge his intentions.

"I can trust you, right?" Tim continued in a whisper. "If I tell you something, will you keep it private? Even if you decide not to take the opportunity—which, let's be real, you'd be a fool not to, and you're no fool."

Catrina, doing her best to suppress her confusion, said, "Of course, Tim. You know I'm trustworthy. What's going on? This isn't like you—you're not usually one for all this preamble."

Tim grinned. "Here's the deal: I'm starting my own company. It's a distribution business—but not any distribution business. This is going to revolutionize the medical device field. I've been working on this behind the scenes for months. I've built the right contacts, secured a key supplier, and already have end users lined up. This is going to be huge, Cat. But I need the right people to help me launch it. People I can trust. Someone like you."

"Wow. Okay," she said, "so you're going into distribution?"

"DeltaTech is too focused on R&D and licensing," Tim said, shaking his head. "That's where they pour all their money. And when they see a product they didn't develop, their solution is to try and acquire the company. Costs the shareholders a fortune. Being the middleman is where the real money is. Let the suppliers invest in development, and we'll connect them with the end users. Pure profit for us—no R&D, no manufacturing, no stock to maintain. Just customer service. That's what I'm good at. What we're good at."

Tim took a brief pause before continuing. "It's about building a streamlined network that makes the current system obsolete. The big players are bloated and inefficient. I've identified the gaps, and if we move fast and smart, we can fill those gaps before anyone else does. You understand the field and know how to handle clients. You'd be my first hire, my right hand. We'd build this together."

Catrina was torn between being flattered and wary of his overconfidence. "Tim, that's . . . ambitious. It's a lot to think about. I need to hear more before I can make a decision."

"Fair enough. I'll show you exactly why this will work. But not here. Meet me at your coffee shop in fifteen minutes."

"The Break?"

"Yeah, the one with that cute brunette barista playing hard to get."

"You aren't her type."

Tim shrugged and trotted off.

As Catrina packed up, her body went cold, which she attributed to nervousness. She didn't love Tim's uncharacteristically hushed tone and refusal to discuss details inside the office, which made her fear Tim's plan wasn't entirely aboveboard.

Nearly a year ago, Catrina had come home to a crisis. She recalled stepping into the stale, musty air of the living room of their rental home; the space was small and dim, the beige carpet worn thin and stained in spots.

Wednesday, September 16, 2009

Sunlight filtered through flimsy, yellowing blinds that didn't fully close, casting uneven stripes across a sagging couch covered in a threadbare quilt. A chipped coffee table sat in front of the TV, cluttered with unopened mail, a half-empty coffee cup, and a stack of magazines. As she let her bag drop onto a chair, Catrina froze midstep. She could hear the faint sound of sobbing.

Following the noise, she found her mother hunched over the scuffed dining table in the kitchen. The room was in a battle with time—linoleum floors curling at the edges, particleboard cabinets with peeling fronts, and an avocado-green refrigerator humming loudly in the corner. Morven sat surrounded by a chaotic pile of bills, her face buried in her hands. A battered box of receipts sat on the edge of the table, its contents threatening to spill onto the dull, chipped countertops. Catrina's eyes lingered on her mother, who was slumped and silent.

"Mom?"

Morven looked up. Her red, tear-streaked face was a contrast to the effortless beauty she usually exuded. Her perpetually optimistic face was missing its signature smile, and she clutched a crumpled letter with unmistakable letterhead:

INTERNAL REVENUE SERVICE

"They're auditing me," Morven said. "They want receipts and records from the last three years. I don't have them, Catrina. I've barely kept anything."

Catrina glanced at the table, where a stack of handwritten receipts sat haphazardly on scrap paper. She picked one up and examined it. The document was crude, scrawled with vague numbers and expenses that wouldn't fool a child, let alone an IRS agent.

Morven sniffled and gestured helplessly to the pile. "I thought that if I wrote down what I could remember, it might work. They don't have time to check everything, right?"

Catrina sighed, pulling out a chair and sitting across from her mother. "Mom, this is ridiculous. The IRS won't buy this for a second. You can't make up numbers and hope for the best."

"Well, what do you suggest I do?" Morven snapped. "I don't have the money to pay them if they reject my deductions. They'll take everything. What if they throw me in jail?"

Catrina sulked because she had seen this before—her mother's chronic inability to plan, her tendency to panic and resort to half-baked schemes. It was exhausting, but Catrina knew she couldn't leave her mom to fend for herself. "Okay," she said, "if you're going to fake receipts, they have to look real. Like, really real. Handwritten notes won't cut it."

"How?"

Without replying, Catrina grabbed her laptop from her bag and opened a design program. She began pulling up templates and creating professional-looking receipts with itemized line entries, plausible dates, and realistic fonts. Mimicking the logos of local box stores and online suppliers, she crafted a narrative for her mother's expenses, piecing together a story that made sense on paper.

A couple of grueling hours later, Catrina handed her mother a thumb drive of PDF files.

"Here. Stick to the story and avoid over-explaining. Use this only if absolutely necessary. If they catch the forgery, you'll be in an even worse position."

Morven took the thumb drive, her eyes welling with fresh tears. "Thank you, Catrina. I don't know what I'd do without you."

Catrina forced a smile, brushing off the gratitude, but as she packed up the laptop, Catrina harbored resentment. She wasn't proud of how easily she had set aside her integrity to fix Morven's fuckups, but she loved her mother. Clinically codependent, they were bound by a tether neither could break.

Monday, October 4, 2010

Catrina was surprised to see Sam behind the counter when she stepped into the Break.

"I thought your shift ended at two," Catrina said.

"It did," Sam said, "but as a manager, I get the honor of covering shifts when people call in sick. I'm here for another hour or so."

"Ugh. That sucks."

Sam reached for an empty mug and set it in the bussing tray, the ceramic clinking against the counter. "No big deal. Still good to run?" Sam asked.

"Yup."

Sam's voice dropped as she raised a touchy subject. "Did you email your new sisters?"

"I haven't, and I'd like to discuss it further with you, but something else unexpected happened today."

Sam smirked as she put another plate in the bussing tray. "Oh boy, so much drama with you."

"Yeah . . . Tim is starting his own company and wants me to join. He says it's a *game-changer*. He's coming to walk me through the details."

"Seriously? Here?"

"Yup . . . Oh! By the way, Tim thinks you're playing hard to get. Want me to set you up?" Catrina joked.

"Definitely not," Sam said, unamused, as she set Catrina's drink down.

Catrina kept stirring her latte, watching the foam swirl into nothing. Across the counter, Sam stood stiffly, her fingers drumming on the edge of the counter.

"He says it's a big opportunity."

Sam leaned forward, looking annoyed. "Big opportunity for who, exactly? Him? Let me guess, he pitched you the 'I can't do this without you' speech? Made it sound like you're the secret to his success?"

Catrina stirred her latte, not meeting Sam's eyes. "He values my work. I'm not just anyone to him."

"That's what these men say," Sam shot back, arms crossed. "Tim's just another overconfident mediocre white man who got tired of answering to a different mediocre white man."

"You don't even know him," Catrina said, sitting up straighter.

"I know enough. He's been in plenty of times. I know the type. Suits that cost more than our entire wardrobe, the bravado cranked up to ten, always acting like they're hosting a TED Talk." Sam paused. "They act like they're self-made, but they're not. They've had all the breaks. More importantly, I know you. You're far more competent than a guy named Tim."

"Tim's different. He comes across douchey, no doubt, but he worked his way up from nothing," Catrina said, her voice softening into a sympathetic tone. "His parents barely looked after him and his brother growing up. When he was ten, he flipped used Beanie Babies at markets and online to keep food on the table. He didn't get handouts or shortcuts. He scraped together enough to get into UC San Diego and worked two jobs to stay there. He got the DeltaTech internship, the same one I had, and then landed a full-time job, just like I did. He has progressed from there and is now in a position to start his own company. He isn't the brightest bulb, I'll admit that. But he is a people person and attacks opportunities."

"I'm not trashing him. He's just another guy who comes in here and hits on me without bothering to learn the most basic thing—I'm gay." Sam paused. "Cat, I'm always on your side and will support you no matter what you do here, but please protect yourself. Make sure you don't get used up and tossed aside."

"I appreciate you looking out for me. I really do. I know how it looks, but I'm not just his assistant. I've been his right hand for two years. I'm not disposable," Catrina said.

"If it were me, I wouldn't make a decision now. Take the night to think about it without him standing over you. Hear him out, then sleep on it. I highly doubt your decision can't wait until tomorrow."

"I agree. He's had months to work on this; he doesn't get to spring it on me and expect an answer in an hour." Catrina glanced sideways out the window. "He just pulled up—wish me luck."

Catrina hustled to the corner table, steeling herself for Tim's arrival, determined to control the conversation. The door jingled as Tim strode in, immediately commanding the coffee shop with his presence. His tailored shirt and overly confident smirk said "salesman," a role he played effortlessly.

"Catnip," he said, dropping into the chair across from her, his arm draped over the back of an empty chair. "Alright, here's the deal: DeltaTech is dying under its heft. They're trying to buy out SidOrtho for their SiddlesCube system, but the deal's dead in the water. They just don't know it yet. I killed it."

"Slow down," Catrina said.

"SidOrtho has been leasing the cages to DeltaTech for distribution for two years. Doctors love them. Makes their wrist procedures easier, and the patients recover faster."

"I know all this."

"Sure. But you don't know that the lease deal is ending and DeltaTech is playing hardball. They want to purchase the patent for the cages, refusing to extend the lease. SidOrtho refused since that patent is their only useful asset. DeltaTech has pivoted and is now attempting to acquire SidOrtho."

"Why doesn't SidOrtho distribute the cages?" Catrina asked, curious but visibly flustered.

"See, you get it. That would be the play, except SidOrtho can't get into hospitals. They lack the necessary infrastructure to distribute and the connections with hospitals and doctors. Remember, all the end users for the cages think they're using a DeltaTech product. They've never heard of SidOrtho."

"I assume that's where you come in."

"Exactly," Tim said, with confidence bordering on cockiness. "I'm going to undercut DeltaTech's acquisition strategy. I've made contact with SidOrtho. They're desperate. Their product is brilliant, but they have nobody to sell it. My company, our company, will act as the middleman—we'll be lean, efficient. I have the contacts to sell their cages to the right surgical facilities faster than anyone else. Hospitals need solutions now, not next year. And I'm the one who can make it happen. Dr. Jones is already on board, and his business accounts for a giant chunk of SidOrtho's sales. He uses the cage in every wrist procedure. And, as you know, his volume is insane."

"What about Dr. Scotbrite?" Catrina asked. "Mary is good to work with."

"Sure, she'll come over. What choice does she have? She needs the cages. She's small potatoes, but, yeah, her too," Tim said.

"Okay," she said unconvinced.

"What I'm doing is a great thing. We'll save the doctors money, help their patients get procedures quicker, and save SidOrtho as a company. The doctors need us to deal with the wholesaler, tracking shipments and ensuring everything is in the operating room at the right time."

"All for a large fee," she added.

"You get it!" he said, with an animated hand gesture.

"You have it all figured out. Why do you need me?" she asked.

"You're smart, organized, hungry, and know how this business works. You're my right hand, Cat. I trust you to keep things running while I build relationships and close deals."

"I'm not sure. DeltaTech has been good to me."

Tim tilted his head, his cartoonish grin fading. "You think DeltaTech knows who you are? You're fresh out of college, working under me. Without me, what do you think happens to you there?"

Catrina sat up straighter. "I've gotten great reviews, Tim. Rachel in HR told me I've been doing an exceptional job. Most interns don't get full-time offers after college like I did. They said I have a bright future at DeltaTech."

Tim laughed, a harsh, dismissive cackle. "Yeah, that's not what they said. I've spoken with management, Cat. You're nothing to them. They don't care about you. They don't notice you."

"That's not true."

Tim lurched forward. "It costs them nothing to pat you on the head and send you back to your desk. But when it comes to promotions? Raises? Real opportunities? They're not thinking about you. You're a dime a dozen, Cat. Without someone like me pulling the strings, you'll stagnate like the dozens of others who came before you."

Tim's words pressed on every insecurity Catrina held. Was he lying, or did he know something? She wanted to argue, to push back, but Tim's tone and the certainty in his words left her questioning herself.

"You stay at DeltaTech, and you'll be stuck in the same position for years—if they keep you at all," Tim continued. "They'll milk you for everything you've got and give nothing back. I've seen it happen over and over. But with me? I'm offering you a chance to build something real. A company that puts you on the map. You'll make more money than you or your mom ever imagined."

Catrina swallowed hard, trying to hold her ground, but his words burrowed deep. She hated the extent of his power over her. Glancing up, Catrina saw Sam in the distance, her arms crossed, wearing an overt look of annoyance.

Tim pressed on. "This isn't an opportunity. It's a lifeline. DeltaTech's a sinking ship. You stay there, and you're going down with it. But with me? We're talking about building a company from the ground up, which will put us at the top of this industry. This is the kind of chance you don't get twice."

"Why now?" Catrina asked.

"Timing," Tim said. "SidOrtho *needs* us right now so they can back out of the acquisition with DeltaTech. They're desperate to avoid being swallowed by a corporate monster. They see what we can offer— agility in distribution, strong connections, innovation, and real results. But this only works if we move fast. We need to start tomorrow."

She wanted to argue, to push back, but she hesitated.

"Look, I get it," Tim said patronizingly, his tone softening slightly. "Big decisions like this can be scary. However, to succeed in this industry, you must be willing to take risks. You don't want to wake up in five years still stuck in a dead-end desk job, wondering why you didn't take this leap."

"I'd hate to leave without notice," Catrina said.

Tim waved a hand dismissively. "DeltaTech won't mind. Hell, they'll be glad to save the salary. And don't kid yourself—there's no loyalty there. It's all politics and profit margins. The only person looking out for you is me. So what do you say?"

"I need time," Catrina said.

Tim's smile vanished, along with his soft, soothing tone. "Time? Cat, this isn't the kind of decision that can wait. Either you're in or you're not. If you're serious about your career, meet me here tomorrow at 7:00 a.m. We'll get started. If not, this conversation never happened, and it was good knowing you."

The finality in his voice left no room for negotiation. He pushed back his chair and stood, towering over her. "Don't overthink it. You've got potential, but potential only matters if you use it. See you tomorrow."

Without waiting for a response, Tim left.

Sam's caution echoed in her head, but Tim's words lingered, too, planting seeds of doubt. *What if he's right? What if this is my only chance?*

Sam walked over and gently rubbed Catrina's shoulders, her touch warm and supportive. "Come on," she said. "Let's get our running gear on and meet at the usual spot. I'm guessing we have a lot to discuss."

Catrina marveled at how Sam's touch relaxed her in a time of stress. As the shoulder rub lasted a few seconds longer than expected, Catrina experienced a slight rush of blood, a tingle she couldn't quite place.

"Sure. See you soon, Sam."

CHAPTER 7

Monday, October 4, 2010 | Carlsbad

Catrina laced her running shoes and left her mom's house. She was relieved her mom wasn't home because she didn't want to talk to her before she could gather her thoughts. The first mile was her time to relax and think. Today, there was plenty to unpack. Tim's pitch at the coffee shop loomed large, bringing a mix of pressure and promise that she was struggling to untangle.

Also, there was the email from her new sister. She needed to decide whether to respond and, if so, what to say. Catrina had spent years without considering her father, and now, with a single email, he had been forced into her life. She picked up her pace, letting her legs do the thinking for her until she saw Sam in the distance, and then her thoughts turned to her friend.

Catrina and Sam had grown close over the years, having attended the same high school in Carlsbad. Sam had started at the Break during her junior year, and what had begun as a part-time job had gradually become a career. After earning her associate's degree from MiraCosta Community College, she had been offered the manager position and hadn't hesitated to accept. The money was decent, and she could support herself comfortably. She occasionally considered returning to school for a degree in social work—something Catrina was confident she'd excel at—but for now, dealing with the customers at the Break seemed to satisfy her talk-therapy itch.

Sam waved as Catrina approached, her bright smile cutting through the mental fog. "Hey!" Sam said. "Good run so far?"

"Yeah, much needed," Catrina said, matching Sam's pace as they fell into step as a middle-aged jogger passed them.

Catrina asked the question she had asked many times over the years. It had been a running joke whenever they passed a male jogger. "Uh, Sam . . . Were you ever, um, attracted to men? Like, a little?"

Sam laughed. "Not even a little."

As their conversation meandered, it came back to Miriam's email. "So I did a little more googling of my sisters, Miriam and Julia," Catrina said. "Miriam has had some serious roles. At first, I didn't recognize her name, but she had a decent part in *Wonder Woman*. The tall blonde girl, remember?"

Sam's eyes lit up. "Wait, *Wonder Woman*? Didn't we see that together? I know her now! That's wild. She's your sister? She's hot! She must be six three. At least."

"Yup, she stole my height genes," said Catrina, who was all of five feet, two inches. "She has won awards for that British comedy show about nurses. We should watch a few episodes."

"For sure," Sam said.

"And the younger sister, Julia, the Australian, was more difficult to track down. She doesn't seem to have any internet or social media presence."

"That's strange for a young woman," Sam said.

"I had to dig, but I found one article."

"What was it?" Sam asked.

"She won a surfing competition in Australia. The picture was hilarious. This tiny little girl was holding a giant trophy, with a surfboard buried in the sand towering above her."

"She's a surfer chick? That's so cool."

"A famous actress and a surfer, my sisters couldn't be any more different than me. It's so strange."

"Do you think you'll meet them?"

"Maybe. I'm not opposed to it," Catrina said. "It's a lot to process. But the whole thing makes me think about my dad, which I'd rather not."

Their run had eased into a jog as they approached the deli in Carlsbad Village, and Sam broached the topic from earlier.

"What are your thoughts on Tim's offer?"

"It's a risk. But I'm leaning toward going for it. If Tim pulls this off, it changes my life. Financially and otherwise. When will I ever get the chance to be on the ground floor of a startup?"

Sam nodded.

"And if Tim is full of shit, or it's otherwise a failure, surely I can get another assistant job somewhere in San Diego County. I have two-plus years of experience. My references would be rough, but I could find something."

"Your logic is solid. If it hits, you win. If it doesn't, you're back to where you are now."

Catrina smiled, appreciating Sam's support. She'd expected her friend to try to convince her to stay at DeltaTech. "I'm not oblivious to Tim's downsides, believe me. But my mom and I . . . We have never . . . had financial stability. This would change that."

As they entered the deli, the conversation drifted back to ephemera, such as discussing the plot holes in their new favorite Netflix series. When they were done eating, Sam gave Catrina a warm smile. They parted ways, walking in opposite directions toward their respective homes.

Catrina's friendship with Sam had always been supportive, warm, and safe, but lately, it had felt different, closer. She loved the little moments—the way Sam handed her a latte, the way Sam's hand lingered on her shoulder at the coffee shop, even the way Sam glowed after a run. Unfortunately, Catrina's mind drifted, unbidden, to Tim—not his unpleasant personality, not the career opportunity, but the unspoken piece to the puzzle she had failed to share with Sam.

Less than a year ago, while Catrina was a senior in college and working as an intern reporting to Tim, she had attended the DeltaTech holiday party.

———

Friday, December 13, 2009

Catrina admired how DeltaTech had transformed into a holiday wonderland. Outside, the building was wrapped in strings of white and multicolored lights, the company's clean, modern architecture illuminated by the festive ambiance. A large wreath adorned the main entrance, and planters usually filled with native flowers now housed miniature Christmas trees decorated with red ribbons and sparkling ornaments.

From the warehouse extended an expansive outdoor patio where heaters kept the crisp winter air at bay. Guests wandered between high-top tables and cozy seating areas, sipping drinks and enjoying the twinkling lights strung around the pergola and over the hedges.

Catrina was caught between awe and amusement as she walked into the party. It was her first corporate gala, and the atmosphere was worlds away from the small gatherings she was used to in college. The mood was contagious, with colleagues laughing and chatting, their usual professional personas softened by holiday cheer and perhaps a few drinks.

She'd dressed for the event—nothing too flashy but enough to be in the Christmas spirit. Tim had encouraged her to attend, saying it was a good networking opportunity. She was excited to spend time with him in a less professional setting. She wanted to know what he was like when he wasn't in businessman mode.

As she made her way through the crowd, exchanging pleasantries with coworkers, she found herself scanning for familiar faces while soaking in the sights and sounds of the celebration. The party was enjoyable, and she relaxed in the joyous atmosphere, spending most of the evening chatting with Rachel, her closest friend at DeltaTech. She had a few cocktails—a peppermint martini and two gingerbread old-fashioneds—but was careful not to get sloppy.

As the night wore on and the crowd began to thin, she decided it was time to head home. Tim appeared as she stood near the buffet table, preparing to grab her coat and head out.

"Leaving already?" he asked. His eyes loitered on her chest a beat too long.

"Yeah, it's getting late."

Tim was casually dressed in a golf shirt that Catrina thought suited his athletic frame.

"You've been avoiding me all night. Did I do something to scare you off?" Tim asked.

"You seemed busy. Figured I'd stay out of your way." She smiled politely.

"Busy, sure, but never too busy to talk to my favorite junior colleague." Tim paused, then said, "You look great. Very festive."

Catrina blushed, caught off guard. "Thanks."

"You've done a hell of a job this year, Cat. I hope you know that. I don't say this to everyone, but you have real potential."

The words hung in the air, heavy with meaning. His tone was casual, but his gaze was piercing. He focused on her as though she were the only person in the room.

She embraced the flattery and ignored the inappropriateness of his hand, now, all of a sudden, creeping down her lower back. "Thank you," she said, unsure where this was going.

"You don't give yourself enough credit. You're smart and talented. You've been keeping me on my toes all year. I admire you."

"You're laying it on a bit thick, Tim," she joked.

"Am I?" he asked. "I'm telling the truth. You're impressive, Cat. You have an aura."

The air between them shifted, and their easygoing conversation took on a charged feel. His gaze trapped her, but she didn't want to escape. She couldn't think clearly because of a pull, a gravitational force, toward him.

"So what do you say?" Tim asked, stepping closer. "One more drink?"

"Sure, okay. But we better hurry. I think the bartender is packing up."

"Forget that bottom-shelf swill. I've got top-shelf liquor in my office. I've saved it for a special occasion, with a special person."

Catrina's instincts screamed no, but she said, "Sure, one more drink."

Tim gestured toward the hallway leading to the offices. "Come on. It'll be quieter. We can talk without everyone hovering around."

Her pulse quickened, but she followed him anyway, the noise of the party fading as they moved farther from the crowd. His office was dimly lit, the party lights filtering through the glass walls. Tim closed the door behind them, and the click of the lock was deafening in the sudden silence.

"Here," he said, pouring two glasses of scotch from an expensive-looking bottle he pulled from his desk drawer. He handed her one, his fingers brushing hers. The touch sent a shiver up her spine. "To you," he said, raising his glass. "For being the brightest part of this place."

Catrina clinked her glass against his, unsure how to respond. Tim stepped closer, and the space between them disappeared. She didn't pull away. This was reckless, and she was aware of it, but surrounded by the comfort of his attention and the haze of the night, she didn't stop his advance.

———

Monday, October 4, 2010

Almost a year later, Catrina was still confused by that night but didn't regret sleeping with Tim at the party or any of the times since. There were far more attractive women at DeltaTech, and his wife was undeniably gorgeous. Why had Tim picked her? She appreciated how he had taken her under his wing professionally, but that made sense. She was reliable and good at her job. She made him look good at work, which had been his original directive at her orientation. But why had he chosen her at the party? Why had he slept with her, and why did he still reach out whenever his wife was away or he felt lonely? Why did she answer his late-night texts?

She couldn't reconcile her behavior.

Neither of them wanted a relationship, but the sporadic sexual encounters complicated everything, especially now. She couldn't ignore the impact of joining his company. Could she work directly for someone she was intimate with? What would happen if she met somebody else? Would Tim get jealous and fire her if she stopped fucking with him? The questions spiraled.

She suspected Sam knew the truth by the way Sam looked at her or avoided certain topics. Sam's emotional intelligence was off the charts—of course she knew. Yet she'd never shamed or judged. Catrina decided she would tell Sam about the affair when they discussed Tim again.

When Catrina returned home, her head was whirring with uncertainty. She kicked off her shoes, threw her keys on the counter, and headed straight for the shower before her mom could ambush her. The steam and heat helped clear her mind. The first decision she made was about the email. She wouldn't respond to her sisters—not yet. It wasn't a no, but it wasn't the right time. There was too much going on, too many decisions. She couldn't add the drama of new family dynamics.

Stepping out of the shower, she felt a strange sense of clarity. She would take the leap and join Tim. Yes, there were risks—she knew precisely who Tim was and what working with him entailed—but she wouldn't abandon him after everything he had done for her. This, more than anything, solidified her decision. It wasn't about DeltaTech, her friendship with Rachel, or her doubts about Tim. It was about loyalty. She owed him.

CHAPTER 8

The following morning, Catrina was sitting at a table at the Break, gently sipping her coffee and scrolling social media, when she noticed Tim outside, peering through the window. Their eyes met, and before she could react, he came storming in. His presence disrupted the cozy calm of the café, and he wasted no time launching into his plan, which Catrina immediately determined was half-baked.

"I knew you would come! I've got it all sorted. Here's what we do," Tim said, fully charged, as he slid into the chair across from Catrina. "We skip work today. We find office space. Then, we buy a couple of computers. After that, we return to DeltaTech, retrieve the necessary files, and contact the clients. But here's the tricky part." He leaned in closer, his tone dropping. "My contact at SidOrtho is demanding a few specific R&D files. They want to see how close DeltaTech is to creating a cage system. Those files aren't on the regular server. I'll have to find a way to access them."

Catrina froze, her coffee cup midway to her mouth. "Isn't that illegal?"

"No more illegal than how I found out about the acquisition," Tim said with a shrug. "In for a penny, in for a pound."

"How *did* you find out?" Catrina asked, unamused by his cockiness.

"I waited until Tom Wilkshire—the general counsel, you know him—went to lunch while his assistant was on vacation. I snuck into his office, accessed his computer before the screen saver activated, and skimmed through his emails. Legal gets all the dirt. I saw the SidOrtho acquisition paperwork and remembered a golf buddy high up there. I got him drunk over eighteen holes, and by the end of the night, we worked out this plan. He pitched it to SidOrtho, and they said if we bring over at least ten high-end doctors to use their cages *and* hand over those R&D files, we're golden. Set for life."

Catrina's mind raced. She took a big gulp of her coffee to keep her composure. The memory of breaking the law for Morven with the IRS flashed in her mind. "Tim, your plan sucks. What you did is definitely a crime. And what you're proposing is a worse crime."

"Cat, don't get bogged down in the details," Tim said. "This is the opportunity. We need to make this happen. Now."

Catrina took a deep breath. She knew too much. "We never discussed my pay or title," she said, trying to regain some control of the conversation.

"There's no time right now. Trust me, you'll be taken care of. How does my plan suck? What would you fix? This is why I need you," Tim said, his smirk returning.

Catrina exhaled, forcing herself to focus. "First, we're going to work today. We act like everything is normal. Then, we compile a list of all the doctors who could use SidOrtho's cages and gather their contact information. At lunch, I'll take Beatrice, the executive assistant in R&D, to lunch. While her computer is unattended, you get the files. At the end of the day, we resign and start calling the doctors."

"Solid plan, Cat, but two changes," Tim said. "First, we're not resigning. We're not giving them a chance to call the doctors first. Before DeltaTech knows what hit them, I want those doctors signed. Second, Beatrice doesn't have access. Only Barry, the head honcho in

R&D, does. I'll bite the bullet and take that bore to lunch. You'll need to get in and grab the files."

"How am I supposed to do anything with Beatrice watching?" Catrina asked.

"Create a diversion," Tim said. "You're good at that. Use this thumb drive to download the following files." He handed her a device and a list.

"I can't do that. I'm not comfortable stealing files. And IT will see what has been downloaded."

"Cat, it's the only way. I'm sure you'll think of something."

She thought for a moment, trying to suppress her rising anxiety. "I could take pictures of the files from the screen. It would be undetectable, and your contact can get what they need from the pictures."

"Perfect. Let's make it happen."

"Wait," she said. "Can we pause for a second? I need to think."

Tim, his momentum unstoppable, got up and grabbed his jacket. "We've got to get going," he said, leaving no room for discussion.

Catrina hesitated, looking toward Sam, who was standing behind the counter. Sam's eyes met hers, a nervous, questioning look passing between them. It wasn't reassuring.

Ignoring Tim's impatience, Catrina took a moment to think. *This is my one chance*, she thought. *This is my one chance to make something of myself and be financially secure.* She didn't want to back out. She owed him. He had taught her the business. He had promoted her from an intern. He had her back when clients were upset. She couldn't shake her sense of obligation toward him. And now, Tim needed her. Without her, the plan would implode; he would mess it up and probably end up in jail.

Catrina got up, packed her laptop bag, and affirmed her decision. She gestured goodbye to Sam, who returned it with an uneasy smile. Without looking back, she walked out with Tim.

Catrina was at her desk, ready for what she had named the Great Research and Development File Heist. She loved naming things. In front of her sat eight disposable cameras. She pre-opened each camera and wound each to the first frame. Using a Sharpie, she labeled each camera with the file name she needed to photograph: *Fracture Stabilization Blueprints*, *Prototype Cost Breakdown*, *System Integration Testing* ... The list Tim had given her was burned into her memory, but she double-checked it one last time. There could be no mistakes.

The disposable cameras sat like a jury in front of her, their labeled surfaces a constant reminder of what she was about to do. Catrina wasn't blind to the moral gravity of her impending actions. This was theft, plain and simple. Not petty theft, but corporate espionage. Fraud. And even if DeltaTech never learned of the stolen files, at a minimum, leaving and contacting clients without giving notice would burn bridges, sever ties, and leave permanent scars on her reputation.

DeltaTech wasn't a faceless corporation to her; it had been a lifeline. A place that had taken her in when she had nothing but college credits on her résumé. DeltaTech had been good to her, better than she deserved. In the aftermath of the financial crisis, when most of her classmates were flipping through want ads and hustling for unpaid internships, she had a job with a generous salary, health benefits, and a 401(k).

She thought of Rachel, her work friend and confidant. They'd spent countless coffee breaks together. Catrina winced, remembering the celebratory lunch Rachel had organized when Catrina had been offered a full-time position after graduation. Rachel would see what Catrina was about to do as a betrayal. And it was. No justifications or explanations would save their relationship. Catrina tried to tell herself it was only business, but the reality stung.

Catrina wasn't naïve. The actions she was about to take were illegal, immoral, and unethical. She'd spent hours staring at the ceiling, reviewing every angle and consequence. The guilt twisted in her chest, but she pushed it down. The promise of what Tim had offered—an executive title and a stabilizing amount of money—was life-changing. She didn't delude herself into believing her actions were righteous. She wasn't a starry-eyed kid being obtuse or impulsive. She was in charge of her actions and had determined that the reward outweighed the damage to her friendships and reputation; however, this mindful awareness did nothing to ease the difficulty of living with the choice.

As she sat at her desk, waiting for Tim to start the caper, Catrina pushed the doubts from her head. The cameras were ready, and the plan was set. She couldn't afford the luxury of indecision. It was time to get to work.

She overheard Tim on the phone, speaking loudly and confidently. "Barry, let's grab lunch at the club today. It would be great to catch up. Echo's team might be there, and you know how those guys like to talk shit." There was a pause, and then Tim added with mock urgency, "I'm serious, Barry. Don't flake on me."

Catrina glanced up as Tim ended the call. He caught her eye through the glass walls and gave her a thumbs-up. The plan was in motion.

At 11:25, Catrina waited outside Tim's office, holding a box of champagne. Or so it appeared. She checked her watch. The timing had to be perfect. Tim emerged, his machismo dialed up to eleven, and strode toward Barry's office. She trailed behind, keeping a safe distance.

"Barry!" Tim shouted, barging into the R&D head's office. "Let's go! We can't let Echo beat us to the club. Those bastards are insufferable. We need to get there first and claim the corner table."

Barry looked flustered, fumbling for his wallet. "I need to finish this email—"

"No time!" Tim said, cutting him off, and clapped him on the shoulder. "Come on, man. This is important. Grab your stuff, and let's move."

Barry hesitated, his hand hovering near his mouse, but Tim upped the urgency. "Barry, seriously, let's go. Bro. Don't fuck me on this."

Caught up in the whirlwind of Tim's exuberance, Barry grabbed his wallet. Tim gave Catrina a wink as they passed in the hallway, signifying that their colleague had left his computer unlocked.

Catrina walked purposefully toward Beatrice's desk, her heart hammering. The R&D assistant was diligently typing away, completely unaware of the heist about to unfold.

"Hey, Bea," Catrina said, hoisting the champagne box onto the desk. "One of Tim's clients sent over a box of champagne, but his fridge is full. He asked me to bring it to Barry's fridge."

Beatrice glanced. "Sure, set it on my ledge."

Before Catrina could respond, an email appeared on Beatrice's screen: *Lucciano's lunch delivery in the break room! It's first come, first served!* Catrina had scheduled the email from the generic admin account for this exact time.

Beatrice's head snapped toward the monitor. Her eyes lit up. "Lucciano's? Oh my gosh, that's the good stuff!"

Catrina smirked, feigning eagerness. "Yep. Chicken parm, cannoli, the works. You better hurry—it won't last long."

Beatrice hesitated, her eyes darting between the champagne and the monitor. "But this box—"

"I've got it," Catrina assured her. "Go. Trust me, you don't want to miss the pasta bar."

That was all the encouragement Beatrice needed. She was out of her chair and headed toward the break room.

Catrina slipped into Barry's office, the door clicking shut behind her. The room was quiet except for the hum of the computer fan. She set the champagne on the floor, pulled on latex gloves, and hit Barry's keyboard to keep the computer awake. Then she removed the top tray of three bottles and pulled out the cameras safely hidden below.

Her gloved fingers flew across the keyboard as she opened the first file. She pulled out a camera and began snapping photos, one file at a time, page by page. Three files were completed without incident, then four. Catrina worked quickly, snapping pictures and clicking pages. She was surprised at how calm she had remained—

until she heard rustling in the hallway. Soon, every noise outside Barry's office—a cough, a footstep, a door creak—was amplified. Every sound sent a fresh jolt of adrenaline through her system.

By the fifth file, the murmurs had started. Close. Too close. Her breath caught as she registered the muffled sounds of conversation growing louder, the cadence of footsteps unmistakably heading her way. Somebody was coming. Of this, she had no doubt. She shoved the cameras under Barry's desk and dropped to the floor beside the champagne, arranging herself to look as if she were casually stocking a fridge.

This was it. She was caught. She was going to jail. And for what? A few disposable camera photos? She made $23 an hour—was that worth federal prison? Dread washed over her as she struggled to catch her breath. All previous risk-reward calculations she had made were instantly obsolete. *I'm so fucking stupid.*

The door creaked open, grating in her ears like nails on a chalkboard. Catrina tried to look normal, whatever that was, her pulse a deafening drumbeat. She scrambled for a casual expression.

"Hey, Cat." Thom, a young R&D researcher, stuck his head inside Barry's office, his eyes scanning the room. "Is Barry around?"

She forced a smile. "He went to lunch with Tim."

Thom's gaze shifted between her crouched position and the champagne bottles. "What are you doing on the floor . . . with gloves on?"

Terror built inside her. She'd forgotten to remove the gloves. She was cooked. There was no talking her way out of this one. Nevertheless, she managed a shaky laugh. "Uh, making room in the fridge for all this bubbly. They don't like our fingerprints on their expensive bottles. I feel like a dental hygienist wearing these silly gloves. Absurd, isn't it? You know how it is—someday, they'll send us the fancy stuff."

He didn't respond. He stood there, his eyes narrowing as though trying to piece everything together. The silence stretched unbearably, every second an eternity. Catrina's mind spiraled—she pictured herself in an orange jumpsuit, her hair butchered by a prison barber. She was lightheaded, sure she was about to pass out.

Thom's silence was unbearable; each second felt like an eternity. She willed him to leave. Her body stayed composed, but her mind broke down. *Say something. Call security already. If this is how I go down—if this is my last day in my twenties as a free woman—get on with it.*

His lips twitched into a faint smile. "Yeah, right. Guess we can dream." He started to turn away, then turned back and said, "Oh, Cat. There's food in the break room. You should hurry. Bea is already down there."

"Good looking out. I'll be down in a minute."

Thom turned and left, the door clicking shut behind him. Relief flooded her, but it was fleeting. She clutched the edge of the desk, her breath coming in shallow, ragged gasps. She couldn't afford another close call.

With shivering hands, she retrieved the cameras and finished snapping the remaining photos, knowing every second was borrowed. As she placed the cameras back in the hidden compartment under the empty champagne tray, she took a moment, her ears straining for signs of life outside the office. She locked Barry's computer, ensuring the desktop looked precisely as he'd left it. Satisfied, she shoved the gloves into her pockets and headed for the door. She got to the hallway just as Beatrice returned from lunch.

"You're still here?" Beatrice asked, eyeing the box. "You're missing out on the chicken parm."

Catrina faked a grin. "Brought the wrong bottles the first time. I had to fix it before Tim noticed. He's picky."

"Good work, Cat. Those men don't want any mistakes with their booze," Beatrice said.

"Have a good one, Bea."

"Later, Cat."

Back at her desk, Catrina took a second to compose herself. Then she splashed water on her face and rubbed her eyes to redden them. She walked into the administrator's office, feigning alarm.

"I'm having an allergic reaction. Were there walnuts in the food in the kitchen? I'm an idiot for not asking. May I run to urgent care?"

"Go. Take care of yourself," she said.

Catrina grabbed her purse and drove to Tim's house, where she stashed the cameras and the list of contact information in his garage. When she returned to the office, Tim was pulling up. He rolled down the window, grinning. The files were secured, and the plan had been executed flawlessly. She gave him a thumbs-up, her smile tight with relief but not pride. Still, the knot in her chest loosened—what was done was done. If consequences came, she would face them. She wouldn't waste time on regret. This was the choice she had made, and she owned it.

CHAPTER 9

Thursday, January 6, 2011 | Sydney

J ulia cleared the dirty plates from table six and wiped down the booth. It'd been three months since she started at Gus's Taverna, and she had proved to be a natural. The work pattern suited her, and she'd grown into her role, juggling her tasks with a quiet confidence that Gus and the rest of the crew noticed. Gus often joked she could run the place if he ever decided to take a vacation—not that he ever would. She never missed a shift, was always on time, and genuinely took an interest in the regulars. She chatted easily and instinctively knew when a customer wanted to be left alone. Gus declared that Julia had the "spirit of the taverna," a blend of toughness, kindness, and unpretentious hard work.

Julia had also made inroads into the Manly surf community. Her two closest friends were Alani and Ginger, both in their early twenties. Alani was attending beauty school, while Ginger lived off her parents. Although they were both immature, they provided a base level of companionship and the safety of a pack at night. Most late afternoons, Alani and Ginger would stop by for a coffee and discuss the night's plans with Julia before the dinner rush. Gus wasn't their biggest fan but tolerated their presence if they left before the dinner rush.

As Alani and Ginger pulled up two stools to the counter, Gus welcomed them. "Greetings, *Kopélas*. I'll call your waitress over."

"Coming out tonight, Jul?" Alani asked while Ginger signaled for a cup of coffee.

"Yeah, definitely," Julia said as she made two flat whites from the large machine and placed the drinks in front of the girls.

"Tonight's the night," Ginger said.

"Going for it?" Julia asked.

"We've been dancing around it for a week. I could use a good shag," Ginger said.

Alani rolled her eyes.

"Good for you, Gin," Julia said.

"I don't know, Gin. Beau has eyes for Jul," Alani said harshly.

"Not true. I don't even talk to him," Julia protested.

"Shut up, Alani. Tonight's the night," Ginger said.

"Have you gotten laid since moving to Manly?" Alani asked Julia.

"Nah. I've never been into surfies. Kinda grimy for my taste. Back in school, I messed around with sportos. I didn't date them, but they were good for a shag," Julia said.

"Except for Beau," Alani said, laughing.

"Of course. Beau isn't grimy. Good luck, Gin," Julia added.

"What about you, chick? Big plans tonight, Ali?" Ginger asked Alani.

"If the bloke with the tat gun comes tonight, I'm going to get the inkie of a koala on a surfboard. Going to work on the sketch after coffee," Alani said.

"Oh, awesome," Julia said. "I've been thinking about getting one of Floating Sky on the back of my shoulder."

"You should!" Ginger said.

Gus interrupted the chat. "Tzoúlia, table four is ready to order." He turned to Alani and Ginger with a big smile. "You two, finish your coffee before the real customers get here."

The familiar closing sounds echoed through the taverna as the small team worked through their final duties. Gus moved methodically through his cleanup ritual, an unspoken routine everyone knew better than to disrupt.

He counted the cash from the register, his fingers quick and precise as he placed the money in the bank bag. From there, he moved to the kitchen, checking the stoves and gas lines with the same care he showed to every corner of the taverna. Julia could hear the soft clang of metal as he ensured everything was turned off and secured.

The chairs were stacked on the tables, the floor was freshly mopped, and the garbage bags were tied and ready by the back door. "Tzoúlia, you've got the front?" Gus called out as he hoisted the garbage bags over his shoulder.

"On it!" she replied, flipping the last light switch and waiting by the front door. Gus appeared moments later, having taken out the garbage, which he did every night—a duty he never delegated. Together, the two stepped outside, the night air warm against their faces.

Gus secured the locks on the front door, testing its security twice before stepping back and surveying the taverna. He gave a satisfied nod and turned toward her. "So how are you liking the flat?" Gus asked.

Julia smiled, tucking her hands into the pockets of her work pants. "It's nice. I enjoy having my own space. Thanks for setting me up."

"Bah, don't mention it. I'd rather you have somewhere safe to rest your head than be worrying about where to sleep. But you're resting, right? Getting enough sleep?"

"I get by during the week. Sundays are my catch-up days—no surfing, no work, just sleep."

Gus gave her a pointed look, the kind only someone with decades of life experience could pull off. "You're burning the candle at both ends, kid. It will catch up to you. Take it from someone who's been there."

Julia nodded, appreciating the concern but eager to move along. "I hear you, Gus. I'll slow down."

Gus didn't look convinced. "Alright, alright. Remember, the taverna needs you." He handed her an expertly packed sandwich. "Tzoúlia, make sure you eat this."

"Thanks, Gus. I'll see you tomorrow."

"*Kalinýchta*," Gus yelled as Julia headed down the street, his Greek accent thick.

"*Kalinýchta*," Julia said without turning her head.

———

The night truly began for Julia when Gus locked the taverna. The comforting predictability of her job gave way to hazy, disjointed evenings—a completely different world she had come to enjoy. She stopped by her studio flat, rinsing the grease and grit of the taverna off her skin, then swapped her work uniform for a loose tank top and ripped jeans. The outfit was comfortable and unassuming, blending into the rowdy crowd she was about to join. She checked herself in the mirror, mildly annoyed at the uneven and disjointed haircut Alani had given her. *Eh, the price was right*, she thought.

Her first stop, as usual, was the surf house, a dingy yet magnetic share house four blocks from the beach. The house was an infamous fixture in the Manly surfing community and was where every night began, some never ending. Its exterior was a peeling mess of faded paint and a sagging roofline, but inside, it was alive with music and chatter. Surfboards leaned precariously against every available wall, and the scent of saltwater mingled with the spilled beer, marijuana, and sweat. The floors were perpetually sticky, dotted with sleeping bags and old couch cushions that served as beds for whoever happened to crash there. Trash overflowed from bins, scattering discarded bottles, takeaway wrappers, and pizza boxes.

The surf community of waxheads, frothers, and surfie chicks circulated through the house, a place to drink, smoke, gossip, and numb out. The party was in full swing when Julia arrived a little before midnight. Music pulsed through the walls, and laughter echoed from every corner. Upon arrival, Julia pulled a small, discreet edible from her pocket, popped it into her mouth, and swallowed it with a few gulps of water from her bottle. Staying hydrated was her way of keeping some semblance of control over the otherwise unpredictable night. Julia wasn't a drinker, and though she occasionally smoked weed, edibles were her favorite.

She spotted Alani and Ginger near a corner where a group was gathered around a makeshift table, rolling joints and talking loudly. Ginger, with her fiery red hair and boisterous personality, waved her over. Alani, who was quieter and more sarcastic, flashed her a smile.

"Late start tonight?" Ginger teased, passing Julia a joint she politely declined.

"Long shift. Any luck with Beau?" Julia asked.

"Ha, this slut hasn't even talked to him," Alani interrupted.

"Working on it," Ginger said.

"Ooh, look. Ink Guy is here," Alani said, pointing.

Julia had seen this man before, with his portable tattoo gun and massage table. It wasn't the most hygienic setup, but making house calls to a party was a good way to pick up business. Alani pulled out a crude sketch and handed it to Ink Guy. She removed her shirt and lay stomach down on the massage table. Ink Guy started to clean the area on her lower back as Alani pointed to Julia and mouthed, "You're next."

Julia swallowed hard. She wasn't against the idea but wasn't excited either. She grabbed a beer from the giant garbage can filled with ice and took a swig as Beau came over.

"Sup, Jul?" Beau asked.

"Nothing. Watching Ali get inked," Julia said.

"Pretty rad. Up for hitting the beach later? Got some quality mushies."

"Yeah, maybe. You need to talk to Gin. She wants to hang," Julia said.

"Gin is cool. Would be stoked to kick it with you too," Beau said.

"Vibe with Gin tonight, and I'll be around. She's *choice*," Julia told him.

As the hours ticked by, the party began to shift. The more casual crowd filtered out, leaving behind the core group of regulars who would ride the night until dawn. Two hours had passed, and Alani was still on the massage table. She appeared to be in pain but expressed excitement every time Julia checked. When she inevitably asked if Julia was next, Julia avoided answering.

Ginger and Beau had gone off to a corner and were making out. Julia was happy for her friend and credited herself with an assist.

For Julia, this was the dance of her nights: immersing herself in the scene's energy while keeping a careful distance. She didn't need to impress anyone or prove herself. She was here on her terms. Like the ocean, the party was unpredictable and untamed, but Julia had learned to navigate it with the same grace she brought to surfing.

"Jul, my ink's done. Take a look before he puts on the bandage," Alani said.

Julia peeked and almost vomited. It was a mess. Maybe it would look fine when healed, but the sight was horrific. "Looks . . . good, Ali," she said.

"Are you next?" Alani asked.

"Uh, not tonight. I've had a bit to drink."

"Yeah, need twenty-four hours from your last drink, mate. I'll be back next week," Ink Guy said.

"Oh, good. Maybe next week. Sorry, Ali," Julia said.

"No worries. How is Gin getting on?" Alani asked.

"She's having a pash."

"Legendary! Since you aren't getting a tat, we should go to the beach. Gin will be game," Alani said.

———

It was after three in the morning, and Beau, Alani, Ginger, and Julia found a secluded spot on the beach. Beau offered the mushrooms, but everyone declined. Instead, Alani pulled out a bottle of Vodka O, raspberry and blood orange flavor, and everyone took a swig as the bottle was passed around. Julia skipped her second and third turns. Within fifteen minutes, Alani and Ginger were fast asleep and Beau turned his attention to Julia.

"You and Gin were getting on," Julia said.

"She's fit. No doubt."

"Sorry she fell asleep."

"All good, mate. Wanted to spend time with you." Beau offered Julia the bottle, his fingers brushing hers in the process.

She declined.

"You were the best part of the party. You have an aura about you," Beau said, taking a small swig from the bottle. He moved in closer to Julia.

She didn't pull away as his hand brushed against her bare arm.

"You're gorgeous, Jul. I've wanted to tell you for a while," Beau said.

Julia struggled to find words, and Beau brushed the back of her head, pulling her closer. He took another sip from the bottle and slowly moved his hand down her back. Julia didn't stop him, her mind hazy from the night of drinking and edibles. As Beau moved from her back to her chest, Julia refocused and asked him to stop. He did and apologized. Before Julia could respond, she heard Alani rustling.

"What's going on?" Alani said, half asleep, and shook Ginger to wake her up so she could also see what was taking place. "Are you two getting it on?"

"No, it's not—" Julia said.

"You fucking slut!" Ginger added, aggressively.

"Nothing happened. I swear," Julia said.

Alani and Ginger got up, brushed off the sand, and left the beach. Julia gave Beau a disapproving shake of the head and followed them.

At first light, Julia was on the ocean, rain or shine, good surf or poor. Dawn was her sanctuary, the world still in bed, leaving the water for those who truly belonged to it. She surfed almost exclusively at Manly, finding comfort in its convenience and familiarity, though now and then, she piled into a van seeking Sydney's other great beaches. On this day, the surf at Manly was poor, disorganized waves and weak sets making for frustrating runs.

Her body ached as the alcohol worked its way through her system—a good reminder of why she wasn't a drinker. Her mind also ached from the pain she had caused Ginger. She planned to tell Miriam about the evening and get her advice.

The surf and her health didn't improve, but Julia pushed through the discomfort until the waterproof Timex that was her tether to the world while on the ocean told her it was eight a.m. On better days, she might stay until ten, but today, two hours was plenty. Julia paddled to shore, ready to get to sleep.

She rinsed off at the beach hut, letting the cool water strip away the salt and sand. Pulling on a loose tank top and shorts, she began the walk back to her flat. The streets of Manly were coming to life—cafés filling with early risers, parents wrangling children, and surfers hauling their boards to the waves she'd left behind.

Her studio flat was modest, a third-story walk-up in a run-down building. The narrow staircase creaked as she ascended, her surfboard barely fitting through the tight hallway. When she reached her door, she unlocked it with a key that stuck a little in the lock.

The studio itself was sparse. A mattress lay on the floor, covered with an old, loosely draped sheet and a flat pillow. In the corner was a used beanbag chair she'd bought secondhand for reading. There was a small kitchenette with a barely functioning burner that she never used. The cramped bathroom had a shower over the bath, and a small vanity basin. The flat had a single window overlooking the alley, which let in enough sunlight to make the space habitable.

Julia kicked off her flip-flops and dumped her damp clothes in a corner, leaving a faint trail of water across the linoleum floor as she made her way toward the bathroom. The shower's hot water was heaven on her sore muscles, and she fought to stay awake long enough to finish. She could barely keep her eyes open when she toweled off. She stumbled to her mattress, collapsing onto it undressed. She set her Timex alarm and trusted it to rouse her from a deadened sleep. No matter how crazy things got, she refused to be late to work.

When the alarm chimed at 1:30 p.m., she groaned, stretching out her limbs as she blinked away her grogginess. The room came into focus as she sat up, rubbing her eyes. She didn't waste time but pulled on her work clothes, combed her still-damp hair, refilled her water bottle, and headed out the door.

Most afternoons, Julia took a brief detour to the Manly Corso, sometimes stopping to do laundry or pick up essentials like toilet paper and shampoo, but today, she was heading straight to the internet café. She treasured her regular 2:00 p.m. calls with Miriam. It was 7:00 p.m. in Los Angeles, and although Miriam had a busy schedule, she usually managed to make it work. The only days Julia didn't call were Wednesdays, when she did most of her errands, and Sundays, her day of complete rest.

The internet café was quiet, and Julia settled into one of the cubicles near the back. She'd arranged a weekly pricing deal with the owner, saving her money. She clicked Miriam's name and waited, her eyes drifting to her inbox. The only new message was from her mum, Alice. Julia hadn't been home since the fight with her father, but she wrote her mum weekly to let her know she was doing well and was safe.

The connection rang a few times before the screen lit up with her sister's face.

"Jules!" Miriam's cheerfulness came through the speakers. "How was the surf today?"

"Pretty bad; I bailed early."

"I want to hear how your night went, but I'm dying to tell you my big news."

"Oh! What is it, Mir?"

"You're not going to believe this—I got the part! The show I auditioned for, they cast me!" Miriam said.

"That's amazing! Tell me everything."

"Okay, so it's called *IRS Rogue* and will be on HBO. Like, real prestige TV! The kind of show that gets Emmy nominations."

"Fancy. So what's it about? A tax-collecting drama?"

Miriam laughed, rolling her eyes. "It's more than that. It's set in Los Angeles, and I play Inspector Claudia Von Haulsteen. She's part of an elite IRS unit that targets high-net-worth individuals and corporations that avoid paying their taxes. And because these individuals have access to vast resources—lawyers, private security, and even hired muscle—our team must think creatively. Think undercover operations, unconventional methods, and, yes, sometimes skirting the law a little."

"So you're like . . . an action star, but for the IRS?"

"Exactly," Miriam said. "It's gritty and intense, but it also has a lot of moral gray areas. Claudia is this no-nonsense, tough-as-nails investigator who's brilliant at her job, but she has a whole backstory—family trauma and personal struggles. You know, the kind of layered character that wins statuettes."

"A far cry from *Night Nurses*. Excited?"

"Excited, nervous, all of it," Miriam said. "This is a huge shift for me. *Night Nurses* was fun, but it was fluffy. This role could redefine my career. Plus, HBO! It's the Holy Grail of television."

Julia couldn't help but smile at her sister's enthusiasm. "When do you start?"

"Soon. We start filming in a few weeks, but I have prep work. They're sending me to an IRS office to shadow real investigators. Can you imagine me in a cubicle?" Miriam laughed at the thought. "But it's all part of the job. I want to get Claudia right."

"Mir, this is huge. You're going to kill it."

"Thanks, Jules. I mean it. It's been such a crazy few months, and having you to talk to, even about the little stuff, has made it all feel . . . doable. You're my rock, you know?"

"You're the one booking HBO gigs. I'm just here surfing and slinging souvlaki."

"Now, tell me about your night," Miriam said.

Julia leaned back in her cubicle chair, grimacing. "So last night was the usual at the surf house. Alani and Ginger were there, and we hung out. Alani got a wretched tattoo and wanted me to go next, but I passed."

"Thank heavens."

"Ginger was pashing with this silly boy. And then we went to the beach. Ali and Gin passed out from the drinks, and the boy tried to make a move on me, but I shut him down. Of course, they woke up, thought I was nicking Ginger's boy, and got mad."

Miriam leaned in to the screen, her expression shifting into maternal. "Jules," she said, "you need to be careful. Some of those 'silly boys' are grown men, and they become dangerous when they've had too much to drink."

Julia rolled her eyes, but it was more affectionate than dismissive. "Mir, I know. You've given me this speech before. Trust me, I'm not stupid. I never stay alone and stick with Ali and Gin. I'm fine."

"I know you're careful, Jules. It's just . . . I worry about you. There is only so much you can control, and some of those guys won't take no for an answer."

"I get it, Mir. Really. But I'm not taking chances, I promise. I've got my safety routines down."

"Alright. Just . . . keep your guard up, okay? And while I'm at it, make sure you're eating enough, too. You're running around all day —surfing, working—I don't want you running on fumes."

"You sound like Gus. He's always shoving food at me. Every day when I start my shift, there's a full meal waiting for me, and he hands me a sandwich when I'm heading out the door."

"Good. It sounds like Gus has the same concerns I do."

"Any ideas what I should say to Ali and Gin to patch things up?" Julia asked.

"They'll be fine. You didn't do anything wrong. Ginger needs to find a new silly boy who prefers her."

"Yeah."

"Last thing, while I'm being preachy: I was twenty once. And I'm not a teetotaler. Far from it. I know you're going to drink and use gear. I'm not being a hypocrite and telling you not to, but please . . . be cautious. They'll become habit. Trust me, I've made mistakes."

"Of course, Mir. I hear you. I appreciate you looking out for me." Julia glanced at her Timex. "Shit, it's already two forty-five. I've got to run to work."

"Alright. Call me tomorrow."

"Love you, Mir."

Miriam's grin widened. "Love you too, Jules."

CHAPTER 10

"Tzoúlia! *Goomorni!*" Gus bellowed. It was one of his endearing quirks, saying "good morning" no matter the time of day.

Julia couldn't help but smile. "*Goomorni*, Gus. You're in a good mood today."

"I am! Big plans tonight!" he said, clapping his hands together. "It's my anniversary. I'm taking Maria into town on the ferry to a fancy French restaurant. Can you believe it? French food! They put the food on plates the size of my palm, but, eh, she loves it. And guess what? I got my shirt dry-cleaned. Dry-cleaned, Tzoúlia!"

Julia laughed, tying her apron around her waist. "That's impressive, Gus. You're pulling out all the stops. I hope Maria appreciates the effort."

"Ah, she will. Thirty years of marriage, and I still try to impress her."

"Thirty years of marriage, Gus. How'd you pull it off?" Julia asked, smirking as she stacked plates by the register.

"Love at first sight, Tzoúlia. For me, at least. Her, not as much."

"I haven't heard this story," Julia said, circulating among the tables.

When she returned to the counter, Gus said, "I followed Maria to Manly. I was working construction in Sydney when I met her. She took the ferry to Manly every morning to clean houses. She'd come back in the evenings, sun on her face, telling me how quiet and beautiful it was."

"You followed her here because she said it was nice?" Julia teased.

"I would come over on my days off and eat lunch with her. I fell in love with Manly, too," Gus said, tapping his chest. "I would've followed Maria anywhere. She was kind and didn't put up with my nonsense."

"What nonsense? You're so laid-back."

Gus ignored the sarcasm and continued, "Maria encouraged me to start my own business after my brother, Nico, died. She believed that if I opened in Manly, the locals would embrace me and eventually, tourists would follow. Also, it's cheaper than Sydney. She was right, of course. She's always right."

"So she's the reason the taverna exists?" Julia asked.

"Absolutely. Everything good in my life started with her," Gus said. "She saw something in me when I was a stubborn immigrant working construction, drinking too much, and grieving the loss of my brother. I proposed the day the taverna opened in 1979, and we married thirty years ago today."

Julia smiled. "I'm glad you two found each other."

As Julia started preparing for her shift, Gus approached the counter. "I'll be working through the dinner rush, but I'll head out with the bank bag afterward. You're closing tonight."

Julia paused mid-step. "Me? Close? Alone?"

Gus grinned and pulled a backup set of keys from his pocket. He held them up, dangling them before her like a prize. "I trust you, Tzoúlia. You've been here six months, never late, never missed a shift, and you work hard. You've seen me do closing a hundred times. You're ready." She reached for the keys, but he pulled them back, wagging a finger. "Not so fast! Recite the protocol. All of it. From memory."

"Alright. First, check the register and count the money. Put it in the bank bag and lock it. Second, take out the garbage. Third, chairs are off the floor; mop and wipe the tables. Fourth, make sure the stoves and gas are turned off. Fifth, lock the back door. Finally, lock the front door after making sure everyone is out."

"Good. But you forgot one thing."

"I did?"

"You forgot to double-check both locks. I always double-check!" he said.

"Yes, I'll double-check that the door is locked."

"Both doors. Double-check both doors," Gus corrected.

"I'll."

"Leave the money in the register; I'll have the bank bag. It shouldn't be much since it will be after the dinner rush," Gus added.

Julia nodded.

Satisfied, Gus ceremoniously handed her the keys.

"Thanks," Julia said, pocketing them. "Have fun tonight, Gus. Your wife will love it."

"Alright, Tzoúlia, get to work. I need these customers to pay for tonight's extravagance."

Julia glanced over to the new arrivals and gave Gus a playful salute. "On it. And don't worry."

The last customers of the night were taking their sweet time. Alone in the taverna, Julia completed every bit of closing prep she could while the customers loitered. The trash was bagged and sitting by the back door, ready to go out. The kitchen floor was mopped, and she double-checked that all the appliances were turned off. The clock ticked relentlessly past 11:00, and the couple showed no signs of wrapping up their conversation.

Alani and Ginger poked their heads in, their impatience palpable. "Jul, hurry!" Alani whispered. "The beach party is epic tonight. We've gotta arrive as a group. Tonight's the night Gin gets her Beau."

"Let's hope, Ali," Julia said.

"Stop adding pressure," Ginger replied.

Julia rolled her eyes and turned toward the customers. "Still working on your coffee?" she asked the couple, hoping to nudge them along. She returned to the counter, wiping it down again though it was spotless, and studied the clock.

Ten minutes later, Ginger came in, looking exasperated, and said, "Still?"

Julia shrugged.

At 11:30, the couple paid their check and stood to leave. Julia smiled as she thanked them and bid them a good night. Before she could exhale, Alani and Ginger bolted inside.

"What still needs to be done?" Ginger asked as they looked around the empty restaurant.

"I need to lock up the register, put up the chairs, and mop the floor," Julia said. "Everything else is done."

Alani and Ginger grabbed chairs and flipped them onto the tables, while Julia sped through the remaining minor cleanup. She halfheartedly mopped the floor while Alani and Ginger hovered near the door, tapping their feet.

After a final inspection, Julia untied her apron and hung it behind the counter. "Alright, we're good," she said as she turned off the lights, casting the taverna into darkness. She double-checked the front door as she locked it, giving it a firm tug to ensure it was secure. Satisfied, she pocketed the keys and turned to her friends, who were excitedly skipping down the street. Julia smiled, and her adrenaline kicked in as she hurried to catch up. It was time to let loose.

After staying out all night and surfing the next morning, Julia was exhausted as she walked to work. She was in a great mood, riding high on the excitement of an epic night and the warmth of her video chat with Miriam. Her sister had also been in good spirits, her energy radiating through the screen. Shooting for *IRS Rogue* had wrapped, and Miriam was optimistic about its reception.

Their chats had settled into an easy rhythm. Julia would begin by recounting every detail of the night before—stories about her friends, the party, the beach, the waves, the laughter, and the stillness of early mornings spent watching the sunrise. Miriam never judged but provided advice when appropriate. Miriam said she valued being treated as a sister, not a celebrity, and liked not having to watch her words and just being herself. Their conversations bridged the twenty-year gap of involuntary separation, drawing them closer than anticipated. For Julia, it was comforting to have someone genuinely invested in her world, and for Miriam, it was a rare chance to share hers without pretense.

On this day, Miriam had noted the dark circles under Julia's eyes, the telltale sign of another night spent without sleep. In a maternal tone, she had suggested that Julia attend Alice's brunch that week. "Maybe you need a home-cooked meal," she said.

Julia had shrugged it off, agreeing conceptually, though she wasn't ready to see Ray. She had no interest in navigating whatever guilt or tension awaited her in Mosman. Miriam hadn't pushed—she never did—but Julia could tell she'd hoped the suggestion would take root. The thought lingered as Julia approached the taverna, her fingers brushing the keys in her pocket. She was running on an hour of sleep, struggling to stay upright. It wasn't the first time she'd shown up to work in this state, though, and she braced herself to put on a professional front.

When she entered the taverna, the bell jingled, but something was different. Gus wasn't at his usual post behind the counter. Instead, all was quiet. Julia frowned, glancing around the room. The regulars were there, their souvlaki and coffee steaming before them, but they were subdued.

"Gus?" she called out, stepping further inside and dropping her bag by the counter. No answer. Her pulse quickened, and she experienced a rush of adrenaline. Something was off. Gus never missed her entrance—it was their ritual, his way of setting the tone for the workday. She scanned the taverna again, her gaze landing on Frank, the busboy, who was stacking plates near the kitchen.

"Where's Gus?" Julia asked him.

"He's in the back. He said he wants to talk to you."

Julia had never been summoned to the back of the taverna. Was something wrong? She walked into Gus's closet-turned-office and was directed to sit in a plastic folding chair. Gus, seated in his decades-old, fabric-covered executive chair, leaned forward, his expression severe yet measured, his thick hands gripping the edge of the table.

"Last night," he began, "you didn't lock the back door."

Julia's blood ran cold. She opened her mouth to respond, but nothing came out. Her mind was racing, replaying the steps she had taken to close the taverna, trying to pinpoint where it had gone wrong.

"I know this," Gus continued, "because when I came in this morning, the garbage was sitting inside the back door, right where you left it. And the register? Empty."

Oh no, the register! she thought. She wanted to speak, to explain, but all she could manage was a weak stammer.

Gus didn't let her off the hook. "I checked the video camera. At about 4 a.m., a homeless man entered, helped himself to some moussaka, and emptied the register."

Julia's face flushed hot with embarrassment and guilt. She gripped the sides of her chair, trying to balance herself, but the shame was overwhelming. Her lips moved, but the words were clumsy, inadequate. "I—I'm so, so sorry," she stammered. "I thought —I thought I did every step, but a couple stayed late, and I must have . . . I messed up. I am so, so sorry."

Gus took a deep breath, crossing his arms. "Tzoúlia, it's my fault."

"What?" she croaked.

"I misjudged the moment. I should've stayed and closed myself. I put too much on you too soon, too young."

Julia opened her mouth to object, to take the blame, but Gus raised a hand to stop her. "Luckily," he said, "there wasn't much money in the register. Only five tickets were sold after I left, and three of them were paid with a card. But it's not about the money, Tzoúlia."

"Am I sacked?"

Gus didn't answer right away. The silence was excruciating, stretching for ages as he weighed her fate. After a long pause, he shook his head. "No. Everyone is entitled to a mistake, Tzoúlia. I'll judge you on how you respond."

Relief flooded her, and her shoulders sagged as she exhaled. "Thank you, Gus. Thank you for not sacking me. I made a mistake, but I'll make it right. I'll work extra hard and make up the money from my tips."

Gus raised his hand. "No, no. I don't want your money." He paused. "But I need you to listen, Tzoúlia. You're running yourself ragged. You're not getting enough sleep, and it's catching up to you. Mistakes like this happen when you're running on fumes. If you don't slow down, you'll make more mistakes. And if that happens . . ." He trailed off. "Well, I won't be able to help you anymore."

Julia swallowed hard. "I understand, Gus. I do. I promise to do better."

"Good. Now, put on your apron and get to work."

Julia didn't protest. She went to the counter, tied her apron around her waist, skipped her pre-shift meal, and stepped onto the floor, ready to dive into work. But as she moved through the taverna, things were different. Gus was polite and professional, but all the warmth she had grown accustomed to was gone. There were no jokes, no playful teasing, and none of his affectionate charm that made the workplace special. It was as if a wall had gone up between them, and Julia felt its chill in every interaction.

The chill stretched every minute into an eternity. She was desperate to redeem herself, working twice as fast, her movements manic. Gus gave her instructions with a curt efficiency, his tone devoid of the usual humor, no twinkle in his eye. Each time he walked past her without a smile or a kind word, Julia was wounded, and by mid-shift, she was holding back tears. She blinked furiously every time her eyes threatened to well up, biting the inside of her cheek to keep herself together. She couldn't afford to break down— not here, not now. But the silence between her and Gus was deafening, and the loss of his tenderness was a punishment she struggled to endure.

When the last customer left and her shift ended, Julia untied the apron with shaky hands and hung it on a hook. She glanced toward Gus, hoping for a sign that things were okay between them, but he was busy with the register.

She swallowed and whispered, "Good night, Gus," before slipping out the door.

As the door was about to close, Gus called out, "Tzoúlia, you forgot your sandwich."

She turned back, and Gus handed her a wrapped sandwich through the door frame. The gesture was simple, but it broke through the wall she had held up all shift. Tears welled in her eyes, and she wiped them away as she took the package.

"Tomorrow is Sunday. Rest. And on Monday, you work," Gus said.

As Julia walked, the day's events looped endlessly in her mind, each replay adding to the significance of her mistake. The disappointment in Gus's eyes had stung the most, a constant reminder of how deeply she'd let him down.

She knew she had to make it right—for Gus and herself—and she resolved to do so one step at a time. And the first step was to skip the evening's party at the surf house and get rest. But Julia didn't want to be alone. Nor did she want to be in Gus's rental flat. She didn't deserve his kindness, not tonight, not after her betrayal. She was miserable and instinctively got on a bus to Mosman.

Julia's legs were heavy as she climbed the stone steps to the Corning residence. Her cheeks were raw where tears had streaked down them during the bus ride. Her unwashed, wild hair clung to her face. The midnight air was cool, but she didn't care. The exhaustion coursing through her veins was physical and emotional. The mental wear of the day made her soul weary. She had almost missed her stop, only jolting upright when the bus driver announced it.

As she approached the door, her nerves were frayed. Julia hadn't set foot here since the day she'd walked out, leaving her father's seething anger and her mother's helpless silence. The idea of returning had been undesirable for so long, yet here she was, driven not by a clear plan but by craving the comfort of her childhood home. She paused briefly at the door, the light from the living room spilling out onto the front porch. Alice would still be awake. It was Saturday night, and she would be up till twelve thirty or one. Ray would be sleeping, she knew, bringing Julia a sliver of calm and reprieve from a confrontation she couldn't handle tonight.

Julia lifted her hand to knock on the door. The gesture felt strange, foreign. She hadn't knocked on this door in years—maybe ever. The sound echoed lightly, and within seconds, the door opened. Her mother was there, her face softening in surprise and concern. "Julia," Alice said, pulling her daughter into a tight, maternal hug before Julia could speak. "What's wrong, sweetheart? Are you okay?" Alice asked.

"I'm just . . . so tired."

Julia crumbled in her mother's presence. Alice didn't press for details. She took Julia by the hand and led her inside. The house was quiet. Alice guided Julia down the hallway, past the family photos and into her old room. To Julia's surprise, it was untouched. The bed was made with the same soft lavender quilt, the bookshelves lined with her childhood novels and trinkets. Alice pulled back the covers and gestured for Julia to lie down. "Come on, sweetheart. Get some rest. We'll catch up in the morning."

Julia didn't argue. She slipped off her shoes and climbed into bed. The familiarity of the thick mattress eased the tension throughout her body. Alice tucked the blanket around Julia and, with her hand, brushed the hair from her daughter's face.

"I'm glad you're here, love," Alice said before closing the door.

"Thanks, Mum."

Julia stirred, her eyelids heavy. When she opened them, she caught sight of the bedside clock illuminating the darkened room: 2:00. She'd slept for fourteen hours, yet her body felt weighed down, as though exhaustion had seeped into her bones. Outside the door, words filtered down the hallway, muffled but unmistakable. Soon her father's voice pierced through.

"How much longer are we going to delay? Brunch is supposed to be at noon or before, Alice. Either wake her up or we eat without her."

Julia could hear the irritation lacing his words, the edge she remembered all too well.

Her mother's response came, calm but firm. "Ray, we don't have any guests today. We'll wait until she's up and has a chance to shower. Our only daughter is back after six months. I don't care if she sleeps till ten. We'll eat with her. And you'll be bloody supportive."

There was a pause, followed by the heavy huff of her father's frustration. Julia listened as his footsteps retreated, punctuated by the closing of his study door with a definitive thud. Julia was put at peace by her mom defending her. With that, she let her body sink deeper into the mattress, and her eyes fluttered shut. She drifted back into sleep, cocooned in the fragile comfort of her childhood room.

When Julia woke again, the clock read 4:00, and she reluctantly swung her legs over the side of the bed. Her body was still wobbly. She hadn't eaten much over the past two days, and the hunger pangs motivated her to move. Alice had laid a towel at the foot of the bed, and a neat stack of fresh clothes Julia had left behind six months before had been placed on the desk chair. It was a thoughtful gesture. Grabbing the towel and clothes, Julia trudged to the bathroom, the warm shower water slowly rinsing away the groggy feeling.

The smell of Alice's cooking wafted through the house as Julia emerged from her room, freshly showered and dressed, hair combed into submission. Her mom had clearly taken the sound of running water as a starter pistol to get the meal ready.

The dining table was as Julia remembered it—immaculately set, with dishes of food spread across like a banquet. Alice stood nearby, setting down a plate, her face lighting up as Julia entered the dining room. Ray was already seated. Julia hesitated before sliding into her old seat, bracing for his first quip.

"Thanks for having me for a Sunday meal," she said, breaking the ice.

Though still carrying his usual air of formality, Ray's expression was tempered—softened by Alice's efforts to set a positive tone. His response surprised Julia. "We're happy to have you home, Julia," he said, his manner pleasant. "You look well."

"Thanks, Dad."

"I heard you're working at a Greek place in Manly."

"Gus's Taverna is what we call it."

"I have been there a time or two. It has character."

"Definitely."

"From what I've been told, you're doing a good job. A hard worker. Next time I'm in the area, I'll stop by for some coffee."

Julia blinked, unsure of how to respond. Ray's words, while kind, carried an awkwardness she wasn't used to. Still, she seized the opportunity to avoid confrontation and offered a small smile. "The coffee isn't bad, and the souvlaki is better."

The meal carried on in the same vein—detached but pleasant, with everyone making a visible effort to avoid conflict. Even Ray, usually quick to provoke, was holding back. Alice, ever the mediator, kept the conversation light, commenting on the quality of the prawns and asking Julia about handling the taverna's busiest days. Julia responded politely, her words measured, and she was careful not to say anything that could lead to a lecture.

"Dad, you look skinny. Are you resting enough?" Julia asked, noticing that Ray, usually full of energy, seemed a bit listless during dinner. She had assumed a conflict-avoidance strategy but was curious if he was under the weather.

"I get regular sleep. School and social obligations have been tiring, but nothing I can't handle. My appetite has decreased, but your mum will fatten me back up."

As the plates emptied and Alice began to clear the table, Julia leaned back and glanced at Ray. "I'll be heading out soon," she said, testing the waters. Then, after a beat, she added, "Do you still watch *Night Nurses* on Sundays?" The question was neutral and polite on the surface, but a subtle jab lurked beneath it.

Ray's expression shifted. He was clearly trying to gauge whether she meant it as a dig. After a pause, he answered, "The new episodes are terrible. The writing's gone downhill."

Julia nodded, taking a deliberate sip of her water. "Maybe tonight will be a rerun," she said evenly, her tone ambiguous.

The resulting silence hung in the air before Alice broke it. "Will you come back next week, Julia?"

Julia turned to her mother. "I appreciate the nap and the home-cooked meal. I'll try to make it more regularly. I'll email you in advance." She smiled, her words a tentative olive branch.

Alice beamed at the response. "Good. I'll make sure there's something special for you."

Ray said nothing, simply folded his napkin and pushed back his chair. Julia could tell he was biting his tongue, choosing to let the moment pass without stirring the pot.

As Julia stood to leave, Alice hugged her tightly, whispering, "Take care of yourself, sweetheart."

Julia nodded, her eyes looking for Ray, who stood at a distance, his hands in his pockets. He gave her a brief nod, neither warm nor cold.

Julia stepped toward the door, carrying a canvas bag filled by

Alice with her freshly cleaned clothes, an extra towel, a fluffy pillow, and proper bedsheets. The house was as Julia had left it six months before, yet everything was different: strained, but not entirely uncomfortable. Surprisingly, the experience had been pleasant. Despite her complicated emotions about the house and its inhabitants, Julia couldn't deny the relief she had experienced from the brief return.

CHAPTER 11

Thursday, October 13, 2011 | Carlsbad

Catrina sat at the Break, sipping her coffee and letting the chatter of the morning crowd soothe her anxiety. The café vibrated with activity, the purr of the espresso machine blending with the customers' animated conversations. Tables were packed with locals and the occasional tourist; some worked on laptops while others scrolled their phones, flipped through paperbacks, or exchanged animated stories over steaming cups.

Sam was in the back, buried in paperwork. They'd spoken for a few minutes when Catrina had arrived, but as the café got busier, Catrina was left to her thoughts. A notification appeared on her phone, reminding her that it was the first anniversary of Brockwell Surgical Sales, LLC, or as Tim called it, BSS. It had been a whirlwind, but successful. She was well compensated and held the title of Chief Operations Officer. She didn't make as much as Tim, but far more than she ever expected to earn at twenty-three. She still lived with her mom, and that had personal complications, but otherwise, life was going well. BSS was the exclusive distributor for all SidOrtho products and had secured a client base of twenty doctors. What had begun as a conceptual partnership had turned into a one-sided arrangement. Tim had leveraged his initial contacts to establish the business but had soon retreated to the comfort of his country club, leaving the daily grind to Catrina. She managed client relationships, resolved logistical issues, and ensured operations were in order. In truth, BSS's continued success was almost entirely her doing, though Tim never acknowledged it.

The office mirrored the illusion of the company itself. Housed within a collaborative workspace attached to a luxury car dealership, it exuded an air of prestige and success despite the office being modest. Clients would walk through the dealership's opulent lobby, featuring marble floors, mid-six-figure sports cars, and leather seating, creating an impression of affluence. Tim's office, with its wooden desk and leather chair, was all for show, rarely occupied since he spent most of his time golfing or networking over cocktails. Catrina took over the office in his frequent absence, using it as her command center to manage the endless tasks that kept BSS running. On rare occasions when Tim was present, she was relegated to her small functional cubicle outside his door.

She had been so naive when she had joined the business; she'd believed Tim's talk of true partnership and shared success. But a year later, she knew the reality: Tim was the face of the company, while she was its engine. The operation would crumble without her, yet the credit landed squarely on his shoulders.

As Catrina was about to pack up and leave for work, Sam emerged from the back room, wiping her hands on a towel, and slid into the seat across from her friend. "You've got that serious look again," she said teasingly. "What's going on in that head of yours?"

Catrina swirled her remaining coffee. "Just . . . work stuff. I was thinking about my last day at DeltaTech, joining BSS . . . and Tim's ego." She rolled her eyes.

"Having regrets?" Sam asked.

"No. Just thinking about sliding-door moments. Things are good . . ."

"But Tim's being an ass," Sam said.

Catrina gave a halfhearted laugh. "When isn't he? It's not that he's a pain. It's just . . . he's so dismissive. No matter how much I do, he doesn't notice. He acts like BSS runs itself while he's puttering around town."

"Like I said, an ass."

Catrina stirred her coffee, the clinking of the spoon soothing her.

"At least you're well compensated. Speaking of, when are you going to get your own place?" Sam asked.

"I want to, but I worry about my mom. I don't like to leave her unsupervised," Cat said, attempting a joke that fell flat.

"Come on, Cat. You let the college scholarship go to help her out. She's doing better now. You can't live there your whole life. The timing will never be right for your mom. You have to let her adjust. It sucks, but that's the reality. And I like your mom. I do. But you're doing her a disservice. She'll survive. You're not abandoning her— you're still in the area."

"You're right. I know you're right. But it's not just her. I've never lived alone. I like the noise of another person milling about. Keeps me out of my head."

"Well," Sam said, "I'm month-to-month. We could find a two-bedroom—"

"Yes. A hundred times, yes," Catrina said abruptly. "I can apartment shop after work today. I'll find a broker, or I can—"

Sam cut her off. "See, together, we make one functional human. I've been thinking about finding a better place for a year, and here you are, ready to shop today."

Catrina froze, her body going cold as she realized how over-the-top she'd acted. She swallowed hard, trying to regain her composure. "You were serious, right? About getting a two-bedroom?"

"Yes. A hundred times, yes," Sam said, mimicking Catrina. "I'll see you after work."

Catrina nodded, trying to keep her expression neutral. Moving in with her best friend excited her, though she dreaded telling her mother. There would be tears.

Catrina sat in her cubicle, flipping through a trade journal. She had been waiting for this article since Tim had been interviewed a month before. Her anticipation turned to disappointment and resentment as she read the write-up. The piece portrayed Tim as a groundbreaking visionary, a self-made entrepreneur who had single-handedly founded BSS and revolutionized the medical device sales industry. There wasn't a mention of her—not her tireless work managing clients, not the logistics she handled to keep the company running, and no nod to her general contributions.

The article left a bitter taste in her mouth. Tim was such a creep. She hadn't been credited for the endless hours she'd spent building relationships after his initial introductions or keeping the business afloat while he lounged at the country club. She hadn't expected him to put her on a pedestal, but to erase her? It was insulting.

Catrina put down the magazine as Mr. Lambert, the office manager, approached her cubicle. His ordinarily pleasant demeanor was agitated, and she sensed what was coming.

"Hey, Cat. Sorry to bother you," he began. "Tim's check bounced again. I've had to chase him down three months in a row."

Catrina sighed. "I'm so sorry, Mr. Lambert. I hate that Tim doesn't let me manage the account. It's . . . it's terribly embarrassing."

"It's not your fault," he said. "But Tim keeps telling me he has some special deal with the dealership. If that's true, nobody informed me, so I'm looking foolish."

"I know," Catrina said, her frustration evident. "I think he'll be in this morning, but I can't promise anything."

Mr. Lambert frowned. "I don't want to talk to him. He lies to my face with that giant smile of his. I need certified funds today, Cat. If I don't get them, BSS will lose access at 5:00 p.m. There will be no exceptions this time."

Catrina hated being caught in the middle of Tim's financial messes. "I understand," she said. "I'm sorry he put you in this position again. Let me write you a personal check. It isn't certified, but I can show you my account balance. It won't bounce. I'll sort it out with Tim personally, so you don't have to deal with him."

"I hate to take your money, Cat. It's not fair to you."

"It's fine," she insisted, pulling out her checkbook. "Any time he's late, just come to me. I'll make sure you're not left hanging, and I'll eventually get reimbursed by Tim. I'm sorry you're dealing with this."

"You're an angel, Cat. I don't know what that guy would do without you."

Catrina smiled as Mr. Lambert walked away, but inside, she seethed. Now her savings were being tapped to cover for Tim's irresponsibility. Her resentment was spilling over.

When Tim arrived at the office, his usual swagger in full effect, Catrina wasted no time. She walked into his office with the article and slapped it on his desk. "Care to explain this?"

Tim glanced at the page. "Pretty great, right? Good press for us."

"Us?" Catrina shot back. "There's no 'us' in this article, Tim. It's all about you. Nothing about the work I do."

"Relax, Catnip. I mentioned you. Of course I talked you up. I told them how important you are to BSS. If they left you out, that's on them, not me. I don't control what they print."

"Stop calling me Catnip."

"Okay, okay. Chill. This is a good day," Tim said.

"Chill? Quit bullshitting me. You didn't even mention me in passing. They would've called me if you had done so, to confirm the information."

"Look, it's not what you think. This is a good thing."

"A good thing?" she repeated.

"Yeah," he said, his hands folded on the desk. "I've been hearing rumors. DeltaTech may be considering legal action over the SidOrtho deal falling through. It's all talk for now, but it's better if you stay under the radar. The less they can tie you to anything, the safer you are."

Catrina blinked. "Legal action? You never mentioned this before."

"I didn't want to worry you," Tim said as if he were doing her a favor. "You know I've got your back. That's why I didn't push to have your name in the article. It's not worth the risk."

Her skepticism lingered, but the logic of his explanation was plausible enough to make her hesitate. She hated how easily he spun things, how effortlessly he turned her doubts against her. But he was her boss, her mentor, and—despite it all—the man who had given her this opportunity.

"Fine," she said. "But next time, I want credit where it's due. I do too much around here to be erased."

Tim smiled, his charm back in full force. "Of course, *Cat*. You're the backbone of this company."

"And you owe me for the rent. I paid it from my account."

Tim nodded, and she left his office, the journal still on his desk. She'd been manipulated again and hated herself for it.

Morven was home, sitting on the couch with a pile of mail spread across the coffee table and an old sitcom playing in the background. "Catrina! Eating here tonight?" she asked.

Catrina dropped her laptop bag by the door. "Just stopping by before I head out. I'm meeting Sam."

"Everything okay?" Morven asked as she shuffled some envelopes and patted the cushion beside her. The room was filled with unopened boxes from their last move, and every counter was piled high with precious junk Morven had accumulated over the years. Morven did have a unique eye for botany, which was displayed with an old pale blue-pitcher with a chipped rim serving as a vase. Inside, a spray of hibiscus bloomed in mismatched glory: broad, delicate petals in blood orange, faded pink, and a single near-white blossom tinged at the edges with lavender. Each flower was open wide, trumpetlike, with its golden stamen curling outward like a flame. The leaves were waxy and deep green, a few still damp from rinsing. The arrangement didn't follow any rules, but it worked—an easy metaphor for Morven.

Catrina sank onto the couch. "We're looking at apartments tonight."

Morven froze mid-reach for a soda on the table, her hand hovering in the air. The sitcom's canned laughter filled the silence. "Oh," she said. "Well, that's a big step."

"It is. It's time. We've got a couple of places to see. Not far from here, though."

"I knew this day would come," Morven said, tears starting to form. "Sam's lucky to have you as a roommate."

"Mom, thank you."

Morven blinked, seemingly caught off guard. "For what?"

"For everything. It hasn't been easy. You sacrificed a lot for me."

"I don't see it that way, Catrina. I really don't."

"I know, but thank you still."

Morven sighed. "I have tremendous guilt. I did a terrible job giving you a stable home . . ."

"That isn't true, Mom—"

"It is." Morven shook her head. "I never made enough money. I never dated the right men. Every choice I made was trash. And yet, somehow, you turned out amazing. That's not because of me—that's because of you. I'm so proud of you."

"My bio dad screwed you over. He should've provided financial support."

"Sure, that would've helped," Morven said, nodding. "But the truth is, I just never got my act together."

Catrina hesitated, then said, "Mom, remember when I broke up with Lonnie in high school?"

"Of course."

"I was devastated. I would've done anything to get him back. Anything. I was ready to make some really bad choices."

"You were?"

"Yeah. I had it all mapped out in my head. But I came home, and you spent hours with me. You put aside every problem you had and focused only on me."

"I remember that night, but I don't recall giving you advice."

"You didn't. You just shit-talked Lonnie."

"That, I do recall," Morven said, a small smirk breaking through her tears.

"You shit-talked him so bad that I was happy to see him go." Catrina laughed. "Without preaching, without telling me what to do, you convinced me to move on."

"Years of my own bad choices, my love. I've made every mistake with men in the book. I got pregnant too young. I never wanted that for you." She wiped at her face. "You're my blessing, and I didn't give you a stable home."

"You were there for me. We struggled financially and moved a lot, but you never let me feel alone. You're a mess, Mom, but I owe you everything."

Tears ran freely down both their faces as they embraced. Catrina had to leave, so she tried to lighten the mood. "You'll be okay," she said, pulling back with a teasing smile. "You'll finally have space to keep your craft projects out without me complaining."

"Maybe I'll take up painting. I've always wanted to put some art on those walls," Morven said with a smile even as tears streaked her cheeks.

Catrina reached for her mom's hand, squeezing it as she stood. "I'll come by all the time."

Morven nodded. "I love you. Don't forget your mother when you're off in your fancy new place."

"I won't," Catrina promised, heading for her room to change. "I've gotta go—Sam's waiting. And I love you too."

Friday, October 21, 2011

Catrina and Sam sat in a corner booth at Divine, a trendy brewery with warm, industrial décor and salads to die for. Exposed wooden beams lined the ceiling, hanging planters spilled greenery over the edges of the concrete walls, and indie rock played over the speakers.

A mix of young professionals, local surfers fresh from the beach, and craft beer enthusiasts filled the space, creating a lively but relaxed vibe. On their table, two half-drunk flights of beer and a nearly empty appetizer sampler told the story of their evening.

Sam raised her hazy IPA, the overhead Edison bulbs catching the amber hue. "To a new chapter," she said with a grin, clinking her glass against Catrina's.

"A new chapter," Catrina echoed, sipping her crisp lager.

Signing the lease for their two-bedroom apartment was a big deal. For Sam, it meant upgrading from her cramped, dingy one-bedroom in a less desirable part of town. For Catrina, it meant stepping out of her mother's house and into her own place—well, mostly her own. She shared with Sam, but that was a feature, not a compromise.

"I can't believe it's happening," Sam said. "No more fighting with a moldy bathroom or neighbors who think 2 a.m. is prime time for arguing."

Catrina laughed. "And no more getting grilled by Mom every time I get home. I love her, but . . ." She paused, swirling her beer. "It's time."

Sam tilted her head, studying her friend. "You okay with it? Moving out?"

Catrina hesitated, tapping the edge of her glass. "Yeah. I am. It's just . . . Mom's been through a lot, you know? And I've been the one holding things together for a while. But she's stronger than she lets on. She'll be fine. And this is the right thing for me."

"You're allowed to want your own life, Cat. It doesn't mean you're abandoning her. It means you're trusting her to figure things out. You've earned this."

"Yeah."

"Speaking of, I made a decision today. I'm done with Taylor," Sam said.

"Taylor? The data analyst?" Catrina asked.

"No. The girl from the salon."

"You and your Taylors."

"We've been out a few times," Sam said while taking a sip of beer. "She's sweet, but . . . a bit of a chore. Never date a hairdresser, Cat. I don't have the patience for it."

"So who's up next?" Catrina asked.

"Remember Florence from run club?"

"I thought she moved to Burbank?"

"She's back. May go see her this weekend."

"What was missing with Taylor?" Catrina asked as she nibbled at the scraps from the appetizer tray.

"Data or salon?" Sam asked.

"Stop it."

"This may sound weird, but she didn't touch me."

"Really? You two didn't . . ."

"Don't be silly. We had plenty of sex."

Catrina giggled.

"The problem was, she didn't touch me outside the bedroom. I like being touched. It's my love language. At least how I like to receive love," Sam said.

"Any place in particular?"

"Head, hair, back, shoulders . . ." Sam lingered on the thought.

"Feet?" Catrina asked.

"No, not my kink. But to each their own."

The conversation drifted into spicier territory as their first flight of beers turned into subsequent rounds of full mugs.

"Can I ask you something? And no dodging. Full honesty," Sam asked.

"Depends. Do I need another beer for this?"

"Ha, maybe," Sam teased. "Have you ever slept with a girl?"

Catrina nearly choked on her sip, coughing as she set the glass down. "What? No!"

"Not even in college? To explore?"

"I've never gone there. Why do you ask?" Catrina asked.

"No reason. Just curious."

Catrina shrugged, avoiding further discussion on the topic. Instead, she blurted, "I've slept with Tim a bunch of times, though."

"Gross!"

"I know," Catrina said, holding up her hands. "I know. Not my proudest moment—moments—okay? But it's . . . convenient, I guess. No strings. Nothing serious. It's not going anywhere, and I'm fine with that."

"Does he know it's not serious?" Sam asked.

Catrina shrugged. "Probably. I mean, he's married. I'm planning to cut it off soon. I just . . . I'm not sure how he'll react. He doesn't handle rejection well."

Sam reached across the table, resting a hand on Catrina's. "First, thank you for telling me. Second, I already knew."

"I suspected," Catrina said.

"I appreciate you opening up. You deserve more than convenient. You deserve someone who's all in, who will give you everything. If this thing with Tim makes you happy right now, okay. I'm not here to judge. But promise me you'll leave room for something better."

"I hear you. I do. But I don't have time to date between work and everything else."

"Well, I'm jealous of the man who wins your heart," Sam said, finishing the beer before her.

"You're so cheesy. And full of it. Jealous? You?"

Sam shook her head, her eyes locking onto Catrina's. "You're different, Cat. You're . . . amazing. The kind of person people dream of building a life with. You're smart, kind, funny, and loyal to a fault. That's rare. And, yeah, I'm jealous of whatever man gets to be on the receiving end of your love."

"And I'm jealous of the Taylors," Catrina said.

"Nobody should be jealous of the Taylors."

"You're right. The Taylors got dumped. You'll have your pick of impressive women whenever you decide to settle down. Everybody in North County adores you," Catrina said just as one of the Break's customers walked by and said hello to Sam.

They sat in silence for a moment, the commotion of the brewery fading into the background.

Catrina broke the quiet by saying, "Do you really think I deserve more than Tim?"

"Of course, Cat," Sam replied, her hand once again reaching across the table to rest lightly on Catrina's. "And I'll keep reminding you of it until you believe it too."

Catrina glanced down at their hands, then at Sam. "Thanks, Sam. For . . . everything."

"Always," Sam said, her grip on Catrina's hand tightening briefly before she let go. "Now, finish your beer so we can get one more round."

Catrina couldn't remember when she had been happier than signing a new lease and having drinks and unfiltered conversations with her best friend. Not to mention the sensation she experienced every time Sam touched her hands.

Sam raised her glass one last time as the brewery began to wind down for the night. "To new beginnings."

"New beginnings," Catrina echoed.

CHAPTER 12

The calm water lulled Julia into a state of peace she rarely enjoyed on land. She had savored a full night of sleep and hadn't gotten on the ocean until 9:30. She sat atop Floating Sky, the board bobbing with the swells, watching as the horizon stretched before her. The next set wasn't rolling in anytime soon, and that was fine by her. Some mornings weren't about chasing waves; they were about the stillness, the isolation, the salty air, and the companionship of the sea.

Drifting aimlessly in solitude allowed her mind to wander, letting her thoughts sway like the water beneath her. It had been more than six months since her mistake with the back door at the taverna, and she and Gus had weathered it. It had taken time, but she had proved herself by arriving early, staying focused, and handling her duties reliably. Gus had started joking with her again after a week. He couldn't stay cold; it was contrary to his nature. If an employee crossed him and truly violated his trust, he sacked them. Gus couldn't have workers around that he didn't treat as family. He had even thrown her a little party for her first anniversary. There had been balloons, a small cake, and a card that all the staff had signed. Alani and Ginger had helped decorate, and Ginger had even brought her boyfriend, Beau. Julia had been surprised by the party and deeply touched.

Gus had asked her to run the taverna on Mondays because Maria had put her foot down and insisted he start taking time off. Monday was a slow day, and Julia had demonstrated the responsibility he required. Gus often complained that the day at home with his wife was less restful than joking with regulars at the taverna, but Julia was delighted to have regained his trust. The one precaution he took was to have another worker stay with her through closing. The other employee, usually Frank, had to take a picture of the locked doors and text it to Gus before he would permit them to leave. If the image was blurry, he demanded a fresh picture.

Her social scene had also slowed. Julia still attended surf house parties, but not every night. She had found that two times a week was a better balance. Friday was her big party night most weeks. At first, Alani and Ginger had been annoyed at her absence, but they had eventually seen the merit in slowing down and had created a healthier balance. It made Friday night more exciting and gave them time to relax. The three of them spent most other evenings watching Netflix and chatting. Sometimes, the three would take a walk on the beach before heading to bed.

Julia smiled faintly as she sat on her board, thinking of how she cherished her video chats with her sister. They talked about everything—Miriam's new life in LA, the progress of her career, and lighthearted topics like fashion or what they had eaten. The conversations grounded her, and Miriam provided a needed role model for Julia. Julia's goal was to save enough money to visit her sister. It wasn't a distant dream but a tangible plan she was working toward. She kept it quiet, though, not wanting Miriam or Gus to give her the money—she wanted to earn it.

Julia had settled into a rhythm of attending Sunday brunch once or twice a month—enough to keep Alice content, but not enough for Ray to pry into her life. Ever the strategist, Alice began emailing Julia early in the week, tipping her off when other guests would join them, knowing it made Julia more likely to show up. Julia would finish her shift at the taverna on Saturday night and take the bus to Mosman. Alice would be waiting, awake and holding the front door open. They would sit down together and start talking, not about anything big: work, surf, or how Alani was handling school. Her mum asked questions without steering the conversation.

Over the past few months, the shape of their talks had shifted. Alice spoke more openly about her life. For the first time, she mentioned her job at a solicitor's office in North Sydney before Julia was born and how much she had liked criminal law. There had never been talk of law school, even though she had shown promise. Alice's father believed university was wasted on girls. Her mother focused on teaching her to iron properly and host events with a personalized flourish that would satisfy her need for individuality and public praise. When she met Ray, he was making rapid progress through the education system. He was bright, popular, and articulate, with no shortage of ambition. Alice saw the match as confirmation that she had done well. Her parents agreed. In their eyes, she had secured her future.

One night, she told a story about a school Ray had declined to run because it was on the west side of the city. Alice had been disappointed. The school was near her parents, close to where she had grown up. She pointed out that the pay was better and the houses more affordable than anything in Mosman, but Ray had made his decision. There had been no shifting it. In the end, she believed he had been right. Their life in Mosman had been "lovely," and she wouldn't have chosen differently.

Julia listened closely. She liked being treated as an adult. She still didn't agree that deferring to Ray all those years had been the right call, but she could now see how her mother had arrived at it.

She had spent years trying to understand the woman who folded Ray's jumpers and passed the gravy with the one who stood silently when Julia was scolded for answering back. As a teenager, it had felt like betrayal. It had read as weakness. These fresh conversations didn't erase the past, but they shifted Julia's perspective. Alice had been raised to believe that a woman's purpose was to support a man's path. She had accepted that her worth was measured through his success. Ray's accomplishments were her accomplishments. Julia still wished her mother had done things differently, but she no longer saw her choices as senseless. They had their logic.

What surprised Julia wasn't the depth of her mother's loyalty but the absence of bitterness. Alice didn't speak with regret. She wasn't revising her life. She shared it plainly, piece by piece, exactly as she had lived it. There was clarity in how she spoke about Ray—his rigidity, his inflexibility, the way he held court rather than conversation. She admitted he could be exhausting. And then she would mention the birthday letter he once wrote, so loving that she had it framed. There had been one obvious rupture between them, a breach of trust that still surfaced during moments of strain, but otherwise, Alice had chosen her life and stood by it, even if it wasn't one Julia would've chosen for herself.

After the chats with her mum, Julia would go to her room, crash hard, sleep through Sunday morning, and wake up in time to join the meal in progress. At brunch, when neighbors and family friends were there, she slipped into the background of polite chatter, avoiding the spotlight.

As Julia bobbed along on Floating Sky, her eyes drifted to the shoreline. A mix of tourists and locals played in the shallows, their laughter carried on the breeze. The children darted in and out of the waves, their parents allowing an illusion of independence. Julia, ever vigilant, kept an eye on the water. Even in calm conditions, rip currents and undertows posed a significant danger. She had seen it too many times: someone wading out too far and suddenly panicking as the current pulled them away from the shore. It didn't take much for a fun day at the beach to turn deadly.

Her gaze fixed on a small group of teenagers splashing near a sandbar. They were fine for now, but the rip in the area was deceptive. Julia hoped the lifesavers onshore were paying attention. Out of habit, her fingers traced the small hand signal she used from her board—a quick, subtle way to capture the lifesavers' attention if she saw trouble brewing. It was a layer of community vigilance shared by surfers and lifesavers.

As she sat there, the sun climbed higher, illuminating the calm water. Julia was content, the calm sea mirroring her internal harmony, but the serenity shattered in an instant when two of the teenagers, caught in the pull of the water, began struggling and crying out for help, their panicked shouts piercing the quiet morning. Julia scanned the shore, searching for lifesavers, but the station was unmanned. Julia flattened on Floating Sky and began paddling ferociously, cutting through the water with powerful, determined strokes.

As the screen lit up and Miriam's face appeared, Julia didn't wait for a proper greeting. "I saved two teenagers from the surf!" she blurted out. Her grin stretched from ear to ear, her cheeks flushed.

"What? Jules, that's incredible! Tell me everything."

Julia bounced in her seat. "I saved two lives!" she repeated, excitement gushing out in one breath.

"Details," Miriam said.

Her words spilled out. "Okay, so here's how it happened: I was sitting on my board, you know, waiting for the next set and zoning out when I saw these two kids—teenagers—struggling in the water. At first, I thought they were goofing around, but I realized they had been caught in a rip and couldn't get back to shore. They were screaming for help."

Miriam listened intently, with apparent pride, as Julia continued, "I looked toward the shore, but the lifesaver station was empty, and I didn't see anyone else paying attention. So I didn't think twice—I laid down on Floating Sky and started paddling as fast as I could. The current pulled them farther out, so I pushed to get there before it got worse." Her hands moved animatedly as she described the scene, mimicking the paddling motions.

"When I reached them, they were panicking, flailing

everywhere, which made it harder to help. But I stayed calm. I told them to grab onto my board and tried to keep them talking so they'd stop freaking out. They were heavier than I expected—two teenage boys! They were coughing and gasping for air, and my arms were burning, but I kept paddling toward the shore. Somehow, I managed to haul them in." She paused for a breath. "When I finally got them to the shallows, I dragged them onto the sand. By then, a few people had come over to help, but they didn't know what to do, so I took charge."

"Wow," Miriam said.

"Mir, all those surf safety courses Dad made me take kicked in. I ensured that the boys' airways were clear and that they were both alert. And the best part? They were stable and talking when the paramedics arrived."

Miriam's smile was as big as Julia's. "Jules, that's incredible. You're incredible. You saved their lives. How does it feel?"

"Honestly, it's the best feeling I've ever had. Like, I can't explain it." Though still thrumming from recounting her beach rescue, Julia shifted the conversation. "I need to catch my breath. I'm still buzzing. Tell me something. Any news on awards for *IRS Rogue*?"

Miriam's eyes lit up. "That puts me on the spot. Having to follow *saving lives*? What a wild morning. You're so brave!" she exclaimed.

"Thanks, Mir, but seriously, what's the latest?" Julia asked.

"I have been nominated for the Critics' Choice, SAG, and a Golden Globe! And my agent says there's talk of an Emmy nomination, too. Can you believe it? Me, up for an Emmy!"

"That's amazing. You deserve it."

"And that's not the best part," Miriam continued. "I learned this week that we're getting a second season."

"Wait, what? I thought it was supposed to be a one-off miniseries," Julia said.

"That's what we were told!" Miriam said, gesturing animatedly. "But the viewership numbers have been insane, and the critics love it, so HBO decided to extend it, and now it's officially a full series. They haven't told me much, but from what I've heard, there's a good chance my character will take center stage next season. Claudia Von Haulsteen might become the main storyline!"

"You're killing it."

"Thanks, Jules. All the hard work is finally paying off, you know? I've been busting my backside for years, and now . . . now it's happening," Miriam said. "The only downside? Claudia's look. I miss my long hair."

"I'm so happy for you. I've watched a few episodes over at Ali and Gin's. They've got Foxtel. Gin puts it on her dad's credit card."

"Foxtel?" Miriam asked.

"Yeah, pay TV that carries the HBO shows down here."

"Did you like it? What did you think?"

"I loved it," Julia said. "It's so intense, but in the best way. And you? You're incredible in it. I mean, I knew you were good, but wow, Mir. Claudia is a badarse."

"Thanks, Jules. Means a lot."

"You're a great actress and all, but it does take me a few minutes to forget that Claudia is on screen, not my sis. I've never had to deal with that before. It's pretty goofy."

"My mum used to say the same thing," Miriam said.

"I'm going to get back over there and finish the season," Julia added. "We're due for a binge night."

"You have got to see the finale. That's where Claudia comes into her own. It's my favorite episode," Miriam said.

Julia nodded, making a mental note to plan her next visit to Alani and Ginger's place.

After a moment, Miriam's expression shifted, a hint of curiosity crossing her face. "I had a weird thought. Mind if I share it?" she asked.

"Go for it."

"Does Dad watch my new show?"

Julia paused, considering the question. "I don't know. He hasn't mentioned anything to me. I don't think he pays for Foxtel. He's a tight old bastard."

The conversation hung, a shared understanding passing between them. For Julia, it was another reminder of how much she valued these chats.

"Jules," Miriam began, "can I confess something to you?" Her face became more serious.

"Of course. What's on your mind?"

"I've been having a hard time sleeping since Mum passed. At first, it was the grief. Then it was the stress of work, all the pressures of this industry. It got to the point where I couldn't function without something to help, so my doctor prescribed Klonopin."

"What's Klonopin?" Julia asked, tilting her head and attempting to make eye contact through the screen. "Are you okay?"

"I'm fine. It's a medication."

"What does it do?" Julia asked, blinking rapidly.

"I don't know exactly. It's like hitting a pause button for your anxiety or stress."

Julia nodded slowly, trying to absorb the information.

Miriam continued. "It's used for things like anxiety, panic attacks, or trouble sleeping, which is why I started taking it. But now . . . I'm still taking it. Daily."

Julia nodded. "How can I help?" Julia asked.

"I don't know. I don't have a point in telling you this. I just needed to tell someone."

"I get it. I'm glad you did."

"Sorry to be a downer. Especially today when you've been a hero. I'm so proud of you."

"You're not a downer. Promise me you'll stay safe, okay? I'm here for you if there's anything you need—anything at all." Julia was touched that Miriam had been able to be vulnerable with her. It revealed their bond wasn't built only on shared blood.

"I'm good. Seriously. But thanks for offering."

"Up for a quick subject change before you go? I have something juicy," Julia said.

"Please."

"I meant to tell you earlier, but it slipped my mind. Last Saturday night, my mum told me about Catrina's mum and Dad."

Miriam perked up. "Wait—you know the story? For real?"

"I do," Julia said. "Mum had too many drinks that evening and was mad at Dad. When I arrived at the house late after work, she . . . spilled it."

"Tell me."

"Okay, so it was in 1988. Dad wasn't a drinker, as he had always been wary of repeating his father's ways, but he had a slip—a big cricket match at the Sydney Cricket Ground. The Aussies had some epic win, and Dad got blasted celebrating with mates. He ended up at a tourist bar at The Rocks. Beyond that . . . nothing. He has no memory of the night."

"Oh. I see where this is going," Miriam said. "Can't be responsible for his actions?"

"That's what he tried to tell Mum," Julia said. "Anyway, a year or so later, Dad got a call from America. A woman named Morven claimed that he was the father of her daughter, Catrina. She described a night at the bar that matched his hazy memory, but Dad insisted he never shagged her. He claimed it was extortion, a shakedown. He dismissed the whole thing, calling it a *malicious fabrication*."

Miriam shook her head. "Unreal. How scummy of him."

"It gets messier," Julia continued. "Dad told my mum about the call. He was covering his arse. He wanted her prepared if Morven or Catrina called or showed up at the door. Dad never heard from Catrina's mum again, but my mum hasn't let it go. She said she reminds him when they fight, like on Saturday. He has no counter to the attack."

"Wow, that's messy."

"Want to hear the kicker? Dad stalked Catrina on the internet. He found pictures of her. And, according to Mum . . . she has to be his daughter. She looks like him. No doubt."

"It's really sad," Miriam said, mouth agape.

"Dad knows what he did but won't own up to it. I can't respect a person like that," Julia said.

"I agree." Miriam glanced at the time on her screen as the call began to wind down. "I have to go, Jules," she said. "I have a meeting in a bit. But we can talk tomorrow, okay?"

"Sounds good."

"And, again, I'm so proud of you for saving those kids. Amazing!"

With a deep breath, Julia grabbed her bag and headed out the door after they ended the call. The sun was bright in the sky, and the ocean breeze lifted her spirits as she approached the taverna. Today was a turning point, and Julia was ready to embrace it.

As she rounded the corner, two people in red-and-yellow uniforms with *Manly Life Saving Club* emblazoned across their polo shirts approached her. Both looked professional yet approachable, their expressions serious but kind.

"Excuse me, Julia?" the older man, in his late thirties with a weathered face and confident posture, called out.

She stopped, startled. "Yeah, that's me."

The man smiled. "We're from the Manly Life Saving Club. I'm Gary, but call me Gazza. This is Lottie, short for Charlotte." He gestured to the woman beside him, who looked in her late twenties, her brunette ponytail swinging as she nodded in greeting.

"We were hoping to discuss what happened this morning with you. You did something incredible out there."

Julia shifted awkwardly. "You heard about it?"

"It was reported to us that you saved those boys. You stayed calm, acted quickly, and saved their lives. That's not something most surfers would do," Charlotte said.

"It was instinct. I scan the coastline between sets," Julia said.

"Exactly. That's a special gift. You're a natural caretaker. Those two boys are very lucky you were in the surf today," Charlotte said.

"Lottie and I believe you'd be a fantastic fit for the Life Saving Club," Gary said.

Julia glanced at her watch. "I appreciate that, but I'm about to be late for work."

"We can make it quick. Or better yet, why don't we drop by Gus's? If you've got a few minutes to chat during your shift, we can grab a coffee and explain everything," Gary said.

Julia paused. "Alright, sure. I usually have downtime at the start of my shift. Come by. I'll be inside in a few minutes."

Julia went around back to get her mind straight before her shift. She saw Frank in the kitchen, and they chatted for a few minutes. When she got to the front, Gary and Charlotte were sitting in a booth, sipping coffee. Gus was behind the counter as she tied her apron and grabbed the order book.

"Who are the uniforms?" Gus asked.

"They want me to volunteer," Julia explained, trying not to make a big deal of things.

Gus perked up. "Volunteer, huh?"

"Yeah. Help them with the lifesaving. I don't know the details."

"You're the best swimmer in Sydney. Makes sense they'd hire you. They can probably pay more, too. I'm about to lose my waitress..."

"Stop it, Gus. It's all voluntary."

"I know. It still pays better . . . Okay, spill it. What'd you do?" Gus asked.

"Nothing."

"You're smiling ear to ear and skipping around. Two lifesavers show up to offer you a job. You did something. Tell me," Gus said.

"Okay. But promise you won't make a big deal about it."

"Me? I don't do that," Gus said.

"I pulled two boys out of the surf this morning. They got caught in the current and were drowning. I dragged them to shore," Julia said, bracing—yet secretly excited—for Gus's impending overreaction.

He didn't disappoint. "Tzoúlia. You did *what*? You saved two childs from the ocean? Everyone must know my waitress is the hero of Manly Beach."

"While you write your fairy tale for the customers, can I talk to them?" Julia asked.

"Yes. Yes, talk to them. You've got time before the rush."

Julia walked over to the booth, and Gary wasted no time diving in. "First, the Life Saving Club performs around ten thousand preventions a year. That's the people we stop from getting into trouble in the first place. And on average, we save two hundred lives annually. What you did today is exactly the kind of initiative and skill we need. We'd love to have you join us."

Charlotte added, "It's a volunteer position, but deeply rewarding. We're currently short-staffed for the lunch shift—eleven to one, Monday through Friday. That was the problem today. No one was on duty when those kids got into trouble."

Julia frowned, thinking about the moment she had seen the teenagers struggling in the water. If she hadn't been there . . . She shook the thought away. "I appreciate the offer, but I work full time. I can't drop everything."

"We get that. But your swimming skills are already excellent," Gary said.

"And I'm CPR certified," Julia said.

"Perfect. Then your training would be minimal, a week or two. And if you're available for the lunch shift, we can work around your schedule," Gary said, with Charlotte nodding beside him.

Before Julia could respond, Gus appeared behind her, his arms crossed. "Do it, Tzoúlia. For the children of Manly."

Julia turned to him. "Gus—"

He held up a hand to stop her. "You've been with me a year now. Never late, never missed a shift, very reliable. It is something you should do. Make our community safer."

Julia was flattered, not about the offer but by Gus publicly vouching for her work ethic and reliability. "Alright," she said. "I'm in. As long as it doesn't interfere with my shifts here."

Gary smiled. "We'll make it work. One thing you should be aware of is that we have a strict no-drug policy." He handed her a pamphlet with a section on drug testing, underlined for emphasis.

She stared at the pamphlet. Julia thought about her party nights at the surf house and visibly cringed. "Got it," she said. She folded the pamphlet and slipped it into her pocket, a determination taking hold. This responsibility mattered to her. If cutting out recreational drugs was required to make this work, that was easy enough. She would stop. It was time to move forward.

Charlotte handed Julia another pamphlet with a breakdown of the training schedule, saying, "We'll get you started with training next week. Welcome aboard."

As Gary and Charlotte left, Gus gave Julia a pat. "You're doing a good thing, Tzoúlia. I'm proud of you. But don't forget to sleep. Lives depend on it."

"Thanks, Gus. I know. This has been a great day."

CHAPTER 13

Friday, October 21, 2011 | Sydney

"Tzoúlia here is having herself a big day!" Gus announced to everyone. Julia shot him a look, but he didn't care. "This morning, Tzoúlia saved two lives in the surf. And now, she's been personally selected by the prestigious Life Saving Club of Manly to save more lives. She'll save babies, children, and old people. Everybody take note—our Tzoúlia is going places!"

Julia's cheeks turned scarlet as she set steaming plates in front of a table of regulars, who were grinning at her as if she had walked off a red carpet. "Thanks, Gus, but that's enough. People are here to enjoy their coffee," she said, willing him to stop.

But he wasn't done.

"I'm telling you," Gus continued, addressing the entire taverna as if making an Oscar speech, "I discovered her. Taught her everything she knows—well, except the surfing. That's her. But here? Natural. An absolute natural."

Julia ducked her head, hiding her embarrassment as she cleared an empty table, but it was no use. Gus had moved on to another group of customers, regaling them with tales of how she had arrived at the taverna not knowing how to balance a tray, and how he'd molded her into the superstar she was today. She could hear the pride in his remarks and feel it in the way he patted her head every time he walked by, like a father showing off his kid's report card.

One of the regulars at the counter, a gray-haired man named Bruce, clapped as she passed. "Didn't know we had a local hero working at the taverna."

"Gus is overselling it a bit."

Bruce chuckled. "Let him. We could use a little excitement around here."

She smiled politely and returned to the kitchen, hoping Gus would lose steam, but then she saw him standing by the register and pointing her out to a couple of tourists. "That's her! By the kitchen. She saved two teenagers from the surf this morning. And look at that apron—sharp as a tack, eh? The *Hero of Manly Beach* works here!"

Julia groaned internally, her face burning with embarrassment. She caught Gus's eye as she walked by, giving him her best stern look. "Gus, knock it off. People are here to eat, not hear your tall tales."

Gus responded with a wide grin and an unapologetic shrug. "What can I say? I'm proud of you, Tzoúlia." Before she could react, he pulled her into a quick, warm hug before disappearing into the back office, muttering something about organizing for the dinner rush.

Julia sighed, shaking her head as she adjusted her apron and returned to the counter to make a coffee. Gus's over-the-top antics might have been mortifying, but they had warmed her. After everything they had been through—the mistake with the back door, rebuilding his trust, and earning her place in the taverna—it was good to know he believed in her wholeheartedly. When she grabbed her next order from the kitchen, her blush faded, replaced by a small smile. The day wasn't over yet, and neither was Gus's bragging, but Julia was content to let him have his moment—their moment.

As the dinner rush subsided, the door jingled open, and Julia glanced up from wiping the counter. A man stepped in, the kind who turned heads without trying. He was tall—easily six foot four—with a lean, athletic build and carried a visible confidence. His movements were fluid and purposeful, commanding attention.

His brown hair caught the light from the taverna's fluorescents, framing a face almost too symmetrical, as though it had been sculpted rather than born. But his eyes struck Julia the most—vivid green and intense, sweeping across the room before settling on her. His outfit was understated yet clean—a fitted shirt that hinted at his physique without flaunting it, and jeans that looked casual yet fit as if tailored. It was as if he had stepped out of a magazine. As he walked toward the counter, Julia caught the faintest scent of cologne, fresh and earthy. Sliding onto a stool, he rested his arms on the counter, his long fingers tapping idly against the surface as he grabbed a menu. Julia tightened her grip on the rag in her hand.

"Evening," he said.

Julia swallowed and nodded, offering a professional smile. "Hi there. Haven't seen you before. First time at Gus's Greek Taverna? Need any help with the menu?"

The man's eyes met hers with an easy, relaxed smile, and he said, "Yeah, first time. I just moved here, actually. From the Moore Park area. Got a little townhouse a few blocks away. I was out for a walk to explore the neighborhood, and the smell of this place stopped me in my tracks. Instantly hungry."

Julia nodded politely. "Welcome to Manly. What's your name?"

"Marcus," he replied, extending a hand across the counter.

Julia hesitated before shaking it, his grip quick and businesslike.

"Nice to meet you, Marcus. I'm Julia." She motioned to the menu in his hands. "Anything catching your eye? Coffee to start while you decide?"

Marcus shook his head. "No caffeine for me, thanks. But I'll have water and herbal tea if you have it."

"I'll get that for you." Julia turned toward the kitchen, then glanced back for a fleeting moment. He was strikingly handsome—tall, confident, and effortlessly put together. Shaking off the thought, she focused on preparing his drinks. She had never been one to flirt, especially on the job.

As she filled the teapot, she viewed Gus in the corner, deep in a hushed conversation with one of the kitchen staff. The sight was unusual; Gus never whispered. He was usually the loudest and most boisterous presence in the room. Julia scowled, confused by Gus's odd behavior, but dismissed the thought. It was a great day, and she wouldn't let herself get distracted.

Returning to the counter, she placed the water and tea in front of the customer. "Here you go. So what brought you to Manly? New job? Closer to family?"

"No, nothing like that. I spent some time here when I was younger, and it stuck with me. There's something about the place—it's got this pull, you know? So when it came time to move, I couldn't think of anywhere else I'd rather be," Marcus said.

"That's nice," Julia replied. "What's your new place like?"

"It's pretty simple," he said. "A townhouse overlooking the beach. Nothing fancy, but it feels like home."

"Good for you," Julia said with a smile. She motioned toward the menu again. "Take your time. Let me know when you're ready to order."

"Thanks."

Julia moved on to check her tables, take orders, and refill drinks, but she noticed Gus sneaking glances at Marcus, his expression giddy. Shrugging off Gus's continued odd behavior, Julia focused on her customers, determined to keep riding the high of her productive and satisfying day.

When Julia circled back to Marcus, he was hunched casually on the counter, the menu still in his hands. "Hey, Julia," he said, his eyes lighting up when she approached. "I've got a few questions about the menu. Mind helping me out?"

"Of course," she replied, standing beside him. "What can I help with?"

He pointed to three items on the menu: moussaka, spanakopita, and souvlaki. "I'm torn between these three. They all sound amazing, but I've never tried any of them. Which one would you recommend?"

Julia smiled, slipping into her role as the expert. "Alright, so moussaka is kind of like a Greek lasagna, but instead of pasta, it's layers of eggplant and ground lamb, topped with a creamy béchamel sauce. It's rich, hearty, and a favorite. Spanakopita, on the other hand, is a savory spinach pie wrapped in flaky phyllo dough. It's lighter but still super satisfying. And souvlaki? That's grilled skewers of marinated meat—lamb or chicken—served with pita and tzatziki. It's simple but packed with flavor."

"Okay, which is the healthiest of the three?" Marcus asked.

Julia considered for a moment. "Go with the souvlaki. Doesn't have a heavy sauce. It's one of our best dishes."

Marcus grinned, his smile warm and disarming. "Souvlaki it is. I'll have the chicken, please."

Julia caught what she thought might be a flirtatious look, but she composed herself, refusing to let it throw her off. "Chicken souvlaki —good choice," she said. "I'll put it in for you."

She turned on her heel and headed toward the kitchen, slipping behind the counter to clip the order ticket. As she did, she glanced at Gus, who was beside the prep counter and watching her with an amused expression.

"What's going on, Gus?" she asked. "You've been acting weird since he walked in."

Gus burst into a hearty laugh, patting her on the head. "Nothing, Tzoúlia, nothing. Make sure you take special care of that new customer, eh? Let's convert him to a regular."

Julia rolled her eyes but couldn't help but smile a little at Gus's playful mood. She returned to the floor, determined to focus on her tables and not overthink Gus's nonsense.

Marcus kept the conversation rolling as Julia cleared a nearby table. "So what do you do when you're not here?" he asked.

"I surf," Julia replied, grabbing a glass of water for another customer.

"Great place to do it," Marcus said.

"Yep, it's the best," Julia said, placing the water on the next table. "Lots of good spots. Some more crowded than others."

"Are you any good?"

Julia shrugged, avoiding eye contact as she placed a napkin on the counter. "I'm okay," she said. "Been doing it my whole life."

Before Marcus could respond, Gus burst out from the back, "My Tzoúlia is the best surfer in all of Sydney!" he exclaimed. "She won a trophy saying so! It was in all the papers."

Julia froze, her face heating up as Gus continued, undeterred. "And not just surfing—she now works for the lifesaving people! Today, she saved two kids from the ocean. She's a hero. We're all so proud of my Tzoúlia." Gus then moved to another table, his enthusiasm dialed up to ten, recounting Julia's feats once again, embellishing the details.

Julia turned back to Marcus, her face flushed. "He gets carried away," she said. "I won a junior competition at Bondi when I was fourteen, which was cool, but I'm not anyone's definition of the best surfer in Sydney. Well, except for Gus." She gave a small, sheepish smile. "But don't try to correct him. He believes what he believes."

"Wait, is he your dad?" Marcus asked.

"Ha. No. Though you can't work here for any length of time without becoming part of Gus's extended family."

"Well," Marcus said, "it's good to know the beaches are safe. I'll swim confidently, knowing we have a hero in town."

Julia heard the overt flirtation in his words and excused herself, retreating to the back under the pretense of checking on an order. Once in the kitchen, she took a deep breath and composed herself. This wasn't the first time a customer had hit on her, but something about Marcus made her uneasy because—this time—she liked it.

When she was ready, she emerged from the back and took a lap around the taverna, topping off water glasses and checking on her tables. She purposefully avoided Marcus until she heard the ding from the kitchen signaling that his order was ready.

Picking up his plate, she carried it with an exaggerated poise.

"Here you go," she said, setting it down. "Enjoy." She refilled his water, offered a polite smile, and turned quickly, not allowing Marcus to rope her into another conversation. Whatever charm he was exuding, Julia wasn't ready to entertain it.

When Marcus finished eating, it was nearing 8:30. Julia kept her distance while he ate, busying herself with other tables, but she returned to clear his plate. He thanked her for the meal, his eyes lingering. When she offered the bill, he asked, "Are there any good dessert options?"

"We've got baklava, galaktoboureko, and loukoumades," she said, preparing to dart away.

"I'll think about it," Marcus replied.

Julia nodded and walked another lap of the taverna. When she returned, Marcus looked up, fidgeting as though debating whether to speak. Then he blurted out, "I've never done anything like this before, but I feel . . . Would you consider going out with me sometime?"

Julia froze, the words hitting her like a rogue wave. She glanced instinctively toward Gus, who was conspicuously straining to hear the conversation from his perch at the other end of the counter. Her brain scrambled for an escape route, but all she could muster was a panicked signal with her eyes to Gus.

Gus appeared in a flash. "Sir, sir," he began, "many a man has wanted to ask my Tzoúlia out over some baklava, but I forbid her from answering such questions while at work. A local hero must not be burdened while on the clock."

Julia mouthed a quick *thank you* to Gus, relieved for the intervention, but her relief was short-lived.

Marcus, undeterred, said, "Well, do you mind if I stick around for dessert and another cup of tea?"

Before Gus could craft more grandiose responses, Julia, to her shock, blurted out, "Of course. Our regulars loiter for hours." She hesitated and then, as if possessed by some outside spirit, added, "I usually get off work between ten and eleven."

Her words hung in the air. She couldn't believe she'd said that.

That's so unlike me, she thought, horrified. From the corner of her eye, she saw Gus's mouth stretch into the biggest grin. Bigger than his *saving childs* smile. She excused herself to the back, desperate to escape the charged atmosphere. And this time, she'd provided the electricity, not Gus.

Gus followed her, his laughter echoing through the kitchen. "My Tzoúlia," he said with delight, "looks like you fancy this Marcus. And he fancies you. Add another love connection to the history of the taverna."

"Gus, stop it."

"Quite the day. Quite the day, indeed!"

Julia pressed her palms to her face, trying to stifle the heat rushing to her cheeks.

The rest of her shift unfolded quietly, a welcome relief after the earlier events. Marcus kept his word, respecting her space and not attempting to engage her while she worked. Instead, he and Gus fell into an animated conversation about cricket. Julia eavesdropped as she moved between tables. To her surprise, Gus knew quite a bit about the sport, easily throwing out players' names and matches. Marcus, for his part, appeared at ease, sipping his tea and laughing with Gus.

Marcus paid his bill directly with Gus, avoiding any interaction that might have pressured Julia or made her uncomfortable. She was impressed by his consideration of the request to leave her alone. As the clock read 10:30, the last customers, besides Marcus, paid their tabs and left. Gus, never one to let an opportunity for drama pass, clapped his hands and declared to all, "Ladies and gentlemen, the time has come! Tzoúlia's shift is officially over!" he added with a sparkle of mischief. "No cleaning up tonight. Go. Relax. This is my decree."

Julia rolled her eyes but couldn't help smiling at his antics. She wiped her hands on her apron, untied it, and hung it behind the counter. "Fine, Gus. You win."

She glanced over at Marcus, who had watched the exchange with amusement. He stood, his tall frame towering over the counter stools, and turned to face her. "Would you consider going out with me sometime?" he asked again.

"How about we take a walk on the beach? I enjoy unwinding with a walk. If you're up for it."

"Now?" Marcus asked.

"Now," Julia responded.

Marcus's smile widened. "I'd like that."

Julia grabbed her bag and slung it over her shoulder. She shot Gus a look as she headed for the door, knowing he was filing this away for future teasing. Sure enough, he gave her a little wink as she passed him.

"Enjoy, Tzoúlia," Gus said, waving her off. "The night is young."

Julia rolled her eyes again but couldn't hide her grin. She pushed the door open, and Marcus followed her into the night. The street was calm as they walked toward the promenade. The beat of the waves greeted them as they neared the beach.

At first, they walked in companionable silence, the faint incandescence of the moon reflecting off the water. Julia glanced at Marcus every now and then. He looked more relaxed out here, the angles of his face softened by the moonlight. She wasn't sure what she expected from this walk, but so far, it was nice.

"So," Marcus said, breaking the silence, "is this your post-shift routine?"

"Usually. The beach helps me clear my head. I go out on Friday nights, but my friends are on holiday this week, and I won't go alone."

"Smart. My mates try to get me to bars on Friday nights. This is much better," Marcus replied.

Julia glanced at him, raising an eyebrow. "City center bars aren't your scene?"

"Not really," he said. "Don't get me wrong, I like going out with mates sometimes, but I've always preferred quieter spots. A walk like this beats a bar any day."

"The beach is my scene. I don't do bars," Julia said.

Marcus stopped walking and turned to face her, his expression more open than she'd seen all night. "You're the most interesting person I've met in Sydney," he said.

"Because I served you herbal tea?" Julia asked, unsure where he was going with this, but generally unimpressed.

"No. Because you don't try," he replied, hands sliding into his pockets. "Everyone's always trying—too hard. They walk into a room, and it's all show. Who has the best job, the flashiest watch, the most expensive shoes. Even how they talk—it's rehearsed, like they're selling themselves." He shook his head. "It's exhausting."

"I try," Julia said, slightly offended.

"I didn't mean you *don't* try. I meant you were normal all night," Marcus said. "I walk into Gus's, and it's like stepping into a different world. You're just . . . real. It's like you don't care who comes in."

"I don't," Julia said. "It's a restaurant. People eat, listen to Gus, and then leave. I'm not trying to impress anyone, just get the coffee and food out hot and pull Gus away when he's annoying a couple trying to have a personal conversation. That's the job."

"That's my point," Marcus said. "You don't have some agenda. You're not trying to impress anyone. You didn't fuss over me tonight when you took my order."

"I was busy," Julia countered.

"I know," Marcus said. "That's what made it so refreshing. Everywhere else I go, people . . . You were just . . . taking care of me. Like I was anyone else."

Julia shrugged. "Because you *are* anyone else."

"Exactly," Marcus said. "I watched you with the regulars. You were joking with them, remembering their orders, giving Gus hell."

"It's just my job, Marcus," Julia replied.

"It's more than that. Trust me, I should know."

Julia grew bored of his fumbling attempt at compliments and decided to change the subject. Her mouth curved into a sly smile, her eyes sparkling with mischief. "You know what's real?"

"What?" Marcus asked.

"A private spot where we can watch the moonlight dance over the waves."

"Huh?"

"It's quite hidden."

"Hidden?"

"Quite. You game to have a go?"

Marcus's face lit up. "Lead the way."

CHAPTER 14

L inda strolled through the aisles of the Pio Pico – Koreatown Branch Library, her fingers trailing lightly along the spines of the shelved books. She paused occasionally, carefully pulling out titles for her annual reading ritual—Hunter S. Thompson's astute, rebellious prose and Horatio Alger's tales of determination and self-reinvention. Today was her personal time capsule. Each book she selected was a thread connecting the person she had once been, her choices, and the person she was today. As Linda moved from shelf to shelf, she lingered in the bittersweet memories of how far she had come. Her fingers brushed over a dusty hardcover, the rough texture evoking a memory from another library—a different world.

Linda entered the world as Liora Edelstein in the Williamsburg neighborhood of Brooklyn. She was immediately immersed in the rules and rituals of the Orthodox Jewish community, where every aspect of life followed strict rules based on long-held traditions. The neighborhood bustled with the measure of observance, the shuffle of feet on Sabbath mornings, the scent of fresh challah wafting through the streets, and the chatter of Yiddish mingling with the distant rumble of the subway. For some, it was a sanctuary of faith and family, but for Liora, it was ornamental captivity.

As a child, Liora's days were structured and predictable, marked by prayer, modesty, and relentless instruction in what it meant to be a *good Jewish girl*. Her mornings began before dawn, the sun filtering through lace curtains as her mother nudged her awake for prayers. She would slip into her long skirt and collared blouse, her dark hair braided, and join her family in their tiny kitchen for blessings over breakfast. The words of the prayers flowed effortlessly, ingrained in her like second nature, yet beneath the surface of her devotion, questions simmered—questions she dared not ask aloud.

The Edelstein household was one of reverence and order. Her father, a respected Talmudic scholar, spent his days poring over sacred texts, his voice rising and falling as he debated interpretations with his peers. Her mother, ever diligent, was a paragon of piety, her hands perpetually busy kneading dough, lighting candles, or mending clothes. Liora admired her mother's strength but couldn't ignore the resignation in her eyes.

For Liora, the real battle began at school. The girls in her community weren't granted the same access to Torah study as their brothers. Instead, they were taught to manage households, uphold traditions, and prepare for marriage and motherhood. While her brothers debated the finer points of Talmudic and rabbinic traditions at the yeshiva, Liora's lessons focused on modesty, respect, and obedience. She remembered the sting of envy as her brother Avi returned home with his satchel full of books, his curious mind alive with the possibilities of learning. By contrast, her books were filled with stale moral teachings and remedial mathematics. It wasn't enough.

The community walls were impenetrable, each boundary enforced by a strict adherence to halacha, Jewish law. Liora learned that questioning those boundaries brought swift consequences. When, at the age of nine, she boldly asked her teacher why girls couldn't study the Torah like boys, the response was curt and chilling. "Because it's not for us. Our role is to honor, not to question." The words echoed in her mind, a reminder that her curiosity was not only unwelcome but dangerous.

And yet, Liora's spirit was not easily quelled. By the time she was twelve, she had mastered the art of slipping out unnoticed and making her way to the library on Division Avenue. It became her sanctuary, a sacred space where she found total peace in the pages of books. Here, under the bright fluorescent lights, she discovered the work of Hunter S. Thompson. His drug-fueled ramblings and alcohol-soaked narratives initially shocked her; his world so far removed from the rigid boundaries of her upbringing. But it wasn't the excesses and flourishes that captivated her—it was his endless quest to experience and define the American Dream.

Thompson's constant references sent her spiraling into Horatio Alger's tales of self-determination. She devoured everything she could find about Alger's rags-to-riches narratives, captivated by the idea that hard work and grit could rewrite a person's fate. For Liora, these stories weren't just entertaining—they were a promise. The American Dream became her North Star, a vision of a better life beyond the walls of Williamsburg, where her fate wouldn't be dictated by male elders but carved by her own hands.

Each night, Liora returned home breathless from the thrill of stolen knowledge. She clutched her library books like lifelines, hiding them beneath her mattress or in the pockets of her dresses. The library was an escape hatch, a portal to a world where women were more than wives and mothers, where the possibilities weren't arbitrarily confined by accident of birth. Thompson's relentless pursuit of the American Dream and Alger's tales of grit and triumph lit a fire within her, one that no amount of rules or expectations could extinguish.

The cost of defiance was steep, however. Her father's disapproval was palpable, and his disappointment loomed over the household. "Liora," he would say, "a girl with too much knowledge is like a bird trying to fly against the wind. It is unnatural and unsafe."

Her mother, though gentler, echoed the sentiment in her way, urging Liora to focus on her chores and leave the rest to the men.

As Liora grew older, the pressure to conform intensified. At sixteen, she was expected to consider marriage prospects, and her family was eager to see her settled within the community. But Liora wanted more—a life driven by the ideals of the American Dream that she had passionately absorbed during her hours at the library. She longed for an education, a career, and a chance to control her destiny—a life not dictated by antiquated norms and sectarian customs.

Her resolve crystallized one summer afternoon when she accompanied her mother to the garment factory where her mother worked part time. The sight of women hunched over sewing machines, their exhausted faces, struck Liora with a deep, unshakable conviction: This was not the life she wanted. Bound by circumstance and convention, these women reminded her of Alger's protagonists—not in their triumphs but in their unrealized potential. She vowed, right then and there, to be one of the few who escaped.

By seventeen, Liora made her decision. It wasn't a choice she made lightly. Leaving the community meant permanently severing ties with her family and abandoning the only life she had ever known. But the thought of staying—living a life she would never embrace—was unbearable. Her dreams were too large for Williamsburg's narrow streets, and her vision of the American Dream was too vivid to ignore. Liora left Williamsburg behind with a few dollars, a small satchel, and the fire of Horatio Alger's ideals.

Liora stepped off the Greyhound Bus in downtown Los Angeles for the first time with copies of *Fear and Loathing in Las Vegas* and *Tony the Tramp* tucked under her arm, two books she had failed to return to the library. The city's dry heat hit her like a wall, but she was undeterred. Industrious by nature, she discovered a small community in Los Angeles that assisted displaced Orthodox women in transitioning to secular life. They provided her with temporary housing and assisted in getting her paperwork in order. They also introduced her to a local synagogue where she could join an open-minded Jewish community.

Liora's first visit to the synagogue was memorable, as she would make a lifelong friend and spiritual counselor. It was late afternoon in Los Angeles, the sky muted as the sun dipped low over the city. The building before her wasn't grand—nothing like Brooklyn's towering, ornate synagogue. This one had a modern, minimalist facade, its clean lines softened by the surrounding greenery. A Star of David sat prominently above the entryway, catching the light. Linda took a deep breath, stepping through the glass doors into an air-conditioned interior that smelled of candles.

Inside, the space opened into a sanctuary with high ceilings and walls painted in earth tones. Light filtered through stained-glass windows, casting fragmented rainbows on the pews below. The elevated and simple bimah was adorned with a modest ark and a single menorah. Linda noted the contrast between the synagogue she had grown up in—rigid and intimidating—and this one, which was welcoming and unassuming. Linda hesitated in the entryway, unsure if she was intruding.

"First time here?"

Liora turned to see a woman approaching. The woman looked to be in her mid-twenties, with dark curls pulled back loosely and a kind smile. Her posture was relaxed, her tone inviting. "I'm Junior Rabbi Yael Hartman," she said, extending a hand. "You look a little lost."

Liora shook her hand, while speaking in her harsh New York accent. "Yeah, I guess I am. I just moved here. My name is Liora. I'm just off the bus from Brooklyn. I left home and . . ."

"Slow down, Liora, slow down," Rabbi Yael said as she put her arm around Linda and motioned toward a bench.

They both sat down, and Liora took a breath. "I've been . . . trying to figure out where I fit here. Back home, in Williamsburg, Judaism was a given—Orthodox family, Shabbat every week, Torah study. But

I don't know, I never really connected with it. It was all rules, no meaning. But I'm not ready to give up my faith either. I thought maybe this house of worship could be different."

Rabbi Yael studied her before speaking. "I get it. Tradition can be heavy when it's forced. But it doesn't have to be that way. Judaism isn't just a set of rules—it's a culture, a community, and a way to make sense of the world. You don't have to leave it behind just because you left Brooklyn."

Liora shifted, unsure of how to respond. "I'm not sure if I'm ready to dive back in. I just ... wanted to start somewhere."

"This is a good place to start," Rabbi Yael said, motioning to the synagogue.

"Your house feels open, but I fear falling into the old ways that I escaped," Liora said, her eyes affixed to the floor.

"This is a unique community, Liora. Unlike any you have experienced. We do things differently. For example, I'm a young woman and a junior rabbi. Is that a shock to you? Where you came from, that would not be allowed, no?" Rabbi Yael said as she put her hand on top of Liora's hand.

"Well, no ... I never met a rabbi like you," Linda said, feeling a unique sense of comfort with Rabbi Yael.

"This community has welcomed me. And now, I'm here to welcome you. Why don't you join us at our next service? No pressure, just come as you are."

"Maybe," Liora said, failing to make eye contact.

"I'm not a saleswoman, Liora. But what's the harm? Experience our community. And even if it doesn't suit you, my office will remain open to you."

"That is very kind, Rabbi," Liora said as they both stood.

"Welcome to Los Angeles, Liora."

Liora's first official act as a Los Angeles resident was to change her name to Linda. It was a small act of severing ties with her past while embracing her new identity. Armed with an unshakable resolve and convinced that education was her path to the American Dream, Linda passed the high school equivalency exam. She took college-prep courses, eventually enrolling in community college. Between classes, she worked multiple jobs near campus—waitressing, stocking shelves, and cleaning offices at night—to pay her bills. Extravagances were out of the question. Linda lived with frugality bordering on asceticism, believing that each penny saved was another brick in the foundation of her future.

Her free time was spent in the library. Linda devoured literature with the voracity of someone starved for knowledge. While she made a point to stay informed on current events and to read nonfiction to sharpen her understanding of the modern world, her true love was the classics. She subscribed to a mail-order program that sent formally bound editions of classic novels each month. *Don Quixote*, *Moby Dick*, *Pride and Prejudice*, Dante's *Divine Comedy*, *Great Expectations*—the titles arrived one by one, each a ticket to a different world. Linda made a personal rule that no book could be displayed on her bookshelf until she had read it cover to cover.

In those days, her apartment began to resemble a library. The smell of paper and ink mingled with instant coffee, the only luxury she allowed herself. Each finished book was a trophy on her shelf, a testament to her intellectual development. The growing collection brought her a sense of pride, the completed books symbolizing how far she had come, the worlds she had explored, and the person she was becoming.

Linda occasionally dated men, although her focus never wavered from her studies. She found more romance in the pages of Austen or Alcott than in any conversation in a loud bar or restaurant. Her dreams were too large for fleeting distractions. Every finished book, every aced exam, and every shift worked brought her closer to the future she envisioned—a future shaped by the freedom to make her own choices, unbound by the constraints of her past. For Linda, the American Dream wasn't about success but about being the best version of herself, fully and unapologetically.

Linda worked her way through community college with unrelenting determination and was accepted to the UCLA School of Law, which she felt was a testament to her drive and commitment to the American Dream. Initially, Linda envisioned a career in community organizing, utilizing her education to help underserved populations fight for their rights; however, a chance internship at a prestigious entertainment law firm during her second year of law school changed everything.

The internship was a whirlwind introduction to Hollywood's glamorous, high-stakes business world. Although the work was miles from her original goals, she found herself fascinated by the complexity of entertainment law and the unique blend of creativity and acumen it required. When she graduated and passed the California state bar exam, Linda was recruited by a top-tier law firm specializing in entertainment contracts.

The job was financially rewarding, and Linda was exceptionally good at it. As the months passed, however, the monotony of drafting and reviewing contracts all day left her feeling empty. This wasn't the American Dream she had envisioned while reading *Phil the Fiddler*. Where was the purpose? The meaning? The impact?

At twenty-seven, with a promising career trajectory in one of the world's most competitive industries, Linda boldly quit her job. She had no plan, no safety net beyond the savings she had built over the years. For several days, she ruminated, unsure of what to do next. She spent most of her time in her small Los Angeles apartment, reading her beloved classics, seeking answers in the words of Woolf, Hawthorne, Dostoevsky, Tolstoy, Flaubert, and Steinbeck. Then, one sleepless night, she decided to take a leap.

With her savings, Linda opened a solo law practice. She expected this would lead to her original calling in community organizing, perhaps working with nonprofits or smaller-scale legal disputes, but fate had other plans. Shortly after opening the law practice, Linda was approached by Rabbi Yael to speak to a member of their synagogue family, the renowned actress Tova Greenblatt. Linda met with Tova, who expressed unhappiness with her studio deal, which locked her into unfavorable terms. Tova was well known for her roles in period dramas and musicals but wanted the ability to pursue more diverse projects. Desperate, Tova asked Linda to get her out of the bad arrangement.

Linda dove into the contract with a ferocity of purpose. She spent nights dissecting every clause and scrutinizing every detail. What she found were several loopholes and arguments that could invalidate the agreement. Linda drafted an aggressive, precisely argued letter to the studio. The response was swift: initial pushback, then capitulation. The studio was beaten, and Tova was released from her obligations.

Tova was elated and hired Linda to negotiate her next studio deal. Linda's meticulous preparation and tenacious negotiation skills secured Tova a lucrative, artist-friendly contract, which also caught the attention of other creatives in Hollywood. Word spread quickly. One satisfied client turned into ten. Within a year, Linda's client roster included rising stars, veteran character actors, and emerging directors.

At twenty-nine, Linda was featured in trade lists as one of the top female entertainment lawyers under thirty-five. Her reputation in the entertainment community captured the interest of a leading talent agency, Goldstein, Hirsch, Rosen & Associates. They approached Linda with a lucrative offer to acquire her practice and hire her as part of their elite team. Linda accepted on the condition that she retain control over her client relationships and work autonomously within the agency. They agreed, and she was installed in the same office she would still be working in some twenty-five years later, representing Miriam Worthington. From that small, scrappy law practice to her standing as one of the most respected agents in Hollywood, Linda built her career the way she built her life —on her terms, fueled by ambition, grit, and an unwavering belief in the power of the American Dream.

Years later, Linda still found herself drawn back, at least in her mind, to the streets of Williamsburg and the life she had left behind. Although her career flourished and her world had expanded far beyond the rigid confines of her Orthodox upbringing, pieces of that past lingered, particularly when she thought of her mother. They hadn't spoken since Linda had walked out in 1972. Over the years, Linda had written three carefully worded letters, updating her mother on her life and asking about her family. She also had written to her brother Avi, now a grocer in Brooklyn. All of Linda's letters went unanswered. The silence was a painful confirmation of the permanence of their divide.

Several years back, Linda had learned of her mother's passing—not through family but from a mutual friend. The news had hit her harder than expected. She had spent many years telling herself she'd made peace with the loss of her family, but the finality of her mother's death had brought a fresh burst of grief, not only at the loss of her mother but also at the loss of any hope for reconciliation, for closure, for understanding.

After her mother's death, Linda created a ritual to honor her mother. Every year, on the anniversary of her mother's passing, Linda kept her calendar clear. She started the day at synagogue, sitting alone in the back row. She recited "El Malei Rachamim," a prayer for the departed's soul, and then the mourner's Kaddish, a prayer for the woman who had given her life and, indirectly, the courage to change it.

After leaving the synagogue, Linda went to the library. Not the pristine modern libraries of Beverly Hills or Hollywood, but the Pio Pico branch in Koreatown. There, she spent hours poring through the works of Hunter S. Thompson and Horatio Alger, the authors who had ignited her passion for the American Dream. She reread passages she had long since memorized, letting their words transport her back to the days when she would sneak into the Division Avenue Branch, defying her constraints for a few hours of freedom.

The day was both a tribute and a release. It was her way of connecting to the mother she loved. It was also a reminder of her journey and how hard she had fought for the life she now lived. And every year, as she closed the final page of *Facing the World*, Linda achieved a bittersweet sense of peace—a recognition that although the past couldn't be rewritten, it shaped her in ways she would forever carry.

Linda sat in the corner of the library, a stack of books beside her, trying to lose herself in *Songs of the Doomed*. The Pio Pico library stood as a beacon in Koreatown, with its clean lines and modern glass contrasting the surrounding storefronts. Inside, the open space was filled with students hunched over laptops, retirees relaxing in chairs, and parents trailing children through the aisles. Linda appreciated its simplicity—a public place where anyone could escape without pretension or cost.

Typically, on this day, her ritual was a comfort, but today, her thoughts wouldn't settle. They circled back to the meeting she had scheduled for tomorrow—a meeting she dreaded.

Miriam Worthington was a star. A force of nature. A client she had painstakingly built into one of the most recognized names in television. Yet Linda had to deliver the bad news—Miriam's time on *IRS Rogue* was over. Season 2 would go on without her, and for all her talent and charisma, the decision had nothing to do with her abilities but with behavior. Miriam's loose tongue and inability to work as part of an ensemble had caught up with her again. The network had been furious at the decision. They wanted Miriam on the show, but the cast and producers had remained firm: Either Miriam was out, or the show would not go on. The network had given in and delivered the news to Linda, who now had to deliver it to Miriam.

This was not *Night Nurses*, where Miriam was tired of the show and happy to leave. Miriam loved working on *IRS Rogue* and was excited for season 2. She was going to take this badly. But Linda would deliver the news with honesty and compassion. She wouldn't coddle. Miriam needed to hear the truth, even if it hurt. This was a crossroads, a moment that could either break Miriam or push her to grow. Linda hoped it would be the latter.

Linda sighed, staring blankly at the pages of *Curse of Lono* now. The words blurred together, refusing to distract her as they usually did. This wasn't the first time she had found herself in this position, coaxing, convincing, and sometimes outright battling for a client who had burned one too many bridges, but with Miriam, it was different. This was déjà vu. History had repeated itself, and Linda was powerless to stop it.

Miriam was fiery, unapologetically ambitious, and undeniably gifted. Linda admired her in many ways, even as she often cleaned up the messes the actress left behind. This time, however, there was no cleanup. The cast's demands were clear, and the network was dropping her. It didn't matter that Miriam had carried the first season on her back or that critics lauded her portrayal of Inspector Claudia Von Haulsteen. The show was an ensemble, and the ensemble had spoken.

Linda leaned back in her chair, rubbing her temples. She knew how tomorrow would go. Miriam would rage and lash out at the cast, the writers, and the producers—all of whom she had alienated in one way or another. But not Linda. Never Linda. Miriam trusted Linda implicitly. Linda had always smoothed things over to make the impossible happen and to shield Miriam from the fallout of her actions. This time, though, there was no shield.

And yet, Linda was sad. She believed in Miriam, not only as a client but also as a person. Beneath Miriam's bravado lay a vulnerability that few people ever saw. Miriam's drive to succeed and her refusal to settle for mediocrity came from a deep insecurity, a need to prove herself to a world that doubted her, a father who had abandoned her. Linda understood that better than most. She also lived it in her own way.

Her gaze drifted to the Horatio Alger book sitting on top of the pile beside her. *Luke Walton.* It was the story of a newsboy who rises to success through honesty and hard work. Linda clung to the tale in her journey, a reminder that success was possible even when the odds were stacked against you. She didn't doubt that Miriam would find her way, as Linda had, but the road ahead would be bumpy, and Linda couldn't smooth it for her this time.

The library's overhead lights flickered, a subtle signal that closing time was near, and Linda gathered her things. As she got up, she allowed herself to reflect. Her mother's memory was at the forefront of her reflections, as it always was on this day, but so were the lessons she had learned since leaving Williamsburg: Life was unpredictable, success was hard-won, and sometimes, the best thing you could do for someone you cared about was let them face the consequences of their actions.

Linda, as she often did, pondered whether she would be a suitable protagonist in a Horatio Alger story, turning it over in her mind. She had left behind the rigid confines of her Orthodox Jewish upbringing and traded the predictable path for a life of independence and adventure. She had clawed her way through community college, UCLA Law School, and the ruthless world of entertainment law, which wasn't designed for people like her. By any measure, she had achieved success.

But had she done enough?

She thought of the bookshelves lining her home. They were packed with the classics that had shaped her worldview. There, nestled among them, was *Ragged Dick,* the Alger story that had captivated her as a young girl. The tale of the ambitious bootblack rising above his station through hard work and determination had always resonated with her, yet now, in her late fifties, she questioned whether her story fit the ideal. Her life had been far from a straight line of hardship to triumph. It was messier, more nuanced, and marked by numerous compromises.

Was her story truly a rags-to-riches tale? The financial rewards were undeniable—her office, her home in the Hills, and the accolades accompanying her name—but Alger's stories were never about material wealth. They were about character, about the ability to stay true to one's principles in the face of adversity. Linda prided herself on her integrity, advocating fiercely for her clients and building relationships based on trust rather than opportunism, yet there had been moments, particularly in the early years, when she had played the game as ruthlessly as anyone. Did that make her unworthy of Alger's ideal?

Linda shook her head, her thoughts spiraling deeper. Maybe his ideal wasn't about worthiness at all. Perhaps the American Dream wasn't a gold-plated destination, a final achievement to be displayed for all to see. It wasn't a plaque or a flashy title. Perhaps it was about the striving—the ceaseless pursuit, the endless quest to define, find, and live that dream, even if it was a mirage on the horizon—a goal meant to inspire, not conquer.

Linda took solace in this thought. The American Dream, she realized, had been bastardized in popular culture and reduced to a hollow formula of wealth, fame, and power. It was commonly defined by stock images of sprawling mansions, red carpets, and corporate empires—symbols of arrival rather than of the quixotic journey—but to Linda, that definition was shallow, a distortion of the ideal's true essence. Linda saw the distorted application of the American Dream play out in her world all the time: actors chasing stardom, moguls chasing money, and people clawing their way up for hollow reasons.

To Linda, the American Dream was aspirational by its very nature, an ever-evolving pursuit of growth and self-improvement. She believed that Horatio Alger and his many literary disciples would agree. His rags-to-riches stories weren't about accumulating wealth for its own sake but about resilience, ingenuity, and character. They were about becoming, not acquiring. The American Dream was about setting goals that pushed you beyond your limits, not materially but intellectually, vocationally, recreationally, and even spiritually. The American Dream had always been about striving for a life of purpose, for something greater than oneself. It was about embracing setbacks, learning from failures, and continuing forward even when the summit is impossibly far away.

The American Dream, she thought, was aspirational by design, a boulder that could never be pushed to the top of the mountain. Its power lay in the effort itself; in the sweat and determination it demanded. But the climb wasn't linear—it was rocky, unpredictable, and riddled with setbacks. Embracing the inevitable failures and disappointments was as much a part of the journey as celebrating the successes. Each stumble provided an opportunity to reflect, recalibrate, and grow stronger. Setbacks weren't failures, not really;

they were proof that the journey was real, that the striving mattered. This was the lesson she would share with Miriam: Her story wasn't finished with this setback; instead, the mark of Miriam's life and career would be measured by how she responded to it.

Linda took a small stack of books to the checkout counter and handed the librarian her Los Angeles Public Library card. The librarian scanned the card, then glanced up with a polite smile. "Have a good night, Liora."

The name on the card caught her off guard, a faint echo of the past. Liora's story might be finished, but Linda's wasn't. And that no longer unsettled her. In fact, she welcomed it. Each day was an opportunity to redefine the American Dream, to pursue a better version of it, and to let it evolve alongside her. Tomorrow would bring a fresh challenge, another opportunity, and Linda was ready— for Miriam, herself, and whatever came next.

Selah.

CHAPTER 15

Thursday, January 5, 2012 | Carlsbad

Catrina and Sam's apartment was modest but comfortable, a two-bedroom, one-bath space with an open kitchen and living area. Their secondhand couch, deep and inviting, sat at the center of the room, its neutral fabric worn but cozy. A mismatched throw draped across the back added warmth, while the coffee table was cluttered with books, notebooks, and Sam's ever-present collection of colorful pens, which she used for journaling.

Sam was curled up on the couch, a thick book resting on her lap, her legs tucked beneath her. Catrina envied her ability to be so at ease. Sam's natural self-assurance was inspiring, and their cohabitation had, in ways Catrina hadn't anticipated, bolstered her own confidence.

Thanks to Sam's prodding over the past three months, Catrina had worked to improve her destructive people-pleasing tendencies. Her mother was fine alone, though Catrina checked in weekly.

For most of her life, Catrina had operated under the assumption that she was the glue. If she didn't call, Morven would spiral. If she didn't show up, bills would go unpaid. Their lives had been so intertwined for so long—Catrina the reliable one, Morven the chaos in motion—that even as an adult, Catrina struggled to see where one ended and the other began. Her mother had never asked her to take on that role. She just left a vacuum, and Catrina had filled it.

Moving out had felt like severing a limb. She had put it off for years, staying through college and even while working, convincing herself it was practical, financially sound, and mutually beneficial. But the truth was more complicated. She didn't know how to live without helping her mom. And Morven had never given her a reason to believe she could manage alone.

Catrina had never expected stability from Morven, but she had also never questioned her resilience. Her mother had grown up in Ohio, the daughter of Scottish immigrants who never quite found their footing in the United States. They came over on a sponsorship from a cousin and spent the next two decades trying to make a living, moving from rental to rental, chasing work, navigating a system that never welcomed them. Morven learned early not to ask for anything. Her parents weren't cruel, simply overwhelmed. There were no bedtime routines, no after-school pickups, no baked goods at the holiday fair. Morven made her dinners by age seven and figured out how to forge signatures on field trip forms by eight.

What she lacked in academic aptitude, she made up for with hustle. She could charm a teacher, flip a detention, and pocket a free meal without anyone noticing. Morven survived not through excellence but by angling. She learned how to cut corners and how to get by.

As a mother, she took a similar tack. What she couldn't provide financially, she made up for by being there. She showed up late sometimes, was often distracted, but was present. She helped Catrina with school projects by suggesting they repurpose something from the cupboard. She filled out free-lunch paperwork without worrying about the embarrassment of living below the income threshold. She once siphoned electricity from a neighbor's outdoor outlet for two weeks until the overdue bill could be paid. Catrina learned that resourcefulness was a virtue, but so was concealment. You didn't talk about what it took to make things work. You made them work.

That lesson stuck. Too well.

Catrina knew how to operate in the gray. She had come to depend on her ability to solve problems without letting anyone see her sweat. It was what made her good in school and then in the medical device field. She understood that, in the workplace, appearing competent mattered more than asking for help. But she also knew where that instinct for subterfuge came from—and how easily it became a trap. Her mother had spent a lifetime patching holes in her life with duct tape and charm, convinced that intention outweighed consequence. Catrina fought against that logic every day. And still, she found herself justifying choices others may not have made.

She had inherited her mother's improvisation, but not the tolerance for it. The past decisions—like stealing the DeltaTech files—stayed with her. They lingered in her conscience, unresolved. She couldn't reframe them as necessary or harmless. They sat with her, heavy and persistent. But still, when the moment called for it, she could make the greasy choice. If required, she didn't flinch.

From a distance, she could see her mother more clearly, not as the woman who had raised her through instability but as a person still learning, still moving forward. Morven was messy, disorganized, and often late, but she was also employed, solvent, and, for once, happy.

It turned out, they were both better off. Since moving in with Sam, the calls and visits with her mother had changed. Not in content—Morven still bounced from topic to topic, often talking through problems she hadn't yet decided were real—but in tone. There was less panic. Fewer requests. She had picked up extra shifts at work and even negotiated a better schedule with her manager. The power bill had been paid on time. The rent was up to date as well. When Catrina offered to help sort out the mobile plan, Morven waved her off and said she'd handled it. Catrina hadn't expected independence to suit her mother. She had assumed distance would lead to her collapse. But instead, it allowed Morven—improbably, and to her credit—to take control of her life.

The tether between them hadn't snapped. It had stretched. And in that extra real estate, both of them had changed for the better. Her mother was no longer in crisis. And Catrina, for once, was focusing only on her life.

What Catrina hadn't recognized, at least not until she moved out, was how much of her people-pleasing wasn't rooted in generosity but in reflex. Sam had started identifying it, gently, over the past few months. Not in clinical terms, but in offhand comments. Why do you say yes to things before you've thought them through? What would happen if you just said no? It wasn't therapy, but the effect was similar. Catrina was starting to see her patterns more clearly. The way she adapted to meet the needs of others. The way she volunteered for discomfort. The way she pretended not to mind until it was too late.

She hadn't solved it yet. Her professional life still rewarded compliance, and her relationship with Tim was built on her accommodations of his needs and whims. She hadn't untangled that fully. But she had finally established firm boundaries. When Tim spent the workday on the golf course, she wouldn't answer his after-hours call demanding a rundown of the day's events; he could wait until morning, during work hours. More importantly, Catrina had stopped rushing to a hotel room whenever Tim had an urge. She'd successfully separated her work from her personal life and avoided blowback from Tim in the process. That, in itself, felt like progress.

Catrina tossed a pair of sneakers into the hall closet and grabbed a dish towel to wipe down the kitchen counter. "I never did respond to Miriam's email," she said.

Sam, putting her book away and standing by the coffee table as she started to work through the mess, glanced up. "Who?"

"My sister. The actress one."

"Oh, yeah. That email still sitting in your inbox?"

Catrina shrugged. "Kinda want to respond, but is it weird if I do it now? It's been over a year."

"I don't think so," Sam said, stacking a few books into a pile.

Catrina walked back into the living room. "I don't know. I'm not looking for a family reunion. I have my mom, I have you, I have friends. My life isn't missing anything."

"Same conversation as last year, if I recall."

"Sure. But as you said last year, what's the harm? At worst, they're pen pals. At best, they're . . . I don't know," Catrina said.

Sam stretched her arms above her head. "That reminds me . . . we should watch *IRS Rogue* on HBO. I hear people raving about it at the shop. Apparently, your sister is awesome in it."

"Ooh. Good idea. I'll do some light stalking, and then I'll email them tomorrow. Or next month . . ."

"How's it stalking? She's on TV. What's your hesitation? Clearly, they're still on your mind."

Catrina frowned. "Guess I'm afraid it will lead to talking about my dad."

Sam picked up a notebook and flipped through its pages before setting it back down. "He raised one of them, right? My guess is, subconsciously, you're worried you'll have feelings if he was a great dad to another daughter. Like, he didn't think you were good enough."

"Come on, not everything is that deep."

"Isn't it?"

"You're insufferable," Catrina said, smiling, as she returned to the kitchen to rinse a glass in the sink.

"And yet, you live with me."

Catrina let the water run, staring out the window above the sink. Outside, the complex's communal pool shimmered in the sunlight, surrounded by a manicured courtyard dotted with succulents and palm trees. Their building, a charming mid-century complex with cream stucco walls and teal trim, was on the nicer side of Carlsbad, not far from the beach. The quiet, laid-back atmosphere suited them both as North County natives.

"Here's the thing," Catrina said, turning to Sam, who had followed her to the kitchen. "Things are going well . . ."

"Can I speak freely? As a friend?" Sam asked.

"Of course."

"I mean, correct me if I'm wrong," Sam continued. "You don't date, at least not since what's-his-name in high school. You avoid most men, which I agree with, by the way. Maybe, just maybe, that has something to do with your dad ghosting?"

Catrina let out a chuckle. "That's some tremendous amateur psychology, Sam. Inspired."

Sam smiled and rubbed Catrina's shoulders. "I do what I can. My point is, when you're ready, you should explore your feelings about your dad. He has affected your relationships with men, whether you admit it or not. Perhaps your sisters could serve as a safe entry point for you to confront those feelings. At least one of them had the same experience, and my bet is the Australian sister he raised isn't his biggest fan either."

Catrina hesitated, running a hand through her hair. "Look, my dad was never in the picture. That's not some deep wound I need to heal. It's just a fact. I've never given him a second thought."

"Which is a problem. It's a wound. You should give it a second thought—when you're ready."

"I don't have a problem emailing or even meeting my sisters. But I don't know anything about surfing. I don't know anything about acting or being gorgeous. We'll inevitably end up discussing the one topic I don't want to think about."

Sam considered Catrina's position and agreed. "You're not wrong. You must be prepared to discuss him if you respond to them. I'm sure they'll be there for you when you're ready. In the meantime, could you please get your IRS sister's number? She's so hot."

Catrina whacked Sam with the dish towel and laughed.

"Watch the moneymaker," Sam joked.

They both laughed as they eased into their routine. The night was set. They would pour some wine, sink into the couch, spread out a blanket, and binge half a season of *IRS Rogue*. Any fear that living together would hurt their relationship had proven unfounded. If anything, it had only strengthened their ability to talk openly—even about touchy subjects.

CHAPTER 16

Julia stretched as the morning sun filtered through the massive glass walls of Marcus's townhome, spilling across the uniform black furniture and the gray cabinetry. The gentle sound of waves meeting the coastline inspired her as she pulled herself out of bed. Marcus's bedroom, with its cold symmetry and neatly folded linens, looked untouched despite her having slept there. She threw on a hoodie and padded barefoot into the open-plan living area.

"Ali," she said, nudging the blanket-draped figure on the leather couch. "Time to get up." While she waited for Alani to move, Julia reflected on how she had become a good friend over the last year. They had several shared qualities; notably, they both had impressive hustle. Alani was the daughter of hardworking parents who had emigrated from the South Pacific when she was a baby. Their ethic wore off on her as she worked, attended school, and still made time for friends. A stark contrast, Ginger was spoiled, lazy, and obsessed with Beau. Yet she was also a good friend who made time for Julia and was supportive of her relationship with Marcus.

Julia was thrilled with the community she'd built in Manly.

Alani groaned and pulled the blanket over her head. "Five more minutes."

"Nope. We went too hard last night, and I need you up before Marcus's place starts smelling like cheap weed and cheaper tequila."

Alani peeked out from under the blanket, her long black hair a tangled mess. "This place is too clean, Jul. No character. You should give it a splash of color."

Julia smirked, picking up an empty water bottle from the coffee table. "I don't live here, Ali."

"Sure you do."

"I agree it's a little sterile. The interior designer had a field day with this one—Marcus hasn't touched it. But the soaking tub and state-of-the-art kitchen make up for the flaws."

Alani sat up, blinking against the sunlight streaming in. "Everything is top of the line. No argument there. This couch was more comfortable than my bed."

Julia opened the fridge and pulled out two bottles of water. She handed one to Alani. "Anything is more comfortable than my flat."

"Why even keep the flat?" Alani asked. "You spend all your time here."

"Nah. I'm just house-sitting while he's off with the cricket team. Summer is their travel season. When he's in town, I try not to sleep here more than one night in a row. I don't want him to think I'm moving in."

"Why not? I'd move in today," Alani joked.

"I barely know the bloke. He's a top guy, but I'm not ditching my flat for a three-month fuck-buddy."

Alani twisted the cap off her water. "I can't believe you only party on Fridays. I understood cutting back to twice a week, but . . . it puts too much pressure on one night."

"It works," Julia said, standing at the dark marble kitchen island. "I need the rest for Gus's and lifesaving. Fridays are enough."

Alani chuckled. "Fair enough. Surfing today?"

"Nah. I slept too late and want to shower and call my sister," Julia said. "Gin and Beau looked happy. Glad they weren't arguing for once. Bet they just went to sleep."

"They're a disaster," Alani said, standing and stretching. "But, hey, good on 'em."

Julia glanced at Floating Sky against the far wall by the door, its vibrant paint contrasting with the townhome's muted decor. "This place really is a museum, isn't it?"

Alani grinned. "Your board's the only thing keeping it from being a showroom."

"Exactly," Julia said, tossing the empty water bottle into the recycling bin. "Alright, time to get moving."

Alani smirked as she slipped on her sandals and asked, "How's the fancy sister? I hate that she's no longer on that IRS show. She was the best part. Who would watch season 2 now?"

"No shit," Julia said. "She's good, though. Gets loads of modeling work. Wish I had her figure."

Alani shook her head and headed toward the door. "Bullshit. If you had gazelle legs, you couldn't stand on your board."

"Fair point," Julia said, opening the door for her. "Thanks for crashing here with me."

After showering, with her hair still wet, Julia settled into Marcus's home office, a space as refined and minimalist as the rest of the townhome. The glass desk, with no drawers, reflected the late-morning sunlight, and the executive-style chair was more suited to boardroom meetings than casual chats. Still, it was private and perfect for a video call with Miriam.

"Jules! You're up early for a Saturday. No surfing today?" Miriam said, brushing a strand of her grown-out hair behind her ear.

Julia chuckled, settling back into the chair. "Got a little sloshed last night, but I've drunk water and showered, so I'm good to go."

"Oh, to be twenty-one again."

"You're not exactly old at twenty-six."

"How is the Manly prince?"

Julia rolled her eyes but couldn't suppress the small smile tugging at her lips. "Marcus is fine. Still traveling. I'm curious how our relationship will go during his off-season. I kinda like this arrangement. It's uncomplicated."

"And how is the arrangement? You two? The whole . . . whatever it is?" Miriam asked.

"It's good. He's good. When he's here, we get along well. He's easygoing, attentive, and, well . . . you've seen him. He's not hard on the eyes," Julia said, nervously wringing her hands.

"Sex still good?"

"No complaints."

"So what's the hesitation I'm sensing? Spill."

"Well, our physical connection is . . . intense, effortless. But I'm not looking to be a *we*. I'm scared he wants to move faster. I'm enjoying life. When he returns to Manly for a long stretch, he's going to want me around, all the time."

"When will you see him next?"

"He's back tonight, but only for a day or so—the perfect amount of time."

"Ha. Miss Independent," Miriam said. "But seriously, Jules, you have got good instincts. If it feels right, don't sabotage it. Let it run its course. If it feels wrong, move on."

Julia nodded. "Enough about me. What's happening with you? How was that last modeling job?"

Miriam offered a small smile. "It went well. Good pay and only a day's work. I need to take an acting job, though. My agent has been sending scripts my way, but nothing has gotten me excited. And, honestly, I'm not well right now."

"What do you mean, not well? How?" Julia asked.

"It's probably nothing, but I've been low energy lately. Even walking up the stairs leaves me winded. And sometimes . . ." Miriam paused. "I don't want to jump to conclusions, so I'm going to see a doctor next week for a checkup. Something is off. But I'm not sure what."

"That doesn't sound like nothing, Mir. Please promise you'll tell me what they say."

"Of course," Miriam assured her. "It's probably stress from losing *IRS Rogue*, but it has been going on for over two months. It's time to see a doctor. I'll keep you updated."

Julia woke the next morning to the soft rustling of waves against the shore. The sun filtered in, casting long shadows across the hardwood floor and bathing the room in the morning light. She blinked, momentarily mesmerized by the view. She sat up and scrambled to find her clothes. Marcus stirred beside her, turning his head lazily on the pillow.

"Where are you off to in such a hurry?" he asked, half groggy.

"I have brunch with my parents today," Julia said, tugging on her jeans as she spoke. "It's been a couple of weeks, and Mum invited old-timers from the Mosman Men's Club, so it's a good day to go."

"You like the old-timers?" Marcus asked.

"I don't care about them one way or the other. But I only go to brunch if there are other people around. Brunch is fine if my dad is entertaining. It's intolerable if I'm there alone and become the topic of conversation. Mum emails me in advance when people confirm. She figured out I'm more likely to come."

Marcus propped himself up on one elbow. "Can I come?"

Julia froze in the middle of pulling her shirt over her head. "You don't have to do that," she said. "My parents—especially my dad—can be . . . a lot. You should relax. Take the day."

He swung his legs over the side of the bed and sat up. "I want to spend time with you. I'm traveling again tomorrow. And besides, parents love me."

She didn't doubt that. If anyone could charm Raymond Corning, it was Marcus. Her initial instinct was to shield Marcus from a Sunday brunch, but another thought crept in. *Dad's face when he sees Marcus. Tall, elegant, professional—the kind of man Dad thinks is too good for me.*

"So? What do you say?" Marcus asked.

Her internal debate ceased, and she sighed. "Fine," she said, grabbing her sneakers from the corner. "But you should know this isn't some big step forward in our . . . whatever this is. The bus should be on the corner in ten minutes."

"Understood," he said. "But no bus. I'm driving the Beamer."

Marcus's 2012 BMW 750Li glided into the driveway of the Corning residence, its jet-black paint catching the sunlight. Julia's fingers brushed against the car's leather interior as she exited the passenger seat. The contrast between the car's opulence and the ranch-style home only heightened her apprehension. Regret bubbled up inside her as she questioned her decision to bring Marcus to meet her parents.

The familiar creak of the door welcomed her, as did the smell of roast lamb and herbs, Alice's signature Sunday brunch spread. The wood-paneled walls of the 1980s-built home stood unchanged, a stubborn tribute to decades past. As oversized as ever, the dining room table loomed in its cramped space, set with Alice's best dishes. It was like walking into a time capsule, the house, the tablescape, the smell—a physical memory she couldn't erase.

Marcus sauntered in behind her, his presence instantly filling the entryway, and Ray's eyes lit up as he turned from the living room. His face broke into an expression Julia had seen only once before—when she had won the surfing competition at age fourteen. Ray's sheer delight and excitement sent a jolt of recognition, accompanied by irritation, through her.

"Marcus Daelmans!" Ray said, rushing forward to shake Marcus's hand with the same enthusiasm he reserved for his Men's Club buddies. "Welcome! My God, Alice, do you know who this is?" Ray didn't wait for her to answer, turning back to Marcus. "It's an honor to have you here, son. Truly an honor."

"Thank you, sir," Marcus said.

"Why are you here?" Ray asked.

Marcus looked at Julia, who said, "We're dating, Dad."

Ray smiled and shook Marcus's hand again. He turned to Alice and said, "This chap is a champion cricketer. And all-around great bloke. The papers call him the 'Golden Boy of the Australian National Team.'"

Julia turned to Marcus with a puzzled look. She'd understood he was part of the national team but had had no idea he was a celebrity—one of the problems with not having a phone. Why hadn't Gus, Alani, or Ginger said anything? They were all in on some elaborate joke, clearly.

"That's impressive, Marcus," Alice said. "How did you meet Julia?"

"A chance encounter at the taverna about three months ago," Marcus said.

"Well, I'm glad Julia hasn't been a distraction. Your form has been tremendous. What are you averaging with the bat this summer? Seventy-five?" Ray added.

"Yes, sir, she's my lucky charm," Marcus said.

"Call me Ray. Please."

"Well, Ray, Julia is remarkable—a testament to how well she's been raised."

Julia gagged and folded her arms to keep her irritation in check as Ray's enthusiasm reached a fever pitch. Marcus, ever composed, met Ray's energy with polite humility that amplified the older man's admiration.

Julia had become a bystander. She'd brought Marcus here as a buffer, a bit of armor to help her navigate the family dynamics, but instead, she'd handed Ray a shiny new toy. *And isn't that perfect? Another trophy for Ray to show off to his friends.* Why had she brought Marcus? Of course Ray would love him; Ray loved cricket.

What the fuck am I doing? she asked herself.

Finally, the welcome banter began to slow down. Ray ushered Marcus into his study—a space Julia referred to as "the museum" for its shrine-like collection of personal accolades and cricket memorabilia—and Julia turned to Alice, who had moved to the dining room and was busy arranging a platter of freshly sliced bread.

"Haven't seen your father this happy in ages," Alice said, not looking up from her task.

"I didn't realize Marcus was such a star. I need to read the papers more."

"You did well. He seems very kind. And respectful to your father. Not hard on the eyes either . . ." Alice said.

"*Mum!*"

"Just a fact, love. Thanks for coming today. I'm thrilled that you brought your boyfriend. This will mean a lot to your dad. He hasn't been feeling well lately. Very low on energy."

"He's never low energy," Julia said. "He never did get his weight back up, did he? He looks very skinny."

"He just needs a checkup. He's been working a lot and needs to have some blood tests. The right vitamin mix should get his pep back."

Julia didn't want to consider why her dad looked frail, so she changed the subject as she followed Alice into the kitchen. "About every seven years, I bring Dad a new trophy, each bigger than the last. I'm not sure how to get one bigger than Marcus. It will have to be a building of some sort."

Alice sighed, setting the bread on the table with a soft clatter. "That's silly. Marcus isn't a trophy."

"Isn't he?" Julia said. "This is Dad's dream day, Mum. A cricketer under his roof, respectfully listening to his stories of past glory."

Alice didn't argue. Instead, she turned back to her preparations. "He's excited. You did a nice thing, whether you want to admit it or not."

"Mum, why did you ever get with him? I'll never understand what you saw in Dad."

"I love your father deeply," Alice said.

"Sure, but why him?"

Alice scoffed. "Are you kidding? All my mates fancied your dad. He was a star athlete, fit, the smartest man in every room—"

"Still is . . . at least according to him."

Alice shook her head with a small smile. "He has a magnetic personality. You've seen how people gravitate toward him. Our brunches are a coveted invitation."

Julia paced the kitchen, trying to settle her nervous energy. She regretted bringing Marcus to brunch and was still working through her feelings. She had heard her mother talk about her father as a young man before, and she could certainly see how charming he was in public. Alice's explanation made sense, especially given her upbringing in a traditional family where daughters were expected to marry well and tend to the home.

Julia stopped pacing and planted her hands on her hips. "You don't find him controlling?" She had asked her mom a version of this question countless times, and the response was predictable.

Alice sighed as she turned on the tap and began rinsing dishes. "He likes things a certain way. He can be rigid. I'm not blind to that, love." She scrubbed a plate, then added, "You'll learn that no marriage is easy. It's work. And I hope you work at it with Marcus— he seems lovely. In many ways, he reminds me of your father."

Julia's body went cold. The comparison sent a shiver down her spine, but she dismissed it as absurd. Marcus was nothing like Ray. Yes, he played cricket, was fit, and was charismatic in public, but that was where the similarities ended. He treated her with respect. He deferred to her. *Wait*, she thought, *was Ray like this at the start?* The thought gnawed at her, lingering as Alice turned off the tap, wiped her hands on a towel, and continued.

"And yes, his need to have things a certain way can be tough. You've seen me frustrated plenty of times. I'm not a robot. But when I step back and balance his flaws against his good qualities, I know I made the right choice."

Julia didn't respond. She appreciated her mother's acknowledgment of Ray's controlling nature. It reassured her that she wasn't imagining things, that her feelings were valid. But Alice's way of measuring her relationship with Ray—by tallying his good and bad traits—was transactional and hollow to Julia.

Thinking about this, Julia left the kitchen in search of Marcus. As she approached the study, she heard Ray's animated cadence punctuated by Marcus's polite replies. Gagging slightly, she turned around and headed for her room. She wouldn't interrupt their mutual admiration society.

––––––––––

As the old-timers from the Men's Club arrived, the house filled with the familiar din of hearty laughter, clinking glasses, and the scrape of chairs. Brunch was uneventful, other than Ray gushing about Marcus at every opportunity. Julia endured it with a blend of disinterest and eye rolls, focusing more on Alice's cooking than the conversation. Ray repeatedly told guests that his Julia had been recruited to join the prestigious Manly Life Saving Club because of her strong swimming and bravery. He took credit for identifying and nurturing her swimming skills from a young age. She hated that he was only proud of her when she did things he could brag about—or because she had brought home the "Golden Boy."

By the time dessert arrived, Julia was done. She nudged Marcus as Ray launched into yet another story about his Under-17 cricketing triumphs. "Ready to head out?" she asked.

"Sure," Marcus said.

As they gathered their things, Ray looked up. "Leaving already?"

"We've got to run. Enjoy your program tonight." Julia's little jab was subtle but caustic. Ray's face fell, but he didn't respond. He got up and ushered Marcus to the door, saying his farewells.

Once outside, Marcus glanced at her, his expression upbeat. "That went . . . well?"

Julia remained silent, but once they were driving away, she asked, "You think that went well?"

Marcus grinned, oblivious to the tension radiating from her. "It was great," he said. "Your parents are nice. I enjoyed the family atmosphere—it's cool that you still go back for Sunday brunch. And your dad? Solid guy. Loves his cricket."

Julia's temper bubbled. She stared out the window, willing herself to stay calm, but her words spilled out in disbelief: "I had no idea you were the Golden Boy. It would've been good information."

"What? Jules, you know I play for Australia," he said. "You don't care about my celebrity. It's one of the many reasons I like being with you. I haven't acted like a big shot around you, have I?"

"Gus and my friends know?"

"They also treat me like anyone else. I feel comfortable with you and your group. Your dad was excited, but he'll chill next time—"

"No, he won't. He hasn't chilled once in the last twenty-one years."

"The day was good, I thought . . . Help me understand. If I messed up, I want to fix it."

"How do you not see it? So many little passive-aggressive barbs."

"For example?"

"Remember when he complimented you on not being distracted by me? That was messed up."

"I didn't catch that, I'm sorry. I took that exchange as you inspiring me to my best season."

"He was saying you did great despite me. But I can see why you didn't hear that. You don't understand him like I do."

"I'm sorry, Jules. I would've stood up for you. I missed it."

"It's not a big deal. This is my baggage. You didn't do anything wrong." Julia took a deep breath. "I need to be dropped off at my flat," she said curtly.

Marcus didn't argue, though he was clearly confused. The car fell into a heavy silence, with only the engine audible as the tension hovered. He didn't press her, and she wasn't going to explain any further. The ride felt long and suffocating, but it passed, and before long, they'd pulled up to her flat. As she got out of the car, Marcus glanced over at her, his face puzzled. "I'm sorry. Again. I want to make it up to you. I'll be back in town soon."

Julia didn't respond.

"Are you watching over my place while I'm away? Or should I make other arrangements?" Marcus said, apparently trying to force a response.

Julia paused, turning back to the open passenger window. She peered in and said, "I'll look after it. Safe travels. Find me when you get back."

CHAPTER 17

Catrina gripped the steering wheel, her knuckles aching from the strain. The day had been a disaster, but not atypical for her as the number-two employee at Brockwell Surgical Sales.

The company had carved out a niche in the market. Tim had leveraged his connections with surgeons and hospital systems to get SidOrtho's cages into operating rooms immediately after leaving DeltaTech. He knew the industry better than most and wasn't burdened by a conscience. His advantage lay in the fact that surgeons, within reason, could choose which surgical instruments they used. In an ideal world, they would select the best product for the patient, but this wasn't an ideal world, as Catrina had learned.

Several factors, including price, ease of use, durability, and customer service, influenced a surgeon's decision-making process. Officially, blatant kickbacks, such as vacations and extravagant gifts, had been banned by regulators; however, soft kickbacks still fueled the industry. Shady representatives like Tim skirted the system by disguising the graft, creating speaking engagements with minimal attendance in Hawaii, Mexico, or Las Vegas—all expenses paid, of course. In return, those same doctors ordered cages from Tim for their procedures. SidOrtho quietly reimbursed BSS for the doctor's fake speaking engagements through under-the-table consulting fees.

Tim spent his time arranging these deals, accompanying doctors on trips, and maintaining strong relationships with surgeons. When he wasn't traveling, he was at the country club, entertaining his best client and friend, Dr. Jones. Tim's role in the company focused on the graft, networking, and the underhanded financial reimbursements. He excelled at it.

At times, BSS felt like a house of cards to Catrina. Most doctors didn't care which wrist cage they used; functionally, all the cages did the same thing. That meant Tim had to continually raise the stakes, which had led to the extraordinary step of securing Dr. Jones, SidOrtho's highest-volume surgeon, a six-figure annual consulting contract with SidOrtho. Whether this was disclosed to his hospital was unclear, but with so much money flowing from Dr. Jones's tireless work ethic to the hospital, any questions they may have had were ignored.

But securing orders from doctors was only part of the operation. Once they agreed to use the product, BSS had to ensure the cages were in the operating room by the time procedures were scheduled. If shipments weren't delivered on time or if parts were missing, surgeons would face backlash from hospital administration, which could threaten the entire scam.

This was where Catrina came in, and she was exceptional. She meticulously tracked every procedure involving a SidOrtho cage, ensured orders were properly registered with the wholesaler, and confirmed deliveries at each hospital. She made sure surgical nurses opened the packages a day or two before procedures to verify that all parts were accounted for. If anything was missing, she drove to SidOrtho, retrieved the part, and hand-delivered it to the operating room. Without her, all of Tim's maneuvering would have been wasted. No matter how much wining and dining he did, hospitals wouldn't allow surgeons to use unreliable products.

On this day, like so many others, Tim had been missing in action. No updates, no thanks, even though Catrina had single-handedly saved two shipments from missing their operating room deadlines. If she hadn't stepped in, there would have been hell to pay, maybe even a loss of SidOrtho's hospital privileges. But since she'd fixed everything before anyone noticed, as usual, it didn't even register as a problem.

She sighed and focused on the road, heading toward her mom's house for their weekly check-in. The commercial sprawl of warehouses and office parks faded behind her as she drove west, the streets narrowing, the buildings shrinking.

Her mom had been doing well since Catrina had moved out, but Catrina still made a point to visit at least once a week. If nothing else, she enjoyed hearing her mom's latest drama—it had a way of making her life feel more put together. Without fail, Morven would ask if she'd found a man yet, and when Catrina brushed it off, she'd offer to set Catrina up with a friend of a friend. It was their routine, a playful back-and-forth, that kept their relationship close without the strain of daily contact.

As Catrina drove, she noted again how striking the coastal neighborhood was compared to industrial Carlsbad: palm-lined streets, stucco homes with bright tile roofs, and the occasional glimpse of the ocean peeking between houses. It should have been calming, but something wasn't right. She had noticed an Acura had been behind her for too many turns. The car, a dull gray older model, had stayed a few lengths back, its driver hidden behind the glare of the windshield. She tried to tell herself it was nothing—plenty of people took the same route through town.

She turned left onto Chestnut Avenue, and the Acura followed. Another right onto Jefferson, still there. She took a longer detour, cutting through the winding residential streets near the lagoon, doubling back toward her mother's street. The car never wavered, always a few cars behind, never speeding, never backing off.

She shifted in her seat, hyperaware of every movement the Acura made. Her shoulders tensed, and a dull ache began to form at the base of her neck. Despite the cool air from the vents, sweat gathered along her hairline. Panicked, she reached for her phone and called her mom.

"Hey, honey, you close?" Morven asked.

"I think I'm being followed."

"What the hell? Where are you?"

"I'm about two minutes out. Mom! What do I do?"

"Don't stop. Drive straight here. I'll meet you outside."

"You sure?"

"Yes. What kind of car?"

"Old Acura. Gray."

"Ignore stop signs and get here quick."

Catrina pressed the gas and cut onto her mom's street. The Acura didn't hesitate. It followed her turn by turn, closing the distance.

She swung into the driveway, tires screeching against the pavement. Before she could open the door, Morven burst from the house, barefoot, wearing an old tank top and yoga pants, wielding an aluminum baseball bat.

The Acura stopped at the curb, the driver's door opened, and a middle-aged, overweight, balding man heaved himself out. He held up an envelope, waving it like a white flag. "Whoa, relax! Don't hit me!" he said. "I'm just a process server."

Morven pointed the bat at him. "One more step, and it's your last, fat man!"

The man froze. "Jesus," he yelled. "I'm just doing my job, lady."

Catrina exhaled and glanced at the envelope, piecing together what was happening. She turned to her mom. "It's fine."

Morven didn't lower the bat.

Catrina walked toward the man, reached out, and took the envelope from his outstretched hand.

"Catrina McDavid, you've been served," he said meekly, wiping sweat from his forehead. "Sorry for startling you. Have a nice day."

Morven took a step forward. "You have five seconds to get out of here before I call the cops."

The man didn't argue. He backed toward his car, slid inside, and sped off.

Back at her apartment, Catrina threw her work bag aggressively on the floor and flopped onto the couch, her arms flailing dramatically.

Sam entered the living room from her bedroom and asked, "What's wrong?"

"Dickhead," Catrina said. "My God, it never stops."

"What now, Cat?"

"DeltaTech sued me! Papers say I owe in excess of $25,000. In excess! That could mean millions!"

"Wait, what? I thought Tim said he couldn't mention you in that article to protect you from this."

"Oh, it gets worse," Catrina said.

"How is that possible?" Sam asked, standing over her.

"It does. Trust me." Catrina gripped the edge of a couch cushion, her knuckles whitening as her nails dug into the fabric, the tension radiating through her rigid shoulders.

"Cat," Sam said, moving toward the kitchen, "breathe for a second. I'll get you some water. I've never seen you this angry."

As Sam busied herself in the kitchen, Catrina sank back into the couch, her legs bouncing with nervous energy. Sam returned with a glass of water and sat beside her.

"I'm sorry," Catrina said, taking a sip.

"For what?" Sam asked.

"Making everything about me. It can't always be about me. How was your day?"

"It isn't always about you," Sam replied. "We talk about my stuff all the time. I didn't get sued today for thousands, so . . . How is it worse? This is killing me."

Catrina set the glass down on the coffee table. "After the process server handed me the documents, I called Rachel at DeltaTech from Mom's house."

"I bet Morven had feelings. What did Rachel say?" Sam asked.

"Yeah, she was fired up. Anyways, Rachel said she couldn't talk to me because of the lawsuit but offered to transfer me to the general counsel, Tom Wilkshire."

"Man, you're brave," Sam said. "I would've hidden under this couch."

Catrina snorted. "Bullshit. You'd march straight to the country club and kick Tim's teeth out."

"Still might," Sam quipped.

Catrina allowed herself a small smile before continuing. "So Mr. Wilkshire. He was . . . actually nice. Said no one at DeltaTech hated me, but leaving the way I did, without resigning, rubbed everyone the wrong way. But they weren't going to include me in the lawsuit originally."

"But you're in it," Sam said.

"Yup. Apparently, during settlement talks—which I didn't even know were happening—Tim informed them that I was the one who had acted improperly. I was the mastermind."

"He threw you under the bus?"

"Completely," Catrina said. "I asked Mr. Wilkshire if I needed a lawyer, and he said he couldn't advise me, but yeah, I'm in serious trouble."

"Have you called Tim?" Sam asked.

"About fifteen times. He won't answer."

"Try him again," Sam said. "Put him on speaker."

Catrina hesitated, her thumb hovering over Tim's name in the call log. She glanced at Sam. Taking a deep breath, she hit the call button and set her phone on the coffee table.

The line rang once. Twice. Three times. Tim's voicemail clicked on, his grating, upbeat message playing: "Hey, it's Tim. You know what to do!"

Catrina hit the red button to disconnect. "Unbelievable."

"Try him again," Sam said. "Don't let him ignore you."

Catrina stared at her phone. Her hands tremored as she typed a message to Tim.

> I'll call you in 2 minutes. If you don't pick up, I'll go to the police station and confess everything.

She pressed Send and exhaled. Within seconds, her phone lit up. Tim's name flashed across the screen.

"Here we go," she said to Sam, hitting the answer button and putting the call on speaker.

"Cat, what the hell are you talking about?" Tim said. Catrina could detect a hint of panic he was trying to mask.

"Are you kidding me, Tim?" she snapped. "I got served with a lawsuit from DeltaTech. My name is on it, Tim. As a defendant. You didn't think I'd want a heads-up?"

There was a pause, and she visualized Tim recalibrating. "I planned to tell you, Cat. I didn't think they'd move this fast. I'm shocked you've already been served."

"That's bullshit, Tim. You blindsided me!" Catrina said, shaking with anger. "You've dragged me into your shit, and now you're throwing me under the bus? What the hell is wrong with you?"

"Cat, calm down. This is all part of the strategy," Tim said in a patronizing tone, making her face burn hot. "Listen, to save the company . . . the lawyers thought it'd be best to, uh, shift the focus. It's a legal tactic, nothing personal. Nothing bad will happen to you. At worst, you declare personal bankruptcy and it shields you. I promise I'll take care of you financially. You know I'll."

"Declare bankruptcy?" Catrina yelled. "You want me to ruin my credit, my reputation, for you and the damn company? And you didn't think to consult me first? What the literal fuck is wrong with you?"

"Look, I didn't want it to come to this. I asked to take the blame—keep the fact that you devised the plan hidden."

"My plan?"

"Listen . . . The lawyers are clever. They've done this before. This is the only way to protect everything we've built. BSS. The doctors. Their patients. They all need us. This is about survival, Cat. Our survival."

Catrina glanced at Sam, whose expression darkened.

"I knew you'd be upset," Tim continued. "But think about it—if you testify that I didn't know anything, the lawsuit weakens, and BSS is free and clear. They can't touch my personal assets."

"What assets? You're broke, you stupid fucker. It doesn't matter how much BSS makes—you spend a little more. It's gross."

"Cat, calm down. You're being emotional. Just stop and listen to me. If BSS survives, you'll be set for life. I'll make sure of it," Tim pleaded.

"You'll make sure of it?" she repeated. "Like you made sure I wouldn't be included in this lawsuit?"

"That's not fair," Tim said. "I've always looked out for you, haven't I? But you need to be practical. Get yourself a solid lawyer—someone legit. I'll recommend a few. But you'll need to pay for it yourself. We can't have anything traceable back to me or the company."

"You want me to pay for a lawyer?"

"It's for your protection," he said. "You don't want anyone sniffing around and tying us too closely together. This is about keeping the company alive, Cat. You've worked hard for this—don't throw it away now."

Tim's ability to manipulate her was weakening—not just in this conversation but gradually, over months. She was no longer the twenty-year-old intern who owed him everything, no longer the girl who dropped everything to rush to a hotel room or smooth over a problem he caused. She was the one who kept BSS running, the one who built its operational backbone while he played golf and took luxury vacations. For years, he had framed her competence as loyalty, but the illusion had worn thin. Since moving out of her mom's house and living with Sam, Catrina had started to see things clearly. She didn't belong to him. She didn't owe him. And now, with a crippling lawsuit in her lap and his voice spinning bullshit through the speakerphone, whatever hold he had on her cracked for good.

"Fine," she said after a pause. "I'll think about it."

She wasn't losing her resolve by saying *fine*; she was buying time. Letting Tim believe he still had control gave her time to think. For once, she was using his expectations against him.

"Good," Tim said, his tone brightening. "That's my Catnip. We're going to get through this. I promise."

The call ended, and the room fell into a heavy silence.

Sam's expression twisted with anger and disbelief. "Catnip?" she asked.

"Yeah . . ." Catrina said.

"Fuck. That. *Pig!*" Sam said as she paced the room. "He is such a piece of shit, Catrina." Cat realized Sam was serious now; Sam never used her full name. "Actually, he isn't a piece of shit. He's the entire cesspool. Only a man like Tim would pull this level of crap, self-serving garbage, and somehow convince himself he's doing you a favor. It's disgusting. He doesn't give a damn about anyone but himself. For a complete fucking idiot, somehow he is clever enough to make you carry all the burden while he plays golf."

Sam's voice rose, the words spilling out in a rush. "And men like him always do this. They don't build anything themselves—they leech off everyone else, especially women like you, who actually work, who actually care, and they throw you under the bus the second they need to save their skin. It's infuriating. It's disgusting. And—" She stopped herself abruptly, biting her lip as if physically stopping the next words from tumbling out.

"I'm not going to protect him this time," Catrina said. "But I need him to think I might. I have to figure out my best play."

"I'm going to give you space to process," Sam said. "I'm so mad. I'm afraid I'll say something that pisses you off. We don't deserve that. Our friendship . . . Tim doesn't get to hurt our friendship."

"Sam, I agree with you. One hundred percent."

"Good," Sam said, noticeably more relaxed than a moment before.

"And I don't want space. I want to do something. With you," Catrina said.

Sam sat back on the couch, the tension in her shoulders easing. "Then come with me tomorrow."

"To the lady golf thing?" Catrina asked.

"Yeah," Sam said. "At Torrey Pines. I've got a room at the

Monarch Ridge La Jolla. You can blow off some steam and hang out with a bunch of fun lesbians. There will be plenty of time to handle Tim and the lawsuit later."

"I don't know anything about golf."

"You don't have to. Just show up, eat overpriced snacks, and laugh at my hilarious jokes."

"Fine, but if anyone hits on you, I'll shoo them off," Catrina teased.

"Don't! My fitness instructor will be there," Sam said. "Now go pack. And for the love of God, leave Tim to stew. I guarantee he's going to spend all night tossing and turning, imagining you walking into a police station. At the very least, he deserves a few nights' shitty sleep."

"You have a way of putting things, don't you?" Catrina said.

"Get packing. And start in my closet. You don't have anything for Torrey Pines."

CHAPTER 18

Friday, March 9, 2012 | Sydney

Marcus had been nominated for Aussie of the Year, and despite her reservations, Julia agreed to accompany him to the ceremony at the Sydney Opera House that evening. His excitement was infectious, and he booked a full day of shopping and styling before the event. Julia was particularly nervous about the red carpet, aware that paparazzi and tabloid journalists would be waiting to capture every moment. This event—the cameras, the attention, the glitz—was far removed from her life, yet she was up for a new adventure.

Gus offered her the day off, insisting she didn't need to worry about the taverna with such a prestigious evening ahead, but Julia refused. She scheduled herself to work the lunch shift from 11:00 a.m. to 3:00 p.m. In jest, Gus gave her a Greek Taverna hat to wear during the event. He preached about the value of free advertising, and the regulars had a good laugh.

It had been a long week, and Julia and Miriam hadn't spoken since Miriam had a minor lung procedure. Though they had exchanged a few emails, Julia needed to see her sister's face. As Julia adjusted the laptop's camera, the clock on the screen read 9:45 a.m.— early for their chats but necessary since Julia had to get to her lunch shift. She pressed the call button, hoping Miriam would be up for talking after a week of recuperation. The sisters had gotten close, but Julia suspected Miriam didn't want Julia to see her struggling.

When Miriam's face appeared on the screen, relief washed over Julia. Miriam looked tired but otherwise the same.

"Hey, Jules," Miriam said.

Julia moved closer to the screen, studying her sister's face and body language. "Mir, you look . . . okay." The words came out more of a question than she had intended. "How are you feeling? How did it go?"

"I'm alive," Miriam said, her expression betraying her fatigue. She paused for a moment, her tone turning more serious. "The procedure didn't go as planned. They drained what they needed to, but now there's an infection. The doctors aren't thrilled, and I have to return for more tests on Monday."

"That's awful," Julia said. "I missed seeing you. I was close to hopping on a plane."

"I'll get through it. Sorry I missed our calls. By the way, Jules, I've been meaning to say I'm proud of you. You didn't let Dad derail things with Marcus, and you're stepping out of your comfort zone tonight. The Aussie of the Year ceremony is a big deal. My agent, Linda, will record it, and we'll watch it in the morning."

"I'll be in the front row with the tall guy."

"I know this isn't your scene, but you're handling it like a pro."

"Thanks, Mir. But let's not get carried away. I'm freaking out. Any tips for dealing with the red carpet? I have no idea what I'm doing."

Miriam's eyes lit up. "Okay, first, posture is everything—shoulders back, head high. Confidence, even if you're faking it. Second, don't try to pose. Keep it natural, like you're having fun. And don't forget to smile—your real smile, Jules, not your *I want to leave* smile."

"Alright, shoulders back, smile. Got it. Anything else?" Julia asked.

"Yes—avoid eating spinach. Trust me, you don't want anything stuck in your teeth when the cameras are flashing."

Julia laughed. "Noted. Avoid leafy greens." As the nervous

laughter faded, Julia shifted the conversation. "It's nice you've had some time off since leaving *IRS Rogue*, though it must be a relief to have the modeling gigs."

"It's a blessing, sure, but I'm itching to get back into acting. I want to be healthy and land a role—a lead role in a studio film or a prominent series. The modeling pays the bills, but the work doesn't excite me," Miriam said.

"It'll happen for you, Mir. It's only a matter of time. You're too talented. Once you're back on your feet, they'll be lining up to cast you."

"Thanks, Jules, I needed to hear that. I've been pretty down lately. But enough about me. Today is a big day. I'll keep my phone on tonight if you need to call me. Don't hesitate to wake me. All I do lately is sleep," Miriam said.

Julia glanced at the clock on the laptop. "I should get going, but I'll try to check in after the ceremony, let you know how it goes."

"Have fun tonight, and remember—no spinach," Miriam said.

As the screen went dark, Julia felt a little lighter. Despite everything Miriam was dealing with, she had found a way to ease her little sister's nerves.

Gus was uncharacteristically quiet for most of Julia's shift, roaming between the kitchen and the counter without his typical barrage of commentary and jokes. Julia hadn't worked a lunch shift before and wondered if Gus was more focused and less playful during the day. She marveled at his stamina, working twelve-hour days five days a week, plus the occasional Sunday. *Where does he get the energy?* she wondered, shaking her head in admiration.

As the clock neared 3:00, Gus emerged from the kitchen carrying a plate of spanakopita; the rich aroma of spinach and flaky pastry filled the air. He placed it down in front of Julia with a flourish. "Eat, Tzoúlia," he said. "Tonight will be busy, and you'll forget to eat."

Miriam's warning about spinach flashed in her mind, but Julia didn't want to insult Gus. She smiled and picked up her fork. "Thanks, Gus." She ate a few bites, the buttery flakiness of the pastry melting in her mouth, balanced by the earthy tang of spinach and creamy feta. She kept licking her teeth, acutely aware of the cameras that awaited.

As she ate, Gus stood at the counter and launched into a disjointed but enthusiastic history of the Aussie of the Year award. "Every year, Tzoúlia, the best of the best. Scientists, athletes, humanitarians . . . It's the whole country watching, yeah? The prime minister is there!" He gestured grandly, and his excitement was as high as if Julia were attending the Met Gala.

"Great," she said, her mouth full of spanakopita, the pressure mounting.

Gus ignored her sarcasm and transitioned seamlessly into a dramatic speech about why *she* should've been nominated instead of Marcus. "Sure, Marcus scored one thousand test runs last year," he said, waving his hand dismissively. "But did Marcus save two lives in a single day? Did he balance a tray of flaming saganaki without breaking a plate? No! Nobody else had a better record in 2011 than Tzoúlia. Nobody!"

Julia couldn't help but laugh. "I don't think *Best Lifesaver-Waitress in Manly* qualifies, Gus."

"*Waitress-Lifesaver*," Gus corrected. "But you're not just a waitress; you're my Tzoúlia. And tonight the whole country will see how amazing you are."

As Gus was wrapping up his performance, Alani and Ginger walked into the taverna. "Ready to be all over the tabloids tomorrow, Jul?" Ginger asked.

"What an awful thought," Julia replied.

"Mrs. Julia Daelmans, who are you wearing?" Alani asked in a fake announcer voice.

"This apron is from Gus's Vintage Collection, 1979 edition," Ginger replied, pointing to the sign on the wall celebrating Gus's opening.

"Enough nonsense, girls, Tzoúlia must focus. Marcus will be here any minute," Gus said hypocritically.

As Marcus pulled up and illegally parked in front of the taverna in his BMW, Julia smoothed her *vintage* apron before untying and hanging it behind the counter. She caught sight of Marcus waving at her from behind the wheel, his grin as easy as ever. Before she could get in the car, Gus, Alani, and Ginger followed her outside.

"Tzoúlia!" Gus called out.

She turned back with a raised eyebrow, faking annoyance.

"Don't bring Floating Sky. There are no surfboards allowed."

"Noted, Gus. Floating Sky stays home."

"Grab me a goodie bag," Alani yelled.

"Me too," Ginger added.

Gus grinned and waved. "Have fun. Good luck, Marcus. Tzoúlia, we're proud of you."

Marcus parked his car with precision outside an upscale department store in Sydney's city center, his confidence layered with an almost imperceptible edge of anxiousness. He checked his watch a few times too many, and his shoulders seemed unnaturally stiff.

"Big day, huh?" she said, stepping out of the car.

"Not really," Marcus replied. "It's just an awards thing. No big deal."

Julia smirked. "You're practically vibrating. Relax, mate. It's just a shiny plaque and a handshake, right?"

Marcus didn't respond as he led her into the department store.

Inside, a well-dressed store assistant greeted them with a rehearsed smile. "Mr. Daelmans, your tuxedo is ready."

Marcus nodded and followed the assistant to the back, leaving Julia to wander among the garish displays of cufflinks and leather shoes. He returned a few minutes later, carrying a garment bag and grinning as if he'd just scored the winning runs against England. "Your turn," he said.

"Oh, joy," Julia deadpanned as she was ushered into the women's section.

A sales assistant named Clara appeared, holding a clipboard and sporting an eager smile. "Ms. Corning, we've selected some options for you."

Julia glanced at the rack of dresses Clara gestured toward—flowing fabrics in shades of red, purple, and blue—and wished Miriam were here to guide her. One dress caught her eye—a light-blue gown with a halter neckline and a long, flowing chiffon skirt. It was simple but elegant. "This one," she said, pointing.

"Excellent choice. Let's try it on," Clara said.

A few minutes later, Julia emerged from the fitting room, brushing the fabric over her hips. Marcus looked up from his phone and gave her a quick once-over. "Perfect. That's the one."

Next came shoes. Julia chose silver heels that looked refined but slightly uncomfortable. She winced as she stood.

"If I break an ankle and can't surf, we're done."

Marcus laughed. "You'll survive. Now on to hair."

"I'm not joking," Julia muttered under her breath.

The salon was a whirlwind of activity, with stylists darting between clients and the drone of blow-dryers filling the air. A stylist ran her hands through Julia's hair. "What are we thinking today?" she asked.

"Make it fancy," Julia said.

An hour later, Julia's hair was slicked back, her neckline accentuated. She caught her reflection in the mirror and thought, *This is ridiculous.*

Marcus, freshly groomed and looking every bit the part of a dashing nominee, smirked. "You clean up well."

"Thanks, mate," Julia said. "Now, let's get this over."

After dropping their bags at the Four Seasons Hotel on George Street, they climbed into a black limo. Marcus fidgeted with his cufflinks as the car rolled toward the Opera House a few blocks away. Julia watched him out of the corner of her eye, biting back a grin. "You're nervous," she said.

"I'm not," Marcus shot back.

"Okay . . . Why not? Loads of people will be watching."

"You're right. It's not about the award. It's just . . . a lot of eyes," Marcus said.

The limo arrived at the Opera House, the building's iconic white sails glowing against the evening sky. The VIP entrance was a flurry of activity, with photographers lining the red carpet and vying for the attention of arriving guests. Marcus stepped out first, his charm switching on like a spotlight. He turned to offer Julia his hand, and she accepted, stepping onto the carpet with indifference, focusing on her steps. The last thing she wanted was to fall on national TV.

"Marcus! Over here!" photographers called. "Who's your stunning date?"

Marcus smiled, his hand resting lightly on Julia's back. "This is Julia Corning, my girlfriend," he said to a nearby reporter.

"What's your story?" a reporter asked Julia.

"I surf and wait tables at Gus's Greek Taverna in Manly," Julia said apprehensively.

"Uh . . . okay," the reporter responded.

"Great coffee if you're ever in Manly," Julia said into the camera, hoping Gus was watching. Julia imagined him ranting and raving about his Tzoúlia being a TV star, and it brought a needed smile to her face.

The photographers' cameras clicked furiously as Marcus paused for interviews, chatting about his nomination and the honor of being recognized. Julia floated to the background, scanning the scene with mild amusement. This was Marcus's world, not hers, and she was content to stay on the periphery.

Inside the auditorium, they were seated in the front row. The air crackled with anticipation as speeches and performances filled the evening. Marcus sat straight in his chair, but Julia noticed his knee bouncing. He was nervous, no matter how much he tried to hide it.

After hours of prattle, they finally arrived at the main event, the Aussie of the Year announcement. Julia imagined Ray watching the show on his couch with Alice, seeing his surfie-bum daughter sitting in the front row between his favorite cricketer and a noted climate-change scientist with a ridiculous mustache. She audibly chuckled.

"What's funny?" Marcus asked as Captain Planet gave her a sideways glance.

Shit, she thought. "Nothing. Shhh. The presenter is coming out," she said. *If Marcus doesn't win, I hope they pick the lady doctor. She looks nice. Bet she saved more than two people last year. Should be the minimum: Save more lives than Julia, the waitress.* She held back a second laugh.

As the announcer took the stage, the room hushed.

"And the Aussie of the Year is . . ."

Marcus straightened further in his seat.

"Dr. Eleanor Bates!"

The room erupted in applause as the pediatric cancer doctor and researcher stood to accept the award. Julia turned to Marcus as he let out a subtle "damn," his first visible crack all evening.

When the applause died down, Julia whispered, "Gus was right, I should've won. I saved two people from drowning."

"What?" Marcus asked.

"Lightening the mood. Sorry you lost."

"It's an honor to be nominated," Marcus said.

"Absolutely. At least it was her, not the grumpy climate guy next to me," Julia said. "He's a bad fish."

"Of course. Child cancer research should win. What a silly . . . At least we can leave. Nobody wants to interview—"

". . . the loser," Julia said, completing his sentence.

They both giggled.

"For the record, I never expected to win. This whole thing was for fun."

Julia gave him a sympathetic hug and said, "Let's go."

"I could use a drink. Or five!" Marcus replied.

The night air sparkled with excitement as Marcus and Julia stumbled arm in arm through Circular Quay, the silhouette of the Opera House still visible in the distance. To Marcus's credit, he wasn't letting the loss affect his mood.

The waterfront teemed with life. Street performers played violins and guitars, their music blending with the crash of water against the pylons. Crowds of tourists snapped photos of the illuminated Sydney Harbour Bridge, its towering arches contrasting against the night sky. Well-dressed couples meandered past, their laughter coexisting with general conversations in dozens of languages. Ferries pulled into the wharves, their engines churning as they unloaded streams of passengers who disappeared into the night. A group of teenagers skateboarded past, their whoops adding to the chaos. Vendors sold ice cream and roasted nuts from carts, the scents wafting through the air. Seagulls hovered above, their squawks adding to the evening's soundtrack.

The afterparty for the awards was held at a high-end private restaurant on The Rocks at Circular Quay, its sprawling balcony offering a panoramic view of the Sydney Harbour Bridge and the Opera House. Inside, the space was spectacular, featuring marble floors, chandeliers dripping with crystals, and floor-to-ceiling windows that showcased the harbor. Waiters moved deftly through the crowd with trays of champagne and canapés while a cover band crucified John Lennon.

Marcus mingled, shaking hands and trading laughs with the attendees. Julia followed, more amused than impressed by the opulence. She sipped her champagne, letting Marcus do the networking while she took in the scene, and slipped out to the balcony where she could enjoy the fresh air and view of the water. Marcus joined her after a while, fresh drink in hand.

"Not bad, huh?" he asked.

"Decent spot, for sure. Are you okay?"

Marcus waved her off, smiling too wide. "I'm fine. It's all good."

She decided not to push him, but Marcus's facade began to crack as the night wore on. His jokes got louder, his laughter forced. The drinks kept coming, and his polished veneer slipped further with each glass. By the time they sat at a small table tucked near the balcony, Marcus was sloppy. "You know," he slurred, "I told myself I didn't care about winning."

"But you did."

Marcus nodded, his gaze fixed on his glass. "I wanted it. Nobody gets nominated more than once in sport. This was my shot."

"You're the best cricketer in the country," Julia said. "You're just not . . . the *Aussie of the Year*."

Marcus laughed. "It's stupid, right? Caring about this."

"No, it's not," Julia said. "Tonight was a big deal. It's okay to be disappointed. Own it."

He nodded, his head swaying slightly. "Look at all these pretentious arseholes. Fuck them. When I stop scoring runs, they'll pretend not to know me."

"Tall poppy syndrome is as Australian as Vegemite," Julia added.

"We looked good tonight. You were . . . really pretty on the rug. Carpet. Rug carpet. Red carpet. Made me . . . proud to have you on my arm."

Julia didn't have time to process his incoherent ramblings as she reached out and caught his drink before it tipped over. "Time to call it a night, mate," she said.

Marcus didn't argue. "You're a good sport," he slurred as they started to walk. "Better than I deserve."

As they left the afterparty, Marcus was drunk, his steps uneven, but his mood improved after he had admitted his disappointment. Julia had never seen him drunk. He waved at a passing couple who recognized him and gave a goofy nod. *People love this guy.* She appreciated his honesty about his disappointment. It was a human reaction, and Marcus dropping the stiff upper lip was endearing.

They reached the Four Seasons, its grand entrance bathed in mellow light, the glass doors ushering them into a world of understated grandeur. The elevator doors slid open, revealing a capsule of mirrors. Marcus pressed the button for the top floor, and the smooth ascent began, accompanied by soft jazz playing through hidden speakers.

The elevator opened to a private corridor, plush carpeting muffling their steps as they walked to their suite. Marcus swiped the key card, and the door clicked open to reveal a room that could have been from a movie. The living area was understated yet luxurious, with plush seating arranged around a low, glass-topped coffee table. A wall-mounted flat-screen television remained dark, its glossy surface reflecting the room's ambient lighting. On one side of the room was a stocked bar under recessed lighting, its crystal decanters and bottles untouched. Beyond the living area, the bedroom was indulgent, with a massive bed draped in high-thread-count sheets, flanked by bedside lamps that lit the room. The marble bathroom had a giant bathtub positioned to overlook Sydney Harbour.

Julia ignored the room, her attention commanded by the panoramic windows in the main living area. The view was breathtaking. All of Sydney stretched before them, glowing against the dark sky. Julia particularly enjoyed watching the late-night ferries coming and going, the passengers scattering into the night.

Marcus tossed his jacket on an armchair and collapsed onto the couch with a sigh, finally at ease. "This," he said, stretching his legs out, "is exactly what I needed."

Julia couldn't help but laugh, shaking her head as she kicked off her heels. "You and your fancy hotels," she teased.

"A little pampering," Marcus replied, patting the spot beside him. "C'mon, let's take it all in."

Julia joined him on the couch, letting herself sink into the plush cushions. She turned to Marcus. "You know," she said, "that tub looks like it's calling our names."

"You love water. Let's do it," Marcus said.

Minutes later, the two of them were submerged in the luxurious tub, warm water enveloping them as the glittering Sydney skyline stretched beyond the glass. The world Marcus inhabited still felt foreign to Julia, and she didn't love it, but here, in this moment, she allowed herself to enjoy it.

Bathtub sex had been new and amazing. Julia's cheeks were flushed from the shower's heat and physical intimacy as she slipped on the soft hotel bathrobe. It was 12:30 a.m., and Marcus's energy was waning. He had gone from the bath directly to the bed, skipping the shower. He appeared to be fighting to stay awake. It was a miracle he hadn't passed out after the long day, alcohol, and a hot bath. Julia, however, was on her second wind. Late nights were her normal, and she wasn't ready to succumb to sleep. She climbed into bed and kissed him lightly, her lips brushing his softly. "Round two?" she asked.

Marcus muttered something unintelligible, but Julia didn't quit.

"I hope I did okay tonight," she said. "I asked my sister for advice —she's a red-carpet pro—but I totally violated her first rule. I ate spinach at lunch."

"You were amazing, Jules. Seriously perfect. I loved . . . it."

They began to kiss again, slow and tender at first, then Marcus paused and spoke, his words mumbled and slurred. "Move in with me?" he asked. "Live with me so I can take care of you."

The words struck Julia like a slap. Her body stiffened as she pulled away. "What did you say?"

"Let's live together," Marcus said.

"The other part."

"I'll take care of you. Anything you need."

"I don't need to be taken care of, Marcus!"

"I didn't mean . . ." Marcus's face fell. "Jules—wait . . . I don't want to take care of you because I think you need it—I want to because I love you. I want us to be together. We looked so good together tonight. The whole country saw us . . ."

"So?" Julia asked, standing by the bed with her hands on her hips.

"We're the next Australian *it* couple. People loved us."

"You really don't get me, do you?"

"What?"

"The dress, the shoes, the reporters. I'm not a trophy. I didn't ask for this, Marcus. I was doing you a favor."

"A favor? Most women would kill to be on a red carpet."

"Wow. I'm going to go."

"Why? What's happening?" Marcus asked.

Julia was unsure what had set her off, but she needed to leave. "The last ferry to Manly is at one o'clock; I can make it."

"Jules, I'm sorry. Stay."

"Call me tomorrow when you're sober." Julia kissed him on the forehead and put on her morning clothes. She left the expensive dress and shoes on the floor and raced out of the suite. The elevator ride was a blur.

She ran through Circular Quay, her flats slapping the pavement as she dashed to the ferry. Her breath came in short gasps from both exertion and the emotions of the evening. She barely made it, stepping on board just as the gangplank was pulled back. Finding a quiet corner, she stood outside overlooking the rail, her chest heaving as she tried to calm down. Her eyes scanned the few passengers until she spotted a middle-aged woman holding an iPhone. Julia approached her. "Excuse me, could I pay you to use your phone? Just for a quick video call?"

The woman, startled, looked at Julia's red face and handed over the phone. "No charge, mate. Take your time."

Grateful, Julia offered a shaky smile and dialed Miriam's number from memory, praying her sister would answer, since it was 6:00 a.m. in Los Angeles—a conversion she did instantly. The phone rang twice before Miriam answered, her expression shifting from anticipated joy to concern.

"Jules? What's wrong?" Miriam asked.

Julia's words came out in a rush. "Marcus and I had a fight, and I left the hotel room and got on a ferry. He wanted me as a trophy, Mir. I'm not a trophy."

Through her mental haze, Julia caught the subtle softening in Miriam's expression. Her sister angled closer to the camera. "Hey, hey. Breathe," Miriam said, her calm tone grounding Julia. "If the situation wasn't good, you did the right thing. Whatever the reason, trust your gut. You aren't anyone's trophy, Jules."

Julia blinked, and Miriam's words settled over her like a balm. She hadn't realized how much she needed to hear them. Miriam wasn't questioning, pushing her to explain or justify her actions; she was there, unwavering and supportive. It was the reassurance she needed.

"I just . . . I don't know what to do."

"There's nothing to do. We'll work it out tomorrow; go get some sleep," Miriam assured her. "Call me from the internet café first thing. I'll clear my schedule, I promise. We'll talk it through, all of it. For now, get home safe. I love you, okay?"

Julia wiped her face with the back of her hand, her breathing beginning to even out. "I love you too. I'll call as soon as the café opens."

Miriam smiled. "I'll be ready."

Julia handed the phone back to the woman. "Thank you, really. Come by Gus's Taverna—I owe you a coffee." The woman smiled, patting Julia's shoulder with understanding.

Turning away, Julia walked back to the railing, her eyes fixed on the dark waters below. The lights of Sydney in the distance and the ocean swell as they crossed the heads brought her peace on this strange night.

CHAPTER 19

Catrina stepped off the shuttle bus onto the grounds of Torrey Pines for her first golf event. Her short ponytail swung out of the back of her UC San Diego hat as she took in the scene. Her running shoes crunched along the gravel path as she tugged at the hem of a navy-blue golf skirt and a snug white collared shirt. Aside from her hat and shoes, everything else was borrowed from Sam's closet. Sam strode ahead in her chic black skirt, lavender polo, and Titleist visor.

The impressive expanse of Torrey Pines stretched before them—manicured green fairways and rugged cliffs that dropped dramatically into the Pacific Ocean. The breeze carried the light scent of saltwater and freshly cut grass. To their left, the deep blue sea glistened under the midmorning sun, waves crashing against the shoreline. To their right, clusters of tall pine trees cast dappled shadows across the grounds. Over the cliffs, three Navy jets tore through the sky in formation, engines screaming as they skimmed the cliffs in perfect synchronicity before vanishing over the Pacific.

Catrina's gaze shifted from the landscape to the throng of women. There were groups everywhere, chatting, laughing, and milling about with drinks in hand. Some wore golf gear, while others sported casual sundresses or sporty leggings. An unsurprising number of rainbow-themed pins, hats, and shirts dotted the crowd, subtle signals that this wasn't just a golf event but a gathering of like-minded women. There was an easy camaraderie and a shared sense of belonging.

Sam was no outsider at this event. As they moved through the crowd, women greeted her with smiles, waves, and friendly touches on the arm. "Hey, Sam!" called one wearing a Callaway cap and aviators. "Looking good, girl!"

Sam grinned and waved back, glowing. Another woman stopped to give her a hug and to chat about how great it was to see her again.

Catrina followed a step behind, watching the interactions with admiration. "Do you know everyone here?" she asked jokingly as another woman gave Sam a bright "Hi!" while walking past.

"Ha. No," Sam said over her shoulder, flashing a smile. "But this is my scene. These are my people."

Catrina couldn't help but grin. She loved seeing Sam in her element, commanding attention in a low-key manner. Sam was the interim mayor of Torrey Pines, and Catrina enjoyed the spectacle. She hadn't seen her in this environment before. Sam's self-assurance was an inspiration and a sight to behold.

The crowd thickened as they approached a large clearing where a handful of the world's most popular golfers were teeing off. Catrina craned her neck to see, catching glimpses of the players through the sea of heads. She didn't know any of their names, but the elation in the air was contagious. Sam pointed out a few of the pros, rattling off facts about their careers. Catrina nodded along, casually listening but mostly soaking in the atmosphere—the cheers, the murmured commentary, the bright colors of the golfers' outfits against the greens and blues of the course.

As they continued walking, Sam slowed and turned back toward Catrina, her eyes sparkling. "What do you think?"

Catrina smiled with a genuine lightness she hadn't experienced in weeks. "It's . . . a lot, but in a good way. I can see why you love it."

"You haven't seen the good stuff yet," Sam said with a wink, pulling Catrina along toward another cluster of spectators. "The real fun starts at the Monarch Ridge bar afterward."

Catrina followed, getting swept up in the day and the lively, welcoming thrill of it all, her curiosity piqued.

———

Catrina and Sam stepped out of the elevator and into the bustling lobby, each dressed in a completely different style for the evening. Catrina wore a simple black dress paired with flat sandals that gave her a casual elegance. Her hair, damp from the shower, was down, and she'd applied enough makeup to highlight her features without being overdone. Sam exuded effortless confidence, wearing a deep emerald-green jumpsuit with a plunging neckline, her strappy heels clicking on the floor. Her hair, styled into loose waves, framed her face, and the delicate gold jewelry she wore added a subtle touch.

The bar was alive with a vibrant blend of tournament attendees mingling with hotel guests. The modern bar design featured floor-to-ceiling windows that offered a view of the terrace outside. Inside, low leather seating was arranged around wood tables, and the bar itself was a centerpiece—an elegant stretch of fine polished wood backed by glass shelves showcasing premium liquor bottles.

On the terrace, tournament banners fluttered in the breeze, and clusters of people sipped cocktails under strings of fairy lights. Conversations ranged from hushed exchanges between sponsors to animated laughter from groups of fans recounting the day's highlights. A musician played acoustic guitar in the corner. His vocals blurred the line between singing and the guttural cry of a strangled cat.

Ever the social butterfly, Sam greeted people with warm familiarity, her pluck evident as she exchanged handshakes, hugs, and jokey banter. Catrina soaked in the lively ambiance and marveled at how seamlessly Sam fit into this world.

"Drinks," Sam said. She led the way to the bar, where the bartender mixed for a waiting group of tournament attendees.

When they caught the bartender's attention, Sam opted for a gin and tonic, while Catrina hesitated before choosing a white wine. They both stood at the bar, watching their fellow patrons obliviously milling.

"This is really nice. Thanks for including me," Catrina said.

"I'm happy you're enjoying it. I love coming here every year."

"I can see why. You're a celebrity," Catrina teased.

"Nah," Sam said. "Ready to see the *good stuff*?" she asked, her playfulness and mischievous grin charming.

Catrina smiled, relaxing as the night stretched out ahead of them, full of possibility.

Catrina was nursing her third glass of wine at the bar while Sam scrolled through her phone. The bar at the Monarch Ridge La Jolla was still juiced, though the diehards were gradually replacing the casual tournament attendees, presumably looking for the *good stuff*. This was the perfect end to the Tim-assisted week from hell, hanging out with her best friend in an atmosphere where she was blissfully anonymous.

Sam nudged her with an elbow, smirking as she glanced toward the people gathered by the terrace. "See the guy in the green blazer? He's been staring at you."

Catrina laughed, shaking her head. "Yeah, sure."

"He is. Don't underestimate yourself, Cat. You look hot."

Before Catrina could respond, a woman walked toward them from the lobby. She was about thirty-five and fit, with closely cropped, partially shaved hair and an air of intrigue.

Sam's face lit up like a Christmas tree. "Here comes my *fitness instructor*," Sam said, drawing out the word *fitness* in a way that made Catrina blush.

The woman tapped Sam on the shoulder, and Sam turned, her grin widening. "That's my cue," she said, glancing back at Catrina. "You good?"

Catrina faked a smile. "Yeah, of course. Go. Have fun. Text me later—I'll be here or upstairs."

Sam gave her a light pat on the shoulder before leaving with the fitness instructor. Catrina tried to hold on to her feigned excitement, but her face dropped as soon as Sam disappeared. She stared at her glass, swirling the wine absentmindedly. Her reaction surprised her. She was inexplicably sad. Disappointed. And she didn't understand why. Sam wasn't ditching her; she wasn't doing anything wrong. Hell, Catrina was the tagalong. She even vaguely recalled Sam mentioning the fitness instructor the night before.

She sipped her wine, trying to rationalize her emotions. Sam had been generous to bring her today, to include her in this beautiful world. *Of course she was going to meet someone. She definitely mentioned a fitness instructor. That was the reason we came. One of them, at least. I should be happy for Sam.* But instead, she was gutted. She ordered a whiskey, hoping to drown the confusing swirl of emotions pulling her under.

As she sipped the fresh drink, her sadness deepened. She told herself it was the exhaustion from the day in the sun, the stress of the week, the dehydration, the wine. Anything but the truth she didn't want to face. Jealousy didn't make sense; Sam was her best friend.

Catrina's thoughts were interrupted by the arrival of a man sliding onto the stool next to her. He looked like a business traveler —mid-forties, neatly dressed, with an expensive watch and a polite, if tired, smile.

"Busy night here," he said, motioning to the crowded bar. "Didn't realize I booked a room during a golf tournament. I thought I was getting a quiet night in La Jolla before work tomorrow."

Catrina gave him a cursory glance and a fake smile. "Yeah, it's been packed all night."

He smiled back, signaling the bartender. "Well, I suppose I can't complain. Makes for interesting people-watching."

Catrina nodded, but her attention drifted. The man appeared harmless, someone trying to make small talk, but she wasn't in the mood. Her thoughts circled back to Sam—her smile, her laugh, how she had sensually touched Catrina's back before leaving with that *fitness instructor*. Catrina understood it wasn't fair to be mad at Sam, but she couldn't shake the feeling of rejection.

"My name is Derek. Are you here for the tournament?" the businessman asked.

"Catrina. Something like that," she replied, taking another sip of her wine. She didn't want to be rude, but she also didn't want to engage. She was preoccupied, tangled in thoughts she couldn't name or understand.

The man nodded, sensing her lack of interest. He turned his attention back to the bartender, and Catrina was grateful for the silence. She needed to think, to sort through the mess of emotions swirling inside her. The more she tried, the more confused she was. Sam's absence pressed her irrationally and undeniably. No amount of wine was helping the feelings go away. Worse, she was sitting with Derek, the business traveler. *Blech. Derek is sitting on Sam's stool. Well, it was her stool. She ditched it for some skank. We should be sitting together, laughing about the day.* Instead, Catrina was alone.

As the sting of Sam's disappearance settled deeper, Catrina pushed the thought aside and leaned into the small talk. "Are you from San Diego County?" Catrina asked.

"Pasadena. I drove down after dinner. Have a meeting tomorrow," Derek said.

They exchanged pleasantries over another drink. Soon, a step past tipsy and done with the noise in her head, Catrina turned to Derek and moved from small talk to flirtation. "How'd you manage to pick the one straight woman in this bar?"

Derek chuckled. "Didn't pick. It was the only open seat."

"A happy accident," Catrina responded, a little sloppy.

After a few minutes, Derek glanced at his watch, paid his tab, and stood. "I should get to bed. Tomorrow is going to suck. It was a pleasure chatting with you, Catrina."

Before she could think better of it, the words slipped out. "Do you want company?"

The man blinked, surprised. "Uh, sure. I could go for another drink upstairs if you're game."

Catrina didn't dither. She paid her bar tab and followed him toward the elevators in a haze of alcohol and impulse.

Catrina lay in bed as the dimly lit hotel room cast a depressing shadow over her black dress on the floor. Derek's snoring cut through the otherwise oppressive silence. It was after eleven, approaching midnight, and shame clung to her like a weighted blanket. She stared at the ceiling, desolate, replaying her impulsive decisions. Her phone rumbled, jolting her out of her thoughts. It was Sam.

> U still at the bar or back in the room? wanna hang out?

Catrina's mood shifted, and she scrambled out of bed. She pulled on her dress quietly to avoid an awkward farewell conversation. Her fingers flew across her phone as she typed.

> Wherever u are, I'll b there.

As she hurried toward the elevator, her phone pinged again.

> One chill drink at the bar? then crash. checkout's not till noon.

Catrina exhaled and stepped into the elevator, her reflection in the steel staring back at her. She didn't recognize herself— disheveled, restless, and suddenly desperate to erase the past hour.

When the doors opened, she nearly collided with Sam, equally disheveled, stepping out of a different elevator. Sam had a flushed, satisfied glow on her face, her hair mussed and her jumpsuit askew. Catrina froze, unsure how to react.

Sam, ever quick with a quip, smirked and said, "Looks like you also got to see *the good stuff*. That's amazing!"

"Yeah, something like that." Catrina gestured toward the bar, eager to change the subject. "Shall we?"

Sam smiled. "Absolutely. Let's go."

As they walked side by side, Catrina's emotions churned in a frantic, unrelenting spiral. Every step was heavier than the last.

The low ambient conversation faded into the background as they settled at a corner table. Catrina nursed a glass of wine, already dizzy and out of sorts, her grip tight around the stem as if it might anchor her in place. Sam was in a great mood, swirling her glass of red wine, her casual demeanor contrasting with the storm of guilt and confusion inside Catrina.

Sam broke the silence, her tone light. "So what did I miss? Meet a guy at the bar?"

"A business traveler," Catrina said.

Sam studied Catrina, presumably waiting for her to elaborate. She did not.

"Not marriage material . . . got it," Sam joked.

Catrina forced a shrug.

"Fair enough," Sam said, letting it drop. She took a sip of her drink. "You wouldn't believe the night I had," she began. "After we left the bar, we went up to her room. We ended up talking for a bit. She plans to hike the Pacific Crest Trail next year." Sam laughed and continued. "And she . . . well, let's say we click, you know? She's very, very good. Excellent, actually."

"Going to see her again?" Catrina asked, visibly annoyed.

Sam didn't seem to pick up on Catrina's annoyance. "Maybe next year, no rush. I'm not in good enough shape to see her more often," Sam said, then took another sip of her drink.

Catrina nodded as Sam continued sharing details, more graphic by the sip.

When Sam finally ran out of steam, she said, "You've been quiet. What's going on?"

Catrina set her glass down. "I . . . I am a mess."

"Sure, but so is everybody else. Sort of the point of this event. Let your freak flag fly."

Catrina clenched her hands in her lap. "I went upstairs and fucked him."

Sam didn't react. "Okay," she said carefully. "And?"

Catrina's words spilled out in a rush. "And I don't know why I did it. He was happy to go to sleep. I invited myself up."

"Good for you. You wanted it, and you got it."

Catrina started crying, surprising herself. "I'm my mother, Sam," she said, tears spilling down her cheeks. Her hands quivered as she clenched them on the table. "I worked my whole life to be better, and I'm not. I'm about to lose my job. I'm about to be bankrupt. I might go to jail. And I slept with a stranger tonight. I've slept with Tim for years. I'm my mother. I'm her all over again."

Her cries cracked into a sob, raw and guttural, as the words poured out like poison. "I worked so hard. I gave up everything. I stayed . . . I stayed for my mom, lost the scholarship, and stole for Tim for this job that I hate. And for what? For this? To end up like this?" Her breathing came in ugly, shallow gasps as she entered the full-on sobbing stage. "I'm Morven. I'm her. I'm going to lose everything, and it's all my fault." Her hands shot up to cover her face, her shoulders heaving as her sobs echoed in the quiet space.

Sam, alarmed but composed, immediately slid into the seat next to her, wrapping an arm around her shaking frame. "You're not your mother, Catrina," she said. She began stroking Catrina's hair, her touch gentle. "You're not her. You've made mistakes, yeah, but you're not her. You're human. You're struggling. But you're not alone, okay? I'm here."

Catrina shook her head violently, her hands still covering her face. "You don't get it," she sobbed. "You don't know what it's like to look in the mirror and hate what you see. I can't fix this. I can't fix myself. I've ruined everything. I'll end up like her—broke, desperate, and completely lost. I committed crimes, Sam."

"It's not that bad," Sam said soothingly.

"I committed *crimes*. It was me. For my mom. For Tim. Crimes.

Federal crimes. They were too dumb to do it right, so I did it for them. I did their dirty work." She let out a strangled sob, quivering with self-loathing. "I'm absolute garbage. Irredeemable trash!"

"Take a breath, Catrina. You're unraveling," Sam said.

Catrina's hands slid down her face, revealing eyes swollen and red with tears, and she looked at Sam as if begging for condemnation, for someone to affirm the ugliness. "Who does that, Sam? Who risks everything for people who use them? I can't blame anyone. I did it. I'm the one who made the choices." Her despair, fueled by years of repression and hours of alcohol, was bottomless, an abyss pulling her under with every word.

Sam tightened her hold. "Catrina, listen to me. You aren't her. You're not. You're allowed to feel like this, but we're not doing this here, okay? We're not sitting in this bar while you fall apart." She stood, guiding Catrina to her feet. "Let's go to the room. Come on, you don't need to do this here. Let's get you somewhere private, somewhere safe."

Catrina's legs began to move on autopilot as Sam wrapped an arm around her shoulders and led her toward the elevators. Her sobs continued, quieter now but still shaking her entire body. Sam held her close, whispering reassurances as they stepped into the elevator.

As the doors closed, Sam whispered, "You're not your mother."

CHAPTER 20

Saturday, March 17, 2012 | Sydney

I t had been a week since the Aussie of the Year fiasco. After a long and open discussion, Julia and Marcus had agreed to leave things casual for now. Marcus wanted to progress the relationship but respected Julia's timeline. It helped that Marcus would be on an international tour with the national team for a few months.

As Julia arrived at the taverna, the smell of grease and coffee hit her like a warm blanket, but the place's meter was off. Gus was behind the counter, flipping through the day's receipts. He looked up as she entered, his expression dead serious. "Tzoúlia," he called out, setting the papers aside. "Your mum called. She's looking for you."

Julia groaned, slipping behind the counter to grab her apron. "Seriously? Did she say why?"

"No, but she sounded . . . upset. You need to call her back."

Julia sighed, reaching for the phone, fearing terrible news. Alice rarely called.

Her mom answered on the first ring. "Julia, finally!"

"I just got to work, Mum," Julia said, irritated. "What's going on?"

Her mother's voice wavered. "It's your dad . . . He's very sick, Julia. You need to come now."

Julia froze, the words landing like a punch to the gut. "What do you mean, sick? What happened? He was fine a few weeks back."

"He collapsed at home and has been diagnosed with pancreatic cancer. The doctors say it's advanced, and . . . there's not much time. Please, come."

"Okay. I'll come tonight after my shift."

"Now, Julia. Now," Alice said.

Julia hung up without another word, staring blankly at the phone as the reality of her mother's words sank in. The last time she had seen her dad was when she had brought Marcus to meet him for the first—and, as it turned out, only—time. He had seemed fine then, his usual stern and commanding self. She recalled Alice mentioning his low energy and going to the doctor, but her mom hadn't seemed worried. Now he was dying? It didn't make sense.

Gus looked up from the counter, concern etched on his face. "Everything okay?"

Julia shook her head. "My dad's . . . dying. I need to get over there."

Gus frowned, taken aback. "I'm sorry, Julia. Has he been sick?"

"Not that I know of," she said. "I just saw him two months ago. He was fine. Mum said his energy had been low, but he bounced off the walls that night. This is . . . sudden."

"Go. Don't worry about the shift. I'll cover it," Gus said.

"I'll be back in a few hours," Julia said, untying her apron. "I just . . . I need to check on this."

"Take your time. Don't wait for the bus. Is Marcus around?" Gus asked.

"No. He's in New Zealand."

"That's right. Here, take my car," Gus said, pulling his keys out of his pocket and placing them in her hand.

Julia held the keys like foreign objects. "I can take the bus."

"You need to get over there. Just go," Gus urged.

Julia stared at him, her emotions swirling too fast to pin down. Gratitude, panic, disbelief. She nodded, gripping the keys tightly in her hand. "Thanks, Gus."

"Go," he repeated, moving to take her spot behind the counter. "And, Julia, if you need anything, call me."

As Julia pulled Gus's 1995 Holden Commodore with its faded green paint and squeaky brakes up to the Corning residence in Mosman, she inhaled, steeling herself.

The scent of hardwood cleaner and freshly brewed tea greeted her as she entered the house, but it did little to settle her nerves. Alice was waiting in the hallway, her arms crossed, and an expression of exasperation etched across her face.

"It's been nine weeks, Julia. Nine whole weeks since you've come home," Alice said.

Julia let out a small huff, taking her shoes off near the entryway. "Nine weeks, and not once did you call or email to say that Dad is sick," she shot back, her irritation bubbling to the surface.

"I wanted to tell you in person," Alice said. "It never occurred to me you'd miss nine Sundays in a row."

"The last one wasn't a pleasant experience, was it?"

"What are you talking about? It went great," Alice said.

"Dad was—never mind."

Alice opened her mouth to continue, but Julia raised a hand to cut her off. "Where is he?"

Alice's shoulders sagged as the fight drained from her posture. "He's in the study. I'm sorry, love."

Julia turned and headed down the hallway, her footsteps heavy on the hardwood floor. She didn't look back, focusing entirely on what awaited behind that door.

She hesitated, her hand gripping the frame as she entered the transformed space. Ray's study, the epicenter of his world, no longer resembled the commanding room she had grown up tiptoeing around. The massive mahogany desk that had once anchored the space was gone, replaced by a hospital bed that was jarringly out of place amidst the relics of Ray's life, and yet, the room retained its essence: a personal museum—soon to be mausoleum—dedicated to the man who had spent his life cultivating an image of control and authority. The built-in shelves, packed with neatly aligned books, loomed over the bed like silent witnesses to his decline. His awards and plaques were prominently placed facing the bed, inscriptions detailing decades of academic and athletic achievements. Framed photographs lined the walls, capturing moments when Ray had stood shoulder to shoulder with notable figures—headmasters, politicians, and cricket legends—each a testament to the life he'd built. On the far wall, cricket memorabilia dominated: bats signed by players, framed scorecards from historic matches, and game-used stumps from the Melbourne Cricket Ground. They were all displayed like spoils of modern antiquity. The study reeked of nostalgia and self-importance, an undeniable reminder of who Ray was, even as he lay reduced and fragile.

The air was thick with the smell of antiseptic. The man in the hospital bed barely resembled the father who had once towered over her. His once-robust frame was gaunt, his skin pale and yellowed, and yet, in this state, his eyes—smart and calculating—still carried authority, the unrelenting expectation that even dying ought to be done his way.

Ray's voice, raspy but deliberate, broke the silence. "Julia," he began, his tone still carrying the cadence of the headmaster, "good of you to finally come. Doctors say I won't last the month."

Julia blinked, startled by the bluntness of the grim prognosis. She moved closer and sat in the chair placed beside the bed, her feet brushing the edge of the rug that had once sat under his desk. "How did this happen so fast? You were fine when I brought Marcus to brunch. Your energy was good."

Ray exhaled, his chest rising and falling with visible effort. "Pancreatic cancer," he stated, as though reciting from a textbook. "Rarely found early. By the time symptoms appear, it's usually too late. Mine . . . mine has progressed aggressively." He lifted a frail hand, motioning vaguely toward the shelves. "Do you know anything about this cancer and its symptoms?"

Julia shook her head, unsure whether he was seeking an answer or preparing to educate her.

"Belly pain that radiates to the sides or back," he began. "Loss of appetite. Weight loss. Jaundice. Light-colored or floating stools." He paused, swallowing hard before continuing. "Dark urine. Itching. Fatigue. Blood clots causing pain and swelling in the limbs."

Julia shifted uncomfortably, the list of symptoms more of an indictment than an explanation. "Dad—" she said.

"It progresses quickly, Julia. Stage four in less than a year. The body turns against itself with terrifying efficiency," Ray said.

She clenched her hands in her lap, resisting the urge to tell him to stop. The scholarly details, delivered in his methodical tone, were unnecessary yet oddly fitting. This was Ray, after all—the man who sought control through knowledge, even in the face of the uncontrollable.

"You should've gone to the doctor sooner," she said. "All those symptoms—"

"I thought I could manage it," he interrupted. "There's always something to be done, something more important than my discomfort." His eyes drifted toward a cricket bat signed by Mark Taylor mounted on the wall. "I've spent my life powering through. But not this. Not this."

Julia bit her lip. This was a concession she had never expected to hear from her father. For so long, he had been the unyielding presence in her life, a man who demanded obedience and allowed no room for vulnerability. She skimmed the room, her eyes landing on the framed photographs that taunted her with reminders of his storied past. "Why here?" she asked. "Why set up the bed in the study?"

"This is where I've spent the best hours of my life," he said. "Where I've achieved, planned, succeeded. This room is me, Julia. If I'm going to die, I'll do it surrounded by the proof of my life's worth."

"This is absurd," Julia said under her breath, unclear whether Ray had heard her. A rush of conflicting emotions threatened to overwhelm her. The room, with its trophies and accolades, was a shrine to Ray's ego, and yet, as she looked at him now—frail and vulnerable, dwarfed by the towering shelves—she realized it was also his sanctuary, the one place where he could hold on to the illusion of control for a little longer. "Is this where you want to be remembered?" she asked.

Ray ignored the question and carried on. "I need to ask you something important," he said. "After I'm gone, I want you and Marcus to honor me at the Men's Club. Speak on my behalf. It will cement my legacy."

Julia, stunned by the sheer audacity of the request, asked, "What? Why Marcus? You met him once."

Ray frowned. "Marcus is a respectable man. The blokes would like to hear from him. Also, he's a good fit for you. A true winner."

"Not always," she shot back. "Aussie of the Year didn't go his way."

"Julia, I raised you better," he said, shaking his head. "Keep up this attitude, and Marcus is bound to leave. A national icon can have any girl. It's a blessing he picked you. Please treat him with respect. You two are the talk of the club. I'm very proud of the young woman you have become."

"*Excuse me?*" she said. "Marcus picking me makes you proud? I picked *him* and haven't decided if I'll keep him yet."

"Why wouldn't you?" he asked. "He is good for you. Stable. Respected."

"Because I'm not interested in being someone's trophy!" Julia snapped. "I want more than a relationship that looks good to your buddies or in the tabloids."

Ray's face hardened, but there was something in his eyes—hurt, maybe, or regret. "You've always been impulsive, Julia," he said. "You're my Child of the Sea—drifting, untethered, always chasing the next wave without thinking about where it will take you."

"That's rich," Julia replied, "coming from the man who spent his entire life building this fortress around his ego."

Ray sighed, lying back against the pillows. "I don't want to fight with you, Julia. I need us to work this out."

Julia sneered. "Work what out, Dad? You've spent my whole life measuring me against an impossible standard. And now you want me to give a public eulogy with Marcus Daelmans about how great you were?"

"I wasn't measuring you against an impossible standard," he said. "I was trying to prepare you for a harsh world that doesn't care about your feelings."

"No, you were scoring me against Miriam," Julia said, her words cracking like a whip. "I know her, Dad. And guess what? She's incredible. Smart, accomplished, charming. You blew it, Dad. You have a daughter like Miriam, and instead of being in her life, you used her as a measuring stick against me."

Ray moaned, the color draining from his pale face. "You don't know the whole story," he said, "and I doubt Miriam does either."

"What's that supposed to mean?"

He vacillated, looking away as if searching the room for an answer. "There are things—complications—you can't possibly understand. Decisions were made that . . . were not mine to make."

"Like your decision to cheat on Mum with foreign tourists? Spare me the cryptic excuses. You made your choices, Dad. You chose your reputation, your career, your precious Men's Club over your family. Over me. Over Miriam. Over Catrina."

Ray's lips pressed together. "You're still an ignorant loudmouth. I was faithful to Alice. You think I would hurt her?" he said. "And I lived with the regret of not knowing Miriam every day. You have no idea what you're talking about."

Julia stared at him, her anger surging. "Why didn't you do something about it?" she asked. "Why didn't you reach out to her? Why didn't you tell me the truth about my sisters?" Julia got up from the chair and headed for the door. She'd heard enough.

"Please, Julia, don't go. I need us to fix this. I can't—" He faltered, swallowing hard, raw with emotion. "I probably won't see you again."

She turned. "If you want me to stay, I need the real story, Dad. All of it. No deflections, no excuses. Tell me about Rosalind. About Miriam. Tell me why you chose not to be part of her life."

Ray's expression shifted, a flash of discomfort breaking through the sorrow etched into his features. "That's not a story you want to hear," he stammered. "It's . . . unseemly and disrespectful to the dead."

"Unseemly? You're dying, Dad. Whatever scandal you're trying to protect, whatever pretense you're clinging to, it doesn't matter anymore. Just tell me the damn truth." She took another step toward the door.

Ray's voice broke through as her fingers brushed the doorknob, his voice halting but resolute. "Wait."

She turned back slowly, crossing her arms and peering at her father. His eyes met hers. She could tell his instinctual pride was fighting against the moment's need for vulnerability.

"Fine," he said. "You want the truth? Here it is." Ray shifted uncomfortably in the bed, the crisp sheets rustling around him. He paused. "It was the summer of 1984. And before I met your mother, I met Rosalind."

"Before?" Julia asked.

"I've always been faithful to your mother," Ray said.

"What about Catrina's mum?" Julia asked.

Ray's face twisted with discomfort. "That lady . . . she's crazy."

"Do you deny the resemblance?"

Ray didn't answer. His silence was all the confirmation Julia needed, and she moved on to the topic of interest.

"What about Miriam's mum?" Julia asked.

"Rosalind Leighton Worthington," he said, the name rolling off his tongue. "She was holidaying in Sydney. A British aristocrat—tall, blonde, utterly captivating. She had this . . . presence. The kind of woman who could walk into a room and make everyone stop and stare." Ray's lips quirked in a bittersweet smile. "I was more than smitten. I was completely taken. She was everything I ever dreamed of in a partner. We spent two months together that summer. She was . . . brilliant, driven, elegant. And for some reason, she chose to spend that time with me."

Julia had never heard Ray speak this reverentially about anyone.

"She loved the ocean, like you, Julia," Ray continued. "We'd walk down to Coogee Beach nearly every evening. She kicked off her sandals and waded into the surf, her laugh echoing over the waves as the water caught her off guard. Once, we rented a small sailboat and spent the afternoon on the harbour. Rosalind was terrible at sailing," he added with a rueful chuckle. "Didn't have the faintest clue what to do, but she insisted on taking the tiller anyway. We went in circles until the boat rental guy towed us back to the dock. She was mortified but laughed about it later over supper."

He paused, staring at his hands as if the memories were playing out on his palms. "One weekend, we drove out to the Hunter Valley for a wine tour. She wore this wide-brimmed hat that made her look like she was out of a magazine. Every man in the winery envied me that day. Rosalind's taste was impeccable—she could pick out the subtle notes in any wine. Me? I was there to enjoy her company and pretended I knew the difference between Tyrrell's Vat 9 Shiraz and McWilliam's Mount Pleasant Homestead Riesling."

"Okay . . ." Julia said, searching for his point.

Ray's smile faded. "I thought it was the beginning of something real. Something permanent. I thought . . . But that's not how it ended."

Julia could see the young, hopeful Ray falling head over heels for a woman he couldn't keep. For a moment, her heart ached, which surprised and annoyed her, but her sympathy was tempered by years of resentment and the lack of personal responsibility in his words.

"And then what, Dad?" Julia asked, getting impatient.

"When she discovered we were pregnant, I was thrilled," Ray said. "I was very happy. It was my duty, my honor, to propose marriage. I planned a life together. I could fit into her world. I offered to move to London immediately."

"And?" Julia prompted.

"And I was a fool. Rosalind refused. Her family disapproved—not just of me but of the whole scandal. Getting pregnant by a bloody commoner from Australia? Unthinkable. We're still viewed as an island of convicts in those circles. She said she would return to England and raise the child without my involvement."

The silence in the room was heavy, charged. Julia stared at him, mouth agape. "So what? You let her go? You didn't fight for her?"

"I protested. She got on the plane anyway. I wrote dozens of letters. Rosalind didn't respond. A year later, I got an envelope with a single photo of Miriam. I mailed a stuffed koala from Taronga Zoo to the return address." Ray broke down. "What else could I do? She was determined. She had the resources, the power, the family name. She claimed it was better this way for Miriam."

"Dad, Miriam—Mir, her friends call her—she still has that koala. To this day. And she knows it was from you. She took it in her carry-on when she moved from London to Los Angeles."

The words landed like a physical blow. Ray's shoulders shook, and for a moment, Julia wasn't sure if he understood her. But then, the sobs came—deep cries that shattered the air between them. Julia stared, caught between her frustration and a pity she wasn't prepared to feel. She had never seen him like this, vulnerable in a way that stripped away all the authority, arrogance, and pride he had worn her entire life.

"Dad," she said, reaching for a handkerchief on the shelf. She handed it to him carefully, unsure if he'd take it.

Ray fumbled for the cloth, his hands jerking as he clutched it to his face. He buried himself in it, his sobs muffled but no less raw. Julia shifted uncomfortably, resisting the urge to look away. She had wanted him to feel something, to reckon with the choices he had made and the people he had hurt—but this? This was too much. Almost.

He drew a shaky breath, trying and failing to compose himself. "She kept it," he whimpered through the handkerchief. "All these years . . . she kept it."

Julia nodded, swallowing hard. "Yeah. It reminded her that, somewhere out there, her father cared."

Ray's sobs slowed, though his face remained crumpled with grief. He lowered the handkerchief, revealing eyes red and glassy, and looked at her with an expression she had never seen before—utter defeat. "I—I wanted her to have something from me. Something . . .

to hold on to. But I never thought . . . Every year, Rosalind sent me a photograph of Miriam on her birthday. I have them all here."

"Photos?" Julia asked.

"Yes. I want you to have them. They're on the sideboard. All the photos of Miriam, and a few of Rosalind and me. When you see Miriam . . ."

Julia stood up, picked up the envelope of photos, and put them on her lap as she sat. "I'll give it to her. Though I can't promise she'll look."

Ray swallowed hard, his head dropping to the bed. "I missed her whole life. The photos weren't enough. But they were all I had."

Julia shook her head with disappointment. "You know what's worse, Dad? You didn't just miss her life; you used her as a mythical figure. A perfect daughter you could hold over my head every time I didn't live up to your expectations. Do you have any idea what that's done to me?"

Ray dipped his head but didn't speak.

"And all those nights watching *Night Nurses*. You couldn't have liked that show. You were admiring and pining for your favorite daughter, weren't you? Watching her succeed and contrasting her with your loser surfie-bum daughter. You see that? You get that forcing us to watch your better, more talented daughter was sick. Right?"

Ray looked up, his eyes filled with tears. "I never meant to—" He stumbled. "Julia, I never meant for my past to hurt us. I love you dearly. I've lived with this guilt every day, and I'm sorry . . . sorry that it came between us."

Julia stood at the foot of the bed, arms crossed, her expression alternating between defiance and exhaustion. "Miriam was the daughter you wanted, wasn't she? Perfect, impeccable, ambitious. I wish you got to know her—not the idea of her, but the real her. She isn't perfect, Dad. She has real, difficult issues. Her mother, your dream girl, died in 2009—and it was very public. Why didn't you reach out?"

"I should've. I regret not doing so."

"She's battled addiction too. Probably inherited from Grandpa. You could have helped her."

"What? I didn't know." Ray looked devastated as he seemed to be processing Julia's words.

"Yes. But she'll beat it. She's strong." Julia took a deep breath. "I'm sorry you missed the chance to know Miriam. She's not the perfect idealization of yours. She's a whole person—with strengths, weaknesses, and everything in between. She's amazing," Julia said.

Ray didn't respond. His head rested against the pillow. His tired eyes closed as though her words were too heavy to bear.

For a moment, Julia softened, letting her anger fade. She studied the lines on his face, etched more profoundly than she remembered, and sat with him for the next thirty minutes as he slept. Each breath he took sounded painful and labored. His lungs fluttered faintly, like waves receding from the shore.

Julia stood. "Goodbye, Dad," she said, bending down to kiss him on the cheek.

The gesture was deliberate, its sincerity pointed. As she turned to the door, for the first time, she saw her surfing competition trophy prominently displayed on his shelf. A tear ran down her face, and she fought back a sob. She walked out of the study forever.

———

Julia returned to the taverna, her eyes unfocused, staring at some distant point far beyond the scuffed linoleum floor. She gripped Gus's keys tightly, her knuckles white against the faded metal, and handed them to him without a word. Her shoulders were stiff, her movements automatic.

Gus looked at her, his brow creased. "You don't have to be here, Tzoúlia."

"I'd rather work, Gus."

He didn't argue, which Julia appreciated. She was raw, emotionally exhausted. Gus stepped closer, and before she could retreat into her usual defenses, he wrapped her in one of his signature bear hugs. It was the kind of hug that didn't need words and made the world less overwhelming. Julia stood still, her arms pinned awkwardly against her sides, but she didn't resist. She let herself be held. Her nod was imperceptible as she pulled back, but it carried a gratitude she couldn't express.

She tied her apron as Gus had taught her seventeen months before. The familiar routine grounded her as she reached for her order pad. With a small breath, she squared her shoulders and stepped back into the flow of the taverna, snapping into work mode as if flipping a switch. Right now, she had tables to serve and coffee to make. And she was happy for it.

CHAPTER 21

Sunday, March 25, 2012 | Sydney

J ulia started her morning by going to the internet café to check
her email. She'd called Alice at the end of her shift the previous
night and had been told her dad wasn't doing well and it was
time to transfer him to palliative care. Julia had asked if she should
come over, but Alice had said he was sleeping and there was no
point. Alice had promised to email an update Sunday morning,
which she had—no change in condition. Julia responded that she
could be called at the taverna if anything changed.

The place was quiet. Dead, really. The recently posted sign read
Closed on Sundays, but Gus often came in for a couple of hours to
serve coffee and day-old sandwiches to the post-church crowd. It was
a tradition that reminded him of when he had first opened the shop
and was running it himself, but as he got older, he did it less
frequently. A table of two regulars sat by the window, mugs of coffee
in their hands, engaged in an animated conversation with Gus.

"Tzoúlia!" Gus called, waving her over. "Sit! Sit!"

Julia smiled but didn't say a word. She'd told Gus the night before
that she might stop in to use the phone.

Gus was engrossed in his conversation, which Julia appreciated because she didn't want to talk. She made herself a coffee and then pulled up a chair and watched the banter unfold.

"Gus, mate," said Bruce, an old-timer with a broad face and a shock of gray hair, "you've been running this place since 1979. The menu hasn't changed once."

"Not a damn thing!" chimed in Perry, the other regular, who had a wiry build. "Still the same souvlaki, the same moussaka, the same baklava. Don't you ever get tired of it, mate?"

Gus crossed his arms over his chest, his mustache twitching as he gave them both a mock glare. "When someone invents better Greek food, I'll update the menu. Until then . . ."

Bruce and Perry roared with laughter as if Gus had just delivered the joke of the year. Julia smirked; she had heard this exact exchange between these men a dozen times. Perry shook his head, wiping a pretend tear from the corner of his eye. "Come on, Gus. You're stuck in the past. You've got the same menu, sign, and decor. And don't get me started on that apron. How old is that thing? Older than Julia here?"

Gus scoffed, waving a dismissive hand. "This apron is a classic! You don't mess with a classic."

"Classic, my arse. That thing's so threadbare, it could qualify as antique linen."

Julia stifled a laugh as Gus puffed out his chest. "This apron is clean. More importantly, it has character. What more do you want?"

Perry wasn't letting up. "And these curtains—what's this? Velvet? You buy them during the Whitlam administration?"

Julia watched the exchange with amusement. This was Gus in his element—bantering, arguing, laughing. It was the side of him that made the taverna more than just a place to eat. It was a community, a little slice of life where everyone had their role to play. And today, her role was to listen, which was what she needed as she waited for her mom to call.

"Hey, Gus. Remind us how you ended up in Australia," Bruce said.

"It's a long story, and I don't want to bore young Tzoúlia," Gus said.

"Please tell it, Gus. We haven't heard the 2012 revisions yet," Bruce teased.

"No revisions. The story has never changed," Gus protested.

"Sure, sure. Remind us, then. We're old, and our memories are failing," Perry said.

"Alright, alright. If you insist, I'll tell it. But you might regret asking. It's not a short tale, my friends."

"We've got time, Gus," Perry said.

"All you have is time, Perry," Gus said, folding his arms across his chest before settling into one of his favorite stories. "I was born in a small village outside Thessaloniki. It was a simple life, you know? My father was a farmer—wheat, olives, a few goats—and my mother, well, she kept the house. I was the second youngest of six. Life was hard, but we didn't know it. It was just . . . life."

"Six kids. Your mum had her hands full," Bruce said.

"She was a saint! And let me tell you, it wasn't an easy time to be Greek. When I was born, the Second World War had ended, and Greece was in a state of chaos. The civil war came right after. My father fought on the side of the government, but not because he wanted to. He had no choice. You fought, or you disappeared. That's how it was."

Bruce raised his eyebrows. "Civil war?"

"Oh, it was brutal," Gus said, his expression darkening. "Brother against brother. The communists on one side, the government backed by the British and the Americans on the other. Villages like ours were caught in the middle. The army would come and take food from us, and then the rebels would come and take whatever was left. There was no peace. People disappeared all the time. My father survived, but he came back . . . different. Quieter. Meaner."

Perry nodded solemnly.

Gus rubbed his chin. "Yes, but it wasn't just the civil war. After it ended, things didn't get better. The 1950s and '60s in Greece were awful. The government was corrupt, the economy was in ruins, and there was no future for people like us. My father worked himself to the bone, but it was never enough. There was always a tax, always someone with their hand out."

Julia shifted in her seat, her eyes fixed on Gus. He glanced at her before continuing. "By the time I was a teenager, I had no future in my village. I worked the fields, sure, but I also took odd jobs—anything to make a bit of money. My brother Nico and I looked for ways to make extra money in the underground economy. My father used to say, 'Gus, you're too clever for this place.' I don't think he meant it as a compliment."

"Did you have to break the law?" Perry asked.

"No. But you had to be resourceful. Find opportunities. Nico and I were teenagers. We did our best."

"And then the dictatorship?" Bruce asked.

"Good history, Bruce. Yes, 1967. The colonels took over. They called it the Regime of the Colonels. At first, they said they were saving Greece from communism, that they were protecting us. But it didn't take long to see they were tyrants. They censored everything: newspapers, radio, books, music. It was banned if it wasn't in line with a 'pure' Greece. Even Theodorakis, our great composer, was outlawed."

Julia listened intently, watching the emotions flicker across Gus's face as he continued. He seemed to speak not to Bruce and Perry but to the past, reliving those formative years.

"So how did Australia come into it?" Bruce asked.

Gus smiled faintly. "The Australian government—they were shrewd. They needed workers, men to build their cities and their infrastructure. After World War II, they opened their doors to immigrants. Italians, Greeks, Yugoslavs—we came in waves. They put out advertisements, promising good wages and a new life. They sent recruiters to Greece, to villages like mine. I remember seeing the posters: *Australia Needs You!* They showed pictures of Sydney Harbour. The Opera House was still under construction. It looked like a dream."

Perry raised an eyebrow. "And just like that, you decided to leave?"

"Not just like that. Leaving wasn't easy. My parents didn't want me to go. 'Stay,' they said. 'Stay and help the family.' But how could I help them if I stayed? There was nothing for me in Greece. I could do more good in Australia, where I would earn and send money home. I was twenty-four. My brother Nico was only twenty-one. He begged me to come. I couldn't say no to him, so we made the decision together. We left in 1972."

Bruce nodded. "Must've been tough."

"It was," Gus admitted. "We sold what little we had. We scraped together enough for the boat tickets. It was a long journey—weeks at sea. But every day, I told myself, *This is the right choice. This is the future.*"

"And when you got here? What was it like?" Perry asked.

Gus's face lit up. "When I stepped off that boat in Sydney Harbour, I felt alive. The sun, the open space, the city's energy— nothing like Greece. Everything was possible here. Nico and I were ready to work and build a new life. We didn't know the language but had our hands and determination."

Bruce clapped him on the shoulder. "You're a tough bugger, Gus."

Gus smiled, his eyes glancing toward the photo of Nico on the wall. "Toughness was all we had. Australia gave us a chance. I'll always be grateful to my adopted country."

The table went silent. Julia let the sound of Gus's voice—and Bruce and Perry's cheeky interruptions—fade into the background as she sipped her coffee. However Gus had gotten here, she was glad his sacrifices and hard work had led to him opening this little taverna she loved.

Bruce broke the silence. "So what'd you do when you got off the boat?"

Gus's face lit up with a smile. "Ah, but that's a story for another day, my friends," he said, clapping his hands together. "Enough of my old stories. Go home to your families. I'm locking up."

At 12:30, Bruce and Perry had paid their bills and gone. Gus went to take out the trash when the phone rang.

"Greek Taverna. Julia speaking."

"Julia?" Alice asked.

"Yes, it's me, Mum."

"Your father is nonresponsive. I called the ambulance. Meet us at Royal North Shore Hospital."

Julia hung up, calm but in a daze.

"Tzoúlia, is it your dad?" Gus asked.

"Yes, he's nonresponsive. An ambulance is taking him to North Shore."

"I'll drive you."

"I didn't make it. He's gone," Julia told Gus.

They were in a stark, utilitarian waiting room with rows of plastic chairs, some scuffed, facing low tables stacked with battered magazines. The harsh fluorescent lights illuminated pale, neutral-toned walls, and an antiseptic scent permeated the air.

Gus didn't say a word. He stood up and hugged her.

"Mum is back there talking to the nursing staff," Julia said. "He died during transport. The doctor just confirmed it. She didn't want me to see him like that."

Gus patted her head as she crumpled against his shoulder.

A few minutes later, Alice emerged, her expression flat, her movements stiff, as if in shock. She had trouble maintaining eye contact with Julia as she sat next to her in the waiting room. Julia tried to speak, to comfort her, but Alice wasn't ready. They sat together in silence until Alice finally said, "Go home with Gus. There's nothing more for you to do here."

Julia protested—she wanted to stay, to help—but Alice shook her head, stating that the next few hours would be nothing but paperwork and it would be rough. Reluctantly, Julia agreed to leave, but before she stepped away, she promised to help with the funeral arrangements after work.

———————

On the drive back to Manly, Julia asked Gus, "Will you finish the story? What happened when you got off the boat?"

"I'm very sorry about your dad. I'll pray for you and your mother."

"Thanks. But, seriously, please finish the story."

"You don't want to hear my old stories today, Tzoúlia," Gus said.

"Please. Your stories help me. More than you know. At the taverna, with Bruce and Perry, that's the calmest I've been all week."

"I understand. But you know this one. I arrived with Nico. We built the Opera House. I met Maria. I moved to Manly and opened the taverna," Gus said.

Julia cracked the slightest smile. "You got off the boat in 1972?"

"Yes."

"The Opera House was finished in 1973. You and Nico worked fast."

Gus shrugged. "Of course, I tell that as a joke because the real story is too painful."

"Oh. I'm sorry, Gus. It's okay. I didn't want to—"

"Only Maria knows the full history."

"I didn't mean to pry."

"No, no. Tzoúlia, I'll tell you. Maybe you need to hear it today. Perhaps it can help in some small way. I also dealt with an unexpected loss of family."

"Nico?" Julia asked.

"Yes, Nico. My baby brother. We arrived at Sydney Harbour with nothing but a suitcase and the clothing on our backs. Nico was full of life, always pushing forward. For the first three years, we did everything together. We lived in the same room, worked the same jobs, and spent our free time exploring this welcoming new country."

Gus paused, his eyes glazing over as the memories surfaced.

"Construction was all we did. It was hard work and long hours, but it paid well, and we sent money back to Greece. We were heroes back home. At first, Nico was like me. He worked and kept his head down. But after a while, he got tired of it. We discussed opening a restaurant, like every immigrant laborer. It was a common dream."

Julia stayed silent, her eyes never leaving Gus.

"He started looking for shortcuts. And in Sydney, there are shortcuts. One of the reasons you and I get along is you don't take shortcuts."

"And I'm stubborn," Julia said.

"Like a Greek mule," Gus said.

"Just like you."

"Yes, like me," Gus said. "Nico found the Greek Syndicate. Organized crime. At first, it was small things—running numbers, taking illegal sport bets, moving a little cash for them. But Nico was ambitious. He advanced quickly and became an enforcer. Muscle," Gus said, pointing to his flexed bicep. Julia noticed his eyes were welling up.

"Nico'd come home late with pockets full of money, wearing a grin that didn't sit right."

"You didn't get involved?" Julia asked.

"Never," Gus said firmly. "Nico tried to pull me in. I refused. He complained that I was too proud, missing out on life-changing money. But I didn't want that life. I didn't want to live looking over my shoulder for the police or gangsters. The arguments started small, but they grew. It created distance between us. Distance we never had before. He started spending more time with them and less with me."

There was a pause, and then Gus continued. "Then we had our biggest fight. I was still sending most of my wages back to Greece. Nico . . . he called me a mug. Said I was wasting money on peasants. He said they were old, that we owed them nothing. I disagreed and yelled at him. Called him a crook. He shoved me to the floor and walked out." Gus shook his head. "That was the last time I saw him. A few weeks later, he died in a construction accident."

Julia's breath hitched. "Gus . . . I'm so sorry."

"But there was no accident. Nico hadn't worked construction in years, Tzoúlia. He crossed the wrong people, and they took their revenge."

"Oh no."

"The gangsters dumped his body at a job site. The police didn't care. Just another dead immigrant. I was devastated."

Julia looked at him in shock. This story was more heartbreaking than she had imagined.

Gus took a deep breath. "I carried guilt for a long time. I should've done more. But the truth is, Nico made his choices, I made mine. I chose to work hard. I moved to Manly, opened the taverna, and married Maria. I chose a simple life. I am not a wealthy man, but I am happy."

Julia stared out the window, her voice quiet. "When—how did you forgive him? You hung his picture in the taverna even after what he said . . . what he did."

"Tzoúlia, you're no longer asking about Nico?"

"I am, but I'm also not. I didn't forgive Dad. We sat in peace together at the end, but he never apologized for how he treated me. Nothing was resolved."

"Nico was my brother. And we disagreed. He made mistakes, but he was still my brother. And I keep his picture in the taverna. To remind me of where I came from. To remind me of him."

Julia nodded. "What about the unresolved stuff?" she asked. "How did you resolve it after he died?"

"Nico is dead. Your father is dead. May God rest their souls. There is nothing more to resolve," Gus said.

"I guess not. So I just . . . what?" Julia asked.

"The story of your relationship with your dad is over. There are no more chapters to write. Now, you choose the memories you keep. When you think about your father, you choose the times he made you happy, made you laugh. Your memories, your choice."

Julia's gaze softened. "Like the picture in the taverna."

"Yes, the picture. Two Greek sons, fresh off the boat, standing in front of one of the most recognizable buildings in the world."

"That you two built in a year," Julia said.

"Exactly! It brings a smile to my face. That's how I remember Nico. The bad stuff is part of the history. I'm not erasing it. I also can't fix it. Our fight will never be resolved. But the picture in front of the Opera House is perfect. I'll cherish it forever."

Julia patted Gus on the shoulder. "I need to reframe the day I won the surf competition. I'm a Greek mule. He was proud of me that day. I gave his pride a negative spin, but that was immature. He was proud of me."

"You have a long time to work on those memories. But today, you must grieve. Be there for your mum. It's natural and important."

Julia's eyes filled with tears. "Thank you for telling me about Nico. It means a lot. Especially today."

"Remember, Tzoúlia, your father is part of who you are. Nico is part of me. We must carry their history, even if it doesn't have a perfect ending."

"Thanks, Gus. After I help Mum, I'll visit my sister in Los Angeles. I want to deliver some pictures to her."

CHAPTER 22

L inda didn't even have time to set her coffee down before the knock came. The door swung open and her agency partners, Ezra, Leo, and Conn, filed in, all of them wearing the same stiff expression that told her this wasn't a social visit.

Ezra spoke first, wasting no time. "Linda, we need to talk about your roster."

"Is that so?" Linda replied, planting her hands on her hips, elbows flared in her familiar adversarial pose.

Ezra adjusted his cuffs. "It's stale. Honestly, it reads like a nursing home directory."

Leo jumped in. "You haven't brought in new talent in years. Your biggest star, Tova Greenblatt, passed away three years ago. You haven't replaced her billables."

"Tova worked until the day she died because she was a professional. As for the rest of my roster? Every single one of them works. They work continuously. My roster's work ethic is unmatched. They're on sets, stages, and in recording studios, earning money for this agency."

"That's not the issue," Conn said. "You've been our top producer for decades, but—"

"But what?" Linda cut in. "I still am. I bring in more money than any of you. My clients are the hardest-working, most reliable talent in the industry. I'm proud of my roster."

Ezra raised his hands, palms out. "No one's questioning your numbers, Linda. You're a legend. However, the industry is evolving, and you must adapt accordingly. We need younger talent, and you're not recruiting. You can't fade into retirement with your clients. You need to continually replenish the agency's pipeline."

"Who said anything about retiring? I'm not going anywhere," Linda said.

"My point is, you can't age with your roster. You need to reinvent yourself," Ezra said.

Linda paused and considered whether this was the time to be conciliatory, stroke their egos, or go on the offensive. She chose aggression. "Why don't you three focus on keeping your clients working instead of worrying about mine?" she shot back. "I'm not interested in filling my roster with bloggers and YouTubers who fizzle out in six months. Conn, your roster is full of empty calories. Zero substance."

"Linda, Tova's billables haven't been replaced. Your numbers are good, but they're down. We're asking you to look to the future. Be in a growth mindset," Conn added.

"I have Miriam Worthington," Linda said. "She's young, talented, and she's proven herself. She was nominated for a Golden Globe and an Emmy. She prints money for this agency by modeling."

Conn scoffed. "Miriam *was* a rising star—until she got kicked off *IRS Rogue*. That setback crushed her momentum, and you know it. Now she's relegated to modeling gigs that don't align with this agency's mission. We're not a modeling agency."

"Those modeling gigs are paying our bills, and she stays visible while waiting for the right role. A big role. Not the fifth lead in a buddy comedy on a third-rate network—like your clientele, Ezra."

"The modeling gigs are a problem for the rest of us," Ezra said.

"That's quite the double standard. Your actors can do stand-up gigs at nightclubs, but it's a problem for a beautiful woman to model? That's absurd," Linda said.

"Our clients aren't getting modeling work. That's the problem. It's creating resentment, and it's affecting relationships," Leo said.

Linda stood, planting her hands on the desk. "Then maybe those clients should ask why they're not getting the high-paying supplemental gigs instead of whining about Miriam. If they don't like opening at the Chuckle Factory, be more talented and work harder. Their jealousy doesn't dictate my business strategy. Miriam will land another role when she's ready, and when she does, this conversation will look ridiculous."

Leo sighed, pinching the bridge of his nose. "We're not asking you to drop Miriam or abandon your roster, Linda. But it's time to look ahead. We'd like you to take on a junior agent, someone to help you scout emerging talent. That's all."

"Fuck no. Have you calculated how many millions I've put in your pockets?" Linda asked.

"And how many millions have we put in yours? It's a partnership. And what does that have to do with taking on a junior agent?" Leo asked.

Linda's glare swept the room. "I won't babysit a junior agent. My clients are my business. I've had autonomy for the last twenty-five years. It's in my contract!"

"Linda, nobody has ever questioned your worth or *value*. We're not giving you a directive. We're asking you to consider refreshing your roster by taking on a junior agent. The rest of us have a junior we mentor. It would be good for your roster and the agency," Ezra said.

"I don't need help," Linda said. "If this agency doesn't value what I do, I'll leave. And I'll take every client with me."

The room hung silent. Ezra exchanged a look with the others before clearing his throat. "No one wants you to leave, Linda. Take a breath. This isn't a fight. We're raising concerns. As your partners. That's all."

"Your concerns are a waste of my time," Linda snapped.

No one spoke. Conn shook his head. "We'll leave it alone—for now."

They filed out, quieter than they had entered, leaving Linda standing behind her desk. She stayed still, staring at the closed door, her mind spinning. She had won this round, but she knew their words had merit. Tova was gone, her roster was aging, and Miriam—her one young client—needed a career reset.

Linda tapped a pen against her desk and stared at the monitor. The meeting with the partners had left her rattled, but it had also crystallized an idea she had been toying with for months. Miriam wanted a career-defining acting role. But what if she'd already had it? She was defined by her eight years on *Night Nurses*. Thanks to streaming services, the show was everywhere. It wasn't the old days, when only people in the British Commonwealth saw BBC shows; her performance was ubiquitous. She was a standout as Claudia in *IRS Rogue*, but people knew her as Greta.

Her mind drifted back to a conversation nearly two years earlier with Nigel, the producer of *Night Nurses*. He'd floated the idea of a spin-off, aiming to capitalize on the show's popularity. The idea had been premature; Miriam's adversarial departure was fresh, as was the fallout from her turbulent eight-year run. Additionally, her relocation to Los Angeles had made it impractical. But now, with Miriam's heightened profile from the award nominations for *IRS Rogue*, the visibility she earned through modeling work, and her negative reputation within Hollywood, Linda wondered if the timing might be right.

She picked up the phone and dialed the producer as her mind raced through her pitch.

"Linda Edelstein. It's been a while," Nigel said cheerfully.

"Too long," Linda replied. "I won't waste your time, darling. I've got an idea, and you're the first person I'm calling."

"What's the idea?"

Linda rested her elbows on her desk. "The *Night Nurses* spin-off. Remember we talked about it? It's time to make it happen. Miriam's star has grown. The award nominations for *IRS Rogue* gave her credibility, and her modeling work has kept her in the public eye. She's a global name. You launch this spin-off with her as the lead, and it's an instant hit. Netflix, syndication—you can sell it everywhere."

There was a pause on the other end of the line. "You know as well as I do that Miriam's reputation isn't exactly pristine," Nigel said. "The rumors about her being kicked off *IRS Rogue* didn't help. And you and I both remember how volatile things got during our eight years working together."

Linda didn't flinch. "Look, I won't sugarcoat it—Miriam can be difficult. But she's also a star. Every show she touches turns to gold. Ratings and awards. The problem wasn't her. You don't put her in an ensemble and expect her to blend in. She needs to lead. Hire solid character actors who know their job is to support the star. Make her a producer so there's no ambiguity about who's in charge. Give her that authority, and she'll thrive. Let me at least give you my pitch."

"Okay, let's hear it," he said.

"It's a spin-off of *Night Nurses*," Linda began, improvising as she went, "but it's a new direction. The show is called *Greta*, and it focuses on Miriam's character, Greta Simmons. It's no longer a hospital drama. She can still work there initially for continuity, but the story extends beyond the medical center's walls: Greta's personal life—her relationships, her misadventures in dating. Think *Grey's Anatomy*, but with more humor. Miriam has the comedic timing and drama chops to elevate the spin-off from the base comedy of *Night Nurses*."

She paused, waiting for a response, but pushed ahead when the producer remained silent. "Greta is well known. She was in *Night Nurses* for eight years. The audience knows her inside the hospital, but they don't know her life outside. That's where the magic happens. We get to build her world—her struggles, her triumphs. She's no longer the comic relief. She's a woman navigating a complex life encompassing love, career, and personal growth. That's what the audience will connect with."

Nigel stayed silent.

"I'm telling you," Linda pressed, "*Greta* will showcase Miriam's talent. She's not designed for ensembles. She's a star. Put her front and center, and you'll cash in."

"Alright," Nigel said, breaking his silence. "If I agree to this, I want a seven-season guarantee. I'm not committing to a concept dependent on one actress without security that she won't get bored again."

"Not happening," Linda replied. "Four seasons, tops. And I want creative control over storylines and directors."

"Five seasons," he countered. "You'll have veto power over storylines and directors, but not full creative control."

Linda and Nigel spent a few minutes haggling over Miriam's rate per episode and other financial details before Linda was satisfied. Then she pressed her last issue. "There's one more thing—short seasons. Six episodes max, shot over two months. That gives her time to live in LA the rest of the year and pursue film projects. It'll keep her from getting bored."

Nigel sighed. "Alright. However, the only studio window I have to launch this is February 2013. I'm confident I can secure a full-season order from the BBC without a pilot, but I need a quick yes before approaching them. Today! No delays. No more back-and-forth."

"You'll have your answer. Go ahead and work with the BBC, Netflix, and anyone else. This is a moneymaker," Linda said, mentally drafting her pitch to Miriam.

Hanging up the phone, Linda exhaled slowly. The deal was excellent, but the hard part would be convincing Miriam.

Linda analyzed Miriam from across the desk, her patience waning. Miriam was a dynamo—brilliant, lively, commanding—but today, she was a shadow of her former self. Her hair hung in limp strands around her face, her mismatched clothes doing little to mask the exhaustion in her posture. Miriam slouched, her usual elegance lost to a deep weariness. Linda's assistant offered coffee, but Miriam declined with a halfhearted shake of her head.

Linda continued to the matter at hand. She had a job to do. "I'm glad you could make it in," she said. "I asked you to come today because I have a promising opportunity. A lead role in a new TV show. It's a surefire hit."

Miriam didn't respond. Her eyes were fixed on the window, distant and unfocused. Her shoulders rose and fell with each shallow breath. No eye contact. No interest. No energy. Linda didn't slow down. Miriam might not be mentally present in the room, but the deal was too important to delay.

"The good news is, shooting won't start until next February, maybe March," Linda said. "That gives you plenty of time to take on a film or relax and focus on yourself. It's up to you. But this opportunity," Linda said. "It's exactly what you need right now."

Miriam's eyes remained on the view. The only sign of life was the subtle quiver of her lower lip. Linda took a cleansing breath, her patience beginning to thin. Normally, Miriam would have latched on to every detail, dissecting the terms, but today, she was silent.

Linda fought the urge to push harder, waiting for Miriam to speak and show signs of life. She straightened in her chair, folding her hands together. "Mir," she said, "what's going on? You're not with me."

Miriam broke her silence, her words disjointed and incoherent: "First my mum, now him . . . I don't know why this happens to me. It's so unfair. He's dead. I can't believe they're both dead. What am I supposed to do?"

Linda sat, stunned, watching Miriam's composure shatter before her eyes. She could hear grief, but the words were tumbling too quickly, too erratically, for her to make sense of them. She'd seen Miriam incoherent in London once, but never this unintelligible. The confident woman who could once command a room had unraveled.

Linda took a slow breath, trying to secure herself before responding. This wasn't a business meeting anymore. She chose her words carefully. "Who died?"

"My father. I never got to meet him."

"What?"

Miriam didn't answer; instead, she stared at her hands in her lap, weeping. Linda offered her a tissue, but Miriam didn't acknowledge it.

After a minute, Linda asked, "Are you back on the Klonopin?"

Miriam didn't meet her gaze. Her hands fidgeted with the fabric of her clothes. "I never stopped, Linda. I . . . I upped the dose after I heard from my sister. About Dad dying."

"What happened? Was there an accident? Was he sick?"

Miriam's words spilled out, disjointed. "He was fine two months ago, the last time Julia had seen him. Then, a week ago, or possibly more, she received a call to rush home. He had pancreatic cancer, and they said he wouldn't last long. Julia called me this morning. He died. Julia was too late to see him one last time." Miriam paused. "Life is so unfair. Losing both parents before thirty. What am I supposed to do?"

"I'm very sorry, Miriam. Sorry for your loss. Sorry for your sister," Linda said with sympathy.

Miriam didn't acknowledge the words. "Julia is going to fly here next week before going back to Dad's memorial. I would go too, but I'm too sick." She paused. "On top of everything else, my lungs are fucked."

"What about your lungs?" Linda asked.

Miriam leaned back in her chair, her hands fidgeting. Her voice, usually composed, wavered with weariness as she began listing her troubles. "It started with the Klonopin," she said, her eyes fixed on the floor. "I thought I had it under control, but I've been . . ." Her voice wavered as she added, "And mixing it with alcohol, that wasn't smart."

Linda listened, trying to make sense of Miriam's words.

"Then there's the infection. It's serious—a buildup in the lungs.

They drained it, but . . . the procedure didn't . . . There were complications. And now, my lungs . . . they're inflated. Overinflated. It's . . . uncomfortable all the time."

Linda gasped. She wanted to offer some kind of comfort, but Miriam's face—a mix of tears and self-pity—left her silent for a moment longer.

Miriam's eyes focused for the first time. "I need lung reduction surgery, but the doctors won't consider it until I'm off Klonopin. I'm starting this weekend so Julia doesn't see me like this."

"Do you have a plan?" Linda asked. "You can't go cold turkey."

Miriam shook her head. "No. But I'll start by going down to one or two a day for a while, then . . . then I'll stop."

"That isn't a plan, Mir. Let's get you into a facility."

"No. Not until Julia comes. I'm not missing her visit. I'll consider rehab after she leaves, if I'm struggling."

"How long do they need clean blood work for the surgery?" Linda asked.

"Six months."

Linda started doing the math in her head, trying to process it all. "And how long is the recovery from the operation?"

"Four to six weeks, best I can remember," Miriam said, sounding tired and resigned.

Linda continued calculating, and the pieces of the timeline fell into place. It would be tight. "Miriam, I think we should pass on this opportunity. Get you well first. Then we can properly reintroduce you to Hollywood."

Miriam's face crumpled, and the tears came. She started to wallow. "It's all so unfair. I can't believe this is happening to me."

Linda stayed quiet, watching as Miriam fought to regain control of herself.

After a long pause, Miriam looked up suddenly. "Tell them I'm in. I'll be there for the first day of shooting."

"I haven't even told you what it is."

"I trust you. You always look out for me."

Sensing her client was tired and ready to leave, Linda didn't want to push her luck, so she gave the executive summary. "The show is called *Greta*. You're a producer. Top-of-the-mark pay per episode. Only six-episode seasons, shot in two months. Plenty of time to live in LA and shoot other projects. You have a say in the story and the directors."

"*Greta*? Sure. Whatever. Tell them I'm in. Thanks, Linda. I mean that." Miriam stood and walked toward Linda, pulling her into a tight hug before heading for the door.

"I'll come by tomorrow to check in on you," Linda promised.

Miriam nodded and left. Linda was at a loss. She needed a win for her partners, but this version of Miriam couldn't be attached to a high-profile project.

Linda was standing alone in the sanctuary of the synagogue, the air thick with the scent of aged wood and burning candles. It was late, well past the time for evening prayers, but Rabbi Yael Hartman had agreed to meet. The now chief rabbi entered, her long cardigan swaying with her slow steps.

"Liora," said Rabbi Yael, the last person on Earth who still called her by her birth name, "what's on your mind?" Rabbi Yael gestured to the bench, and they both sat.

"Everything, Rabbi. I don't know where to start."

Rabbi Yael sat beside her, folding her hands in her lap. "Start with the beginning. What's troubling you?"

"My partners are complaining about the age of my roster again and want me to take on a junior agent."

"Why's that a problem, Liora?" Rabbi Yael said. "Wouldn't a young person help?"

"In an ideal world, of course. However, these men are only thinking of their wallets. They want a young agent they control to get into my book of business so they can start transitioning me out of the agency without losing my clients. It's an age-old tactic, and I won't allow it."

"Liora, you find yourself in a den of snakes. But you don't really seek my counsel on this. You have always handled these men. What spiritual concern led you to the synagogue after evening prayers?"

Linda sighed, and then her words tumbled out. "It's a client. She's unwell—medication, drinking, a serious health condition—and she's falling apart. But she has an opportunity, a career-saving opportunity—"

"Slow down, Liora, slow down." It was the rabbi's typical instruction to Linda when they conversed.

"If I tell the producer the truth about her struggles, she'll be unemployable, maybe forever. Addicts aren't tolerated anymore. But if I lie, I betray my ethics and risk my reputation. Not to mention, I need her working on a big project to maintain my standing at the agency."

Rabbi Yael studied Linda for a moment. "So you're trying to find the path where you don't compromise your integrity, and no one gets hurt."

"Yes," Linda said. "But I'm not sure that path exists."

Rabbi Yael nodded and placed a hand on Linda's shoulder. "Let me ask you this: What's this client to you? Is she only a client, or something more?"

"She's . . . more. She's family. I've been with her since she was in her teens. I've seen her at her best and her worst. And right now, she's at her worst."

"Family complicates everything, Liora. When we love someone, their struggles become ours. But love doesn't mean shielding them from consequences."

"I know. But if I tell the producer about her health and addiction, they'll write her off as uninsurable. My business isn't forgiving. And if I lie—overtly or by omission—I'm betraying my principles and risking my reputation. If I sign the deal and get her the job, it will destroy my credibility if she doesn't get well and fails."

Rabbi Yael tilted her head. "Do you think lying is the only alternative?"

"What do you mean?" Linda asked, looking down toward the floor.

"What if you delay?" Rabbi Yael suggested. "Not a lie, but a pause. Give the client time to show she's serious about recovery. Time to prove she's ready for this opportunity. You don't need to make a final decision today."

"They want to move fast. The producer wants a decision."

"And you want to move slow. Cautious. This isn't a lie. You want to see the client beat her problems. You can sell the producer on patience. If the deal is truly good, the producers will wait. What's a few weeks? This is what you do, just like you handle the partners at the agency."

"What if that doesn't work?"

"Then you'll know you did everything you could. Liora, you're not responsible for the client's choices. You can guide her, support her, but you can't carry all her burdens."

She glanced at the rabbi. "If I wait, I'm risking the deal falling apart and my partners' wrath."

"Yes, but isn't that better than risking your integrity? Or your client's career if she isn't ready to get healthy?"

Rabbi Yael's words struck Linda. They reframed the very tension she'd been wrestling with. Linda was trying to juggle loyalty, business, and damage control, believing she had to choose one at the expense of the others. But what if she didn't? The thought unsettled her. It meant letting go of control, trusting the unknown. "So I stall. But what do I tell the producer?"

"Tell him you're waiting on your client," Rabbi Yael said. "It's not a lie. It's the truth. You are waiting for her to get clean. Get healthy. He doesn't need to know the details. Neither do your partners. Tell them a deal is in the works. It's all true."

Linda was contemplative. "I agree."

"And in the meantime, encourage the client to take steps toward recovery. If she doesn't, it may be time to end the professional relationship and embrace your role as her family. Give her the unconditional love of family without letting her harm your professional reputation."

Linda let out a shaky breath, a sense of clarity settling over her. "You're right. I'll give her a chance. But I won't shield her forever."

"No, you can't," Rabbi Yael agreed. "But you can give her the tools to stand on her own."

They sat in silence. Finally, Linda turned to Rabbi Yael. "Thank you for this. Thank you for your long friendship and counsel."

CHAPTER 23

C atrina was typically resilient but now felt overburdened. It had been three weeks since her unraveling at the Monarch Ridge bar, and she was at a breaking point. She wasn't eating and barely left the apartment except to go to work. Her deposition was scheduled in two weeks, but she had put the matter out of her mind. She sat alone on the couch, waiting for Sam to get home from work. She couldn't get her best friend out of her thoughts.

She looked at their bookshelf and marveled at Sam's innate curiosity. Sam was an avid reader, and their bookshelves were filled with biographies, histories, and the classics. Sam particularly loved the classics and had mismatched paperbacks of the great female literary novelists, which she would pick up secondhand. The shelves were lined with beat-up copies of the works of Jane Austen, Elizabeth Gaskell, Louisa May Alcott, Kate Chopin, and Margaret Mitchell.

The same independent streak that defined Sam's reading tastes also shaped her approach to dating. Sam had avoided serious relationships in her personal life, enjoying the freedom and fun of casual dating in the local lesbian scene. North County's laid-back culture suited her perfectly, as she could be herself without judgment or pressure. On dates, she was forthright about her lack of interest in a long-term relationship, and most women appreciated her honesty. Her independence was admirable, and she was never lonely.

Still, her life wasn't all work and dating. Sam had cultivated a close-knit group of friends over the years, people she could count on for anything. Of all her friends, though, she spent the most time with Catrina. They were opposites in many ways—Catrina's usual grounded, practical nature diverging with Sam's free spirit—but they balanced each other. Catrina would hack away at her laptop while Sam journaled with her assortment of colored pens or read one of the classic novels she loved. When it was time to relax, they fell into a cozy rhythm of enjoying a bottle of wine, watching cheesy reality TV, and engaging in playful gossip about annoying café customers. Catrina didn't know what she'd do without Sam.

When Sam unlocked the door to their apartment and pushed it open, she found the living room dimly lit, the curtains drawn. She paused inside the doorway, her eyes scanning the room. Catrina was sitting on the couch, staring at nothing.

"Cat?" she asked, slipping her bag off her shoulder and setting it by the door. She took a step closer. "What's going on? You okay?"

Catrina looked up, her face etched with exhaustion and vulnerability. "I . . . yeah, no. I don't know," she mumbled, her voice shaky. She rubbed her temples, exhaling slowly. "It's just . . . a lot."

Sam perched on the armrest of the couch. "Do you want to talk about it?"

Catrina hesitated, her eyes darting away. She shook her head. "I don't know . . ."

Sam straightened up, clapping her hands decisively. "That's it. We're going on a run. Get your shoes on."

Catrina blinked, caught off guard. "I'm not sure I'm up for that," she said.

"Not an option," Sam said. "Let's go."

Catrina sighed, realizing there was no point in arguing. She pushed herself from the couch and shuffled off to change.

On their run, Catrina kept pace with Sam, who started out faster than usual, her steps hyper. They jogged in silence for a while, the sound of their sneakers on the pavement filling the quiet.

"Julia emailed," Catrina said.

Sam glanced over at her. "Julia—the Australian sister?"

"Yeah. She told me . . . our dad passed away. Pancreatic cancer."

"Oh, Cat. I'm so sorry. That's . . . Are you okay?"

Catrina shrugged. "I didn't care about him. He rejected Mom and me. Screw him." Her voice faltered, but she continued, her tone softer now. "But at the same time . . . I liked having the option, you know? If I ever wanted to . . . to change my mind, I could. Now I can't, and I guess I'll process . . ." She paused her words to catch her breath, her gaze distant. "I'm not going to make the same mistake with my half sisters. I emailed Julia. They're both in California next week. We agreed to meet for lunch at Nate 'n Al's."

"In LA?"

"Yeah. I hate LA, but I figured why not? I might as well get a new blazer on Rodeo Drive. Gotta look good for my execution—deposition."

"Wait, hold on. Is the sister from the new *Wonder Woman* movie going? She's a babe!" Sam asked, playfully.

They fell into another stretch of silence, their footsteps echoing off the quiet streets.

Sam glanced over at Catrina again. "You're handling this pretty well. I mean, reaching out to your sisters? That's a great step." After a few more paces, Sam continued, "And I'm sorry about your dad. It's a real loss. Please don't neglect your feelings about it. It may not hit you for a few weeks, but be prepared."

Catrina hesitated before responding. "Eh. Maybe. We'll see. I don't know if meeting my half sisters is the right step, but it's . . . a step. At least Julia can tell me about my dad."

"Definitely. But meeting them before the deposition—does that make sense? Won't it add to the stress?"

"Maybe. But I need the distraction," Catrina said untruthfully—she wasn't remotely thinking about the deposition. She didn't even care about meeting her sisters, though she wasn't opposed. They seemed friendly, and Miriam was certainly interesting. How often can you have lunch with a Hollywood actress? Still, Catrina had accepted the invitation because she wanted an excuse to go to Rodeo Drive and pick out a new outfit. She was the one who had suggested the Jewish deli in Beverly Hills. She feared her days with a generous salary would end soon and wanted to splurge. Maybe it wasn't responsible, but she needed . . . something.

As they turned onto a quieter street, Catrina spoke, her tone hesitant. "Sam, I did something I'm not proud of."

Sam glanced at her. "What do you mean?"

Catrina slowed her pace. "I called Tim."

Sam stopped in her tracks.

Catrina stopped, too, avoiding Sam's eyes. "Yeah. I didn't know when you'd be back from work, and I felt . . . alone. So I called him to talk. Just talk."

"Cat?"

Catrina ran her hand through her sweaty hair. "At first, it was fine. But he suggested meeting at a hotel. When I told him I wasn't looking for that, that I wanted to talk, he . . . he lost it."

"What do you mean, lost it?"

"He said I was leading him on, misleading him. Then he just . . . unleashed. Called me manipulative, cold, ungrateful." Catrina's voice cracked. "I tried to defuse it. I apologized, but it made him angrier. I repeatedly blamed myself for everything to get him to stop yelling."

"Cat, that isn't okay. None of that's okay. You know that, right?"

Catrina nodded. "I know. But in the moment, I didn't know what else to do."

Sam stepped closer, placing a hand on Catrina's shoulder. "Tim's a shit, Cat. You can't let him keep—"

"I know. I just . . . I felt so alone."

As they restarted the run, the tension between them mounted, the spring air doing little to cool the simmering heat of their exchange. Catrina set a slower pace while Sam ran ahead, her frustration evident. For several minutes, neither spoke; the silence was punctuated only by the sound of their feet hitting the pavement and the occasional rustling of leaves in the breeze.

"Cat, remember our housewarming party?" Sam said over her right shoulder.

"Yeah," Catrina said, remembering the evening after they'd moved in together. It had been a typical low-budget affair—bags of chips hastily torn open, store-bought dips plopped into mismatched bowls, and a smattering of cheap wine and beer scattered across the counter. Their circle of friends had mingled easily in the modest space, the hum of conversation and laughter filling the air. Catrina remembered how excited she had been that night. Moving into the apartment with Sam had been the start of a new, fresh chapter.

Sam continued, "All our friends were there, and you weren't entirely present. Your eyes kept darting toward the door, checking your phone every minute. You were waiting for Tim, ignoring everyone else."

"Okay . . ." Catrina said while catching her breath. The pace had quickened, and she hadn't exercised in over a week. She wondered where Sam was going with this trip down memory lane.

"Tim arrived two hours into the party, making his entrance like a celebrity gracing us with his presence. The energy in the room shifted as he walked in. He greeted people he didn't know as though they were old friends and made rounds like he owned the place. It was obnoxious."

"I recall," Catrina said, getting annoyed and wishing Sam would make her point.

"You transformed when he arrived. Your shoulders straightened, your voice softened, and your demeanor shifted like you were calibrating to match his mood. Tim's presence turned you into someone smaller, lesser. Tim lapped it up. I hated watching it."

"That's harsh," Catrina said while racking her brain for what had come next that night. Then she remembered. She and Tim had had sex, and then he had gone home to his wife.

"Do you know what Tim said to me that night?" Sam asked.

"No."

"'Have we met?' Can you believe that?"

"No way. He knew you. He even told me you were hot. I mentioned you at the office all the time," Catrina said, intentionally slowing the pace of the run so she could give more than one-word answers.

"It was calculated. He sensed that I saw right through his bullshit and wanted to keep me at arm's length. It made my blood boil."

"That's shitty."

"Tim didn't mingle long. After a few rounds of playing the guest of honor, he focused on you. Without checking with you or seeing what you wanted to do, he grabbed your hand and took you back to the bedroom. Painfully predictable." Sam took a deep breath and continued, "I could still see the wedding ring on his finger as he strutted into your bedroom. I wanted to storm after you and tell you not to be reduced to this. But I didn't. I bit my tongue."

"He can be an ass, but I wasn't taken advantage of," Catrina said, offended by the notion she'd been used that night. *Why is Sam, of all people, being such a prude?* she thought. She couldn't believe Sam had been holding on to all this for months. It was petty. *Why would she care who I slept with? Wait, why did I care who she slept with at Monarch Ridge?*

"Forty-five minutes later, as the last of our guests were leaving and I was cleaning up, Tim came out of your room. His shirt was untucked, his hair a little mussed, and he gave a casual nod and left. You appeared minutes later and wouldn't look me in the eye."

"That's an exaggeration. I was cleaning up." Catrina debated whether the heat in her head was from running or anger. Sam could be direct, but this was a whole new level. She hadn't shit on Sam for taking that awful fitness instructor to bed—same fucking difference.

Sam was undeterred by Catrina's silence. "I wanted to tell you that you deserved better, that Tim wasn't worth the heartache. But I didn't—for the sake of our friendship. I didn't want to risk pushing you away. But I was a bad friend. I did you a disservice. I messed up. I should've been direct."

"You're really mad at me, aren't you?" Catrina asked.

Sam glanced over her shoulder and increased her pace. "Yeah, I am, at what you let Tim do to you."

"Slow down, Sam. Please," Catrina said.

Sam slowed down, falling into stride beside her. "Cat, I just . . . I don't understand why you keep doing this to yourself. You know what he's like. You've seen how he treats you. Why is he the person you turn to when you're vulnerable?"

Catrina focused on the ground. "I don't know. It's like . . . it's a reflex. A bad one. But I wasn't thinking. I was alone, and he was—"

"You know who else was available? Me. I'm here. And unlike him, I don't make you feel like crap."

"I get it," Catrina said, bringing the pace down to a fast walk.

"You numb your feelings so much, I'm not sure you can identify them without a man explaining them to you," Sam seethed.

Catrina's face hardened. "That's not fair. You don't know what it's like for me. I don't have it all figured out like you. I'm trying, Sam."

"Trying? How is calling Tim trying? Running back to your abuser? That's not trying, Cat. That's pathetic."

"You're over the line," Catrina snapped. "At least he doesn't judge me."

"Of course he doesn't. He doesn't give a flying fuck about you. There's a minimum level of giving a shit needed to judge. You give him everything he needs, and it costs him nothing."

Catrina rolled her eyes. "I don't need this from you, of all people," she said, picking up her pace to pull ahead.

Sam quickened her stride, closing the gap. "Oh, you don't need this from me? Who else is going to tell you the truth?"

"I don't want your pity! I'm not your project," Catrina said. "You don't get it, Sam. You've got your life together. You're strong. You don't know what it's like to constantly fall short, to—"

"To what? Sabotage yourself? I'm tired of watching you do it. I'm done ignoring it or pretending it's okay."

They ran a mile in tense silence, the sound of their footsteps the only thing breaking the quiet between them. Catrina couldn't remember seeing Sam this angry before, and it unsettled her. She replayed the conversation in her mind, trying to piece together why the news of her calling Tim after her dad had died had triggered such an explosive reaction. It didn't make sense—wasn't she allowed to reach out for support?

What stung even more was her best friend's lack of understanding. Instead of offering comfort, Sam had gone straight to anger. Catrina had just lost her father, but somehow that fact had been overshadowed, swallowed up by Sam's frustration with Tim. A part of Catrina wanted to snap back, demanding an explanation, but another part worried that would only widen the rift between them. Instead, she focused on the path ahead, each step pounding with the questions swirling in her mind. *What difference does it make to her who I slept with?*

Why am I so hung up on who she slept with?

Catrina considered playing the dead-dad card but decided it would be manipulative. She didn't really care about her father dying. Not yet at least. Not today. She suspected that would come, but it wasn't what had led her to Tim. That had been a pretense, an excuse to call him. Had she done so solely to pick this fight with Sam?

That would be preposterous, she told herself. *Why can't I stop thinking about Sam sleeping with the fitness instructor?*

Finally, Catrina decided to see if she could lower the temperature of both the run and the argument. "You're right. I should've called you. But you were at work, and I didn't want to bother you."

Sam stopped running and turned to face Catrina. "Bother me? Cat, I work at a coffee shop. I talk to strangers about their problems all day. It's what I do. It's literally my job."

"I get it, okay? But I wasn't ready to sit there while strangers walked in and out. I was falling apart. I didn't want to do it in public for the second time in a month." She hesitated, her voice softening. "But yeah, I messed up. I should've come to you instead of . . . him."

Sam threw her arms up in exasperation. "You're damn right you should've! Cat, I don't care if you're falling apart. You could've shown up mid-meltdown, and I would've pulled you into the back room and talked. You're not just someone I live with, Cat; you're my best friend."

Catrina swayed as she listened, lost in thought. *Why am I pissed? Why did I call Tim? Is it because of the fitness instructor?* She became convinced that she'd subconsciously manipulated this fight. Calling Tim had been a futile act. She'd known he wasn't going to comfort her in any meaningful way. And then why bring it up to Sam? Was she trying to make Sam jealous? Why would Sam get this mad about her calling Tim? Annoyed, sure, but she was *angry*. It didn't add up. Sam was a hypocrite; she could sleep with whoever she wanted, but Catrina couldn't call Tim when her dad had died? It was ridiculous.

The run was mercifully over, and Sam stayed outside to stretch. Or to pretend to stretch. Catrina didn't care. She walked inside, fuming.

Catrina rested her head against the tile wall of the shower, letting the water beat against her skin as a storm churned inside her. Her whole body clenched. *What did Sam expect?* She gritted her teeth, replaying the argument. *She left me at the bar. She was the one who abandoned me. And now she's angry because I called Tim? Tim didn't ditch me.*

As the water cooled her body, the truth became evident, jarring, and undeniable. Catrina straightened and pressed her palms flat against the slick tile. Tim was a mediocre man who treated her like an ATM and sometimes sex toy. And she let him. She invited it. She called it harmless, but that was a lie. Sam was right: Tim was a shit.

The water streamed over her back as she beat herself up, telling herself she had no boundaries, no self-driven purpose. Catrina's life was at a crossroads. Her people-pleasing and misplaced loyalty had led her to certain ruin. At the very least, she would be jobless and unemployable. At worst, she was in criminal jeopardy. Distracted by other feelings, she hadn't thought about her legal predicament for the past three weeks. The mind's ability to avoid and ignore problems was impressive, she realized. She hadn't even called a lawyer.

In a rush, her pent-up fear and loathing flooded in. She wasn't angry at her mom, the lawsuit, or the fitness instructor, and certainly not at Sam. She *was* angry at Tim, but he deserved it. Regardless, she accepted that she was the common denominator: She was to blame. She'd understood that she'd have to accept any consequences when she stole the files, and now that the fallout had arrived, she couldn't play the victim.

And yet, even now, as she stood in the shower, a rush of fear and panic washed over her, and she couldn't focus on Tim, the deposition, or her impending legal repercussions. All her thoughts led to one person: Sam—her best friend, refuge, and safe place, unconditionally.

But Sam wasn't her therapist, her muse, or an infinite well of patience to absolve her of every mistake. She was the person who showed up for Catrina time and time again, yet Catrina was too selfish to reciprocate. When Sam had wanted to sit at the bar and recite the play-by-play of her sexcapades, Catrina had refused to engage and had made the night about herself. She was a lousy friend, and that sucked. She'd spent her whole life overaccommodating her mom, her high school boyfriend, and fucking Tim, but when it came to the one person who made her feel safe, Catrina was uncharacteristically selfish. Sam's harsh and unapologetic disapproval during the run hurt, but it was warranted. It was fair.

Her shoulders slumped as she closed her eyes. Catrina hated this version of herself, this fractured, indecisive wreck of a person who dragged shit into every corner of her life. The same version that had waited over five years post-high school to move out of her mom's house despite it being an unhealthy environment. The version that had blindly followed a man to start an ego project, leaving a great company that had treated her well.

Sam had seen and nurtured the better version of Catrina—the

responsible, independent, yet still fiercely loyal version that understood the importance of self-care. But today, when Catrina had flagrantly undermined her better self and called Tim, Sam had finally snapped. She had carried Catrina through so much without judgment and had asked very little in return. Catrina relied so heavily on Sam's unwavering support that she had failed to stop and ask if she deserved it. And the girl at the bar, the fitness instructor— why did it hurt? Why did Catrina feel betrayed? Why did she harbor bad feelings? Why, with her professional life crumbling, had she spent the past three weeks obsessing over Sam?

She pressed her forehead against the cool tile, letting the water cascade over her as she, again, thought about the small moments— the latte orders, the nights Sam had stayed up to hear her vent, the way Sam always knew when to push and when to back off. The way Sam's cornball jokes made her laugh. The way Sam's hand brushed hers—and the unexplained tingling sensations. Catrina drew a solitary conclusion: She was in love.

Catrina's hands shook as she hovered near the kitchen entryway. Sam stood at the kitchen counter, an empty wineglass in front of her, eyes fixed on something in the distance. The silence between them was palpable.

Sam slammed shut the cabinet door, gripping the bottle of wine so tightly that Catrina was afraid it would shatter. As she yanked open a drawer to grab the corkscrew, her gaze bounced from counter to floor to sink and back to the floor. Her feet were shifting in place. She poured a heavy glass of wine and downed half of it in one gulp. She opened the fridge, scanning the shelves with blunt, jerky movements. She grabbed grapes, cheese, and some prosciutto and slammed the door shut, slapping the items onto the counter with a force that echoed.

Catrina watched as Sam sliced through a block of cheddar with more force than necessary, the knife slamming against the cutting board. Her legs were planted wide, and her red face simmered as her head jerked from side to side. Catrina feared it wasn't just anger. Did Sam feel betrayed? Rejected? She was the one constant in Catrina's life, the one who never judged no matter how messy things got, and now she wouldn't even look Catrina's way.

Sam scattered the cheese and meat onto a tray haphazardly. She threw a handful of almonds onto the tray as well, the sound of them scattering breaking the silence. She grabbed her glass, refilled it, and slumped on the counter, staring at the assembled board. She closed her eyes and took another drink.

Catrina couldn't wait any longer. She had to say it.

"I'm sorry."

The words fell into the gap between them. Sam didn't move. Catrina searched her face, desperate for a response, but Sam's expression remained unchanged. Catrina understood she didn't deserve forgiveness, but she couldn't bear to leave things broken.

"Sam," she said, "I know I hurt you. I've been selfish, and I see that now. I took you for granted, your patience, your love— everything. You're the best thing in my life, and I've been too self-absorbed to see it. I'm sorry for being so . . . fucked up. You don't deserve it."

Sam's lips pressed together, her jaw clenching ever so slightly. It wasn't much, but it was enough to give Catrina hope. She stepped forward, her legs wobbly beneath her, and stopped just short of the counter. "I don't deserve it . . . your friendship. How you care for me. I don't deserve you. I'm so sorry."

Sam's lips betrayed the slightest hint of a half smile. Catrina seized the small opening, crossing the remaining physical distance. She reached out tentatively, wrapping her arms around her friend. At first, Sam's body stayed rigid, her arms hanging at her sides, but Catrina didn't let go. She pressed her face into the curve of Sam's neck, her grip firm but gentle, an embrace that carried all the words she couldn't say.

Seconds passed, each stretching painfully, and then she felt Sam's shoulders slacken and the tension melting away. Sam raised her arms and rested her hands on Catrina's back. At first, the touch was hesitant but grew firmer, more deliberate. Sam's palms pressed against Catrina's shoulder blades, pulling her closer. Relief surged through Catrina, so overwhelming it almost brought her to tears.

Catrina's hand moved instinctively, stroking Sam's hair in soft, repetitive motions. She had done it before during quiet moments on the couch, but it wasn't absent-minded this time. It was purposeful, an offering of comfort, of love. Sam let out a small breath and leaned into the touch, then started tracing slow, soothing circles across Catrina's back.

Catrina pulled back slightly, just enough to look into Sam's eyes; Sam's anger seemed to dissolve. Catrina's hand slid from Sam's hair to her cheek, her thumb brushing gently against the edge of Sam's jaw. The warmth in Sam's gaze was back, but now there was something else there, something raw and vulnerable. And then Catrina saw it—passion. It hit her like a lightning bolt, illuminating everything she hadn't dared to acknowledge. Sam wasn't just her best friend. She was her person, the one who saw her completely.

Catrina didn't know who moved first, and it didn't matter, but suddenly their lips were touching, tentative at first, then sure. The kiss deepened, and everything else disappeared. Her hands moved instinctively, cradling Sam's face and sliding around her waist, pulling her closer. Sam's hands mirrored hers, holding Catrina as though letting go wasn't an option.

The world narrowed to this connection. Their lips moved in sync, exploring, searching, discovering. When Catrina's tongue brushed lightly against Sam's lips, they parted without hesitation, inviting her in. The kiss was slow but intense, every movement deliberate, every touch filled with meaning. Catrina was alive for the first time in weeks. This was real, this was right.

As they finally broke apart, their foreheads rested against each other, breaths mingling in the room's silence. Catrina didn't need to say anything. Everything she wanted to convey was in the way Sam looked at her; Sam's hand lingered on Catrina's cheek, and Sam's lips curved into the softest, most genuine smile.

Catrina's brain went white. For the first time in days, months, maybe forever, the churn of thoughts, the tension from the run, the looming anxiety of her deposition, and the anticipation of meeting her half sisters were all gone. In their place was a serene clarity. This was perfection. She glanced at Sam, whose energy was magnetic and her confidence palpable, and felt reassured. Catrina didn't analyze or overthink. She let Sam take the lead, surrendered control, and soaked in the experience.

Catrina lay on her back in bed, staring at the ceiling in the dim light, her mind restless. Sam was curled beside her, breathing peacefully, her features relaxed. The sheets were tangled loosely around them, a testament to the night's passion.

Catrina had experienced a swirl of emotions she was attempting to untangle. Had this been a mistake? A fleeting moment of vulnerability? The intimacy they had shared was unlike anything Catrina had ever experienced. It hadn't been only physical; it had been rooted in years of friendship and trust. But what if Sam woke up with regrets? She avoided long-term relationships. Would she turn away from Catrina?

And what if Catrina regretted it? What if this was unexplored grief? What if she was experimenting or seeking comfort amid her ruinous professional life?

No, Catrina decided, she didn't feel that way. Not at all. She had no regrets. This was the best night of her life.

CHAPTER 24

Sunday, April 1, 2012 | Los Angeles

B efore Julia could speak, Miriam wrapped her arms tightly around her, the embrace immediate and unreserved. Julia dropped Floating Sky to her side, caught off guard. It was minutes before they pulled apart.

Miriam's hands lingered on Julia's shoulders as she stepped back to take her in. "You're here," she said, her voice thick with emotion. "Come in, come in!" She grabbed Julia's duffel bag and slid it aside near the entryway as Julia bent down to rest Floating Sky against the wall. "You brought her all the way here, hmm?"

"Of course," Julia replied.

Miriam's house was nothing short of impressive. Perched on a hillside, it was a stylish, modern retreat, all clean lines and minimalist elegance. The exterior featured a mix of smooth stucco and warm wood accents, complemented by drought-resistant plants arranged in the landscaped garden.

"You look good. Tired, though. Long flight?" Miriam asked.

Julia shrugged, stepping inside. "Middle seat, Qantas economy. So, you know, luxury," she quipped, earning another laugh from Miriam. "But they had all these movies and shows. I didn't know what to pick."

"Oh no, don't tell me you watched *Night Nurses*." Miriam cringed.

"Nope, skipped that one. But I did see you in that *Wonder Woman* movie. And then plowed through *IRS Rogue* again."

Miriam's face lit up at the mention of *IRS Rogue*. "Well, thank you. But next time, let me pick you up from the airport, okay? No more buses."

"I like the bus. Gives me time to settle into a place."

As they moved through the entryway, Julia took in the mansion. The high ceilings and open layout immediately struck her. Miriam's house was everything Julia imagined—classy, modern, and sophisticated, yet warm. The concrete floors reflected the soft natural light streaming in through floor-to-ceiling windows, giving the space an airy, almost ethereal quality. On a side table sat a tall glass vase filled with English roses—blush, cream, and pale apricot—each bloom full and layered like silk.

"This is the living room," Miriam said, gesturing toward a sprawling sectional sofa positioned around a minimalist fireplace. The walls were adorned with curated art pieces, each bold and distinctive without being overwhelming. "I don't use the fireplace, but it looks nice, right?"

Julia nodded, running her hand along the smooth surface of the couch as they passed. "Very LA."

"Wait until you see the view."

She led Julia toward the dining area, which opened onto a massive terrace. Julia stepped out, her breath catching as she took in the sweeping panorama of Los Angeles. The city stretched out endlessly below, its lights overtaking the sky as dusk settled. The infinity-edge pool at the terrace's edge shimmered in the fading sunlight, its waters blending seamlessly with the horizon.

"Wow," Julia said. "It's like you're on top of the world."

Miriam leaned on the railing beside her. "Not bad, huh? It's a great spot for clearing your head. Or hosting parties." She gestured to the outdoor kitchen and fire pit tucked into the corner. "Though I don't do much of either these days."

Julia glanced at her, noticing the hint of something behind

Miriam's bright demeanor. "Well, maybe it's time you started," she said.

Miriam's smile wavered, but she changed the subject. "Come on, there's more to see."

Back inside, Miriam pointed out the media room, with its plush seating and giant screen, and the home office, lined with custom shelving and bathed in natural light. "This is where I pretend to be productive," she joked, though Julia could see the stacks of scripts and notes on the desk.

As they moved through the house, Julia couldn't help but compare it to her dumpy studio flat back in Manly. Everything here was so elegant, so deliberate, yet despite its luxury, the house felt lived-in, personal. It was a reflection of Miriam—bold and sophisticated but with layers. Her house was what Marcus's townhouse aspired to be when it grew up.

Julia sat at the kitchen counter, refreshed after a long shower and a change of clothes. She had unceremoniously dumped the clothes she'd been wearing into Miriam's high-tech washing machine, a device so advanced she thought it was going to offer her a cup of tea while doing the laundry.

Miriam set a platter of sushi and a pizza box on the counter. "Figured I'd play it safe," Miriam said, motioning toward the spread. "Sushi for me, pizza for you—or vice versa. No judgment."

Julia grabbed a slice of pizza. "Both work for me. This is better than plane food."

Miriam slid onto the stool beside her, folding her hands around a glass of water. "How are you holding up? It has been . . . a lot. The flight, Dad . . ."

"I'm good. Really. I was so busy making arrangements with Mum that the time flew." Julia glanced down at her plate, picking at the crust of her pizza. "We had a small ceremony at the funeral parlor for family and close friends. Gus came, which helped me. The big celebration of his life will be at his club next week. I'm dreading that one."

Miriam nodded as she listened.

"What about you? You look . . ." Julia tried to choose her words carefully. "Tired."

"That's putting it nicely. It has been a rough few months. I'm working on a plan to get help with those prescription meds so I can get the surgery. It's . . . a process. A lot of phone calls and paperwork."

"Surgery? What kind of surgery?" Julia asked.

Miriam launched into a simplified explanation. "I developed a lung condition from an infection. I forget the official medical diagnosis. Regardless, it caused complications, and now my lungs are hyperinflated. Makes breathing a challenge. The doctors won't consider surgery until I've been off Klonopin for six months."

"That sounds hard."

"It is," Miriam said, "but the only way to get better. Once I'm through this, I can have the lung-reduction surgery, do the recovery program, and get back to normal. Well, as normal as I can be. I just want to work. My career is everything, and sitting here without an acting job is killing me." Miriam stood and grabbed a small box. "Here," she said, handing it to Julia.

"What's this?" Julia asked, opening the box.

"My old phone," Miriam said. "It's still on my plan. Use it while you're in LA. Put your email on there. And before you ask, it's not charity," Miriam said. "It's a hand-me-down from sister to sister. Totally different."

Julia studied the phone, softened by the normalcy of sisterhood. "Okay. Thanks. It'll be nice to have something for the bus rides."

"Exactly," Miriam said, her relief evident.

Julia relaxed in the passenger seat, humming a song as Miriam drove toward Dodger Stadium. The silence in the car was comfortable, but Julia's mind raced. The past few days had been spectacular, not just because of the places they'd visited but also because of how naturally she and Miriam had bonded. They hadn't tried to make up for decades of lost time; instead, they had just existed together, and it worked.

Julia had embraced the chance to be a tourist in Los Angeles. The first day had been a whirlwind. Hiking to Griffith Observatory wasn't her typical idea of fun, but seeing Miriam push through the trail, stopping only to catch her breath, had left Julia impressed. Once they were at the top, the city had stretched endlessly before them, a grid of streets and buildings fading into the horizon.

Julia had turned to Miriam, who had looked worn but content. "This place is insane," she'd said, snapping a few selfies with her sister, their laughter echoing across the hillside.

The next day had been more leisurely. Pasadena wasn't Julia's scene—too calm, too buttoned up—but the morning at the Huntington Library and Botanical Gardens had been fun. The Japanese garden, with its delicate bridges, koi-filled ponds, and perfectly pruned trees, had left her in awe. Among the retirees and camera-toting tourists, the sisters had stuck out, which they found amusing.

Julia couldn't resist teasing Miriam as they navigated the stepping-stones in the pond. "We should start a YouTube channel," she had joked, watching Miriam wobble with uncharacteristic clumsiness.

"*Clueless Sisters Tour Botanical Gardens*," Miriam said with a mock glare.

The afternoon at the Getty had brought a different vibe. Julia expected to breeze through the galleries but was caught off guard by how they had drawn her in. Miriam had led the way, pointing out subtle details in the paintings—the texture of a brushstroke, the emotion in a subject's eyes, the story behind a sculpture. She had been trained by her mother to appreciate the fine arts from a young age. "It's not just about what you see," she had told Julia, standing in front of a portrait. "It's about what the artist wanted you to feel."

Julia had lingered in front of pieces that caught her eye, asking questions and being drawn into Miriam's world. Miriam's appreciation for art had been eye-opening, a side of her sister she hadn't known, and Julia hadn't been in a rush to leave.

Today had been slower paced, a welcome change from the busy days exploring Los Angeles. They'd spent the day lounging on Miriam's patio, enjoying the stillness. Miriam had read scripts while Julia had played on her new phone. As Julia had stretched out, her thoughts had drifted to the next day—her surf day in Malibu. She couldn't wait to get back into the water. Miriam had spared no expense, renting a house perched high above Surfrider Beach that was straight out of a dream, offering a breathtaking view of the crescent-shaped shoreline. Julia had teased Miriam about the extravagance, but deep down, she was touched by the gesture. She could already picture herself riding the waves with Miriam watching from the patio, Julia's laughter carrying over the sound of the ocean every time she wiped out.

And then there was Friday, their last day together. Julia planned to be on the ocean at first light, experiencing the surf in her favorite way. Afterward, they would travel to Beverly Hills, followed by lunch with Catrina. Julia had resolved that any relationship with Catrina would be a bonus, though she wasn't sure about her other sister. She understood but didn't like that Catrina hadn't responded to either her or Miriam for two years. Julia was willing to meet her, but she wouldn't force it if Catrina didn't want a relationship.

The car inched through traffic as the ballpark came into view on the horizon. LA traffic on a Wednesday night was its own special tourist experience.

"I'm surprisingly enjoying all this outdoorsy stuff," Miriam said from the driver's seat.

"Who knew you had it in you? Tomorrow, I'll teach you to surf."

"Let's not go too far," Miriam said. "But you might be rubbing off on me."

"So what's the plan for tonight? Hot dogs and foam fingers?" Julia asked, mildly scared of Miriam's dicey driving abilities.

"Not quite. Linda has us set up in a luxury box. If you're not into baseball, it's the best way to experience a Dodgers game. It was Linda's idea," Miriam said, jerking the steering wheel. "She's a sports fanatic. She wanted to take us to a Lakers game too, but I opted for the outdoor sport."

"Luxury box seats? Beats the plastic ones at the Sydney Cricket Ground."

The sisters sat in silence for a few minutes until Miriam asked, "Penny for your thoughts?"

"I'm nervous about meeting Catrina. What if I like her better?" Julia joked.

Miriam chuckled. "The two younger sisters gang up on the eldest. A story as old as time."

Julia laughed. "Never. You'll always be my favorite."

"What's actually on your mind?" Miriam pressed.

Julia exhaled. "Dad told me about your mum. Just before he . . . you know."

Miriam's hands tightened on the steering wheel. "What did he say about her?" she asked.

"Something different from what Rosalind told you. He said it wasn't a one-night stand or a fling."

"What do you mean?" Miriam asked. "What did he say?"

"Before I tell you . . . do you *want* to know? I mean, this could—" She stopped herself, searching for the right phrasing. "It could change— It's more complicated than I expected."

"Do you believe him? Ray. Did he tell you the truth?" Miriam asked.

"Yeah. I think so," Julia said. "He had his faults—plenty of them —but he wasn't a liar. He would embellish a story, but this one didn't make him look good, and he was embarrassed on his deathbed to tell me. But he wanted me to understand, to know what happened. And I ... He didn't make this up. He had details."

Miriam was silent as they approached Dodger Stadium.

"What do you want me to do, Mir?" Julia asked.

"Let me think about it. I want you to focus on having a good time tonight. Linda is my guardian angel. I want you to see how great she is," Miriam said.

———

When they arrived at Dodger Stadium, the atmosphere was electric. Julia took in the towering lights, the swarms of fans in blue jerseys, and the faint aroma of popcorn and hot dogs wafting through the air. A woman was waiting for them near the premium seats entrance; her Dodgers hat, jersey, and oversized sunglasses made her look like the team's number one fan.

"This must be Julia!" the woman said, pulling her into an enthusiastic hug. "It's great to finally meet you. Miriam's been singing your praises. Come on, let's get you inside. You're in for a treat."

As they made their way through the VIP concourse, Julia couldn't help but marvel at the stadium's sheer scale. The manicured field, a perfect emerald green, was framed by the hills beyond. Linda kept up a lively commentary on the walk, pointing out the best snacks and souvenirs, and Julia peppered her with questions about the game. Julia got a blue interlocking LA Dodgers hat and wore it proudly, quickly becoming their second-biggest fan.

When they reached the corporate box, Linda opened the door with a flourish. "Welcome to baseball, LA style."

Julia stepped inside, mesmerized by the spread of food and the prime view of the diamond below. "Okay, this is ridiculous," she said.

"I told you. Linda doesn't do anything halfway," Miriam said.

As the game began, Julia found herself engrossed. Linda enthusiastically explained the rules, and Julia asked questions, her curiosity growing with every pitch. Miriam, meanwhile, sipped her tea and watched the two of them with amusement and apparent joy.

During a break between innings, Julia turned to Miriam. "You know, this city is nuts. There is so much going on all the time. It makes Sydney feel like a small beach town."

"It's a lot. But I love it," Miriam said.

Julia enjoyed baseball. It was much faster than cricket, and with superior snacks—no sausage rolls or meat pies. When the game ended, Linda joined the communal rendition of Randy Newman's "I Love L.A." to commemorate the Dodgers' win.

As they were about to leave the stadium, Miriam turned to Julia and whispered, "I don't want there to be secrets between us, Jules. Tell me about Mum. Tell me everything."

The following morning, Julia wore her new Dodgers hat as she turned on the kettle and started rummaging through Miriam's pantry. Eggs, bread, tea. She cracked two eggs into a bowl and whisked them, her hands moving with the muscle memory she had built over years of taverna shifts. She was a waitress by trade, but Gus made sure everybody could work in the kitchen. She wanted to pay back Miriam for her kindness and generosity with a home-cooked meal, something Miriam rarely enjoyed. The skillet hissed as she poured the eggs in and worked through her thoughts.

When the clock hit 10:00, the smell of bacon and eggs filled the kitchen, and Julia heard soft footsteps enter. Miriam appeared in the doorway, her hair slightly mussed and her expression calm but groggy. "Morning," Miriam said.

Julia smiled as she set down two plates. "Morning. Tea's ready. Breakfast is served."

They sat down together, the sound of forks scraping against plates the only interruption for a few minutes. The silence was comfortable, as if they were holding on to the moment, reluctant to let it pass.

Miriam's eyes wandered to the door, where Julia's duffel bag and

Floating Sky leaned against the wall. "I love having you here," Miriam said. "I'm not ready for you to leave."

Julia's fork hovered in midair. "I love it too," she said. "It's been . . . easy, like we've done this a hundred times."

Miriam nodded, her gaze fixed on the packed bag. "This house— it's yours, Jules. That guest room is no longer a guest room. It's your room. Anytime you want to come back. No warning necessary. I'll give you a door code."

"A door code? Seriously?" Julia joked.

"I mean it," Miriam said. "I'll come to Australia when I'm cleared to travel. But this place? It's yours whenever you want it. I have so many airline miles from all the transatlantic flights. You can use them. I don't need them. The studios pay for my flights." She picked at the remaining food on her plate, and her eyes drifted back to the door. "I hate seeing your bag there," she muttered. "It feels like you just got here."

The silence stretched between them, the unspoken goodbye filling the room. Julia shifted uncomfortably, clearing her throat as an idea came to her. "We still have two days together," she said.

"I know. But we'll be in Malibu. This is our last bit of time here, playing house like sisters."

"Hey, Mir, I have something for you. I'm nervous about it," Julia said.

"Don't be nervous. I can handle it."

"It isn't bad."

Julia went to her duffel and pulled out an envelope, then handed it to her sister. Miriam opened it and found eighteen pictures of herself, each with a date on the back, and a few shots of her parents from 1984. Her mouth opened, but her expression remained unchanged. "Where did you get these?" she asked.

"Dad."

"Mum sent these?" Miriam asked, flipping through the pages, stopping to show Julia a baby picture.

"Every year on your birthday."

"And he saved them?" Miriam asked in apparent shock.

"Yup. And those with your mum. Locked in his safe."

"Can I keep them? They're the only . . . *anything* of my parents together," Miriam said.

"Of course. He asked me to give them to you," Julia said, studying Miriam for any reaction.

None came. Her sister was stone-faced.

The two sat silently as Miriam looked at the photos and Julia scrolled through her phone. Although she had only had a phone for a week, she was already on social media, sharing photos of the trip with friends. She connected with Gus on Facebook. He commented on every post.

"Hey, about the phone," Julia said. "Do you think . . . I could maybe keep it? I don't know how it'll work in Australia, but it's been . . . nice having it. I've been texting with Ali and Gin. They're intense texters."

Miriam waved her hand. "Of course you can keep it. I'll keep it on my plan for now. We can figure out the international stuff later. Let's get packed up and head to Malibu."

CHAPTER 25

I t had been more than ten days since Linda had pitched the *Greta* project to Nigel, the producer in England, and his patience was gone. Tired of the endless delays, he demanded a copy of the signed agreement by the end of London's business day, or his production company would move on to other projects. Linda had stalled, first with strategic delays over minor contract details, then by having her legal team tangle the agreement in a bureaucratic maze. Rabbi Yael's advice to *buy time without burning bridges* had been wise, but time had run out. Bridges were about to be burned, and Linda's hands were tied. Today was the day.

The Malibu rental house was perched high above Surfrider Beach, its modern architecture blending seamlessly with its natural surroundings. Linda could see Miriam on the patio through the expansive glass walls. She had been anxious about this meeting, given that Miriam was at a crossroads. Miriam appeared composed, even serene, but Linda knew better than to trust appearances. The actress had been her old self at the Dodgers game, sober, present, and charming. Julia's visit had clearly stabilized her, but this new dynamic would soon come to an end, and Miriam would be left to her own devices once more.

Linda stepped toward the patio, her heels clicking against the concrete floor. She carried two documents in her work bag: a Series Lead Casting Agreement and a Termination of Representation Agreement. Only one would be signed, and Linda shuddered at the thought of ending their decade-long professional relationship. She was willing to do it if it meant saving Miriam's life—her job was to protect Miriam, even if that meant letting her go as a client—but it wasn't a decision she had come to lightly.

The wooden deck was lined with teak loungers and a low dining table, perfectly staged against the backdrop of the endless ocean. Miriam was bundled in an oversized sweater, a steaming mug of tea cradled in her hands. The silence was broken only by the rush of water.

"Good morning," Linda said, easing into one of the chairs beside Miriam. She spotted Julia in the water, paddling out with confidence. Her skill was evident; the way she glided through the water was impressive. Even the famously territorial local Malibu surfers moved around her and didn't seem to object to her selecting choice waves.

"She's something out there," Linda said as Julia finished a run and was near the shore.

"She's incredible," Miriam replied. "Watching her . . . it's otherworldly. I could never." She glanced at Linda before turning and watching Julia paddle out again. "She told me more about Ray and Rosalind."

"What did she say?"

"Ray said their relationship wasn't a fling. He cared about her. He proposed marriage. Offered to move to London. He wanted to be part of my life. Mum shut him out. She was the cold one."

"You never really bought her explanation of a fling."

"No, it never made sense. Nothing about her was impulsive. It's far more in line with her character to fall in love and then make a calculated decision to ditch the man for being too common. I buy it."

"Sure."

"Julia also gave me these," Miriam said, handing Linda the envelope.

Linda opened it and thumbed through the childhood pictures of Miriam before landing on one of Ray and Rosalind in Sydney. "How do you feel about these?"

"They're fantastic. Seeing my biological parents together makes me emotional. They were in love, and how they looked at each other. Linda, it makes me happy."

"You were the product of love. Even if things went sideways after."

"Exactly. And they also confirm my dad cared about me. He kept these photos and watched me on the telly every Sunday. He should've done better, but he respected Mum's wishes and deserves some credit for that."

"How does this information change things for you?"

Miriam paused in thought. "It complicates my feelings toward him. But still, he should've reached out, especially after Mum died."

"And Rosalind?"

"She had her flaws, but she was my anchor. She could have handled it better, for sure. But one untruth stemming from personal embarrassment doesn't erase all the good. She gave me everything. She put me first, always."

"I'm impressed at how well you're processing it all. It's a credit to you."

"I'll talk to my therapist next week, but I currently have more positive feelings than negative," Miriam said, her eyes fixed on the Pacific.

Julia and her surfboard were sitting, relaxed, on the water. Her hair shimmered in the sun. She started paddling with purpose, positioning herself as the next breaker approached. As it began to crest, she popped to her feet in one motion, her knees bending to absorb the energy of the water. She carved a crisp turn along the face, the edge of her board cutting clean lines into the water. A spray of white foam trailed her, catching the light as she transitioned into a graceful bottom turn.

The coastline stretched endlessly in both directions, the jagged cliffs framing the crescent of sand below. Seagulls hovered above, their cries blending with the current. Behind Julia, the iconic Malibu Pier jutted, its wooden beams weathered by salt and time. On the beach, a few surfers watched her ride, nodding in respect as she executed a final sweeping cutback, her board slicing toward the breaking swell. Julia rode the wave to shore, stepping off the board as if dismounting from an Olympic balance beam. She caught Miriam's and Linda's gazes and waved.

"She's one with the ocean," Miriam said. "Untamed but in total control. I love her so much."

"She's very impressive out there. The local surfers getting out of the way and watching is proof of her talents. She's quite the athlete. Oh, speaking of sisters, did Catrina confirm lunch?" Linda asked.

"I haven't heard from her. But I'm not worried about it. If she doesn't show, I'll take Julia to a proper Rodeo establishment."

"She'll show. I can't wait for your report on the Jewish deli. Grab a black-and-white cookie for the road."

"Yeah, no thanks," Miriam said. "Let me ask you something: When I visited your office a couple of weeks ago, the staff looked at me strangely. Did I do something wrong?"

"You're too beautiful, is all."

"Seriously . . ."

"My partners are pissed because their clients can't get modeling work like you can."

"They can take my gigs."

"No, they can't, which is the problem. They want me to mentor a junior agent to steal my clients and force me out. The bad vibes you felt were directed at me. I'm sorry."

Linda took a deep breath; it was time to force the conversation— the one she had dreaded. Miriam looked fine, which was encouraging. Being clearheaded two days in a row was a start, but Miriam needed a treatment plan. Linda glanced at her. There was a fragility in her posture, one she rarely saw from the woman who had built her career on commanding attention and exuding confidence. "How are you doing, Mir?"

"Better. Having Julia here has me settled—clean." She hesitated.

"But I'm nervous about what happens when she leaves. It's easier when she's around. When it's just me ..."

"That's why we need a plan. Have you given more thought to rehab?"

Miriam sighed, setting her mug down. "I have thought about it. The idea of going somewhere public—no thanks."

"It's not public," Linda said. "Rehab gives you the best shot at getting better. You've got a lot riding on this, Miriam. Your health, your career ... your life."

Miriam didn't respond right away. Her eyes stayed on Julia, who had just caught a wave, her movements fluid and precise as she carved through the water.

Linda shifted in her seat. "Speaking of your career, I haven't finalized the *Greta* deal yet."

Miriam's head snapped toward her. "What? Why not? I told you to do it."

"I couldn't, Mir," Linda said. "Not until I knew you were serious about getting better. Signing that deal puts a lot of people's money at risk. If you're not in the right place to follow through, it will end your career."

"So you don't trust me?"

"It's not about trust," Linda said. "It's about protecting you. Protecting your reputation. If we move forward and you're not ready, it could ruin more than this deal—it could ruin everything you've worked for."

Miriam looked back at the ocean, her shoulders stiff. "I told you I would do it. That should be enough. Is it not your job?"

"No," Linda said. "It's not. It's my job to guide your career, not take orders. I've been by your side for years; I'm not going anywhere. But if you don't take the steps to get better, I can't keep representing you. I'll always be your friend, but I can't be your agent if you won't get clean. Starting today."

"You would let me go?"

"I'd never abandon you, but I'll not represent you if it means I can't tell you the hard truths," Linda said. "I prayed on this with

Rabbi Yael. I won't avoid the shitty conversations anymore. You're too important to me for that. I don't care if I never make another dime from your career; I need you to be healthy."

"Linda, I have a confession." Miriam paused, and Linda straightened, not knowing what to expect. "Two things have kept me alive: my career and that young girl out there," Miriam said, pointing to Julia, who was sitting on her board, taking a breather. "After Mum died and I was stuck on *Night Nurses*, my career on autopilot, I lost control. I was taking Klonopin like they were Skittles and drinking every night. I have large gaps in my memory from that period."

"Mir, that's scary."

"Remember when I cut my hair before the season finale of *Night Nurses*?"

"I do. The producers ripped my head off."

"Well, I was high. I recall the stylist coming to my flat. After that, no memory. When I woke up, I was in shock. I cried. I panicked. When I calmed down, I convinced myself it was intentional, the best thing for my career, and put on a confident show. But . . ."

"I don't have words."

"If I had stayed in London, I would've died. Two things gave me a purpose and a reason to keep going. The first was moving to Los Angeles and auditioning for bigger roles, and the second . . ."

"Julia?"

"For sure. If she hadn't called me that day, I'm not sure where I would be right now. Our daily calls kept me sober. I was still taking the medication, but I stopped drinking. I made sure I was right by seven each evening for the video chats. I never wanted her to see me messed up."

"What happened after you lost *IRS Rogue*?"

"The drinking started again, and that meant missing calls with Julia. She thought it was because of my medical procedures, but I missed most of them because I was in bad shape."

"And the botched procedure?"

"You can't drink on that medication, Linda. It was all my fault."

"What about rehab? Surely you see it's time."

"I'll not go to rehab."

They watched as Julia paddled hard, her arms slicing through the glassy Malibu water as a wave rose behind her. She popped onto her board, carved into the face, the wind rushing past her as she shifted her weight to ride the curve, but as she tried to pull off a cutback, her back foot slipped, sending her tumbling into the crashing whitewater, the wave swallowing her whole.

"Oh my . . . is she okay?" Linda asked, panicked.

Miriam grabbed her binoculars and scanned the ocean, then pointed to Julia, who emerged, sputtering and laughing, with Floating Sky bobbing nearby.

"I've watched her for two sessions and hadn't seen her wipe out before."

"There's a strong metaphor here, but I'm not clever enough to come up with it," Linda said as she checked her watch. She needed to decide which agreement to pull out of her bag.

"Don't sack me, Linda," Miriam said. "I'm still a good bet. Julia being here has opened my eyes. I want to get better for my career, for you, so I can have a relationship with her."

"It's not about me, Mir. This is about you."

"I have disappointed you over the years. I have been a miserable client. I'll get better, please believe me. I'll regain your trust. I want the *Greta* show. I need to work."

Linda heard Miriam's eagerness to get clean and her insistence that their professional relationship would continue, but she knew better than to take those promises at face value. She had dealt with addicts before—they promised sobriety while taking no actionable steps. Miriam's sincerity didn't equate to readiness, and Linda couldn't afford to gamble her reputation. She needed evidence—actions that backed up the promises. She had seen Miriam sober at the Dodgers game and heard her speak about wanting to change, but she had heard no evidence of a plan, no concrete steps beyond talk. Without that, Linda's decision was clear. The *Greta* deal was too significant to risk on wishful thinking.

Her heart ached as she reached into her work purse for the

Termination of Representation Agreement. Ending their business relationship was the hardest decision of her career. She cared for Miriam and wanted to believe in her, but nothing Miriam had said or done had given Linda another choice, as far as she could tell. This was about protecting Miriam's future, even if it meant stepping away as her agent.

As Linda pulled out the papers, Miriam leaned back in her chair and slid a thick folder out from under her seat, placing it on the patio table between them. Linda raised an eyebrow as Miriam flipped it open to reveal its contents. "What's this?" she asked.

"This," Miriam said, "is everything I'm doing to get better."

Linda thumbed through the folder. Each section was labeled: medical assessments, therapy agreements, a nutrition plan, and signed schedules. Her eyes widened at the signatures. "Is this . . . ?"

"A commitment," Miriam finished. "I have a doctor, Dr. Conway, overseeing everything. He specializes in addiction recovery. We've set up a plan for detox and regular at-home physical check-ins. I start tomorrow after Julia leaves."

"I've heard of him. He's well regarded."

"The detox period will be ugly. Dr. Conway said there is no way around it. He'll visit my house daily to monitor my vitals and assess my progress. He's assigned two full-time nurses to work in shifts until I get through the nightmare period."

"A night nurse? Poetic."

"Indeed . . ."

Linda's fingers hovered over another document. "This is your therapist?"

Miriam nodded. "Yes, Dr. Leah Caldwell. Three sessions a week for the next six months. She specializes in addiction and works with actors, so she understands our unique pressures."

Linda turned to another page. "And this? Nutritionist and trainer?"

"I need to rebuild my health, Linda. The nutritionist, Katie Marsh, has tailored a plan to help me recover my energy and repair the damage. And the trainer . . . well, they'll keep me honest."

"I'm impressed."

"Also, a yoga instructor will alternate days with the trainer."

Linda sat back, stunned. "You've already signed all of this?"

Miriam nodded, her tone firm. "Every single one. Deposits were paid to each provider. This is what I'm doing, starting tomorrow after lunch. It's going to be hell."

Linda scanned the pages again, disbelief giving way to admiration. "I can't believe you did all this, Mir. I've never seen you this . . . prepared."

"I had to be," Miriam said. "I can't lose *Greta*."

Linda pressed her lips together. "This is a great plan. Never in my wildest dreams—"

"I have let you down before, but not this time. My career is everything."

Linda hesitated, then said, "Ask Julia to stay with you for the next six months. She's been good for you."

Miriam's expression softened. "I wish she wasn't going home. I would do anything for her to stay."

"Ask her, Mir."

Miriam shook her head. "As I said, she can't be tamed. She has her own life."

Linda rested her hand on Miriam's. "Mir, don't decide for her. Ask her. Let her decide."

"What's that?" Miriam asked, changing the subject and pointing to the papers Linda had pulled from her bag.

Linda paused and glanced at the ocean. Julia was emerging from the water, her surfboard trailing in the sand. Her pace was leisurely, but her imminent arrival meant it was time to act. Miriam's presentation had been thorough, featuring signed agreements, credible timelines, and tangible steps toward recovery, and Linda's reasonable doubts were no longer justified. Miriam wasn't only making promises; she'd taken action.

Linda was more than satisfied; she was relieved, elated. She returned the Termination of Representation Agreement to her bag and replaced it with the Series Lead Casting Agreement. "Miriam,"

Linda said, setting the freshly pulled papers on the table, "before I go, I've got some papers for you to sign. It's the *Greta* contract. Terms are what we discussed."

Miriam's face lit up as she reached for the pen. "Nice," she said, scribbling her signature without bothering to read the document. "Thank you for believing in me. I'll not let you down."

Linda checked the signature and stood while putting the papers back in her bag. Miriam's head was clear. The last eighteen months had been a struggle, but everything was turning around.

As Linda walked out, Miriam said, "Oh, and Linda, take a junior agent."

Linda stopped and turned. "What? No thanks."

"Seriously, get a mentee. Today."

"Why? I'm not playing their grubby game."

"Linda, trust me. Get a junior agent—just not *their* junior agent. Find your own. A young woman. Only a woman. Either from your synagogue or referred by someone you trust. She'll lighten your daily load. She'll recruit young talent. And eventually, you'll have a protégé to take over . . . in thirty years, when I retire."

CHAPTER 26

A fter a life-altering week with Sam, today marked a return to reality.

Catrina hadn't labeled their relationship, and neither had Sam, but that didn't matter. In her mind, she was her girlfriend. Lately, Sam occupied every corner of her attention. Sam moved through the apartment with a calm that grounded Catrina. The intimacy they had discovered had pulled her into its current so completely that she had gone days without thinking about the deposition or her dad. That inattention, however comforting, couldn't continue.

Today, she was going to Los Angeles to have lunch with her half sisters. After that, she would deal with DeltaTech. She had scheduled an appointment with an affordable attorney in Carlsbad, but she hadn't paid the deposit. She remained undecided because she didn't know what version of herself she wanted to bring to the deposition.

When she had taken the files and walked out of the building, she had been clear-eyed. No self-delusion. No rationalizations. She had known exactly what she was doing. She had committed a crime—probably more than one—and had told herself, in that moment, that she would face the consequences. That was the cost. That was the deal. But now that the fallout had arrived, her resolve had softened. Hiring a lawyer felt disingenuous. A defense team would draft a narrative where she had been pressured, manipulated, and caught in someone else's design. Tim would become the sole architect. She would become incidental. It wasn't the truth, and she didn't know if she could stomach pretending it was.

She was of two minds. Her entire life had taught her to choose the expedient option, to anticipate what others needed from her and deliver it efficiently and invisibly. If she walked into the deposition and did what was expected—covering for Tim, blurring her involvement, minimizing the scope of the theft—she might emerge with limited damage. It was the same strategy she had followed for years, one she knew how to execute. But she was trying to change.

Her relationship with Sam, however early, had become a testament to that effort. She wanted to be someone who earned trust, not someone who manipulated it to her advantage. She wanted to be able to sleep at night without the familiar churn of self-doubt— without the persistent loop of second-guessing and moral editing. She wanted relief from the waking guilt that crept in before dawn, the mental inventory of choices she could no longer defend. She wanted to live in a way that didn't rely on clever framing or plausible deniability.

Maybe the answer was to walk into the deposition and tell the truth. Tim would be ruined, publicly and professionally, and she wouldn't come out clean either. Her consequences would be substantial—possible criminal charges and the unraveling of her career. Her savings might be wiped out. She could lose everything. She would be forced to navigate a life that looked a lot like the one she had watched her mother survive: piecemeal jobs with overdue utility bills. Still, there was a chance the authorities would distinguish her from Tim. And it had been his idea. She was younger. He was the boss and had all the power. He made most of the money.

But wasn't that just another gray zone? Hoping to be seen as the reasonable one, the good actor, the naïve girl who cooperated unwittingly? Wasn't that still a performance—another form of self-preservation? If she leaned on that narrative, was she changing at all?

Even if she told the truth, even if she took the hit, no version of this ended cleanly. She would still be dragged through years of legal proceedings. She didn't know if she had the endurance for it. Worse, she didn't know if Sam would stay. Sam had options, a life rich with family who loved her and friends who adored her. Why would she choose to tie herself to someone spiraling through personal and professional ruin?

Catrina didn't have the answer. None of the options offered clarity. Each one asked her to weigh who she had been against who she wanted to become. Each one threatened to strain the most meaningful relationship in her life. And none of them made her feel like the person she hoped Sam saw when she looked at her in the morning.

Catrina pushed the thoughts aside. She needed to meet her half sisters with a clear mind, or at least as clear as it could be under the circumstances. She still hadn't allowed herself to fully consider what it meant to lose her father, the biological parent who had rejected her outright. Maybe the lunch would begin that process. Maybe it would even conclude it, allowing her to box it up and move on with one less thing to carry. Either way, she had to get out the door. She needed to stop by Morven's before heading to Los Angeles. A fresh crisis had emerged.

The more things changed, the more they stayed the same. She had woken to an urgent text from her mother asking her to stop by before leaving town. Catrina hadn't asked for details. She knew the tone well enough. As much as she didn't have the emotional bandwidth for another problem, she decided it was easier to stop by than to deal with it later. But her mind wasn't on Morven. It was on Sam.

Catrina had no frame of reference for what was happening between them. She'd dated boys in high school—movie nights, group hangouts—but not much since, other than the occasional one-off dates, and Tim . . . College blurred into coursework and part-time jobs. By the time she started at DeltaTech as a junior, her career was her priority, not men.

There was no single moment she could point to, no flicker of recognition or sudden knowing. It was the accumulation of small shifts: the way Sam moved through their apartment, the way she listened without waiting to speak, the way she offered affection. Catrina had never been in a relationship like this—not as a woman, not with a woman—and the novelty of it was both exhilarating and disorienting. She kept catching herself watching Sam's fingers wrapped around a mug, the way she laughed mid-sentence, the profile of her face while reading.

The strangeness wasn't in being with Sam. It was in how natural it felt. As if her body had known long before her mind allowed the possibility. She wasn't confused about wanting Sam. The disorientation came from how new it all was—being in a relationship, being in a relationship with a woman, being in a relationship with her best friend. It was equal parts exhilarating and terrifying.

Morven had her laptop set up on the kitchen counter with her phone out. She was practically running in place, her energy at a ten.

"What's going on, Mom?" Catrina said, preemptively annoyed, standing in the threshold of the kitchen. "I have to get to LA. I want to shop for a blazer before lunch."

"Your father's widow sent me a message on Facebook. Look."

Hello Morven,
I imagine you heard the news as Julia told Catrina about their father. I have been carrying tremendous guilt for my husband's actions and my complicity for over twenty years. I want to say sorry. Sorry for everything. You don't owe me anything, but if you would like to talk, my contact information is below.
Alice Corning

Catrina froze, stunned. Her mind blurred, unable to form coherent thoughts, let alone feelings.

Morven continued. "Can you believe this woman? The nerve. I ought to call her and give her a piece of my mind. Say all the things I was going to say to your father, had our paths ever crossed."

Catrina sank into a chair, her mouth slightly open as she tried to make sense of the message. Her thoughts ricocheted between Sam, DeltaTech, Tim, and the upcoming lunch with her sisters. She was already at capacity.

"She and your father deny your existence, and now she wants me to give her closure? Wants me to relieve her guilt?" Morven paced the kitchen, voice rising.

"Call her," Catrina said, eyes fixed ahead. "Put it on speaker."

"For real?"

Catrina nodded.

"How do you want me to play it?" Morven asked, sitting down again.

"Nothing to play. Just hear her out. Maybe you'll get out some of your anger, and she'll get rid of some guilt. Win-win," Catrina said. "And if it goes badly, who cares? We'll never hear from her again."

"And maybe you have some inheritance."

"Stop it, Mom."

Catrina pulled out her phone and opened the clock app. "Wait— it's two in the morning in Sydney. We should call her later."

"Not a chance," Morven said, dialing.

After a few rings, Alice answered. "Corning residence."

"Alice? This is Morven. I've got Catrina with me."

"Oh my, thank you . . . Let me gather my . . . I'm sorry, I need to—"

Catrina cut in. "Mrs. Corning, Julia told me about your husband. I'm having lunch with her in a few hours. I'm very sorry for your loss."

Morven said nothing. The *I'll give her the what-for* bravado evaporated.

"I'm glad you three are connecting," Alice said, her voice

struggling. "I only reached out to apologize. On my behalf. On your father's behalf. You deserved better. I should've done better. I—"

Catrina cut in again, losing patience. "Mrs. Corning, I appreciate the sentiment. I'm looking forward to meeting your daughter today. You don't owe us anything. My father chose to reject me, sight unseen. I'm fine with it. Truly. Don't spend another minute of your life worrying about me. If anything, his passing opened a small window. If he were still alive, I wouldn't be going to lunch today."

Catrina could hear soft crying on the other end. Morven stayed silent.

"Please, Mrs. Corning. Get some rest. We do appreciate the message. We don't hold anything against you."

"Thank you, dear. You and your mother are very classy. I'm so, so sorry."

The call ended. Catrina looked over at Morven, who still hadn't spoken.

"What happened to giving her a piece of your mind?" she said, mocking Morven on her way to the car, leaving her mother to spiral.

She appreciated Alice's sincerity and was naturally empathetic to the new widow but was surprised by how little the call affected her. She didn't care about Alice, or her apology, or the fact that she'd never met her father and, now, never would. It was all a big nothing.

Catrina considered skipping lunch, keeping her half sisters as permanent strangers, and instead spending the morning hanging out with Sam at the Break.

CHAPTER 27

M iriam was relieved. She had nearly lost her career and stood on the edge; in that way, the Malibu rental house overlooking the cliff was an easy metaphor for her life. She was ready to get healthy. She wanted to save her career, repay Linda for her unwavering faith, and be the big sister Julia deserved. She also wanted to meet her mother's standards of success—both as an actress and as a person. But most importantly, she wanted to get healthy for herself, a realization that had solidified as she watched Julia surf.

As she sat across from her sisters in a corner booth at Nate 'n Al's, sipping refilled coffee and picking at the plates of food in front of them, she was content. The deli bustled around them, waitstaff weaving between tables with trays piled high with pastrami sandwiches, matzo ball soup, and towering plates of roast beef.

"Tell me about our dad," Catrina requested.

"What do you want to know?" Julia asked.

Miriam was surprised by Catrina's sudden directness after an hour of casual small talk, which had revolved around Catrina's work, Julia's boyfriend, and Miriam's health.

"Pick anything," Catrina said. "I didn't know him."

Julia exhaled and shrugged. "He was . . . a difficult person to live with. Strict, expected you to do things his way. He worked hard. Followed his routine. He spoke like you would expect a headmaster to speak. He was very academic but had an explosive temper. Not the warm-and-fuzzy type, if that's what you're asking."

"No . . . not really," Catrina replied. "What was he like as a father?" she pressed. "What was it like growing up with him?"

Miriam spoke up. "Yeah, Jules, what did we miss?"

"It sucked," Julia said. "It really sucked. I hated it. I was glad I moved out. My biggest regret is not leaving earlier. I should've trusted my ability to survive on my own when I finished school."

Catrina smirked. "I get it. I stuck around my mom's after graduation when I shouldn't have."

Julia nodded at Catrina and then continued. "He was controlling, critical, impossible to please. Everything had to be his way, done exactly how he wanted it. And if you didn't live up to his expectations, he would spend entire meals telling you so. If I did something well, he would then criticize me for not doing it earlier or more often. There was no winning. It was easier to do nothing and be called a bum than to try and then be told that my attempt wasn't the right kind of trying." The rawness in her voice silenced the table. Julia's gaze dropped to her coffee, then up to Miriam, with whom she had shared some things about Ray during their video chats.

Miriam gave her a warm smile to reassure her as she continued. "American coffee is shit compared to Australia," Julia said.

"You should try my girlfriend's place in Carlsbad and see how it compares," Catrina said. "Don't rate us on diner drip coffee."

"Anyways, the only two times he cared—the only times he ever looked at me as if I was worth a damn—were when I won a surf competition and again when I brought my boyfriend to brunch. He couldn't wait to tell all his friends, colleagues, and neighbors that his daughter had won a surfing competition and was dating a famous cricketer."

Miriam's eyes softened, but she stayed quiet.

"I kept thinking, *Maybe this time he'll say he's proud of me*—the person, not the shiny trophy I won or because of the person I was sleeping with. But it never happened. He thinks he raised me, but . . . It doesn't matter—there's no fixing it now."

Miriam reached across the table, her hand brushing Julia's. "I'm sorry, Jules. If it matters, I think you're worth a lot of damns."

"You're the one he loved, Mir. He worshipped you. Every Sunday, he watched your show. You were the daughter he wanted. I was . . . an annoyance. A daughter he had to manage and failed to motivate. A disappointment. You were perfection in his eyes."

Miriam frowned. "He didn't love me, Jules. Watching my show wasn't love. He watched out of regret. Out of guilt. But not love. If you love someone, you reach out, even if it might not go well. He wasn't man enough to handle rejection, first from my mum, then he feared it from me. His fragile ego couldn't risk a second Worthington rejection. It's quite pathetic."

"I was with him on his deathbed; he loved you, Mir. He did," Julia said.

"He thought he loved me—but his actions told a different story."

"And I was the one he denied," Catrina added, seemingly bitter. "Though his refusal to acknowledge my existence made life easier. Don't get me wrong, not having a father—or at least a father paying child support—sucked. My mom was a disaster, and we never had money. A financially supportive father would've made a significant difference. But I never felt an emotional loss. I never sat around and worried about a man who pretended his drunken night with my mom didn't happen."

"He knew," Julia said.

"Knew what?" Catrina asked.

"He stalked you online. He saw your picture. Of the three of us, you look the most like him. He knew—my mum confirmed as much," Julia said.

"Isn't that worse? Was he a coward or in denial?" Catrina asked.

"Both," Miriam said. "My guess is that he didn't remember that night with your mom. And he used that as an excuse to deny everything. But he is also a coward. He could have taken a test. He could have acknowledged the resemblance in the pictures. I've known you for an hour, and I can tell you he missed out on an amazing person. His loss."

"From Julia's description, I didn't miss much," Catrina said.

"Maybe not, but you and your mother deserved financial support. My mother iced him out, but her family's resources made that possible. It sounds like your mother had to scrape by, which is unfair," Miriam said.

"He denied me sight unseen. It oddly didn't feel personal. That's how I've accepted it all these years. I wrote him off as a deadbeat and moved on. I don't see myself doing much work on this topic. I've boxed up my feelings and am happy to leave it alone," Catrina said.

Julia and Miriam nodded.

"I hope you realize that ignoring Miriam's email wasn't personal," Catrina told them. "I just . . . had a lot going on in my life and wanted to avoid unwrapping my neat little box," she finished.

The waiter stopped by to offer another coffee refill, clearing away the plates of half-eaten food. None of them had eaten much, their appetites dulled by the conversation.

"We've spent too much time discussing him," Miriam said. "Julia, tell us about Alice."

"Mum is frustrating," Julia said. "She always covered for Dad, making excuses for his treatment of me. I hated how she let him treat her. She never had a life outside the house and existed solely to make him happy. I was pissed that she didn't tell me I had sisters. I'm still mad about it a year and a half later."

"I'm sorry," Miriam said.

"Not your fault," Julia said. "I should lighten up on her. It wasn't easy balancing those secrets against Dad's shame. But she shielded me in her way. She tried to add warmth to the home, especially when Dad and I were fighting. She would do little things that were just for me—a favorite dish at a formal meal or packing a bag of towels and linens for my flat—she considered my needs in a house dominated by Dad."

Catrina took the baton. "My mum, Morven, was . . . is . . . a mess, if I'm honest. Financially, emotionally, all of it. She created chaos everywhere she went—always scrambling to fix whatever was falling apart that week. And she was scared of everything falling apart. But no matter what, her love is constant. I feel it every day. Looking back, I should've set firmer boundaries, but I also can't blame her for leaning on me. She had no support. It was the two of us."

"She had it hard," Miriam said.

"Yeah, but she was there for me—when I broke up with my high-school boyfriend, she sat with me for hours, holding me while I cried, and shit-talked the guy to comfort me. And when I screwed up, at school or wherever, she took my side. She would defend me—even when I was wrong. Her love was—is—unconditional," Catrina concluded, looking toward Miriam.

"Rosalind," Miriam said, taking her turn, "she wasn't warm, not like Alice or Morven. She didn't show love with hugs or words but made up for it in her actions. Every decision she made was for me. She worked tirelessly to help me succeed and provide me with every advantage. I don't agree with her choice to keep him out of my life— it was selfish. She wanted to avoid a scandal. I'll never understand why she thought anyone would care. It's such a regular occurrence."

"It really is," Catrina said.

"She grew up in the British upper class. They have their rules and are old-fashioned. I didn't have to deal with any of it, thanks to her. But if she was leaving the aristocracy anyway, why not let me have a relationship with Dad? It doesn't make sense." Miriam paused. "But I can't deny how much she sacrificed for me. Her path of least resistance would've been to have an abortion. She could have gone ahead with her life, and nobody would've known. She gave up her family, friends, and societal standing to have me . . . I miss her so much." Miriam's eyes reddened as she sipped her coffee. After a few seconds, she glanced at her watch and then stood, smoothing her outfit. "I'm out of time."

"Nice watch. Did you model for Patek Philippe?" Catrina asked.

"Yeah, half-day gig—came with a free watch. It's a Calatrava series."

Miriam's phone buzzed—a message from her doctor with notes about her in-home evaluation that afternoon. Anxiety coursed through her, but she didn't want her sisters to see her distressed. Forcing herself to stay calm, she let her mind race in silence. She sat back down, letting her two younger sisters steer the conversation for a minute.

"What's next?" Julia asked Catrina.

"I'll head back to Carlsbad. Want me to drop you at the airport?"

"Nah, I enjoy a bus ride. I enjoy people-watching and seeing the city unfold before me."

Miriam smiled; she enjoyed watching Catrina get a taste of Julia's stubborn side.

"I get it. Forces you to slow down a little," Catrina replied.

"Exactly. So are you nervous about your legal thingy next week?" Julia asked.

Catrina shrugged. "Yeah. I need to decide before Monday's deposition."

"What's jamming you up?" Julia asked.

"The short version is that if I answer the questions truthfully, my boss will be screwed. He'd get arrested and lose everything."

"Good. From what you mentioned earlier, he deserves it," Miriam interjected.

"No doubt. But here's the problem. If he gets in trouble, I'll have to deal with the fallout. I'll have to go to court and talk with prosecutors. At best, it will be a three-year drain on my time and emotions. At worst, I could be prosecuted for my involvement."

"That would suck," Miriam said.

"I'm in a great place with my girlfriend, and I don't want his baggage to hang over us. The only time Sam and I argue is when we talk about him."

"So what's the other option?" Julia asked.

"I take the fall. I say it was all my fault. I deny committing any crimes and hope they prosecute me. My boss claims he'll take care of me financially if I accept responsibility in court. So potentially, I wouldn't be financially ruined. But trusting him isn't a safe bet, obviously."

"What a shit option," Miriam said, glancing at her phone. She needed to get back home but hated losing time with her sisters.

"Both options are shit," Catrina said.

"Maybe I'm thick, but why are there only two options?" Julia asked.

Catrina paused. "Fuck, you're right, there has to be a Door 3."

"Door 3?" Julia asked.

Deep in thought and looking right past them, Catrina mused, "Another way to do this. A better way. I might be able to remove him from my life—today—and keep myself out of trouble . . ."

"Uh, do that one," Julia said, smirking.

Out of time, Miriam announced she had to go, then leaned over to hug Catrina, saying, "Stay in touch." Then, moving to Julia, she pulled her sister's head close and kissed her temple. "I love you very much."

"I love you too, Mir," Julia said.

"Are you sure I can't drive you to the airport?" Miriam asked, knowing it was a futile offer she didn't have time for anyway.

Julia shook her head. "I'll call you before I board."

Miriam didn't argue. She grabbed the check, waved goodbye, and walked to the register to wait in line. Behind her, she could hear Catrina shifting the conversation, turning the questioning onto Julia.

Miriam listened carefully, glancing back at the table as Catrina slid into the seat Miriam had vacated. She watched as Catrina leaned forward, locking eyes with Julia. "Why don't you stay and live in Miriam's mansion?"

"I don't know. Back in Sydney, I have a job. I do surf rescue, and I have a boyfriend."

Catrina scooted closer. "You can do all that here, and Miriam needs you."

"I don't want to be a burden. She has enough on her plate."

"It isn't charity, Julia. You're her favorite person in the world. The way she looks at you—pure adoration."

"I hear you. I'll come back. She offered me her air miles. I'll be over real soon."

"Julia, skip your flight. Stay in Los Angeles."

Miriam paid and walked out, giving one last wave to her sisters. Her throat tightened as she fought back tears. For a split second, she wanted to turn back and beg Julia to stay. But that would be selfish. Julia had a life waiting for her in Sydney, and the next few weeks would be brutal. The detox program wasn't something a young girl should have to witness. Letting her go was the right decision, but it didn't feel that way.

CHAPTER 28

Door *3 . . . there's always a Door 3.* The idea had taken root during Catrina's conversation with Julia and had blossomed into a fully formed plan. No more ethical compromises or submissions to Tim's manipulative games. This time, she would leave clean, on her terms.

On her way to Carlsbad, Catrina pulled into a convenience store in Anaheim. The place was a relic of a bygone era, its neon sign humming, the letters struggling to stay lit against the midafternoon sun. Inside, the aisles were cramped and mismatched, with dusty shelves displaying an odd assortment of items—chips in faded packaging, off-brand energy drinks, and the usual clutter of lottery tickets and candy bars. Behind the counter, a cashier in his early twenties sat slouched on a stool, earbuds hidden under shaggy brown hair. His eyes didn't lift from his phone as Catrina grabbed a prepaid cell from a rack near the register—a basic smartphone with enough functionality to pass as modern, loaded with 1,000 minutes and one gig of data. A device marketed toward travelers, digital minimalists, drug dealers, and those who needed a fresh start.

Catrina paid in cash, brushing off the cashier's apathetic "Have a nice day" as she slid the purchase into her tote bag. She darted to her car, a muted-silver Lexus hybrid that was practical but had lived through better days. Tossing the phone onto the passenger seat, she started the engine, her mind racing ahead to the second step of "Door 3." Catrina loved naming things.

While stuck at a standstill on I-5, Catrina pulled out the prepaid smartphone and set it up. She registered and linked a new email address to a virtual fax line. Every connection point was untraceable to her old job, thoroughly erasing any digital breadcrumbs that could connect to BSS. The hybrid's air conditioning whirred as she worked, her mind calm and calculating despite the highway's disarray. She took a bite of the remnants of her pastrami sandwich from the carryout container sitting on the passenger seat, the smoky saltiness of the meat mingling with the sharp tang of mustard and the slight chew of the rye bread.

Catrina was surprised at her calmness as she grabbed the prepaid and dialed Sam, hoping she would answer the call from the unfamiliar number.

"Hello?" Sam answered hesitantly.

"Sam, it's me. I know you're finishing your shift, so I'll be quick. This is my temporary phone number. I wanted you to have it."

"New number? Everything okay? How was lunch?"

"It was good. I'll fill you in when I get home, but I need to go to the office first."

"Why? Your deposition is Monday. Take the rest of the day and breathe. I'll be home soon, and we can do that thing . . ."

"Uh, yes to *that thing*, but hold tight. First, I need to get Tim out of my life, *our* life. Permanently. I have a plan. I named it 'Door 3.'"

"Yes! You're finally burning Tim down, aren't you? And of course you named your plan," Sam said, speaking rapidly.

"No," Catrina said confidently. "Burning him at deposition guarantees he stays in my life. I have a better plan—to remove him forever, starting today."

"What's the plan?"

"Door 3 will play all sides against Tim. Do you like 'Door 3,' or should it be 'door C'? I can't—"

"*Cat*, who cares about the name? I'm worried about you. Promise me you won't create more regret."

"Door 3 it is. And I won't. I'm clearheaded. Either this works and Tim is gone for good, the lawsuit is dismissed, and I don't have to sit for a deposition—or I'll go on Monday, tell the whole truth, and accept the consequences."

"You sound level."

"I'm at peace. With you, my dad, and now this. Whatever happens, I'll be fine. I just pulled into the office. Wish me luck."

"Go, go, go! Let me know if you need anything. I'll be thinking about you."

Catrina placed her stuff in an empty cubicle at the shared workspace and logged onto her laptop, her movements deliberate and focused. Reaching into her bag, she turned off her main cell phone, cutting off any potential distractions, and placed the new prepaid on her desk. Before she could start her plan, there was one thing she needed to do—the step she regretted skipping when she left DeltaTech.

The resignation letter came together quickly and was short and professional—no dramatic explanations, no parting shots. Only the facts: "Effective immediately, I resign my position at BSS." Her words were direct, and she felt immediate relief. She printed the letter at the communal printer, retrieved it, and placed it on Tim's desk. The gesture was symbolic—walking into the lion's den one last time and walking out with her head held high.

She emailed it to him as well, under the bland subject line *Correspondence*. Tim wouldn't read it. It was Friday afternoon, and he was at the country club, probably on the back nine, drink in hand, spinning bullshit tales for his buddies.

With that done, Catrina was no longer employed by Tim and BSS. She was amazed at how thoroughly the simple act lifted her shoulders and quieted her head. Catrina took a full breath. The Rubicon had been crossed; there was no turning back. She summoned the determination to succeed in the task that was now her charge. She set up for the long afternoon and evening ahead, and her focus sharpened as she prepared for the required four-way manipulation. But unlike Tim's past deceptions, Door 3, if successful, would benefit all involved, even Tim, though he wouldn't agree.

The first call was to Karen, her main contact at SidOrtho—a bright, no-nonsense operations director who had been straightforward in their previous dealings. Dialing Karen's number on the prepaid, Catrina took an exaggerated breath. When the line connected, she greeted Karen.

"Hey, Cat," Karen said. "What's going on?"

"Karen, BSS is going under, probably as soon as Monday," she said. "I don't want SidOrtho to get dragged down with Tim, especially considering how much of your sales come through his accounts."

"Are you serious?" Karen asked, sounding surprised and curious.

"I wouldn't call if I wasn't." Catrina pushed forward. "Look, you've known this was coming. Tim's been coasting for months. He's burned through client goodwill and dropped the ball on deliveries. Getting the cages to the operating rooms on time has been a train wreck."

"That's the truth. We tolerate him because of you and the doctors. Dr. Jones alone accounts for nearly thirty percent of our volume."

"Exactly," Catrina said. "And that's why I need you to act now. If SidOrtho pulls out today, you can save your doctor relationships. I'm offering you a clean exit where you can save those accounts—without Tim in the way."

"What's your angle here, Cat? Are you starting a new distributor? Are you making a play?"

"No play. No games. I'm out. This is my last day in medical device sales. But I don't want SidOrtho, the doctors, and especially the patients caught up in Tim's wreckage. I can't save myself, but I can limit the collateral damage."

"I'm blindsided. I don't even know how to respond."

"Want to hear my idea? Can't hurt, right?"

"Sure. What are you proposing?"

"I'm proposing that you allow me to shop your distribution agreement to a more reputable, better-established company with greater resources than BSS. If I can find an acceptable landing spot and get the doctors to agree today, then SidOrtho can continue business as usual. If you wait till Monday, all hell will break loose, and I can't predict what happens to SidOrtho."

"This is all very dramatic. We've been monitoring the lawsuit. The executives here are very worried. They don't tell me the specifics, but the rumor is Tim crossed lines and—"

"I was on the inside. Tim did cross lines. And SidOrtho benefited from it. At the deposition, I'm going to tell the truth. It will be a bad day for me, for Tim, and for BSS. That's the reality. BSS won't survive. And if SidOrtho wants to survive, it needs to get out of the Tim business—today."

"Look, I don't have the authority to make this decision, but I hear your urgency. Everything you're saying rings true. Tim is a ticking time bomb; if we can get away from him without any business disruptions, we need to consider it. Let me speak with the decision-makers."

After hanging up, Catrina busied herself, awaiting a callback. She organized her paperwork and set up a crisp, professional email signature for her newly registered email account. Every minute counted, but she forced herself to channel the waiting into productivity.

Thirty agonizing minutes later, Karen called back. "Alright, we're open to moving," she said, "but here's the deal: First, we don't want another startup. The new distributor must be well established. Second, we need at least sixteen of Tim's twenty clients to commit, or the switch isn't viable. Third, we don't want to lease our product as we did in the past. This must be a distribution agreement."

"I have a company that will be more than acceptable. Now that I have your sign-off, I'll get the company to agree and report back to you. As for the clients, I'll get sixteen commits by the end of the day."

"And Cat? We need Dr. Jones. Without him, the numbers won't work."

The mention of Dr. Jones sent a shiver down Catrina's spine. He would be the hardest to flip—his friendship with Tim ran deep, and they were probably golfing together—but the demand was reasonable. Catrina had feared his commitment would be required and wasn't caught off guard by the stipulation. "Understood. I'll make it happen," she said, trying to portray confidence. Door 3 had sounded more fun in her head; now it was an albatross. But she took the win. Stakeholder one of four was in, provisionally at least.

"Thanks, Cat. I'll push our legal team to expedite the distributor agreement for the new company," Karen said optimistically.

Catrina's next call was to her old friend Rachel at DeltaTech. She knew her reputation there was in tatters after Tim had discredited her to management and because she'd left without giving proper notice. Of all Catrina's regrets, DeltaTech was at the top of her list. The company had treated her well, and she'd repaid them by pillaging their files and converting their customers. She hoped Rachel, still a friend—though primarily online—would take her call and pass the pitch up the chain of command.

"Rachel," she said as soon as the other woman had picked up, "here's the deal. I resigned from BSS earlier today. If I can deliver a SidOrtho exclusive distribution agreement and at least sixteen of Tim's clients, including Dr. Jones, would DeltaTech be interested?"

"Cat, is this for real? What's going on?"

"My deposition is Monday. Tim and BSS won't survive it. I don't want the doctors and their patients to suffer. SidOrtho makes a really good product. I don't want the doctors and patients to miss out because of Tim. Because of me."

"How are you going to do this?"

"Tim checked out months ago. I have the relationships with the doctors. Most of them, anyway. I can sell them on DeltaTech's superior support systems and operational capacity. It's a no-brainer. Tim isn't providing any value."

"What's the catch? What's in it for you?"

"All I want is for DeltaTech to drop the lawsuit and cancel my deposition. I'll then exit the scene, and nobody in the industry will have to hear from me or Tim again."

"This is intense."

"SidOrtho no longer wants to work with Tim. They gave me a day to find a new distributor and to move the doctors before they cancel Tim's agreement and become free agents. I would love for the destination to be DeltaTech, but I understand if my reputation kills it."

"If DeltaTech says no, what are you going to do?"

"I'll go to the deposition on Monday, tell the truth, and accept the consequences. But DeltaTech should consider this proposal. Tim brings in a significant amount of money distributing SidOrtho cages, and DeltaTech has the infrastructure to do it more efficiently. It also solves their cage development issue."

"You mean the designs you and Tim stole," Rachel said.

A cold shiver went down Catrina's spine. "If the higher-ups want to prioritize retribution above profits, that's their right. I did things I'm not proud of, and I'm willing to accept the consequences. But DeltaTech is a publicly traded company. There is a lot of money to make here."

"Your plan is . . . ambitious."

"I know. If I have any goodwill left with you, please see if this can happen. You're my only play," Catrina pleaded.

"I'll escalate it. Hang tight."

As Catrina waited for the call from DeltaTech, she spotted Sam approaching through the lobby, carrying a grocery bag and a thermos. She was dressed in a yellow sundress, and her wavy hair swayed with each step.

"Hey, Cat. Brought some coffee and snacks. I won't stay and bother you."

"You're sweet. Pull up a chair if you have a minute. I'm stuck waiting until I get a callback."

Sam's unannounced visit couldn't have come at a better time—manna from heaven. She was in her usual upbeat mood, and her presence relaxed the tension that had been building on Catrina's shoulders. "How's it going?" she asked.

"So far, so good. I'm waiting for DeltaTech to call me. If they agree to my proposal, I'm in the game. If not, well, I don't have another idea."

"I'm sure they'll go for whatever you're cooking up," Sam said. She appeared to have blind faith in Catrina's abilities to pull this off. Her nonchalance gave Catrina a jolt of confidence.

"How was lunch? Your sisters cool?" Sam asked.

"They were fun. I got along with Julia, the Aussie. She's a ball of energy. No filter between her brain and mouth. We hung out for a bit after Miriam left."

"And how was the famous actress sister?"

"She's like a different species of human. So tall, perfectly dressed, not a hair out of place, and with flawless makeup. She's intimidating, but I like her. Julia is an easier hang, though."

"Will you stay in touch?"

"Julia is going back to Sydney today. She wants us all to go to Disneyland during her next visit."

"How fun! I'll dig out my Minnie ears."

The phone rang, and Sam shot up. "Good luck. Text me updates. See you at home."

Catrina waved goodbye and answered the phone. "Ms. McDavid," began Mr. Wilkshire, DeltaTech's general counsel, "I'll be blunt. This all sounds very far-fetched."

"As I told Rachel, DeltaTech has every reason to ruin Tim and end my career. I won't deny it, and if we go to the deposition on Monday, I'll tell the truth, I promise. But, fair warning, the truth will cause a lot of embarrassment—DeltaTech's lax security while the R&D department is out to lunch, for example. Investors and shareholders won't like what I have to say. My career will be over, no question, but the whole truth doesn't make DeltaTech look good either."

"We know Tim is the crook. Tell the truth, and you won't get in trouble. Not much, at least. Why would we drop the lawsuit?" Wilkshire asked.

"Because it's a loser. Tim spends two dollars for every dollar he makes. A judgment against him is useless. I was born broke and am resigned to dying broke. A judgment will bankrupt me, but that's fine. I'm well suited to living on the margins."

"What's your point?"

"The point is, DeltaTech is spending $750 an hour on attorneys to chase broke people. It's a waste of time and money. Instead, do a deal with me today. Scoop up Tim's clients, distribute the cages, and make money. It's a win for DeltaTech. The only win available. Unless watching Tim and I go down in flames is more important than money. But if that were the case, you wouldn't have called me back."

"We're open to it, but getting all this done today is unlikely."

"I can do it, sir. Give me a chance."

"How about this? You deliver SidOrtho and Tim's clients, we'll drop the lawsuit against you—but only you. You'll still need to testify against Tim. He doesn't get off free."

"Mr. Wilkshire, with respect, I loved working at DeltaTech and wanted to stay there for my entire career. Tim told me you would fire me after he left, and I was scared. Not making excuses, but that's the truth. I still did what I did; I'm not an innocent patsy. It was his idea to leave, but I made it work."

"I believe you. But nothing you're saying makes me want to let Tim off the hook."

"I need the lawsuit dropped. Not for Tim—for me. I can't testify. I can't sit in a room with Tim ever again."

"It's not that easy. We don't just drop lawsuits."

"You're influential. DeltaTech management listens to you. This is a good deal. If it wasn't, you wouldn't be talking to me on a Friday afternoon."

"True."

"I don't testify, and the lawsuit is dismissed—in full. That's the deal, and it's nonnegotiable."

"I'll talk to the leadership," Wilkshire said. "No promises."

Catrina compiled a list of BSS's clients, ranking them from easiest to convert to hardest. Unsurprisingly, Dr. Jones was at the very bottom of the list. Catrina kept checking the prepaid, willing it to ring. She had no idea if DeltaTech would take the deal, though she took the delay as a sign they were open to it. A *no* would have been fast. Unless the *no* was a blowoff.

As Catrina spiraled, the prepaid lit up. It was Wilkshire.

"Catrina, management is conflicted. We called SidOrtho, and they confirmed they would sign a distributor agreement. There are some bad feelings about the acquisition falling apart a couple of years ago, but a distribution agreement makes sense for all involved. We have customers who want cages. The lawyers are working on the details."

"Great."

"You have the rest of today to bring over Dr. Jones and company. If you do, then we'll drop the lawsuit—no deposition, no testimony. If you can't, we'll make other arrangements with SidOrtho, and the lawsuit will proceed as scheduled."

Catrina agreed, then hung up.

Even though Dr. Jones was the most critical doctor to sign, Catrina couldn't call him first. Contacting him was tantamount to telling Tim directly, and she needed the other doctors converted before Tim started calling them.

She started with the safest call: Dr. Mary Scotbrite, a kind and pragmatic physician with whom Catrina had built a strong rapport.

"Dr. Mary, I'm sorry to call you on a Friday. It's important."

"What's wrong, Cat?"

"Not sure if you heard, but Tim and I are being sued, and come Monday, BSS will be out of business."

"Oh, my goodness, I'm so sorry to hear that. Are you okay?"

"I'm scrambling for sure, but BSS has been a disaster, as you've noticed."

"It has, but those cages are essential to my practice."

"That's why I'm bothering you. I'm working with SidOrtho and DeltaTech to ensure all BSS doctors have uninterrupted service. You have a bunch of procedures scheduled. I don't want you and your patients to have delays."

"Cleaning up Tim's messes again . . . Sorry to hear you're caught up in all of this. I need those cages, but I don't need Tim."

"Will you commit to transferring your purchasing to DeltaTech? They're a better company, and combining them with SidOrtho's product will make your life easier."

"I agree. I'll transfer my purchasing to DeltaTech. No issue."

"I'll start the paperwork right now."

"Will you still be my contact?" the doctor asked.

"No. After working for Tim, I'm unemployable. I fear I'll be out of the medical device field."

"I'm so sorry. I've been in the field for decades, and you're the best surgical rep I've had."

"I made my bed by going into business with Tim. Sorry to be pushy, but I need you to sign a transfer form. It's one page."

"Send me the form. I'll sign it. I'll also put in a good word for you. Maybe they can make you the client contact."

"Thank you, Dr. Mary. I truly appreciate it, and I'm sorry to rush you, but I need it as soon as possible."

"You'll have it within the hour," Dr. Mary assured her.

One down, fifteen to go. It would be a long afternoon, but at least she was in the game. Door 3 had earned proof of concept—three major stakeholders were on board, including both companies and one doctor. The remaining doctors would be a grind, but she believed nineteen of the twenty would eventually sign. The real question, the one that would determine her fate, was whether she could convince the doctor who was currently playing golf with Tim.

CHAPTER 29

J ulia wedged herself into the narrow bus seat, leaving Beverly Hills and heading toward LAX, Los Angeles International Airport, via Santa Monica. She settled in, her fingers tracing the edges of Floating Sky's smooth surface absently, a tactile habit that calmed her nerves. The board was a constant, reliable barrier between her and the literal ocean of water below her feet. Her life had been a journey, and Floating Sky had been her protector, physically and emotionally, but this was no longer true. Over the past two years, she'd accumulated a cadre of people who watched out for her—who loved her.

First, there was Miriam. Their daily video chats had kept Julia grounded as she had adjusted to life on her own. Then there was Gus, who had taken on the role of a parent and taught her work ethic, responsibility, and how to build a community. She had a core group of friends. Alani and Ginger had initially come across as immature, but once she had cracked their party-girl exteriors, she had discovered layers of depth. Alani came from a poor immigrant family and had worked her way through beauty school, never complaining about the long hours. She had inspired Julia to get through the long shifts at the taverna.

Poor Marcus. He had treated her with kindness and generosity, and she had been nothing short of a pain. Her tantrums would have —should have—driven him off, especially considering his standing in Sydney. He was a good man, and he also had her back. Of that, she had no doubt.

And there was her mum, Alice. Julia was frustrated by Alice's willingness to let Ray control the house and the secrets she kept, but as Julia had told her sisters, her mom had considered her needs and looked out for her. Without Julia realizing it, Floating Sky had gone from being the most important character in her story to just a surfboard—though a surfboard she loved dearly.

It wasn't the most direct route to LAX, but the detour to Santa Monica was worth the effort. She wanted one last in-person glimpse of the Pacific Ocean before the long flight back to Sydney and everything that awaited her there.

Julia shifted in her seat as the bus rumbled down Wilshire Boulevard. Beverly Hills' palm-lined streets gave way to the glass of Century City. She saw the ultramodern Westfield Mall, its glossy surfaces reflecting the afternoon light. She imagined walking through the mall with Floating Sky, the raised eyebrows and disapproving stares she would draw, and smirked.

Her attention shifted to the bus's passengers as the bus turned down another busy street. They were as varied as the city itself: a man in a suit furiously typing on his laptop, a group of teenage Korean girls scrolling on their phones, an older woman clutching a bouquet, her face serene. Across the aisle, a young couple whispered animatedly in Spanish, their conversation punctuated by occasional laughter. Julia felt a pang of affection for the city's patchwork of cultures and lives, all crammed into this bus on their way to who knew where. It reminded her, in a way, of Sydney—chaotic, alive, full of diverse people.

But her thoughts drifted to the Mosman Men's Club and the celebration of life for her father. She sighed. What was she going to say? How could she stand before a room full of his peers—his uptight, self-satisfied friends? Honoring Ray seemed a betrayal of everything she'd endured. How could she praise the man who had never thought she was good enough, who had made her watch *Night Nurses* without telling her why? The father who had elevated her hidden sister into an untouchable ideal while dismissing her as a bum?

And yet she couldn't deny there had been more to him. His passion for education and his tireless work to rise above his troubled upbringing were admirable. When the love of his life had shut him out, he had settled for Alice. He had settled for Julia. His preferred family lived in England. Every Sunday, on the couch watching the TV, Ray had transported himself to London and a better life with Rosalind and their daughter, Miriam. Maybe it wasn't gross, she realized. Maybe it was just sad.

The bus slowed for a red light, and Julia glanced out the window. They were nearing Santa Monica, and the atmosphere outside had shifted. Century City's glass and steel were giving way to low-rise buildings and tree-lined streets. The air was cooler and lighter as they approached the coast. Julia could catch the scent of salt on the breeze, faint but unmistakable from the open window.

A jolt from the bus brought her attention back inside. Floating Sky slid slightly, and she grabbed it. The older woman sitting across from her gave a warm, amused smile. Her hands rested on a small woven shopping bag, and her hair was tucked under a floral scarf. She rocked forward. "You carry that with such confidence," she said, nodding toward the surfboard.

"Oh, uh, thanks."

The woman smiled. "Confidence is good. Strong."

Julia smiled and nodded back.

"You have a gentle smile and eyes full of tenderness. I can tell you take care of your mother. You are a good girl."

The words stayed with Julia as the bus rolled into a Santa Monica neighborhood. She glanced down at Floating Sky, its surface reflecting so many memories. The board had been with her through it all, a constant in a young life full of shifting tides. She worried the board wouldn't make it through the flight unscathed, stowed away in the plane's cargo hold. The idea caused anxiety, but she pushed it aside. *What did she mean about taking care of my mother? Alice doesn't need caretaking.*

Julia caught a glimpse of the Pacific as the bus turned onto Ocean Avenue. The water stretched endlessly beyond the sleeping sand, its surface glittering in the afternoon sun. Santa Monica Pier jutted into the waves, the Ferris wheel spinning lazily against the horizon. She lost herself in the view, the ocean soothing her nerves.

When the bus pulled up to the stop, Julia hoisted Floating Sky under her arm and got off the bus. Reaching into her back pocket, she pulled out a crumpled napkin where she had hastily scrawled the instructions for her transfer. She traced the next steps with her finger: the cross street for the connecting bus, the line number, and the approximate time the bus was expected to arrive.

With a sigh, Julia folded the napkin and stuffed it back into her pocket. Looking up, she watched the Pacific, its waves rolling in slowly, methodically. She paused for a moment, savoring the salty breeze that drifted through the air. It wasn't Bondi or Manly, but it was still her ocean—a different edge of it.

She walked briskly toward the next transfer stop, the bus for Route 3 pulled into view as she neared it. She slowed her pace as the doors hissed open. Floating Sky shifted awkwardly as she adjusted her grip, her other hand reaching into her pocket for her fare, but as she stepped closer to board, she caught another glimpse of the ocean beyond the street. The waves rolled gently to shore, just as they had always done, unchanging and eternal. She froze, her feet rooted to the pavement. She looked back at the bus driver, who was eyeing her impatiently. Instead of stepping forward, she took a step back. "I'll catch the next one," Julia said.

The driver shrugged and closed the doors, the bus pulling away and leaving her standing on the curb, Floating Sky resting against her side. She let out a long breath and turned back toward the beach.

She embraced the undeniable pull of the water, the sea that understood her innately. "Ocean Child," she whispered aloud, a twist on the nickname her parents had given her, now reshaped into something uniquely her own.

———

The sun was high in the sky as Julia sat on Floating Sky, casually bobbing up and down on the water. She had no idea how long she had been out there—time was slippery when she was surfing. Santa Monica wasn't a surfer's paradise; its waves were gentle and small, perfect for beginners or a mellow ride. But Julia didn't mind. She wasn't chasing adrenaline; she was seeking the solace of the ocean, a place to get lost in thought.

Julia wondered what the woman on the bus had meant by saying she took care of her mother. Her mother had already leaned into her garden club for support, and Julia suspected Alice would marry one of the eligible widowers from the Men's Club. Her mom was fine. Julia took a shaky breath as her eyes widened.

Miriam.

The woman had been talking about her sister. Her sister was going through a health nightmare. And as Catrina had explained, Miriam, in her proud and proper manner, was asking for help.

Julia did her scan of the swimming area and didn't see anyone in distress. This lifelong habit had become hypervigilant since she had become a trained lifesaver. Her eyes moved back to the horizon to see if any waves were worth riding. They were not. Julia returned to her thoughts, specifically to her conversation with Gus after Ray had died and how he chose to remember his brother, Nico. The beautiful picture in the taverna didn't erase the bad memories, but Gus chose to remember his brother in front of the Opera House. Julia had not landed on the good memory of her dad. What would become her version of Gus's taverna picture. She suspected the memory—the image—would come in time. They had reached an understanding in his study, not a resolution. There had been no apologies or acknowledgments of wrongdoing, but they had managed to understand each other for at least an hour. Maybe this would be her lasting memory? It was still unclear. But standing in front of the Mosman Men's Club as a human trophy wasn't it.

———————

Julia propped Floating Sky against a nearby restroom, sand sticking to her skin as she padded barefoot across the warm pavement toward a shady bench. She looked at the clock on her phone and did the math—it was 11 a.m. on Saturday in Sydney. Gus would be opening the taverna and preparing for the midday rush. Julia decided to call.

"Gus's Taverna, how can we help you?" Gus answered. She pictured him standing by the counter, wiping his hands on his ever-present relic of an apron.

"Gus, it's me, Julia."

"Tzoúlia! How is LA? Been a crazy week here. Frank keeps messing up my orders. The regulars want to know when you'll be back. Monday can't come fast enough."

"You're letting Frank take orders? That's on you, Gus."

"Fair enough. Everything okay?"

"That's why I'm calling."

"What's wrong, Tzoúlia?"

"I was irresponsible and went surfing . . . and now I'm going to miss my flight. I might be late on Monday." She paused. "I'm sorry, Gus."

"This is why you call? Surely not," Gus said dismissively. "What's the real reason?"

"It's my sister, Gus. She's sick. She lives alone. And when she's alone . . ." Julia paused again while fidgeting on a bench overlooking the Strand, a wide pedestrian and bike path that connects the coastal communities around Santa Monica. "She makes bad decisions," she finished.

"Ahh," Gus said. "Then you must stay."

"But if I stay, I let you and the taverna down," Julia said as a jogger pushing a double-wide baby stroller went by. "You're my family in Manly."

"Tzoúlia, you're indeed family. Can I tell you a story?"

"Sure, take your time. I already missed my flight," Julia joked, settling in for Gus's story time.

"Before you dropped into our lives from the sky two years ago, I was done. Decades of running the taverna had worn me out. I had nightly conversations with Maria about selling. I had lost my passion and motivation."

"I never would've guessed. You bring everything to the taverna every day," Julia said as she felt a lump in her throat.

"I cracked. But you arrived and brought your special energy. Changed my whole outlook," Gus said haltingly, as if fighting back an emotion.

"Come on, Gus. I've been nothing but headaches."

"Yes, Tzoúlia, you make mistakes. You forget orders—"

"One time, Gus. One time!" Julia said, feigning outrage.

"You weren't perfect. You often came to work without sleeping."

"Is this a performance appraisal now?"

"No. My point is that you revitalized the taverna. Younger people in the community started to become regulars. That was because of you. My taverna was filled with Bruces, but you and your friends reintroduced the taverna to a younger crowd."

"I didn't realize," Julia said as a tear ran down her cheek.

"Tzoúlia, you revitalized me, too. Three in the afternoon was my favorite time of the day. I started to hate the lunch shift. Nothing fun happened until after you arrived."

"That's very sweet," Julia said as tears began to flow more freely.

"Ask Maria—she came to the restaurant to watch with all the regulars—when you mentioned the taverna on national TV at the awards ceremony, I cried like a baby," Gus said, sounding like he was also choked up.

"You do love free advertising."

"That isn't why I cried. When you saved those lives in the surf and became Aussie of the Year, I was filled with the pride of a father."

Julia, at this point, lost it and was openly sobbing, though she was trying to keep her voice steady. "Gus, I never won Aussie—"

"You were the Aussie of the Year," Gus said. "The entire taverna watched you in that blue dress on TV. Nobody can tell me different."

Julia laughed through her tears. "Aww, Gus."

"Tzoúlia, you're family. And now you must leave. Your sister needs you. Family can't be kept in the house forever. You have a gift. Your presence makes people happy. Your sister needs your energy to overcome her struggles."

"I know," Julia said. As usual, there was truth in his ramblings. Miriam needed her.

"Yes, you'll miss your shift Monday—and many shifts after that. But you left your mark here."

"I would also miss Dad's memorial thing," Julia said as a run club of fifteen athletes rumbled through like a swarm of bees.

"I'm sorry your late father didn't understand your power. But I promise that was his loss, not your burden. Focus on your life and spend it with people who love you. Don't leave a sister in need to work a shift. And certainly not for a ceremony."

"I understand, Gus. I agree. I'll stay until she gets better."

"You saved the taverna with your passion. Help is a two-way street. I gave you a job and a place to sleep—well, sometimes. You gave me the purpose to come to work. This is the way. A relationship needs give-and-take. Your sister understands that. You're finally seeing it."

Julia's tears flowed without control now, her words jumbled. "When I get back to Sydney, you're my first stop."

"And whoever replaces you as waitress will be on the sidewalk," Gus quipped, masking his emotion.

Julia laughed through her tears. "*Antío*, Gus."

"*Antío*, Tzoúlia."

She set down the phone. Gus had given her more than just a job —he had given her the courage to face hard decisions. She wasn't going back to Sydney. Miriam needed her . . . and she needed Miriam.

After taking a minute to compose herself, she called her sister.

"Julia? Where are you?" Miriam asked, seemingly stunned. "Your flight was supposed to board an hour ago. I've been tracking it on my app, and everything is on time."

"Yeah, about that," Julia said, grinning. "I, uh, missed my bus transfer."

"By five hours?"

"Well," Julia said, now audibly giggling, "I went surfing."

There was a pause, followed by a dry chuckle. "Of course you did. You're impossible, you know that?"

"Can't argue."

"Where are you?"

"I'm in Santa Monica, watching the bikers, runners, and skateboarders fly by. Great people-watching."

"You're unbelievable. So what now? Do you want a ride? Help rebooking?"

"Nah, I'm good," Julia replied. She glanced at Floating Sky, still covered with seawater and sand.

"And Dad's memorial?"

"I, uh . . . will ask Marcus to speak on my behalf. He plans to be there. He's good at that kind of thing."

"Julia. Seriously?"

"Dad loved a trophy. If Mum brings the surfing one, all my accomplishments will be displayed. No reason for me to show up."

"You're something else, Sis."

"Is that offer to live with you still available?"

"Of course," Miriam said. "I would do anything for you to live here."

"What's my door code?"

"Ha. We'll get that sorted," Miriam said. "But, Jules, fair warning: It's going to get hairy. I met with the doctor today. We're starting the detox process tomorrow. It will be ugly."

"We'll get through it—together."

Julia grabbed Floating Sky and headed to the bus stop for her journey to West Hollywood. Out of the corner of her eye, she saw a young Hispanic girl, maybe fourteen, awkwardly tugging on a wetsuit as she sat on a towel on the beach. Julia slowed her pace, her gaze falling to the girl's surfboard—a battered mess at least two decades old, its edges frayed and its surface riddled with dings and scars.

Julia approached the girl. "G'day! How's it going?"

The girl looked up, startled at first but disarmed by the Australian accent. "I'm good, I guess," she said. "I got out of school, and the bus from the Valley was super late. It took forever, and now I've only got, like, an hour to surf before it gets dark."

Julia knelt, holding on to Floating Sky for support as she studied the girl's face. There was determination, an undeniable spark. Julia smiled. "I'd like you to have this," she said, holding out Floating Sky.

The girl's eyes widened, darting between Julia and the board. "Are you serious?"

Julia nodded, her throat tightening as she fought back more tears. "Yes. This board . . . she's been with me for ten years. She's been my support, my protection, in this very ocean. But it's time for her to embark on a new journey."

"Is this for real?"

"Let her take care of you," Julia said as she handed the board over to the girl, her fingers brushing against it for the last time as it left her hand.

The girl broke into the biggest smile Julia had ever seen, her whole face lighting up. Before Julia could react, the girl threw her arms around her in a full-body hug, her gratitude spilling out. "Thank you, thank you, thank you," she said. "I'm going to name her Morning Moon."

Julia blinked back tears. "That's a beautiful name. You'll love her."

The girl beamed, cradling Morning Moon in her arms as if it were the most precious treasure in the world. Julia stood, offering the girl and the board one last warm smile before turning toward the bus stop with renewed determination and a new purpose.

CHAPTER 30

Friday, April 6, 2012 | Carlsbad

Door 3 was dragging into its fifth hour. Catrina had secured fifteen signed agreements and was exhausted from an afternoon of intense sales calls, but her confidence was high. The back-and-forth with each doctor had been similar. They all expressed a need for the surgical cages but not for Tim, and their self-interest in avoiding delays to their lucrative high-dollar surgeries outweighed their loyalty to him. The signed forms rolled in, and Catrina forwarded each one promptly to SidOrtho and DeltaTech, building momentum with every deal closed.

Now it was time to speak to Dr. Franklin Jones. He was the linchpin, the most challenging client to sway, and the last obstacle between her and success. She couldn't wait any longer; time was slipping away, and the later it got, the more likely the doctor would be too deep into his evening drinks to focus, let alone sign a form.

"Dr. Jones, this is Catrina McDavid. I worked for Tim at BSS."

A brief silence followed, the faint sound of background chatter confirming what she had suspected—he wasn't alone.

Dr. Jones finally responded with condescension. "Caitlyn, the secretary, right?"

He knew her name, but she resisted the urge to correct him, instead focusing on the task at hand.

"Dr. Jones, I'm reaching out because there's a situation you need to be aware of."

"There is?"

"Very much so. BSS is on the verge of collapse, as early as Monday. When that happens, there won't be anyone to fulfill your orders for your upcoming surgeries—through the rest of the year, and maybe into the first quarter of next year—"

"That's quite a claim," Dr. Jones interrupted.

Catrina continued, undeterred. "As one of SidOrtho's most valued users, I can offer to transition your account. They have reached an agreement with DeltaTech to distribute their surgical cages, and I just need your signature on a simple one-page form to avoid any service interruptions."

"Uh-huh . . ." Dr. Jones said.

"Your practice relies on SidOrtho's surgical cages, and I've spent the day working out a solution to ensure you're not left scrambling, canceling dozens of procedures and eating the costs of empty time slots in your operating room," Catrina explained. "DeltaTech is a significantly more reliable distributor, but I need your written agreement today. Fifteen of BSS's former customers have signed the form and switched their business to DeltaTech."

"I don't have time for this. I'm not transitioning anywhere." Catrina could hear muffled voices in the background. "You're on speakerphone. Tim is sitting right here. Talk to him."

Catrina's blood ran cold as Tim's voice cut in, dripping with venom.

"Well, well, if it isn't the treacherous Catnip. I read your quitting email. Do you understand how stupid you sound? Cold-hearted bitch. You're trying to steal my best client? My friend? This is ridiculous."

"Tim—"

"I took you in when you were nothing—eating ramen on your mom's fleabag couch, barely scraping by like the white-trash, working-class piece of shit you are and will always be. I gave you a job when you had no credentials and taught you everything you know, and this is how you repay me? You're nothing without me. You don't have the brains or the backbone to pull off this little stunt."

"I'm not pulling off anything," Catrina said. "I'm getting nothing out of this. I'm transferring the doctors to a company that will exist in a week. And fifteen have signed."

"Who put you up to this? You're being used."

"Nobody."

"God, I hate you. Clueless dumb whore. What's your master plan, huh? Flash a smile, open your legs, and get these doctors to hand over my business? You're disgusting."

Catrina knew she had him cornered. She could tell he was scared. His derogatory language and loudness betrayed him. When confident, Tim spoke with a low volume and slow cadence. His hyperactive insults let Catrina know she was on the right track and that it was time to make the final push. Tim was the only way to get Dr. Jones to sign.

"Tim, I don't expect you to hear this right now, but try to listen."

"Why would I ever listen to you, gutter trash?"

"I'm not stealing your business." Catrina took a dramatic pause and counted to three. Before Tim could fill the silence with vitriol, she said, "You already lost it. It's gone."

"The fuck it is."

"How many of the doctors you've been texting while we're talking have responded? Any?" Catrina asked.

Tim's silence was confirmation that he was beaten.

Catrina continued in a calm tone, trying to contain the adrenaline surging through her system. "Tim, again, hear me. I'm not stealing from you. I'm saving you. The quicker you embrace this concept, the better."

"This is rich. You? Saving me? From what? Whatever you're plotting will blow up in your face."

"Tim, on Monday, at my deposition, I'm telling the truth."

"What?"

"I am done repeating myself. Please listen. If I have to testify on Monday, I'll spill every detail. Do I have your attention?"

"You wouldn't."

"I told Tom Wilkshire about the stolen R&D files."

"Why the fuck would you do that?"

"Wait till I give him all the details. Do you know what happens after that? Do you, Tim?"

He didn't respond.

"We both go down. Indicted. Corporate espionage, wire fraud—take your pick. It'll be game over for you, Timmy. No country clubs. No golf trips. Orange jumpsuits and prison cells. You've always loved that CEO title. Well, guess what? Prosecutors love nothing more than plastering it across their press releases."

"You're bluffing. You wouldn't dare. You're a coward above all else."

"Wouldn't I?" Catrina shot back. "Think about it, Tim. Who do you think the government will strike a deal with? The crooked CEO or his so-called 'dumb whore' assistant? You've always underestimated me. Trust me, I have no intention of going to prison. If I testify, it will be the end of your charmed country club life."

"After all I've done for you. I treated you like family. You've made more money with me than you and your poor, janky-ass mother could've ever dreamed of in three lifetimes."

"You have all the power," Catrina said.

"Of course I do. I'll always have the power," Tim responded.

"Great. Use it wisely. Here's the deal: If you want to stay out of jail, you're going to convince your good buddy Dr. Jones to sign the Acceptance of Transfer form. If he does, DeltaTech will drop the entire lawsuit—Tom Wilkshire confirmed it. Call him if you don't believe me."

"This is ridiculous."

"Call him. You're right, you have all the power. If you ignore me, well, you know how the deposition will go. But if Dr. Jones signs, you walk away. No lawsuit. No prison. Clean." Catrina let out a small, audible snort that would have irritated Tim further. "Well, not entirely clean. Your business—yeah, that's finished. And your reputation—um, that's fucked beyond repair. But at least you won't be in prison with an astronomical judgment against your name."

"Fuck you, Cat," Tim spat. "Seriously, fuck you."

"This is the most important sale of your life, Tim. Don't blow it." Catrina hung up without waiting for a response. She replayed the heated conversation in her mind and then refreshed her inbox. She knew Tim well but had no idea what he would do. She would give him thirty minutes to calm down and then would drive over to the club to try in person to convert Dr. Jones. She wasn't giving up.

Just as she was about to pack up and head to her car, an email appeared in her inbox.

Subject line: *Fuck you, whore.*
Attached: *Dr. Jones's signed transfer form.*

Catrina exhaled, her relief palpable. She changed the subject line, forwarded it to SidOrtho and DeltaTech, and wrote: 'Deal complete.'

She received a prompt reply: a hearty thank-you from SidOrtho and DeltaTech, along with formal confirmation of the lawsuit's dismissal and her deposition's cancellation. Relief washed over her as she read the words. She could breathe.

Glancing at the clock, she saw it was 9:00 p.m. The day had been long, grueling, and emotionally draining, but she had done it. She had pulled it off. Door 3 had been a success.

But her sense of victory was fleeting.

I'm unemployed. Fuck.

Her phone vibrated in her pocket. She fished it out and glanced at the screen. It was Rachel from DeltaTech. "Can you come in on Monday at 9:00 a.m.?"

———

Monday, April 9, 2012

Rachel was waiting by the elevators, a warm smile spreading across her face as she extended a hand. "Cat! It's so good to see you. Come this way. I want to show you something."

Rachel led Catrina to the elevator, and they rode up to the third floor. Once they stepped out, Rachel guided her down a long hallway before stopping in front of a closed office door, gesturing where Catrina read the nameplate:

Catrina McDavid
Director of Client Relations

"This is your new office," Rachel said, opening the door and stepping aside so Catrina could take it in.

"Uh, what's happening?" Catrina asked as she walked into the office to look around, her mouth agape. The space was expansive and modern, with new furniture, an entire wall of windows overlooking the landscaped courtyard, and enough room to breathe, think, and work.

"We want you to come home."

"Me? Work here again?"

"We've put together a compensation plan and want you to be part of our customer service team. HR approved it, and you'll report to the VP of Customer Service. It's a good offer."

Catrina was speechless, her throat tight as she fought back tears. She ran her hand over the smooth edge of the desk, still trying to understand what was happening.

Rachel continued. "Seriously, Cat. After what you pulled off on Friday, you've earned this. And, selfishly, we need you to service all the new clients. Every single one of them—well, except Dr. Jones—asked us to bring you back to run their accounts. We want you to be here."

"But I did some things that . . . I'm not proud of how I left."

"Every member of our C-suite has done worse. If anything, it raised your profile. But you better believe IT is monitoring your movements on campus."

Catrina laughed but realized it probably wasn't a joke.

"So . . . when can you start?" Rachel asked.

———

"There she is! Director McDavid!" Sam said, putting *Little Women* aside and bouncing in her seat. "How was your first day? Tell me everything. What's your office like? Who did you meet? What are your responsibilities? And most importantly," she added with a sly grin, "any juicy Tim-bashing?"

Catrina laughed, walking toward the couch and shaking her head. "Do you save all your energy for the second I get home?" she teased, sinking onto the couch.

"Always," Sam said, hyper. "Now spill. Did anyone trash Tim?"

"Oh, you'll be pleased. His name did come up—someone referred to him as Dipshit."

Sam laughed, clapping her hands. "Dipshit! That's perfect."

"You need to come visit. I have a beautiful office. I'm going to get my own intern."

"And you'll stop the cycle of intern abuse, which is important."

Catrina sat on the couch next to Sam.

"I'll be busy for a while transitioning the former BSS clients. I'm lucky they were forgiving."

"They weren't forgiving. They need you to make this work. All those doctors told them how valuable you are; they had no choice. Please don't view this as them doing you a favor."

"You're right. Mutual benefit. I need a job, and they need someone who understands these doctors."

"Exactly."

"And when they get settled, I'll take on more customers from other sales reps. This can be a career. It's stable. I fell ass-backward into my dream job. This makes up for all my mom's shitty luck over the years."

"You'll be a vice president in five years or less. You took the hard path, the risky path, but you did it with integrity, and it paid off. It's nice when the good guys win."

"Thanks, Sam." Catrina shifted closer. "Sam," she repeated, taking Sam's hand, "I need to talk to you. It's important."

Sam straightened. "Uh, what is it? Everything okay?"

Catrina nodded but looked down at their joined hands as though searching for words. "I've been thinking about us," she started. "About how we've been . . . *private* for the past few weeks. And I get why we started that way, but . . . I love you."

"I love you too, Cat."

"Yeah, but I want to love you openly. I want everyone to see that I love you."

Catrina felt Sam's hand tighten around hers. "Are you sure? This is a big step. You've presented as . . . straight. This is going to change a lot of things for you. Have you talked to your mom?"

"I don't need to talk to my mom. She supports me and will support us. Not financially, of course. Ha. Shit, you got me off track."

"Take a breath."

"I love you, Sam. And I want to be with you, not in secret, not with disclaimers. You and me, out in the open."

"Cat, I don't want you pressured into this. You're in a good place. Brand-new job . . . I don't want to complicate things for you."

"If you're not ready to settle down, I understand."

"No, that's not what I'm saying. I mean . . . coming out is a big deal. It changes your life."

"Affix whatever label to it. It's unimportant. You're the best thing in my life, Sam. I want to be with you."

"You mean that?"

"I do. I love you."

Catrina melted as Sam leaned in, and their lips met. The kiss was soft and unhurried. When Sam pulled back, her hand lingered, cupping Catrina's cheek with warmth. Catrina couldn't breathe, her eyes on Sam's, brimming with unmistakable certainty.

Sam paused. "I'm all in."

"Good. Because I told everyone at work."

EPILOGUE

Saturday, December 22, 2012 | Los Angeles

Linda's voice cut through the air, commanding attention as she raised a glass from the fireplace. "Ladies and gentlemen, if I may have a moment," she began. The room quieted, heads turning toward the woman who was never shy to speak. "Tonight, we're here to celebrate what Gentiles call Christmas, but it's also fitting that we celebrate Miriam's remarkable recovery."

Julia stood in the corner of Miriam's spacious Los Angeles house, nursing a glass of sparkling water as Linda started her speech. Miriam's home had been transformed for the holidays; a towering Christmas tree stood in the corner of the living room, its branches decorated with white lights, glass ornaments, and a few playful nods to Julia's personality, notably surfing-themed kitsch. Miriam floated effortlessly through the crowd, radiant as ever, her health visibly restored and her laughter filling the room. She moved from guest to guest, her silver dress catching the light as she poured champagne, making each person feel like the center of her attention. She was a natural host. On the patio, Catrina and Sam sat close together, holding hands and angled into each other as they whispered. The twinkling lights above them reflected off the pool, adding a soft, magical quality to the party.

Julia took it all in with pride and awe. The house, the decorations, the atmosphere—all of it spoke to Miriam's resilience and Julia's knack for bringing people together. Her gaze swept across the house to the guests, who were laughing, chatting, and enjoying the night. For all the sisters' challenges, this gathering was a victory —a poignant reminder that joy and connection were still possible even in the darkest times.

Julia had spent many difficult days and nights over the past eight months fighting to get her sister back to this place, to being the life of the party. Miriam's recovery had been a long, grueling journey, and Julia had been there for every harrowing step. She remembered the nights when Miriam would wake up convulsing, drenched in sweat, her body racked with the pangs of withdrawal. Those nights had been terrifying, Miriam's anxiety spiraling out of control, her pulse racing, her mind consumed with doubts that she couldn't survive without a pharmaceutical crutch. Julia had stayed by her side, talking her through the worst of it with an endless well of patience, especially when Miriam's shaking had become unbearable.

The days following the surgery had also been exhausting. Miriam had required around-the-clock care, and though the nurses had been attentive, Julia had taken on much of the responsibility herself. When Miriam had been discharged and begun her six-week outpatient pulmonary rehabilitation program, Julia had become her chauffeur and cheerleader.

Applause broke out, but Linda raised a hand to silence it. "No, no, hold your clapping for a second. While Miriam's strength and determination are unmatched, someone else in this room deserves credit. Someone who quite literally saved Miriam's life."

Julia froze as Linda's eyes locked onto hers.

"That's right," Linda continued. "Julia Corning. I don't think I've ever met anyone as steadfast."

"You mean stubborn," Gus yelled out, interrupting.

"Ha. When Miriam was at her lowest, Julia never wavered. She stood by her through every hairy night. And let me tell you, that was no small feat."

The crowd erupted into cheers, and Julia felt her face flush as Miriam wrapped an arm around her shoulders. "She's right, Jules; I wouldn't be here without you."

The room began to settle as Linda cleared her throat again. "And since tonight is about announcements, let's not bury the lede. Miriam has exciting news to share."

Miriam beamed, stepping forward. "Thank you, Linda. And thank you, everyone, for being here tonight. I couldn't ask for a better family or group of friends." She paused, her eyes scanning the room. "So here it is: All *Night Nurses* fans can rejoice. I'm going to London in February to do the spin-off."

Another round of applause filled the room. As it started to fade, Miriam made another announcement. "I have another sister who has big news. Cat and Sam, come up here."

Catrina and Sam, who had come inside for the speech, came forward, drawing the group's attention.

Sam's voice jittered with emotion as she spoke. "Yikes. Put on the spot." She paused, a radiant smile spreading across her face. "We're engaged."

The room erupted in cheers as the couple held up their hands, the matching engagement rings elevating the moment. Julia came over and hugged them both tightly.

The evening continued with drinks and stories, the air filled with warmth and joy. Morven arrived late, arm in arm with a new boyfriend. Catrina said she was pleased that her mother was so put together this evening and that her life had found some semblance of stability, at least for now.

Meanwhile, Alice was in her element, co-hosting the party with the precision that had made her Sunday brunches legendary. Alice had left her Men's Club boyfriend in Sydney, but Julia suspected that after the first anniversary of Ray's death, her mother would remarry.

Julia wandered through the party, enjoying the conversations she overheard between people she had never expected would gravitate toward one another. Miriam was in the corner, absorbed in a conversation with Morven, her expression animated and engaged.

Morven asked for a selfie to show her friends back in Carlsbad that she had hung out with a celebrity in an LA mansion. Miriam obliged with a professional smile.

Gus and Alice made for an odd but effective team in the kitchen, preparing food and charming everyone who passed by with their hosting skills. Gus was happy to tell anyone who would listen about his Tzoúlia, and Alice was pleased to hear someone complimenting her daughter.

By the fireplace, two young professionals discussed getting their feet wet in their new trades. Talia Bernstein had downloaded to Alani about her first six months as Linda's junior agent, and Alani was reciprocating with tales of beauty school and getting an apprenticeship in Manly. In the middle of the room, Ginger and Beau were receiving much-needed relationship counseling from Rabbi Yael. Julia chuckled.

She loitered near the patio door, listening to Linda and Sam. Linda's voice carried as she spoke. "I'm not sure if you get to LA often, but my book club could use some new blood. We're a bunch of old women prattling about the classics."

"I love the classics. I can't get into contemporary YA when the OGs did it better."

Linda laughed and patted her on the shoulder.

"But I'm not sure I can cut it in your book club—I'm a community college kid," Sam said.

"So am I. Community college is the cradle of the American Dream."

"Really?" Sam asked. "That's encouraging to hear. I loved my time at MiraCosta."

Julia smiled, amused by how two very different people had found common ground. Next, she wandered toward Gus, who was holding a plate of Greek cookies and wearing a ridiculous Hawaiian shirt he had bought at the airport, and looking relaxed.

"Tzoúlia, if Miriam is going to London, are you . . ."

"Yup. I'm coming home."

"I'll remove the tenant from the flat immediately."

"No need, Gus. I told Marcus I'd live with him. Trial run. But . . ."

"Yes, yes. The waitress job is yours. The new girl isn't working out."

"I'm sure she's fine."

"She gone." Gus scanned the perimeter of the room. "Tzoúlia, where's Floating Sky?"

"Oh, I've got a new board. Want to see it? It's in the garage."

"In the garage?" Gus asked, his eyebrows shooting up in shock. "You still surf, right?"

"Every Sunday."

Julia raised the garage door, and she stepped inside with Gus close behind. She crossed the concrete floor and pulled the board off the wall. It was white, with pink accents adding a playful touch. With a flip, she turned it around to reveal the bold airbrushed inscription "Greek Mule," accompanied by a cartoonish mule balancing on a wave, its ears flapping in the wind.

Gus let out a loud laugh, clapping his hands together. "Tzoúlia, you've outdone yourself!"

As the night wore on, Julia sat on the patio, a light breeze brushing against her face as she gazed up at the stars. The distant hum of conversation from inside the house mixed with the faint chirping of crickets, creating a rare stillness amidst the night's celebrations. She wrapped her arms around her knees, letting the calm seep into her.

Miriam slipped into the chair beside her with a cup of spearmint tea. She looked tired yet radiant, and her recovery was evident in her appearance and the ease with which she moved. The night air carried a hint of jasmine from the garden, and for a moment, neither of them spoke, content in the shared silence.

The soft click of the sliding door to the cozy, heated patio caught their attention. Catrina stepped out, a fresh glass of wine in hand. Her cheeks were flushed, and she was tipsy, but her expression was relaxed and playful.

"Room for one more?" she asked, pulling over a chair.

"Always," Julia said. "Where's Sam? I thought you two were joined at the hip."

Catrina smirked, settling into the chair and crossing her legs gracefully. "Oh, I left her inside. She's interrogating Morven's new boyfriend in her barista way. You know that polite but probing tone she uses to get people to confess their deepest secrets while they order a latte."

Miriam raised her teacup in mock salute. "Cat, did you hear Jules's big news? She's returning to Sydney after New Year's for nursing school."

"No way! That's amazing, Jules. I didn't know you'd decided."

"The paperwork's done, and I've been accepted. It feels right. After everything . . . I like helping people," Julia said.

Catrina reached over, squeezing Julia's arm. "You'll be incredible. I have no doubt. Now our honeymoon has to be in Sydney."

"It's a great place for a honeymoon. I can show you two around during the day and leave you alone at night."

"Perfect."

Julia was grateful for the few weekends she had spent with Catrina and Sam exploring Southern California. She had seen the depth of Catrina's love for Sam—how it softened her and made her tougher. Sure, life would throw challenges their way—no couple was immune to that—but she knew Sam and Catrina had the shared resilience to weather whatever came next.

Her gaze shifted to Miriam. Her older sister had progressed further than Julia had thought possible when they had started this journey. But her worry about Miriam lingered. How would her sister fare with life's demands and distractions when she was alone in London? Would the old anxieties, which had driven her to the brink, creep in? Julia resolved to check in often and to make sure Miriam never felt isolated. She would make time to visit her sister. Miriam would undoubtedly be a massive success; her talent and determination guaranteed it. But Julia hoped she could find a way to balance that success with the happiness and stability she deserved.

As for herself, Julia was excited for the future. Nursing school in Sydney was the perfect next step, a challenge she was ready to embrace. Gus, the supportive friend and boss, had adjusted her shifts so she could attend classes, still have time to study, and, as he insisted, sleep. Her Saturdays would be spent volunteering at the Manly Life Saving Club, continuing the work that kept her grounded. Her schedule was set, and she still had time to surf on Sundays. As for Marcus, she would let their relationship evolve naturally. He had respected her boundaries, and moving in felt like a logical progression.

Julia looked at Catrina and Miriam and felt a surge of love. What would Ray think of his three daughters, who had grown up oceans apart, relaxing on the same patio, the one he had raised sitting with the one he had loved and the one he had denied. Despite his failures and the pain he had caused, they had found each other. For now, that was enough.

ABOUT THE AUTHOR

M. E. Flatow is a seasoned trial attorney with a passion for storytelling that extends beyond the courtroom. With a career dedicated to advocating for clients—particularly women—M. E. has spent countless hours crafting compelling narratives to present before judges and juries. The ability to distill complex emotions and circumstances into powerful stories has made M. E. a sought-after voice in the legal profession.

When not in the courtroom or crafting the next story, M. E. Flatow enjoys life in Charlotte, North Carolina. A lifelong traveler, M. E. has explored cities across the globe, with favorites including Amsterdam, Sydney, London, Paris, Munich, and Vancouver. These rich experiences, combined with a passion for human stories, are seamlessly woven into the writing, bringing a vivid sense of place and perspective to each work.

www.ingramcontent.com/pod-product-compliance
Lightning Source LLC
Chambersburg PA
CBHW030245120726
47903CB00005B/1634